Nicholas DelCorso was one of modern warfare's camp followers: a news photographer paid to record the horrors of war. A man obsessed, addicted to the action, driven again and again onto danger's razor edge to get an 8 x 10 glossy of all that was best and worst in man.

In Vietnam, as Saigon fell—then in Lebanon, a land running mad with blood and violence—DelCorso joined the rest of the press elite . . . to get drunk, find a woman, dream of home, and wage war against war with a camera—trying not to think about the consequences . . . knowing too well that sometimes the consequence was death.

DelCorso's GALLERY

——

PHILIP CAPUTO

A DELL BOOK

Published by
Dell Publishing Co., Inc.
1 Dag Hammarskjold Plaza
New York, New York 10017

Special thanks to Eddie Adams, Philip Jones Griffiths, Don Kincaid, Lawson Little, and Don McCullin for explaining the ABCs of photography to a novice and for their insights into the complexities of the war photographer's mind.

Dell® TM 681510, Dell Publishing Co., Inc.

ISBN: 0-440-11842-5

Reprinted by arrangement with Holt, Rinehart and Winston, CBS Educational and Professional Publishing, a division of CBS, Inc.

Printed in the United States of America

First Dell printing—November 1984

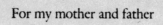

For my mother and father

From time to time God causes men to be born—and thou art one of them—who have the lust to go abroad at the risk of their lives and discover news. . . . These souls are very few; and of these few, not more than ten are of the best.

—Rudyard Kipling
Kim

DelCorso's
GALLERY

PART
ONE

—

1975

1

HE WAS COMPOSING a shot of O'Brien casting into the pool below the falls when he heard, above the water's rush and hiss, a sound like nothing he had ever heard before. Lowering his camera, he turned and saw a hill in the distance changing from green to white. Margaret, beside him on the riverbank, stood and said in the breathless voice he'd once found charming, "Look at that, Nick, it's like somebody's pouring a pitcher of cream over the hill. You've got to get a shot of it." She hadn't finished the sentence before DelCorso, in a single movement, snatched his camera bag from under the poncho that protected it from the rain, changed lenses, and started running toward the ford upstream. He didn't buy Margaret's simile of the cream pitcher—he made his living recording things as they are—but there was no arguing the necessity to get the scene on film. Hearing that unfamiliar sound, his eyes on the solid mass of white spilling down the smooth, treeless hill, he knew he was witnessing a moment he had to capture before it vanished forever.

Hopping across the rocks at the ford, holding the camera tightly against his chest, he climbed the path leading up the opposite bank and started across the fence-broken fields. His hip boots conspired with his bad leg to make him run over the uneven ground with the comic, lurching gait of a drunk.

He slipped several times on the wet grass. The sound, a high quavering as steady as the sibilation of the salmon river behind him, grew louder; the white mass, which looked like an eruption of milky lava if it looked like anything other than what it was, a vast flock of sheep, had flowed halfway down the hill before he was within a hundred yards of the stone fence from which he wanted to shoot the picture. Running, DelCorso made some quick time and distance calculations: with the 50-mm lens, he could get the shot if he made it to the fence before the flock reached the road at the bottom of the hill. He was good at estimating how far he could run in a given span of time for the simple reason that his life had often depended on it; and because his livelihood depended on his ability to estimate the ranges at which various lenses were most effective, he was good at that as well. Too far and you don't have the picture, too close and you won't be alive to take it. Dunlop had told him that a long time ago, and regardless of what he thought of Dunlop now, it was the soundest advice anyone had ever given him about his peculiar profession.

Not that DelCorso was now in danger of losing his life. The only risk was the risk of losing the moment he hoped to arrest and preserve for years, for decades, for all time if he did his work well enough. A rock concealed under a clump of grass tripped him in the midst of this dream of immortality. Breaking his fall with one arm, holding the camera up and to one side with his free hand, he executed a neat shoulder roll and got back to his feet. You earned that one, DelCorso said to himself, his left leg throbbing. Pretense was a mortal sin in his private moral system, and as one who believed that sins have consequences, he considered his fall a punishment for thinking he could do anything that would last forever. Photography isn't art, he reminded himself, and none of your pictures are going to hang in the plastic galleries of the next century.

Like an infantryman taking cover, he flung himself behind the fence and, using its cold, wet stones as a rest, focused on the hill. Through the viewfinder, he saw quick, alert dogs trotting at the edges of the flock and two shepherds wading waist deep through the bobbing, ever-moving whiteness. He clicked off several frames quickly, his hands trembling from an unfamiliar excitement. There was beauty here, of a kind he was not used to photographing, beauty in the swift turns of the agile dogs, in the sheep surging over the green hill, in the bleak light of the overcast afternoon, in the wind-reddened face of one of the shepherds, his mouth open to utter a cry to the flock, in the way the whole great mass suggested a force of tidal power. DelCorso increased the shutter speed to freeze the lunge of a dog, its hind legs stretching, forelegs tucked under its chest, like a horse clearing a hurdle; then he stopped down to bring the entire scene into focus. He imagined himself a wizard, manipulating motion and light, in control of the event he was recording, though he knew that sense of control was an illusion. He controlled nothing but the little box of mirror tricks in his hands, and he wasn't even sure about that under these circumstances. He was working out of his usual element, so his instincts, which almost unfailingly told him when his camera was recording what he wanted, responded uncertainly. He tried various settings to create a photograph that would capture the sense of irresistible momentum, the impression that men and animals were one thing, the feeling that the hill was being—the word *overrun* occurred to him, but it had so many unpleasant associations that he dismissed it—was being engulfed by living flesh. For that, he needed enough detail to present the fact of the event, but not so much as to destroy the essential mystery underlying the fact. He sought mystery above all; not mystery in the sense of an enigma or a puzzle, but in the sense of magic. He wanted the photograph to do what the actual event had done to him. Men and dogs driving a flock to pasture was an ordinary occurrence here in the west of Ireland; and yet it had made DelCorso ache inside, filling him with the wonder of a time traveler who had been transported back to the age when all men were nomadic herdsmen, wandering over a wild earth.

Then it was gone. The last of the flock straggled onto the road; the hill looked no different than it had before, except for the flattened grass, already ruffling in the wind. The feelings of magic and wild wonder deserted DelCorso like the emotions of a dream after awakening. Sheep, shepherds, and dogs still made a picturesque sight as they moved in a dense column down the road; but it was merely picturesque, a scene lacking the power to evoke anything more than passing interest. It would have made a good travel poster for the airline that had sent him here on assignment. He could see it hanging on a travel agency wall. VISIT IRELAND ON ERINAIR.

He slung his Leica and headed back to the river from which

O'Brien, an account executive for Erinair's ad agency, had been trying to coax a salmon that DelCorso was supposed to photograph if and when it leaped. He could still hear, diminishing behind him, the tremulous bleating of the sheep, the rebuking barks of the dogs, and wished he'd been able to capture those sounds. But you could not suggest sound with a camera. With the right tricks and filters, you could do heat and cold, even smell, but not sound.

He reached the ford, but instead of crossing, sat on the bank and lit a cigarette. His left leg aching from the fall and the run over broken ground, he needed a short rest before he could trust it on the marble-smooth rocks. He also needed a few minutes to get his mind into the right frame for the business of watching O'Brien attempt to convince a fish that a hook and a hank of hair were edible. The airline wanted photographs of leaping salmon to use in a promotional campaign aimed at persuading wealthy American sportsmen that the Republic of Ireland was not, like the six northern counties, a land of crazed IRA bombers and British paratroopers peppering mobs with rubber bullets. DelCorso had taken the assignment for a number of reasons: for the money, for something to do, for Margaret, who wanted to see her ancestors' native soil. He hated every minute of it; he was a news photographer, primarily a war photographer, and regarded commercial work as idolatry, even though his income would be halved without it. Smoking, he looked at the river, which had the color and clarity of the whiskey they drank here, then at the fields whose green undulations reminded him of Verdun, where acres of old trenches and shell craters still showed under a covering of unusually bright grass. The memory brought a fleeting realization that war photography also was not without its financial rewards: death, destruction, and suffering were DelCorso's bread and butter. He flipped his cigarette into the damp wind, his elation of a moment ago having dipped into a mild depression. Maybe the somber weather was getting him down, although this mood reminded him of the way he often felt after he'd made love to Margaret—not dissatisfied or disappointed so much as troubled by an awareness that something had eluded him or had been withheld from him. But nothing had been held back from him a few minutes ago; nor could he think of what might have eluded him. The sight of the sheep coming over the hill had provided everything any photographer could have asked for: movement, color, and the raw energy of life; so why did he feel this nagging sense that he had missed something?

"Photographing wars has not destroyed my faith in beauty." He remembered speaking those words to Margaret two years ago in Spain, where he'd been sent to cover Franco's resignation. Margaret, who had a master's in art history and a self-appointed mission to refine her husband's tastes, had dragged him through a succession of museums after he'd finished the assignment. DelCorso had been bored to distraction by the endless parade of Spanish kings, dreamy-eyed saints, benign madonnas, and bleeding Christs until, in the Prado, he saw the great Goya's sketches, *The Disasters of War*. Margaret, who thought the sketches were tasteless propaganda, suggested to DelCorso that his work had destroyed his capacity to respond to anything except gore and horror. That was when, to reassure her that he was not some camera-toting Patton, he'd said that photographing wars had not destroyed his faith in beauty, by which he'd meant his faith in his ability to appreciate what was beautiful in the world.

Now, sitting on a riverbank in gloomy Ireland, he wondered if he'd made that affirmation to reassure himself. Perhaps Margaret was right. Perhaps he had become as gutted inside as those burned-out tanks he'd seen up on the Golan Heights. It wasn't beauty that had eluded him a few minutes ago, but the conviction that he was responding to it for its own sake. He had, it seemed to him, responded to his fear of losing his ability to respond. He'd gone chasing across the fields to prove something to himself: that he could photograph, with skill and control, something other than wounds and death. Christ almighty, why this morbid self-examination? He lived in a world where men acted; he wasn't the sort who continually put his psyche under a microscope or worried about every irregular beat in his emotional pulse.

The wind rose and it began to rain again.

"DelCorso. *DelCorso.*" O'Brien's shouts were just audible above the sound of the waterfall. "Damn it, where are you? I've hooked one."

DelCorso stood and slipped his Leica under his foul-weather jacket. He started to cross the ford when the ankle of his bad leg turned on a bowling ball of a rock, sending through him a jolt of pain sharp enough to make him draw in a breath. He looked for a stick to use as a cane; finding none, he stepped into the rushing water with the caution of a man stepping onto a high wire. He could not afford to fall now; his Leica, an M3D, had been designed as a combat camera and was now worth over a thousand dollars if you could find one; the last model had been made in 1958.

Though it came no higher than his knees, the stream had concentrated force, tugging and shoving at his boots as if its only purpose were to knock him down and drown him. With his leg wobbling, each step became an act to be performed with the greatest delicacy. It reminded him of the way he'd walked down the mined trails in Vietnam; and this memory brought a flash of an unreasonable and unresolvable anger at the faceless machine gunner whose bullet had turned the bones of his ankle and calf into broken crockery. That was nine years ago. Jesus, nine years and the leg still wasn't right. It never would be, which stood to reason: a lot of things hadn't been right since then and never would be.

"DelCorso, he's making a run! He'll jump at the end of it! Where the hell are you?"

DelCorso, who was in midstream, felt some of his anger flow toward O'Brien, an upper-crust Irishman who spoke with a Rolls-Royce British accent. He took a few more careful steps: then a slick, flat rock beneath him shifted and the current picked up his bad leg, pulling at it as if to tear it from his body. He saw the leg, floating in the gold-white swirl, the expanding rings of raindrops in the smooth water below the ford, the rapids below the ford, foaming before they slid over the twenty-foot falls. Margaret was coming up the path, lifting her poncho the way old-fashioned ladies used to lift their skirts when crossing a muddy street.

"Nick," she called. "O'Brien wants you."

Tottering on one leg, all DelCorso could think about was an irreplaceable Leica going under, and, if his hip boots filled up and the current swept him over the falls, his irreplaceable self going under with the camera. Fighting for balance, he stretched his left leg against the force of the stream toward a sandbar a couple of feet away. He managed the trick, but when he shifted his weight to bring his right forward, pain rocketed from his left ankle to his head with such scalding intensity that he could feel the color draining from his face.

"Nick, he's hooked a fish and he wants you to get a picture."

Through a curtain of spots, flashing pinwheels, and roman

candles, DelCorso saw Margaret on the bank above, less than thirty feet from him. A hot, salty lump clogged his throat.

"What's wrong?" Margaret asked.

"Leg," he answered, forcing the words through the lump. "Went out again. Bad."

"Is there anything I can do?"

DelCorso paused momentarily. He was the sort of man who hated to admit dependency on a woman. He hated to admit dependency on anyone for that matter.

"Yeah," he said. "Yeah."

The waves of agony began to abate as he stood storklike on the sandbar, his left leg hooked over the right. Margaret sidestepped down the clay bank, still holding up the hem of her poncho as if it were a gown. Her knee-length leather boots showed with elegant incongruity. A fashionable pair that would have been adequate for walking down a damp street in, say, London, they were useless in this rough country. She had refused the waders O'Brien had offered her because they were clumsy, uncomfortable, and, worst of all, unattractive. The poncho was also unattractive, but she'd had the choice between it and getting drenched. And she looked beautiful in it regardless; even its shroudlike folds could not completely conceal the contours of her marvelous body.

DelCorso watched her step into the stream as gracefully, he imagined, as she had stepped into the limousines in which her boyfriends had driven her to the parties and cotillions that had been her life before she married him. Margaret Delaney Fitzgerald, the eternal debutante. She came on across a bed of rocks, nearly pitched forward, recovered her balance, then stopped at the end of the channel the stream had cut between the rocks and the sandbar. The channel water was flowing like a sheet of golden glass. Margaret stared into it.

"Nick, that's over our heads."

"It just looks that way. Won't come halfway over your knees."

"My boots only come to my knees."

"That's why you should have worn the goddamn waders."

"DelCorso! Damn you!" O'Brien's voice boomed on the wind. "He's jumped twice."

"Damn him," Margaret said, tentatively stepping into the channel. She drew her leg back when she felt the water's cold shock.

"It's freezing."

"Wouldn't be if you'd worn those waders."

"It's like ice."

DelCorso said nothing. Life had not treated him gently, he had never treated himself gently, so he could feel nothing but contempt for this delicacy of hers. It was not a physical delicacy—she was a tall, well-built young woman—but a frailty of spirit that made her reluctant to suffer any kind of discomfort or inconvenience. Then her hood was blown back by a gust of wind, and her hair, whipping out in wild waves of red, her white skin, oval eyes, and slightly pouting mouth made her look as lovely as one of Botticelli's women. DelCorso's contempt dissolved instantly into enchantment. Because his profession demanded an eye for symmetry and proportion, beauty was more than skin deep to him. As far as he was concerned, a woman who looked like Margaret could be forgiven anything short of a class-one felony.

Lowering his leg, the silent fireworks again bursting when he put his weight on it, he waded across the channel. The trickle of cold water that spilled over the top of his boot temporarily broke the circuit of pain pulsing from his ankle to his thigh and back to his ankle. When he got to the other side, Margaret put her arm around his waist and helped him limp to the bank. He lay down, amazed at how deeply his old wound could exhaust him when it acted up.

"What happened?" Margaret asked, gently rubbing his ankle.

"Don't know. Turned the ankle on a rock. Bone fragment must have worked loose and pinched a nerve. They're in the camera bag, in the compartment with the lens tissues."

"Was it worth it?"

"I'll know when I see the prints."

"It was marvelous, wasn't it? Just like somebody pouring a pitcher of cream. Who knows, if it's good, it could be a start."

"A start?"

"A new start. Maybe you could start doing landscapes instead of that awful stuff."

"They're in with the lens tissues. And bring the flask."

"Nick . . ."

"Maggie, get the flask and the goddamn pills."

She turned to face him, her green eyes demanding contrition for speaking sharply to her.

"Sorry," he said. "You know how I get when the leg gets like this."

"I know," she responded in a forgiving tone. "I'll get them."

O'Brien was with her when she came back. He skidded down the bank, his twelve-foot rod in one hand, a silvery salmon in the other. With the rod, the fish, and a tweed hat to which bucktails and streamers clung like garish insects, he was a figure out of a nineteenth-century lithograph of the gentleman sportsman. He dropped the heavy-bodied fish in the mud next to DelCorso. "Ten pounds," O'Brien said. "Respectable fish for this water. Took a Thunder and Lightning."

DelCorso said nothing. He was not an angler, and O'Brien's talk of Thunder and Lightnings, Silver Doctors and Royal Coachmen bewildered him.

Margaret opened the bottle of Percodans and handed him a capsule with the hip flask.

"You're not supposed to mix them with alcohol, Nick."

Ignoring her advice, he popped the capsule into his mouth, washed it down with two healthy belts of the whiskey, then handed the flask back to Margaret.

"How do you feel?" O'Brien asked perfunctorily.

"I'll feel fine in a few minutes."

"Your wife tells me you injured your leg." O'Brien completed his sporting-gentleman costume by taking a pipe out of his pocket. He lit it, cupping the bowl against the lightly falling rain. "Hope it isn't serious."

"No."

"Your wife tells me it's an old war wound."

"That's right."

O'Brien chewed the pipe thoughtfully, as if he'd been let in on a grave secret. Then, pointing to the salmon:

"What do you think of it?"

"Well, like you said, it's a respectable fish. It looks so respectable it could probably join one of those clubs you guys belong to."

"Nick, that isn't clever."

"I was speaking of its qualities as a photographic subject, young man."

DelCorso bristled at the condescension in "young man." He was a few months short of his thirty-third birthday, but knew that growing old was not necessarily a matter of turning sixty-five.

"As a photographic subject, I'd say it sucks rocks. It's dead."

"Yes, that's—"

"But then, I've made a career out of photographing the dead."

He was beginning to feel the effects of his Percodan and whiskey cocktail, a lessening of pain and a loosening of inhibitions.

"DelCorso, I was about to say that that was my point." There was a crackling sound as O'Brien drew on his pipe. "The salmon is dead, but we hired you to get pictures of living salmon, living bloody leaping salmon."

Feeling nothing now but numbness, DelCorso smiled.

"Did I just say something amusing?"

"No, I'm just feeling good. Nothing, O'Brien, feels so good as feeling real good after you've felt real bad."

"I'm pleased to hear that. Now look, I got two or three fine jumps out of that fish. They would have made splendid shots, but you weren't there at the critical instants. Your wife tells me—"

"My wife tells you." DelCorso, irritated by O'Brien's tone, sat up. "My wife tells you this, she tells you that—"

"Your wife tells me you were photographing sheep," O'Brien went on patiently.

"That's right."

"Mr. DelCorso, we're paying you to take photographs of salmon fishing. Why in the hell did you run off at the critical instant to photograph sheep?"

DelCorso, repressing an impulse to make another wisecrack, considered the question.

"I did it because I'm a thief, O'Brien."

"How's that?"

"All photographers are thieves," DelCorso said, looking at the raindrops in the water. "They steal moments."

"What the devil are you talking about?"

"He means," Margaret interjected, "that the photograph was important to him as an artist."

DelCorso glanced at her, pleased that she was sticking up for him, annoyed that she had both called him an artist.

"What the devil are you both talking about? We're here to take photographs for magazine advertisements."

"Moments. Instants," DelCorso said. "Something happens in a moment. It might be something as simple as a flock of sheep coming over a hill, but it means something to you, it moves you, and you want it to move other people. And if you're going to do that, you've got to get it the instant it's happening. A photographer can't take pictures of his memories. He's got to take it right then, otherwise it'll be gone for good."

O'Brien tapped the tip of his venous nose with the stem of his pipe.

"Look, Mr. DelCorso, let's come to an agreement. We'll try this again tomorrow. Maybe the weather will change and improve the fishing. Whatever, I'd appreciate it if you would do what we're paying you to do, and not go running off after these moments of yours."

"Photos of salmon fishing, right?"

"Right."

"Living, leaping salmon."

"That's the ticket. How's the leg?"

"The leg's rotten, but I'm fine."

"Feel well enough to walk? Here, I'll help you up." O'Brien clapped him on the shoulder and extended a hand—intimate, condescending gestures that made DelCorso want to break the man's jaw.

"Don't need it," he said, hoisting himself to his feet and thinking, I don't need any of it, I don't need this assignment, I don't need to deal with this jerk, I don't need to take pictures of fish, who in the hell wants a picture of a fucking fish anyway? The whiskey and the Percodan had kicked in, and the river in front of him seemed to rise on one side, then fall and rise on the other, like soup sloshing in a bowl.

"Let's be off then." O'Brien again tapped his pipestem against his nose, which looked like a miniature transparency of the human vascular system. "If we get back now, we can give the fish to the chef and have it for dinner this evening. He makes an excellent salmon à la russe. What do you say to that?"

"What do I say to that? I don't have a thing to say to that."

DelCorso moved toward O'Brien, who took a step or two backward, raising his rod as if to defend himself with it. The display of weakness incited DelCorso into one of his fits of outrageous behavior. Bending low, he picked up the fish by the tail and tossed it, then pretended to photograph it where it lay on the bank.

"There it is, O'Brien. You wanted a picture of a salmon, there it is."

O'Brien, too startled to speak, just stood there, pointing his rod like a fencing foil.

"I forgot. You wanted a living *leaping* salmon. Okay, one more time."

DelCorso took hold of the salmon in both hands and with Margaret crying, "Nick, stop it, Nick," spun around several times in the manner of hammer thrower and flung the fish into the river. For an instant, as it tumbled through the rapids, it appeared to achieve the miracle of resurrection. Then it turned belly-up and washed over the falls.

"There goes our finny friend, O'Brien. You want salmon à la russe, swim for it. Then you can shove it up the same place you can shove this assignment."

Dizzy, DelCorso turned to face the other man. His head suddenly felt as if it had been pumped full of helium. He saw the riverbank coming up toward him and managed to flip the Leica behind his back before he lost consciousness and fell face-first into the mud.

2

AS HE TOWELED HIMSELF DRY, DelCorso watched Margaret sitting in front of the mirror, brushing her hair and humming to herself in a tone brittle with the tension between her anger and her need to mask it under an outward calm. Her artificial composure irritated him. Although he did not belong to the let-it-all-hang-out school of emotional exhibitionism, he did think there was a difference between self-control and self-repression. He lay down on the bed and, propping his swollen ankle on a pillow, continued to watch her, his eyes on the brush that swept through her hair in long, crackling, violent strokes. At the end of each stroke, her voice rose an octave, sounding as if it were on the verge of a scream. DelCorso wished she would scream at him, or throw the brush at him, play the fiery Irish maid and vent her anger now; otherwise, it would fester inside her for weeks, growing into an abcess that would burst in a fit of unrestrained fury. Then she would lash him, not only for his behavior toward O'Brien this afternoon but for every misdeed he had ever committed, every ill-chosen word he had ever spoken. In the end, her eruption of spleen, the cracking of her usual containment, would fill her with a remorse that she would blunt with a week-long binge of Valium and liquor. For the sort of Irish Margaret came from were not the Irish of fiery maids, mad poets, and saloon brawlers, but the laciest of lace-curtain Irish, people who had turned themselves into Catholic imitations of the Cabots and the Lodges and who regarded the mere existence, let alone the expression, of certain feelings as impolite.

"Come off it, Maggie. Say it and get it over with."

"Say what?" She put the brush down and stood, every sculpted curve showing through her slip, her red hair reaching halfway down her back.

"You know what. That I acted like an asshole this afternoon."

"If that's the way you want your wife to speak to you, you should have married one of those street sluts you grew up with."

"All I want is a little honesty," he said, gazing at the wall.

Out of the corner of his eye, he caught a glimpse of Margaret slithering into her panty hose. The unequivocal indicator of lust began to rise and push against his tight-fitting underwear; but he had been married to this woman nearly seven years and knew better than to try anything when she was in one of these moods.

Buttoning a tweed dress over her slip, she said:

"Hadn't you better get dressed, Nick? They stop serving at nine."

"Think I'll skip dinner. I'm still hurting."

"If you could climb the stairs, you can go to the dining room."

"No kidding, Maggie. My ankle hurts like hell."

"I'm not going to eat alone with all those men down there. Not after the way you embarrassed me this afternoon. Or do you consider having dinner with your wife a punishment?"

DelCorso glanced at his foul-weather jacket, caked with the dried mud into which he'd collapsed.

"All right," he said, swinging his feet to the floor. "All right, I'll go."

In the dining room, they ate in a strained silence broken only by Margaret's comments on the beef wellington, which she found excellent. Who said the Irish couldn't cook? Every now and then, she looked over his shoulder at O'Brien, eating at a nearby table with some of his fishing pals. They listened attentively to his description of his fight with the salmon. DelCorso overheard him say that he'd lost the fish as he was bringing it to net.

"Well, that was decent of him," Margaret said. "I couldn't

look any of them in the face if he told them the truth. I think he thinks you're insane."

"I don't give a damn what he thinks."

"You will when he talks to his ad agency." Maggie spoke in her breathless voice, which once had a captivating, girlish quality but now sounded like a mimic of Jackie Onassis. "Anyway, it's your career."

"What is that supposed to mean?"

"I imagine he'll tell his agency about your . . . your display this afternoon. The word will get around and then you'll have a hard time getting commercial assignments. Nick DelCorso is a madman. I suppose that's the sort of reputation you want, isn't it?"

"Just say it, Maggie. Stop talking around it."

"What you did this afternoon was your way of burning bridges. With a bad reputation with the ad agencies you won't get as many commercial assignments. You'll have to take news assignments. Then you don't have to keep the promise you made me. Very clever."

DelCorso said nothing. Impetuous by nature, he often did things without the vaguest idea of why he did them; so her theory about his motives was as plausible as any. The promise to which she referred was the one she'd extracted from him last summer, after he'd returned from Cyprus. He and Bolton had spent the first day and night of the Turkish invasion of the island trapped in a Kyrenia hotel under mortar and machine-gun fire. After they'd escaped and made their way to Nicosia, shells falling on the road, napalm exploding in the Kyrenia Pass, Bolton filed a graphic account of their adventure. Most of the papers in the United States picked up the story. Two days later, DelCorso received an urgent telegram from Fiona, Margaret's English *au pair* girl: MAGGIE SERIOUSLY ILL IN HOSPITAL. KIDS ALL RIGHT. RETURN IMMEDIATELY. When he got to New York, he found Margaret in the psychiatric ward of NYU hospital, where she'd been taken with what her doctor called an "acute anxiety reaction." After she'd read Bolton's story in the *Times,* Fiona told him, she'd fallen apart and overdosed on V-and-Vs—Valium and vodka cocktails.

Seeing the lovely Margaret locked up with schizos and drug addicts made DelCorso feel low enough to crawl under a door on his back without scratching his nose. When she was released, he readily, even eagerly gave in to her pleas never to put her through such an experience again. He turned down an offer from *Newsweek* to cover Belfast, another from *Time* to go to Ethiopia, and, just last month, another *Newsweek* assignment to photograph the most recent North Vietnamese offensive. Instead, he did promotional campaigns like the one from Erinair, corporate annual reports, and—his low point—a photo essay on Goldie Hawn for *People* magazine. It was whoring, but of the call-girl rather than the streetwalker variety. Even when he deducted his agent's forty percent and the inevitable kickbacks to account executives and art directors, he'd made more in the past eight months than he had in the previous two years. The money, for a while, mitigated the way commercial work made him feel about himself. Margaret had meanwhile made a rapid and, according to her psychiatrist, impressive recovery. DelCorso had not found it so impressive; for weeks before Cyprus, she had been badgering him to get out of the news business since the news business, for a freelancer, almost always entailed risk. She didn't want to be a widow, which was understandable; he didn't want her to be one either. He'd told her he knew how to take care of himself. In all his years of photographing wars, he hadn't been scratched. None of his reassurances helped, and he had a feeling that her breakdown, like so much of her behavior, had been at least partly contrived, a bit of theater. He said as much to her doctor, who admitted it was a possibility, but pointed out that even if she had been acting, a woman who took so much pride in her self-control must have been desperate to go to such lengths to make her point. DelCorso saw his logic; still, he felt the victim of a scam, emotionally blackmailed, enslaved by her weakness.

They continued eating in silence. The waiter appeared, a small man with a broad, red turf-cutter's face. He pulled the bottle of Château Latour from its bucket, and, with a flourish, bent over to refill Margaret's glass. To show she had a tight rein on herself, she put her hand over the rim, giving DelCorso a brilliant, winning smile that would have helped crown her homecoming queen had she gone to a school that held ceremonies so vulgar as homecomings.

"Would you care for any more?" the waiter asked.

DelCorso nodded.

"Has everything else been satisfactory?"

"Oh, more than satisfactory," Margaret answered.

"I shall mention that to the chef. Where in the States are you from, if you don't mind my asking?"

"New York."

"I've an American cousin in New York. In the Bronx. He teaches at university there. Fordham, I believe."

"That's interesting," Margaret said in a tone suggesting it was anything but. The waiter stood awkwardly for a moment, obviously curious to find out if they knew his American cousin. Then Margaret dismissed him with a slight turn of her head, the subtle gesture of a woman who had learned very early how to deal politely but unequivocally with those who had been put on this earth to serve her.

"That was great," DelCorso said.

"What?"

"The way you blew him off."

"Nick, waiters are not supposed to lurk around their customers talking about their cousins." She paused to scoop up a forkful of peas in the European fashion, mashing them against her fork with her knife. "And don't tell me that makes me sound like a snob."

"All right. It doesn't make you sound like a snob."

"I'm not a snob. I simply have standards."

"You have money, Maggie."

"You used the wrong tense."

She said this in her airiest voice, the regal smile shining on him to show she intended no malice.

"We've done all right this year," DelCorso said in defense of his abilities to provide her with at least a semblance of the life she'd known before marrying him.

"I know that. Anyway, it doesn't make a difference to me how well you do financially."

"How in the hell can you say that with a straight face?"

"Because it's true."

"Look. You wanted that town house in Brooklyn Heights and you got that. You wanted an *au pair* girl and you got her. You wanted a private school for Danny next year and he's going to one. You wanted a maid to come in twice a week and she's coming in—"

"Not so loud." She cocked her head toward O'Brien's table.

"All I'm saying is that it makes one helluva difference to you how well I do. Christ, the mortgage and the taxes on that house run me nearly a thousand a month."

"I thought you liked the house."

"Did you hear me say I don't?"

"All right, then." She ran a finger around the edge of her

glass. "It would be less of a strain if you didn't rent that place in Soho."

"Photographers need labs."

"You could set up a lab at home. We've got nine rooms."

"I don't like working at home."

"I see. As if you're home so much. You're hardly ever home. I want another glass of wine, Nick."

"Maggie—"

"And I don't want any of your AA lectures."

DelCorso felt a cold, stabbing sensation in his chest; he'd been able to turn a blind eye to her episodic drinking problem before her breakdown; since then, it made him nervous whenever she drank more than a glass of anything alcoholic.

"Signal the waiter if you're not going to pour it yourself."

He grabbed the neck of the bottle as if it were a chicken he meant to strangle and filled Margaret's glass.

"*Grazie, Nicolò,*" she said, touching the stem with her white fingers, the nails trimmed into perfect ovals.

"*Non fa niente,*" he answered. "Don't mention it."

Chairs scraped and squealed against the polished wooden floor as O'Brien and his friends left their table for the bar.

Later, when he and Margaret finished dinner, DelCorso moved quickly to Margaret's chair and helped her from the table. The traditional social courtesies were important to her. He tried to perform the gesture gracefully, but felt awkward, especially when she stood. In her stocking feet, Margaret was five-nine, only an inch shorter than he; in the kind of heels she had on tonight, she rose to six feet and made him feel more like a younger brother than a husband and lover—an ugly younger brother at that. With his overly muscled physique, perpetual five o'clock shadow, and eyebrows joined by a tuft of hair on the bridge of a nose that had been flattened in a Golden Gloves fight years before, DelCorso could not even be described with the euphemism "ruggedly handsome." He sometimes took perverse pleasure in the reaction the contrast between Margaret's beauty and his ugliness drew from others. Now, walking past the bar toward the front desk, he saw O'Brien and his friends glance at her with impotent lust and at him with baffled envy, as they might at a man who climbs out of a Ferrari dressed in a secondhand suit. Margaret was certainly a Ferrari of a woman, and in those rare moments

when he wondered why he'd married her, he had to confess
that pride of possession had something to do with it. He
also had to confess that possession exacted its price: maintaining her had turned out to be more financially and
emotionally expensive than he'd expected. The emotional
costs came in small but frequent installments. He paid
one now. Entering the small lobby, Margaret excused
herself to go to the ladies' room. A snake of anxiety
crawled through DelCorso's gut; the ladies' room was in the
bar.

"Why don't you use the one in the room?" he asked.

"It's freezing in the room."

He didn't think it was that cold and, watching her walk
away, wondering if she was taunting him, he resisted the
temptation to follow and make sure she didn't sneak a quick
shot. He couldn't be her policeman every time she got within
label-reading distance of a bottle.

DelCorso went instead to the front desk, to check for messages. The clerk handed him a cable from Northstar, his agency
in New York. As he read, a sensation like the onset of a high
fever came over him.

APRIL 1 2030 GMT
NICHOLAS DELCORSO SPORTSMAN'S INN LEENANE IRELAND
NORTH VIETS HAVE CARRIED OFFENSIVE BEYOND BORDER
PROVINCES. TOOK DANANG YESTERDAY. CERTAIN TO TRY FOR
SAIGON NEXT. NEWSWEEK RENEWING OFFER OF ONE THOU-
SAND WEEKLY PLUS EXPS FOR YOU TO COVER MAIN STORY.
WILSON TO BE BACKUP. IF YOU ACCEPT UPWRAP ERINAIR AND
REPLY ASAP EST. HAVE YOU BOOKED ON AIR FRANCE 612 LVG
ORLY NINE A.M. PARIS TIME THURSDAY. FYI DUNLOP IN VIET
FOR TIME. RGDS KAPLAN.

No problem about wrapping up the Erinair assignment, he
thought, his hands tingling with a pleasant terror as they held
the cable. It could not have arrived at a worse moment as far
as his relations with his wife went, but he knew immediately
what his answer would be. Christ, if the North Vietnamese
took Saigon, it would be the biggest foreign story of the decade.
It occurred to him that he should talk things over with Margaret before committing himself, but, afraid she would ensnare
him with tears or implied threats of self-destructive behavior,
he borrowed the clerk's pen and quickly wrote his reply:

3

MARGARET SHIVERED against the cold the night wind drove through the cracks in the window frames. Slipping out of her dress, which she hung immediately, she put on her green monogrammed dressing gown and a pair of furry white slippers that resembled two decapitated rabbits. DelCorso marveled at how even those failed to make her look unattractive. She shuffled into the bathroom, where she began the ritual she performed each night before going to bed: brushing her cover-girl teeth, then her hair again, one hundred strokes exactly, then, with the tap running, cleansing her face as prescribed in the beauty manuals, with a circular motion of the washcloth.

Taking his camera bag, DelCorso fell into one of his own routines—organizing his equipment. He would have to offer Margaret a logical explanation for taking the *Newsweek* assignment and he hoped the familiar, mechanical process of sorting out his lenses, light meters, filters, lens tissues, cameras, and film would bring some order to his thoughts. Like many impulsive people, he often tried to justify his impulsiveness by inventing sound motives for decisions made on the spur of the moment. He was usually good at these after-the-fact rationalizations, but tonight his thoughts were careening inside his head. The plane was leaving Paris for Saigon on Saturday. *For Saigon.* I'm leaving for Saigon on Saturday, he said to himself, as if he did not fully believe it was possible to do such a thing. *For Saigon.* All his instincts told him this offensive was it, the last show, and he was obliged to be there to record the final scenes and images of the longest war in American history. He would feel like a deserter if he didn't go. Would that obligation make sense to Margaret? Of course not.

She was standing by the rain-spattered window, her arms folded under her breasts, elevating them into a white, cleaved ridge beneath the neckline of her dressing gown.

"Now I know why my great-grandparents left this country," she said. "It's beautiful enough, but, God, what a dreary climate."

Her voice was little more than background noise, piped-in music playing in his ear while he concentrated on practicalities. Practicalities. He had all the cameras and lenses he would need, but not enough film. He could buy film in Saigon. There was always plenty of film in Saigon. Most photographed war in history, every GI an armed tourist packing his Minolta into combat and taking snapshots of corpses to show the folks back home. The GIs were long gone, but the markets had stocked enough film to last a century.

"I guess the climate made O'Casey and Yeats write the way they did," Margaret went on, looking out the window. "It's hard to imagine Greece or Italy producing an O'Casey or a Yeats."

Who the hell was O'Casey? His clothes. He'd forgotten about his clothes. Bending over the luggage rack, DelCorso rummaged through the suitcase. Turtleneck sweaters, flannel shirts, corduroy trousers. Nothing that would be of use in Vietnam except a pair of Navy denims, a fatigue shirt, and his old jungle boots, the same pair he'd worn in the Airborne. He could have Mr. Minh sew up a couple of shirts and buy trousers in the Ben Thanh market. Margaret could take his warm clothes back to New York, along with the film he'd shot here. He thought briefly of the picture he'd taken in the afternoon and felt a pang of regret that it would be weeks before he would see how it had turned out. He put the regret in its place and started packing.

"Nick?"

"What?"

"Have you heard a word I said?"

"Something about this being a lousy climate."

"What're you doing?"

"Packing."

"We don't have to leave just because you made a . . . just because you're off the assignment. We've got enough of our own money to last a few days."

"I know."

"Let's salvage something out of this trip. Explore around. We haven't had a vacation together in two years. Not since Spain."

"I thought you said you didn't like the climate."

"I don't, but I wouldn't mind exploring a bit."

The tenor of her voice reflected a true calm, and DelCorso hated the idea of upsetting her. Moreover, her suggestion appealed to him for a passing moment. They would explore this country of misty landscapes, stone villages, and gray lakes and, perhaps, recapture the harmony they had known the first year of their marriage. He put the notion in its place as well, and, before he lost courage, said:

"We've got to drive to Dublin tomorrow. Got a wire from Kaplan when you were in the bathroom downstairs. Another assignment."

"Is it that urgent?"

"It is. *Newsweek* . . . the hell with it . . . read this."

He handed the telegram to her. She read it, folded it slowly and neatly, and gave it back to him.

"I thought you weren't allowed back in Vietnam."

"That was five years ago. Anyhow, Wilson's there. I can wire ahead to him. He'll straighten out any problems."

"So, you've answered Kaplan already."

"Yes."

"That certainly was asap. You might have taken a second or two to talk to me about it."

DelCorso said nothing.

"Instead you present me with this *fait accompli*. That was considerate." Now her voice crackled like the rain against the window. "And it was very considerate of Kaplan to book the flight for you. You're lucky to have such a considerate agent."

"Maggie, look. I know I promised, but this isn't some bongo war. It's too big to pass up."

"Is it worth your life?"

"No, but I've got a responsibility—"

"*Don't* talk to me about your responsibilities. I don't want to hear it. What about your other responsibilities? To me and Danny and Angela. If you want to talk about responsibilities, talk about those."

"Yeah. All right. Let's talk about them. A thousand a week. *Newsweek* takes a lot of color, so Kaplan can sell the black-and-whites they don't use. If this assignment lasts a month or more, there's something wrong with me if I don't clear, say, eight grand."

"You can make more—"

"Yeah, I know. Taking pictures of Goldie Hawn, but eight grand isn't exactly pocket change. Eight grand helps us keep the house and your *au pair* and the private school so Danny doesn't have to learn readin', writin', and 'rithmetic with a bunch of spades and spics."

"Stop that!"

"Sorry. I meant blacks and Hispanics."

"Are you finished?"

"No. What I'm telling you is that this is what I do. This is what I'm best at, whether you like it or not."

"Go on."

"I expect to finish this assignment. I don't expect to get another telegram telling me that you're in the hospital. I won't buy that act a second time."

DelCorso had discovered the secret formula, the solution that dissolved the iron lace of Margaret's reserve. In other words, he got his fiery Irish maid, who lunged and slapped him hard enough across the mouth to draw blood.

"Act!" she shrieked. "You miserable son of a bitch, you think it was an act? An act spending ten days in that awful ward."

Her eyes glinting like green stones, she came at him with the other hand. He blocked it and stepped back, though he was secretly delighted by this cathartic outburst.

"It was an act to spend ten days locked up with maniacs, ten days separated from my children? Goddamnit, Nick, when I read that story, my only thought was, What do I tell the children if he's killed over there? What do I tell them if that happens? 'Your father died for a color photograph in *Newsweek* magazine'?"

"Maggie—"

"I could put it on your tombstone. 'Nicholas DelCorso, 1942–1975. He gave his life for *Newsweek*.' "

"You're breaking the rule, Maggie. No talk about tombstones before one of these assignments."

"It seems to me you broke something by taking this assignment."

"I explained why," DelCorso said, aware that he hadn't really explained a thing.

"I don't care why. All I know is that I gave up a lot for you and I don't seem to be getting much in return. And don't give me any talk about the house and Fiona and the private school. I mean emotionally."

"All you gave up was a life you didn't want to lead."

With the tip of his little finger, DelCorso wiped the trickle of blood from the corner of his mouth. At this gesture, Margaret softened. Daubing his lip with a Kleenex, she apologized for striking him. The apology was offered to herself as much as to him. To regain her control, she went into the bathroom, where DelCorso heard her open a prescription bottle. Valium, which helped Maggie DelCorso play Margaret Delaney Fitzgerald. She came out, opened a drawer, and started packing, folding her clothes just so; it was as though she found something therapeutic in meticulousness. DelCorso went back to his suitcase, and there were the two of them, packing up within five feet of each other but with so much distance between them that they might as well have been in separate rooms. They were, in a manner of speaking, packing up emotionally, preparing for the moment of departure. Logically, they should have continued to do so, exchanging no more than small talk, but life is seldom so tidy.

Offhandedly, while scrutinizing the wrinkles in the brown skirt she planned to wear for the drive, Margaret asked, "Nick, what's wrong with me?"

DelCorso, unsure of her meaning, did not reply.

"Well, Nick? I do try to keep you reasonably happy."

"I know you do," he answered, still uncertain.

"I take care of the bills so you don't have to worry about them and can concentrate on your work. I try to manage the house so it's pleasant for you when you're at home. I think I do a pretty good job raising the children, and I try to make sure they don't bother you after you've come back from an assignment."

"Maggie, I know all that."

"And there've been nights when you've been away that

I've wanted you so badly, I was almost ready to take any man to bed, any man, just to have a man there, but I've never cheated on you."

"Is that a threat?"

"*No.* I would never—all I'm saying is that nine out of ten women wouldn't stand for their husbands being away six months a year, let alone stand for them taking the risks you do."

"I suppose not."

"All I've done wrong is break down. Just once, and it wasn't an act. When I read that story, I thanked God you were safe. But I couldn't sleep that night, and then my heart started beating so fast I thought I was having a heart attack, hot flashes, all of it—"

"Okay, let's not go over that again."

"I do everything I know how to make you happy, and you're still unhappy."

"Who said I'm unhappy?"

"If you weren't, you'd spend a little more time with the children and me when you're at home. But you're never home even when you're at home. You're in that damned lab."

"Maggie, where are you going with all this?"

She didn't answer immediately, but went into the bathroom and draped her skirt over the heated towel rack, to hang out the wrinkles.

"I'd like to know what is so wrong with me that you've got to spend most of your time away from me," she said, turning and standing in the doorway, a look of resolve in her eyes he hadn't seen before.

"Wrong with you?"

"Yes, what's wrong with me?"

"There's nothing wrong with you," he answered, his heart pumping faster when he saw that this reply did not satisfy her.

He had asked for this. He'd wanted to know where her questions were leading, and, now that he saw where, he wanted to go no farther. For they had led dangerously near a truth about his innermost motives that he had no wish to face. It was not "the truth." No one does anything for a single reason, and, in fact, several boilers powered the engine of his restlessness, his compulsive attraction to danger and states of extremes. His sense of obligation was one of them, but he knew, in a way he could not express in words, that a chronic, incurable discontent was another. He couldn't say that Margaret was its cause. Her catalog of her traditional wifely virtues had not only been accurate but incomplete: out of humility and propriety, she'd not mentioned her beauty or her skills as a cook and in bed, though the latter were somewhat limited by the rigidity of her Irish Catholicism. Nevertheless, something was seriously wrong, perhaps with him, perhaps with the way the two of them were together. Whatever its source, his unhappiness drove him out of the house and literally to the ends of the earth. He didn't know why, nor did he wish to know. Finding out would require painful self-examination, for which he had not the time, the talent, or the inclination. He also had an instinct—and he'd learned to trust his instincts—that such a probe might lead to the discovery of a fault in the foundation of his marriage, one that would demand costly repair work beyond his emotional means or demolition of the entire structure.

"You heard me, didn't you, Maggie?" he asked to break the uncomfortable silence.

"I heard."

"It isn't you. There's nothing the matter with you."

"That's good to hear." She forced a smile and he saw the determination in her glance fade. She didn't want to cross into uncharted territory any more than he. "So don't you think you should have at least consulted me before you answered Kaplan? It's not as though you're a salesman, going off to Dubuque to peddle socks."

"I guess I should have. Just didn't think, that's all."

"I know. That's the way you are. You never think beforehand."

Stifling his resentment at her tone, the same tone of affectionate exasperation she used when the children misbehaved, DelCorso embraced her waist and kissed her chastely on the cheek.

"I'll do better next time, all right?"

She turned stiffly in his arms, then moved away and continued packing in her orderly manner.

4

A PLANE CRASH. They had pulled him out of Beirut, flown him across the whole damned Asian continent, and his first major story after arriving had been a plane crash. Granted, the disaster had its dramatic aspects: in the middle of the biggest offensive of the war, an American transport packed with Vietnamese orphans had gone down minutes after takeoff from Tan Son Nhut. But it had been nothing more than a disaster, the kind of story he would have jumped at in the days when he was chasing fire engines but had no interest in now. It should have been covered by Grey, the overeager, overcocky young staffer he wanted to send to the crash site, not by Harry Bolton, who considered himself a war correspondent first and foremost, the best, as far as he was concerned, since Pyle and Hemingway had pounded their Underwoods across Europe. In an age of specialization, he was a master of a specialized and dangerous craft and, like all specialists, intensely proud of his unique abilities. So, when New York telexed him to take Grey off the plane crash and cover the story himself, he'd felt insulted to the point of humiliation. It was as though a highly trained electronics expert in a guided-missile factory had been told to rewire a light switch in the men's room.

Being a good soldier, he had done as he was told. Now, sitting in Laxalt's old office with his size thirteens on the desk, he picked up the clipboard with the outgoing copy and checked it for errors. There were none, but as Bolton reread his lead, anger seated itself in his guts, the throne of his emotions.

> SAIGON—AT LEAST 178 PERSONS, MOST OF THEM VIET-NAMESE ORPHANS 8 MONTHS TO 12 YEARS OLD, DIED SAT-URDAY WHEN AN AMERICAN C-5A GALAXY FLYING THEM TO SAFETY IN THE UNITED STATES CRASHED SHORTLY AFTER TAKEOFF FROM SAIGON'S TAN SON NHUT AIRPORT.
>
> THE GIANT PLANE, CARRYING 243 ORPHANS, 44 ESCORTS, AND 16 CREW MEMBERS, WAS ON ITS WAY TO THE PHILIPPINES ON THE FIRST LEG OF A MERCY MISSION TO TAKE THE CHIL-DREN TO THE U.S. FAMILIES WHO HAD ADOPTED THEM. THE AMERICAN EMBASSY IN SAIGON SAID ABOUT 100 ORPHANS AND 20 ESCORTS SURVIVED THE TRAGEDY.

Bolton tossed the clipboard across the desk. Mercy mission. Tragedy. Journalistic buzz words he used because editors expected them. What bullshit.

"Grey," Bolton called into the other room, where teletypes stuttered above the gurgling death rattles of two very old air-conditioners.

Grey sauntered through the door, on which a metal sign read INTERNATIONAL PRESS SERVICE—SAIGON BUREAU. Below that, in the space where Laxalt's name had been, hung a piece of cardboard with the hand-lettered words, "Harold W. Bolton, Acting Bureau Chief. *That Which Is Not Prohibited Is Mandatory.*"

"What've you got?" asked Grey, a small, long-haired twenty-three-year-old who'd been in the eighth grade when Bolton was hosing down landing zones with an M-60.

"Here's the crash story." Bolton handed the younger man the clipboard. "Call the embassy for an update on casualty figures, then sub the lead."

"Okay."

"And take 'tragedy' out of the second graph. Make it 'ca-tastrophe,' 'calamity,' 'dire misfortune,' 'king-size fuck-up,' anything but 'tragedy.' "

"Okay. Y'know, I've heard a lot about you but I never heard that you were a wordsmith."

Bolton felt the dull anger in his belly honing itself into a sharp-edged rage. Grey was cocky in the way of a punk who has never lost a fight because he's never been in one. Bolton did not like him.

"Listen, if I tell you to change something in a story, you change it without making any comments."

"Hey, I didn't mean anything by it."

"I don't give a shit what you meant or didn't mean. I'm not Laxalt and this bureau isn't going to be a goddamned democracy anymore. They sent me here to stop this outfit from playing catch-up."

"Jesus. Okay, y'know?"

Bolton, his hand-tooled boots still on the desk, leaned back in the swivel chair and gazed at the mildewed ceiling.

"Grey," he drawled with a threatening undertone. "Just get your sorry young ass on the phone, call the embassy, and sub the lead."

"Yeah, okay, Horseman, okay."

As Grey walked out, Bolton's rage felt like the business side of a Wilkinson sword. Swinging his feet to the floor, he strode into the newsroom and spun Grey around by the shoulders.

"Listen, you little SOB. I don't know who told you that's my nickname, but get this. It was tagged on me by a dude named Gillette, a mulatto dude from New Orleans and the best crew chief who ever flew choppers in this war. He was about your size, Grey, but let me tell you, if Gillette was standing in a foxhole with a hard-on and you were standing on a twelve-foot ladder, you still wouldn't be tall enough to lick the end of his dick. I flew about twenty missions with him, and on one of them, he ended up splashed all over half of I Corps, right about the time you were having your first wet dreams."

Astonished, Grey looked up at a broad face, rough as a wood carving. Then his eyes flicked around the room, which was empty except for the two day-shift teletype operators and Hoang, the bureau's driver and interpreter. Hoang did not look up from the newspaper he was reading.

"Jesus. I mean, Jesus, Bolton—that okay? Bolton?—I know you were an army hero and all, but this isn't the army and I'm not some buck private."

"You wouldn't have lasted a Detroit second in the army, but I'll make you eligible for a Purple Heart you ever call me Horseman again. There's only one man in this business who has the right to call me that and it sure as hell isn't you."

Grey brushed back a length of his straight hair and shifted his weight from one foot to the other.

"Sure. It's okay, y'know. I'll cool it."

"You'd better. When a small man has a big mouth, he'd best have the hands to back it up, and something tells me that you couldn't punch a hole in a Chinese lantern."

Then Vincent came in, turning Bolton's attention away from Grey. Vincent, the bureau's full-time stringer, was an old hand. He'd been in Indochina for fifteen years in one incarnation or another, and was valuable for his contacts, a value diminished by the bad habits white men like him inevitably acquire when they stay too long in places they should never have gone to in the first place.

"Welcome back," Bolton said, looking with benign disgust at the heat-rumpled clothes hanging loosely on a frame wasted by opium and alcohol.

"Got to her, Harry," Vincent said, unable to keep the guilt out of his voice. He was referring to the Santa Monica woman who had been one of the escorts to survive the crash. Her local newspaper, an IPS client, had asked for a story about her.

"Way it looks to me, the only thing you got to were a few not-so-quick quickies at the Caravelle."

"Honest to Christ, Harry. I talked to the lady in the hospital. It's all here." Pulling a creased notebook from his hip pocket, he pretended to be in a great rush to get to his typewriter.

"Vinnie, I'm not the snotnose you knew in 'sixty-eight. I'm thirty-five, and I say you had a few quickies. Your eyes are as pink as a rooster's prick."

"All right, Harry. All right. But after the interview."

"After the interview. Vinnie, you've been stringing for us ten years, so why do you have to be reminded every time that we've got deadlines? This is a wire service, not a high school annual."

"I'll get it out, Harry. No problem."

Vincent, lighting a cigarette yellowed by his boozy sweat, sat at his desk, opened his notebook, and made a pretense of trying to write a lead. Bolton stood behind him and picked up the notebook.

"You're an opium-head and a juicer, Vinnie, but I like you. You don't have to put on any shows for me."

"What show, Harry? I interviewed the broad."

"I'm not talking about that. We both know that you couldn't write a bad check when you've had a few. Give your notes to Grey. He'll do the story."

Vincent, his gaunt and sallow face turned toward Bolton, shrugged noncommittally.

"You hear that, Grey? You take Vincent's notes and do a couple of takes on our heroine from Santa Monica."

Grey, on the phone to the embassy, nodded.

"All right, troops, I'll be at the Shelf if anyone needs to reach me," Bolton said.

"You need ride?" Hoang asked.

"Maybe later. Stick around for now. Vincent might need you to drive him out to Cho Lon for a few happy-hour pipes. How many does it take to get you high these days, Vinnie? Two dozen?"

Vincent, with eyes the color of denim that's spent a week in a tub of Clorox, stared vacantly out the window over the jumble of tin and red-tile roofs toward the rice fields beyond the Ben Nghe canal.

"You know, Harry, when I met you in 'sixty-eight, I knew you had the potential to become a first-class asshole and you've lived up to it."

"Ain't it nice when somebody lives up to his potential."

"I'll call you at the Shelf if anything comes up."

"And if you can't reach me there, I'll be where I don't want to be reached."

"Be sure to bundle up so you don't catch anything."

"It ain't what you're thinking. I've only been here a couple of days, but the Horseman rides fast. I might, I say *might* be onto something that'll make the competition start playing catch-up for a change."

Outside, the air clamped over Bolton's nose and mouth like a chloroformed rag. Saigon. The humidity was in the nineties, the temperature threatening to break a hundred, and the traffic strangling both sides of Le Loi Boulevard was spewing enough poisons to give an environmentalist nightmares for the rest of his life. Bolton walked slowly toward the Continental Hotel; he had plenty of time before he met Christensen, and the heat wouldn't allow him to move any faster. He was sweating already. Piercing through the polluting haze, the sun crackled off sidewalks on which pimps hawked fellatio artists, free-lance pushers offered nickel bags of Cambodian Red, street vendors peddled rice cakes and duck eggs, watches, trinkets, Montagnard bracelets of hammered silver, bits of jade and pieces of junk, transistor radios, tape decks, cameras, film, cigarettes, condoms, and soap, their voices chorusing, *you buy you buy.* Saigon was the consumer society gone berserk. She could give you anything you wanted and a lot of things you didn't need. Bolton kept walking, stopping now and then to dole out a few worthless piasters to the crippled veterans who begged from him, to the freaks like The Crab, a man whose limbs were twisted into the curlicues of modern sculpture and who moved with a sidling motion; to Smiling Jack, limbless, the nerve damage to his face freezing his lips into a perpetual grin; to Needle Tracks, the smack-shooting hooker, only twenty-one and so gone with disease she couldn't hook for it any longer, just panhandled in the ghetto jive she'd learned from the GIs who'd turned her on to the stuff, *hey, man, lay some bread on me cuz I just gotta get well;* to Fast Eddie, whom he'd known for years, an ex-Ranger sergeant who'd lost his legs in a battle no one remembered anymore and who got around on a go-cart, propelling himself with his arms and looking like a midget on a wheeled raft. Saigon.

After he passed the National War Monument—a huge, incredibly bad piece of sculpture depicting two Vietnamese soldiers in action, one bent at the waist in the posture of a charging infantryman, the other behind him in the same position, his concrete crotch almost touching the first soldier's buttocks, thus giving the statue its nickname, "The National Buggery Monument"—Bolton waited to cross Lam Son Square at the intersection of Le Loi and Tu Do. Over the roar of motorbikes, motor scooters, taxis, cars, cyclos, and trucks, loudspeakers mounted atop the streetlights blared speeches and music. Since the fall of Danang, to inspire the Saigonese to defend their city, President Thieu had ordered the broadcasting of patriotic songs and slogans at all major street corners. That was his way of meeting Hanoi's offensive. Meanwhile, he remained in his palace, ranting, like some Asian Lear, at the Americans for refusing to send him any more B-52s. And despite songs and slogans, his subjects remained obdurately uninspired. They went on hawking and hustling, bargaining and cheating, though Bolton detected something new in the commercial frenzy: the beginnings of real panic, a growing recognition that the end was coming combined with a paradoxical determination to go on with business as usual. Saigon. Maybe she had once been the city the guidebooks called the Paris of the Orient. She hadn't looked bad when Bolton first saw her in 1964. But she was now like a syphilitic old madam who knew a raid was coming but who was too weak and sick to do anything about it except get what she could out of the last customers before the vice squad shut her down.

Running through the traffic—it was like returning a kick-off through a demolition derby—he climbed the steps to the terrace of the Continental. It was known as the Continental Shelf, but Bolton preferred to call it Vultures' Roost. It was the wateringhole-*cum*-feeding-trough for the newsmen who had come from a dozen different countries to record Saigon's collapse. There were the special correspondents from the big newspapers, the specials with their fat salaries and expense accounts; the wire-service men, whose salaries, like Bolton's, kept their heads above the poverty level, provided they knew how to tread water; magazine writers, photographers, light-men, soundmen, cameramen, and the leading men who reported for the networks in Abercrombie and Fitch safari suits; stringers working for obscure newspapers like the *Sun Valley Sun*; weirdo adventurers using press cards as a cover for operations involving the export of certain cash crops: and an assortment of self-styled free-lancers who would have been arrested for vagrancy if the Saigon police hadn't had more important problems to deal with. There was even an attractive young woman from *Rolling Stone*. What interest *Rolling Stone* had in the North Vietnamese offensive was anyone's guess. Maybe, Bolton thought, they were planning a piece on Saigon's Top Forty. The whole mob charged the air with a tawdry excitement that made Bolton's stomach feel like an ad for an acid-indigestion remedy. Out of the lot, you could count the true professionals on both hands with a finger or two to spare. The rest were thrill seekers and voyeurs and headline hunters who couldn't tell the difference between a tank and an armored personnel carrier, had no idea how many men were in a battalion, and thought a fire-fight had something to do with sirens and bright red trucks. Elizabeth St. John, for example: a tall, gorgeous Englishwoman, a former concubine of British royalty now attached to a famous BBC reporter with whom she toured the rice paddies dressed in resort wear, a Nikon hanging from her willowy neck to lend herself the appearance of legitimacy. Fucking Saigon. Wouldn't it have been a kick in the ass if this gang had been in Rome when the Visigoths were knocking at the gates?

He despised them because professionalism was his religion. In eight years with the International Press Service, he had covered Tet, the invasion of Cambodia, and the North

Vietnamese offensive in 'seventy-two. He had been in Israel
when the Egyptians surprised everybody, the Israelis especially, by breaching the Bar Lev line; he had choppered into
the bush with the Rhodesian African Rifles, had listened to
the crackle of sniper fire in Londonderry, and, by sheer chance,
he had been standing in the middle of the drop zone when
Turkish paratroopers paid a visit to Cyprus. In the interims
between those major bouts, he'd kept in trim by reporting on
obscure uprisings in places like the Ogaden Desert and the
Western Sahara, on airline hijackings, terrorist attacks, coups,
riots, rebellions, and revolutions. Bolton followed wars the
way a migrant worker follows harvests.

His work had won him a Pulitzer and two Overseas Press
Club awards, cost him his marriage, and gave him a view of
human nature somewhat at odds with the prevailing Western
liberal opinion that man is essentially good. He regretted the
divorce, didn't care if others thought him cynical, and cared
still less about the prizes. He hadn't even bothered to frame
those pieces of paper, which did not confirm his talent any
more than the Silver Star he'd won as a helicopter door-gunner
confirmed his bravery. Talent, like courage, had to be reaf-
firmed each day. In the service, yesterday's hero could be today's coward; in the news business, the old cliché, you're only
as good as your last story, was still true, and no amount of
Pulitzers or OPCs would change it. Anyway, those journalistic
medals were given out by the sort of men Bolton despised,
pompous editors who made Rotary Club speeches about the
first amendment and the mission of a free press in a democracy. He had no illusions about missions. He simply saw himself as a consummate professional, a man whose work was
justified by his skill in performing it. The way Bolton saw
things, Willie Sutton should have been made president of Chase
Manhattan instead of thrown in jail.

Nature had designed Bolton for his work. He was a big
man, nearly six-feet-four and two-twenty. Growing up in the
mountains of western North Carolina had made his legs hard
as ironwood, and the hunting and fishing he'd done in his
boyhood had taught him more about cover, concealment, and
terrain than the best tactics manuals. He'd studied the art of
war at the Citadel, which he attended for two years before he
was expelled and joined the army, and had walked over a dozen
Civil War battlefields, Lookout and Kennesaw mountains, Cold
Harbor, Fredericksburg. He could "read" a battlefield as well

as the best generals he'd known, could look at a map and know how an attack or defense should be executed, and he could translate his knowledge into a clear, concise story and get it on the wire ahead of the competition. With his acute hearing, a sense he considered more important than sight because modern armies often fought without seeing each other, he could distinguish by the sound alone an M-16 from an AK-47, an artillery piece from a tank gun, its range from the target. He also had the nerve and stamina to live up to Winston Churchill's motto, a motto he'd adopted as his own, that a war correspondent's duty is to go as far as he can as fast as he can. Harry Bolton almost always went farther faster than the rest of the pack, and had survived because he had the horse sense to know the difference between far and too far, fast and too fast.

He spotted DelCorso sitting with Wilson and staring at a table in a far corner, where, over wine and sandwiches, Dunlop was holding court with his usual entourage of hangers-on and gofers. Not above self-dramatization, Bolton drew himself to his full height and walked across the terrace with the swagger of a gunslinger in a saloon full of sheepherders, his boot heels clomping on the tiles.

"Say, Harry," called a dissipated English correspondent he knew vaguely, "saw you coming across the square. Appear to be getting slow in your old age."

"Not half as slow as you are when you try to get it up, Purcell. Whatever you need, I haven't got it."

"Just wondering if IPS has something on the crash it would be willing to share with us. Word is the Americans haven't ruled out sabotage."

Fucking limey. He covered a story by interviewing other reporters. Bending over, Bolton whispered into Purcell's ear:

"All right, I've got something, but I'd appreciate it if you kept it to yourself for the next hour or so. Till it's out on the wire."

The Englishman nodded solemnly.

"It was sabotage. Turned out that one of the girl orphans was really a member of a suicide squad of Viet Cong midgets. Soon as the plane was airborne, she set off a bomb hidden in her Barbie doll."

"Thank you, Harry Bolton," Purcell said, raising his glass, "you've been helpful as usual."

"Anything for the mother country."

At DelCorso's table, Bolton pulled up a chair and ordered a thirty-three from the waiter.

"So how was your day?" Wilson asked. DelCorso, sipping a citron pressé—he was one of those self-disciplinarians who never drank on the job before sunset—said nothing.

"Been rode hard and put up wet."

"Sounds like a ruralism," said Wilson. "What's it mean?"

"In my case, it means I fly six thousand miles to cover a war and end up covering a plane crash. It means I've got a wise-ass staffer named Grey who thinks he's the next Peter Arnett because he's got a degree from some journalism school, another staffer, a guy called Dalman, who's floating around with a refugee column and hasn't been heard from in two days, and Vinnie for a stringer, who's in Lotus Land half the time. With that crew, no wonder Laxalt went bonkers."

"Laxalt. Heard anything more about him?"

"No. Just that they put him on a plane with enough Thorazine in him to put a cage full of hyperactive monkeys to sleep."

"Another casualty."

"What the hell, Mark, Laxalt never did have it for this. They should have kept him in Washington, rewriting press releases. Anyway, did the lab process your stuff all right?"

"So-so," Wilson shrugged. "It's that junkyard of equipment your boys have. They can't control the temperature and the water's filthy. Looks like it's piped in from a sewer."

"That's because it is piped in from a sewer. Saigon."

"Yeah, but Conklin over at AP let us have a look at the stuff Dunlop sent through them. Looked a helluva lot better than ours."

"What can I tell you? If I had AP's money, I could buy new equipment. I could hire labmen who don't accentuate the positive and eliminate the negative. But IPS is still run by Lou McDaniels, Lieutenant General, Retired, who's as tight with his money as he's conservative with politics. I mean, here I am with a photo lab, but the son of a bitch won't spend the money to send me one staff photographer. I've got to buy junk off some half-assed stringers."

"Maybe now that you're the number one, that lab'll get squared away," DelCorso said, breaking his silence.

"Nick, you know a bureau chief doesn't have much control over a lab. All I do is pay their salaries."

"The way those prints looked, whatever you're paying them is twice what they're worth."

Bolton took a long swallow of the bitter-tasting beer, wiped the foam from his blond mustache, and leaned forward with his elbows on the table.

"Just what the hell is bothering you?"

"The prints looked real bad. I don't like breaking my ass to get the best stuff I can and then have a lab screw it up."

"Right. But that isn't what's bothering you."

DelCorso took a cigarette from the pocket of his shirt, an old chalky green fatigue shirt with his name stenciled above the left pocket.

"Tired, that's all. Four days ago, I was taking pictures of some clown fishing in Ireland. Ireland, for Christ's sake. I've got terminal jet lag."

"We've all got that."

"The truth is," Wilson said, "Nick had a little tiff with Dunlop about half an hour ago."

"Thought so. He hasn't taken his eyes off the old man. What happened?"

"Nothing."

"When it comes to you and Dunlop, nothing never happens."

"I'll tell you what happened," said Wilson, a thin smile breaking on his face, which, with its fine bone structure, looked like a face that should have been on the other side of a camera. "Seems that Dunlop found out we'd been looking at his stuff. He wasn't pissed or anything. He just strolled over here and said that he'd heard we'd taken a peek and wanted to know if we were getting nervous. Deecee said, no, we weren't nervous. Then he gave a little grin and said he was surprised to see Nick here, that he'd heard Nick had gotten so scared in that thing you two went through in Cyprus that he'd quit the business to take pictures of actresses. Well, you know our golden guinea. He jumped up and poked Dunlop in the chest and told him if he didn't take a walk that minute, he'd quote get his teeth shoved so far down his throat he'd be shitting fillings for a month. End quote. Dunlop just kept grinning. But he did take a walk."

DelCorso felt the red curtain of embarrassment rising up his face.

"Nick," Bolton said, shaking his head, "why in the hell do you let that son of a bitch get to you so easy?"

"I don't let him. He just does."

"Yeah, and I'll tell you why. It isn't terminal jet lag you've got. It's terminal ambition."

"Ambition for what?"

"Your ambition is to be Dunlop."

"*What?*"

"You're the ranked contender who wants the belt."

"Jesus Christ."

"Think it's time for me to go," Wilson said.

"No, stick around, Mark. The Horseman thinks I want to be Dunlop. How about you? Would you want to be that jerk-off?"

"Wouldn't mind having his money."

"Yeah, his money's good. His work isn't. He hasn't done anything new in twenty years. More like thirty. He's still doing the same old crap he did in World War Two because he hasn't got the imagination to do anything new, and now he's gone yellow."

"I'm not one of his fans," said Bolton, "but I'll say this for him—he isn't yellow."

"The hell he isn't. P. X. Dunlop has now become P. X. Dunlop, Incorporated. He's got two people working for him, two of his newest protégés, one in Phnom Penh, the other one here. They cover the routine stuff and sell him their negatives for nickels and dimes just for the privilege of working under the master. Of course, the pictures go out under his credit line, so their stuff has to conform to the master's principles. You know, lots of graininess, plenty of shadow, all that smoky-dawn crap, that war-is-hell-but-it's-dramatic garbage. And while those two are getting shot at, the master lays back in Saigon and plays the great man. He had lunch with the ambassador. The word is, the ambassador's going to get him into the presidential palace to photograph Thieu. It'll be a perfect piece of *Time* magazine propaganda. 'South Vietnam's embattled President plans defense of Saigon against the Communist onslaught.' And you're trying to tell me that I want to be like him. I don't know why you brought this up, but let's drop it before I forget that you're a friend of mine."

"I'm not sure why I brought it up," Bolton said. "I'm as competitive as the next guy, but whatever you two have going, it isn't competition. It's hate, and it's liable to get your ass shot off."

"You ever known me to take a risk that wasn't worth taking?"

"You came close in Israel after Dunlop screwed you out of your exclusive. I should say, after you *thought* he screwed you. That car you were in was halfway to Damascus. The way I heard it, you were the one pushing the driver. Keep going, keep going. You ended up in front of the Israeli lines. You were damned lucky you got out with everything you went in with."

"It wasn't luck."

"What was it, then? Your good looks and winning personality?"

"It wasn't luck."

Bolton gave him a puzzled look; then he tilted his head and brought it forward, pretending to bang it on the small table.

"Wait a minute."

"Drop it, Harry."

"No, wait a goddamned minute. I don't believe you still believe that cockeyed idea that your . . . your whatever you call it, your personal mission kept you from getting killed."

DelCorso glanced nervously at Wilson and said nothing.

"Christ on a crutch, you still do, you superstitious guinea. Nick, you've got a high school diploma, this is the last quarter of the twentieth century. If you really believe that horseshit, why not go all the way and start doing astrological charts, throw an I Ching, wait up for the Easter bunny?"

"We've all got a snake in our heads and that's mine. Let's leave it at that, okay? I'm here for a reason and it isn't to run races with P. X. Dunlop."

"Yeah, I know. You're going to take the war photograph to end all wars. Out of six thousand years of recorded history, there've been about two hundred of peace, but Nick Del-Corso's going to put a stop to it with his Leica."

"Would you two like to take a break and have another round?" Wilson asked.

"Sure."

Wilson signaled the waiter and ordered beers for himself and Bolton, a citron pressé for DelCorso.

"I don't get it," DelCorso said after the drinks arrived. "First you bitch because you think I've got nothing on my mind but whipping Dunlop. When I tell you that's not the case, I'm a superstitious guinea. What do you want?"

"An attitude. A professional attitude. We do this because we're good at it, not because we're going to change anything. We're supposed to record what's happening, not make something happen. That social-activist shit is what those lefty professors feed the troops in journalism school."

"Thanks for the lecture. If my work's good, my attitude shouldn't make a dime's worth of difference."

DelCorso idly blew a smoke ring at the ceiling, where it wavered, then vanished in a puff of air from the overhead fan.

"Anyhow, when was the last time I told you how to write a story?"

"Okay, Nick. I shot my mouth off. Let's drop it."

"You shot your mouth off, all right, but let's not drop it. Let's talk about my attitude. I'd say I was the one with the professional attitude when I got those shots on the Suez Canal."

He was referring to the time when, to avoid the censors, he tried to fly out of Israel with his film hidden inside his radio. The border police were waiting for him when he got to the airport, and knew right where to look. They confiscated his film and sent him back to the Hilton with a warning that he'd get the boot if he tried anything like that again. Later, he'd heard rumors that Dunlop, having found out what he had and how he planned to smuggle it out, had tipped off his contacts in the Ministry of Information, who alerted the police. The pictures were exclusives of the Israelis' counterattack. They would not have won any Pulitzers, but would have gotten wide distribution and made DelCorso a nice piece of change. Dunlop might as well have lifted his wallet.

"I know the story. I also know you could never prove he did that. You just put two and two together and came up with five."

"Bullshit. You tell me why a guy like Dunlop would pull a cheap stunt like that? His reputation's safe even if he never takes another picture, he's got two Pulitzers, a hundred thou a year, he has lunch with ambassadors."

"Hell, if he did do it, it's obvious why," Wilson interjected. "He's scared. Getting old, legs starting to go. You're twenty years younger and even he'll admit you're one of the best."

"*One* of the best? If he's so scared of the competition, why doesn't he pull that bullshit on the others?"

"Maybe because you used to be one of his boys, one of the inner circle, like that mob sitting with him now."

"You're close, Wilson, but you know the real reason. I

5

DELCORSO WATCHED Bolton walk off. Lean-hipped, broad-shouldered, the shoulders sloping into long arms that suggested extraordinary leverage, Bolton's presence made Del-Corso glad he was here. They had met a decade ago, when both were in uniform, Bolton a door gunner, DelCorso an army photographer attached to the 101st Airborne. Since then, they'd covered a lot of assignments together, usually in those parts of the world where the Geneva Convention has about as much application as the mandatory eight count does in a street fight. And in the crucible of shared dangers and deprivations, they had learned to rely on each other implicitly. A special bond united them, the bond that unites all survivors: the intimate knowledge of death.

The same bond united him to Wilson, who had been his classmate in Army Photographer's School. They shared little else. A rich, thrice-divorced Californian, Wilson approached photography as he did the act of getting married: it gave him something to do when he got bored. DelCorso liked him nevertheless, and sometimes envied his lightheartedness.

Across the terrace, Dunlop was adjourning court. He and his entourage stood to leave and had moved only a few steps before a gang of the ragged street kids who hung out near the hotel leaped over the low terrace wall to scavenge the scraps left on the plates. They leaped back into the street when a waiter came at them, snapping his napkin like a whip.

"There it is," DelCorso said as Dunlop walked toward the lobby. Bull-necked, gray hair shaved to a stubble, dressed in camouflage trousers and safari jacket, he looked like one of the generals whose portraits he was fond of taking. "And there it goes."

Wilson rubbed his temples as if he had a headache. "You and that old bastard take each other too seriously."

DelCorso didn't argue. He had always taken Dunlop seriously. When he was with the Airborne, he'd carried copies of all four of Dunlop's books with him: the pictures in them seemed the real stuff, what war photography was supposed to be all about, not like the for-home-consumption junk Del-Corso had to do for the army and *Stars and Stripes*. Dunlop's pictures got it all in: the mud, the rain, and the filthy-looking grunts, the bodies in the body-bags, and a mysterious dramatic quality—DelCorso thought then that war was mysterious and dramatic, despite what he had seen the Airborne do at a place called Rach Giang. He loved to look at Dunlop's pictures. He'd look at them for hours, trying to figure out how he did it. When he came back to Vietnam as a free-lance in 'sixty-eight, he attached himself to the older man and practically begged him for lessons.

Dunlop, who loved playing teacher, obliged. In the field, he used the same equipment, technique, and film as all photographers. It was in the lab that he revealed his talents. He painted his pictures, painted them with light. He'd heat up the development, pushing the film through to get the graininess that was his trademark. He would dodge, burn, and flash for hours. DelCorso once saw him go through fifty sheets on a single print before he got the sky just right, a gray that looked like a winter sky over the Baltic. Darkened skies were his specialty. A vintage Dunlop looked as if it had been shot at dusk or in the rain, even if the actual exposure had been made on a cloudless day at high noon. That was what he taught DelCorso and that's what DelCorso did through Tet and afterward. It was imitation Dunlop, but he did all right, earning twenty-eight thousand that year. Dunlop helped him there as well, putting him onto stories and in touch with agencies.

In the two years between the Tet Offensive and the Cambodian invasion, DelCorso covered the antiwar movement, every sit-in and campus riot from Berkeley to Harvard. The one conflict he photographed was Biafra, which forever rid him of any notions that war possessed drama and mystery. Biafra, with its slaughter and starvation, reminded him of the lesson he'd learned at Rach Giang: it was his job, and every other combat photographer's job, to put themselves out of business.

He wanted to disturb people. At the very least, he wanted to make the powerful pause and reflect before they acted out their napalm fantasies. The trouble was, his work hadn't changed. He was still doing Dunlop-style smoky dawns, which didn't disturb anybody. Along came Cambodia. Dunlop and he went in together with the 11th Cavalry. Dunlop had meanwhile published *My Objection*, his fifth book, a halfhearted attempt to catch up with the antiwar mood in the United States, a hawk's book with a dove's cover. DelCorso had a copy with him and was amazed to see that it had forty pages of text. Knowing there had to be something wrong with a photographer who needed forty pages to explain his photographs, he studied the pictures and tried to figure out what it was. Then it struck him: there was nothing objectionable about them. You could look at them and not feel there was anything objectionable about the war. They were dramatic, mysterious, and, in their way, as much for home consumption as the work DelCorso had done for *Stars and Stripes*. Dunlop made the mud, the rain, and the misery look attractive. He even made violent death appear acceptable. In his pictures, the dead were in body-bags, or tastefully masked with skillful burning-in. You knew they were bodies, but you felt a distance, you felt, perhaps, a little sad, you could almost hear the sweet mournful notes of Taps; but you didn't feel the way you really feel when you see some pile of slop with his guts bulging out or his legs gone or his skin the yellow-green color of death. You could look at those pictures and still think it fitting and proper to die for your country. Dunlop's live subjects, no matter how raggedy, all looked Hollywood heroic, bearded warriors in their foxholes. That was because he specialized in the elite outfits, avoiding the ordinary rifle companies whose ranks were filled at that time with weirdo hippie killers, peace symbols on their necks and murder on their minds. They didn't fit Dunlop's idea of what GI Joe should look like. Hell, they didn't fit anybody's idea of what anything should look like.

DelCorso decided to do something different. Out of all the pictures he'd taken during his imitative period, the only one he liked was of a shell-shocked marine that ran in *Esquire*. He'd photographed him in Hue, after the Marines retook the city's citadel, and still thought it the best photo anybody had ever taken of battle fatigue, the old thousand-yard stare. The best, he came to realize, not because he'd played Pablo Picasso in the lab, but because he'd stayed with the marines through the whole rotten mess. Three weeks with the 5th Marines, who took *sixty* percent casualties. Those who were left were crazy, real crazy, in-another-universe crazy, and DelCorso was just as crazy. He'd got the reality of shell shock across because he was shell-shocked when he took the picture.

Going into Cambodia, he knew he would have to stay with the cavalry through the entire operation, live the experience if he was going to get it right. And shoot from up close. He didn't care what kind of long lens a photographer used, the lie of distance came through in the print. Instead of mist, smoky dawns, and mystery, he wanted clarity, the kind of clarity you get staring into the sun with a five-star tequila hangover, the kind that hurts. Wanting people to see what a traumatic amputation looked like, he took a close-up of a Chicano kid who'd been hit in the groin. The background of the photo showed a few soldiers playing cards on the hood of a jeep. It was the kind of detail Dunlop would have left out. DelCorso left it in to show that what happened to the kid was not extraordinary, but an everyday event. He shot him and the freaks with their long hair and peace symbols: a grunt with a prick tattooed on his arm and a bloodstained belt around his waist—he'd ripped it off an NVA he'd killed in a fire-fight—taking a smoke break with a stick of Red; a sergeant looting a temple, grinning as he walked off with a little stone buddha. Then DelCorso paid a visit to the rear. Let the folks back home see what the brass were doing while their sons and lovers were killing and looting and getting their genitals shot off. He wormed his way into a command generals' mess and sneaked a few shots of bald old men eating lobster thermidor. Then he put everything together, selling it as a series of photo essays to *Life* and the *Times* Sunday magazine. Sold it at standard rates; he didn't give a damn about the money. He just wanted the pictures in print to register his own kind of objection.

The high command at MACV objected. The word was, the brass wanted to revoke his press credentials but were afraid of causing a flap. Instead, they sent P.X. to talk to him. He came into DelCorso's room at the Miramar carrying copies of the magazines and acting like an understanding father whose kid's in trouble with the cops. He wasn't angry at DelCorso, he said, but at *Life* magazine. He was on contract with *Life*, and even though they weren't bound to take only his material, it was understood that they would. The only reason they'd bought DelCorso's was because it hadn't cost them anything beyond standard rates. DelCorso said, What do you mean, the only reason? Dunlop replied, The pictures weren't photographs; they looked like snapshots. DelCorso said he wanted them to look like snapshots. No more shades and shadow and darkroom portrait painting. Everything should be clear. Manipulating an image after an exposure, Dunlop responded, was what distinguished great photographers from the run-of-the-mill. Almost anybody could learn to take a respectable picture in a few weeks. It wasn't DelCorso's view. Manipulation was justified if you were doing artsy-craftsy stuff, pictures of snowflakes, but a war photograph had to be straight.

That was when Dunlop's wraps started to come loose. Was DelCorso accusing him of not being straight? What had DelCorso done to him? Done to you? DelCorso asked. What the hell do you mean, *done* to you? And Dunlop answered that everyone, meaning the men with eagles and stars on their shoulders and lobster thermidor in their mess kits, knew DelCorso had worked with him and were giving him flak for DelCorso's pictures. DelCorso had dishonored the American soldier by taking pictures of a few bad apples smoking dope and looting temples. He'd been callous to sell photos of American boys with their testicles blown off. Realism was realism, but that picture was in bad taste, to which DelCorso replied that the war was in bad taste. The way he saw it, bad taste and dishonor were not the true sources of Dunlop's agitation; he was bothered because DelCorso had outsold him by giving the editors Vietnam while Dunlop was still giving them World War Two, relying on tired formulas that no longer worked. He had no more idea of how to photograph the war honestly than his four-star friends had of how to fight it effectively. With that, Dunlop's wraps came loose. Dishonest? Tired formulas? He'd given DelCorso the benefit of twenty-five years of experience because he thought the younger man had the talent to carry on his work. *His* work. He hated to see DelCorso prostitute himself just to satisfy the whims of a few left-wing editors. And with that, DelCorso's wraps came loose. *Pros-*

6

ATABEGA, a dim, cool replica of a provincial French inn, wasn't crowded. A German camera crew sat at one table, a couple of French plantation owners at another. A third was occupied, in every sense of the word, by two Corsican gangsters who were undoubtedly involved in the cultivation of an agricultural product far more profitable than rubber. Wilson, DelCorso, and two other photographers, Conklin and McCafferty, sat near the Germans. For the next hour, over onion soup, Nha Trang lobster, and several bottles of chilled Montrachet, DelCorso listened to the three photographers entertain each other with war stories about the fall of Danang. Conklin said little, but Wilson and McCafferty spoke with the locker-room camaraderie of men who had done something dangerous together and escaped without injury. Their conversation was not a conversation so much as it was a contest, a series of competing monologues to discover who had seen the most horrifying sights, taken the greatest risks. They talked about the Vietnamese marines' panicked flight onto landing craft, about refugees crushed to death in the wheel wells of evacuation planes as if these events had been personal adventures. DelCorso felt out of things; he hadn't been at Danang and had nothing to say. He would not have had anything to say regardless.

There was something boring and self-conscious about macho bull sessions like this one. Still, he hung around listening to it because he did not want to be alone. He had spent most of the day photographing charred, broken dolls that had once been children, and wasn't ready to face an empty hotel room and the thoughts he knew would haunt him there.

It was dark by the time the four men paid the check and left for the Miramar, Wilson's emporium of prime nooky. He hadn't exaggerated. The girls in the top-floor bar were as beautiful as he had described. The sight of them, with their black hair and saffron skin, their enchanting eyes, their slim bodies covered by floral *ao-dais*, the silk trousers revealing the line of a thigh here, the curve of a buttock there, almost made DelCorso forget that he'd taken a vow of chastity for this trip. Like most spouses who travel a lot, his belief in marital fidelity was often assaulted by loneliness and lust. For the first four years of his marriage, he had remained completely faithful to Margaret by making love to figments of his erotic imagination. When, as he'd known it would, the solitary rite of masturbation proved inadequate, he made the usual compromise. He would take women when necessary so long as there was no temptation to commit emotional betrayal, the true mortal sin according to his personal code. Let his cock wander where it might, his heart would remain at home. He confined himself to prostitutes, following some advice his father had given him long ago: "Nick, the women you have to pay will cost you the least." On this assignment, however, he would forgo even the solace of whores. He felt guilty about breaking his promise to Margaret and, the product of a Catholic upbringing, had need to do penance.

He and the others took a table near the window, through which they could see the lights of the city bleeding away into the flat darkness of the delta, illuminated occasionally by a flare. Compared to the savagely commercial hookers who had worked the Saigon bars in the old days, the Miramar's were ladylike. They hovered near the table, demurely waiting to be asked to sit down. The one exception was a girl in a bright orange dress who immediately walked up to Wilson and, standing behind him, began to stroke his neck with practiced fingers.

"Weirson," she cooed, "you soooo pretty."

"Tuyet Hoa," Wilson said, taking her by the wrist and spinning her around onto his lap. Tuyet Hoa perched there proprietorily, warning off the competition with a sudden-death look in her black eyes. Then her fingers worked down from Wilson's neck to his crotch.

"Ah, Tuyet Hoa, you are sooo talented."

"You such pretty man, Weirson."

"What the hell is this?" asked McCafferty in his South Boston accent. "A meeting of the Mark Wilson fan club?"

"Don't feel slighted, McCafferty. It's not your fault and it's not mine. God gave me this face, just as he gave you one that looks like ten miles of bad road."

"Yeah, and if you'd been brought up where I was you wouldn't've kept that face very long. Tell Tootsiewa to stop giving you a hand job and bring us a round."

"It's Tuyet Hoa, you ignorant Mick. It means Snow Flower. Beautiful name, don't you think?"

"It sure is but she's still a fucking bar whore and it's her job to get us a round and not sit there telling us how god-damned pretty you are."

"*Au contraire*, Frankenstein. It's her job to bring *me* a drink. It's your job to pick one of these lovelies for your very own and it'll be her job to bring you a drink."

"I know how it works."

McCafferty turned his battered face toward the lineup of girls, choosing one with short hair that swept over her cheeks like ravens' wings. Smiling, she sat on McCafferty's lap and clasped her hands around his muscular neck. He took them and pressed them to his groin. The girl giggled.

"There you go, darling. If Tootsiewa can play with hand-some, you can play with an ugly SOB like me. What's your name?"

"Mmmmmm?"

"Your name. You got a fucking name, don't you?"

Wilson, whose three marriages included one to a Vietnamese, asked the girl her name in her language.

"Minh Duc," she replied.

"Just your luck," Wilson said, laughing. "Her name means Virtue."

"Yeah? Well, I don't guess she's got any of that, or anything else, either."

"No sweat. The girls in this bar are as clean as the tiles in a Scarsdale bathroom, though I would advise the usual precautions." Wilson paused. "Well, that leaves Conklin and DelCorso to choose their consorts."

"Since when did you start pimping?" asked Conklin, a staff photographer for AP who, with his flaxen hair, clear complexion, and roll of midriff fat, looked like an out-of-shape college sophomore.

"Since my last visit to Times Square, where I saw a gentleman of the Negro persuasion driving a gold Cadillac that must've cost more than I make in a year."

Conklin laughed and, in the manner of a pasha in a harem, beckoned to one of the four remaining girls.

"Nick?"

"I'll pass. All I want is a nightcap."

"*What?*"

"A nightcap. I don't feel like getting laid."

"You don't feel like what?"

"Read my lips, Wilson. I . . . don't . . . feel . . . like . . . getting . . . laid."

"But you're the golden guinea. You have a responsibility not to be taken lightly—upholding the reputation of your ethnic group as cocksmen."

"I'm breaking the stereotype."

"Nick," Wilson said gravely, "you just got here, so you probably don't know that things have changed. These ladies are the *crème de la crème* and they're giving it away. They know that Charlie's coming to town and that if they don't get out real soon, they'll end up sewing red stars on pillows at the Light of Lenin Home for Wayward Girls. All you have to do is give them the impression that you'll marry them and get them a visa to the States and they'll screw your brains out for next to nothing. You don't have to make any definite promises, understand. Just give an impression."

"That your latest scam, Wilson?"

"It's not a scam—"

"Look, I'm not interested in getting engaged to one of these sluts just for a piece of ass. What I want is a couple of drinks and then I'll hit the sack, alone."

"All right, Nick. You're missing a great opportunity, but maybe you'll change your mind in a few days. Danger, as we all know, is an aphrodisiac."

"Just tell Snow Blossom—"

"Snow Flower."

"Tell Snow Flower I'll have a double Scotch straight up. Incidentally, when the hell did it ever snow in Vietnam?"

"On December ninth, 1238 A.D., sixty inches of base were reported on the slopes of Black Virgin Mountain."

Dispatched by Wilson, Tuyet Hoa and the other girls brought a round of drinks. Perfectly behaved little whores, not too aggressive or demanding, they sat on their customers' laps, occasionally nibbling an earlobe or fondling a crotch, and waited patiently for the men to tire of drinking and talking and take them to their rooms. The chatter picked up where it had left off after dinner; when the events at Danang had been exhausted as a topic, it turned to past wars. DelCorso heard stories he had heard enough times before to catch Wilson and the others in a few embellishments. There were the horror stories—of the time a Nigerian officer executed a Biafran for the benefit of McCafferty's camera; of Dunlop's famous shot, which won his second Pulitzer, of Pakistani soldiers bayoneting a Bengali outside Dacca. There were funny stories like the one about Conklin's run-in with the IRA in Londonderry: a gang of Provos commandeered his rental car at gunpoint; when he filled out the insurance forms in the Hertz office, he wrote, in the space asking the reasons for the loss of the vehicle, "lack of British resolve." And there were the obituaries—Thompson burned to death in a half-track struck by an antitank missile in Syria, Aaronson executed by the Khmer Rouge, Leland dropped by a sniper in Quang Tri.

They droned on until, beginning to repeat themselves, they fell into a long silence and then opened negotiations with the girls. DelCorso, working on his third double and a good drunk, got the impression that Tuyet Hoa and company were not yet ready to dispense their favors in exchange for a vague promise of wedding bells and a visa. They held out for cold cash because mama-san, the madam behind the bar, had to have her cut. In the midst of the haggling, Conklin drifted off into a private world. Staring out the window at the flares that hung over the edge of the city like a bouquet of huge, bright carnations, he spoke a word that seemed to sum up his opinion of everything in general:

"Shit."

"Easy, Frank," Wilson said. "You can always charge this off to entertainment on your expense report."

"I'm not talking about that. I mean just listen to this shit."

"Do you find these commercial discussions unromantic?"

"I mean all this bullshit we've been talking." Conklin

turned from the window and finished his beer. He regarded his companions with aqueous eyes that, somehow, still retained a look of innocence. "First it's Biafra this, Belfast that, and now it's so many piasters for a short-time, so many for all night. It's all bullshit."

"Exactly what is bullshit?"

"This is, we are. We call ourselves photographers, photojournalists when we get high-toned about it, but what are we really? Mercenaries who carry cameras instead of guns."

Wilson rolled his eyes.

"That sounds like one of DelCorso's lines."

"If anybody had dropped in on us a few minutes ago, he would have thought that we think war's glamorous."

"Well, ain't it?" McCafferty asked.

" 'Isn't it,' McCafferty. If you don't learn to speak correctly, you'll never get an assignment from the *Times*."

"Fuck you, Robert Redford."

"You think this is glamorous?" asked Conklin.

McCafferty screwed up his face. A wide face more Slavic than Irish, it had the cramped, pinched look of someone who expected to be punched or whipped at any moment, a face that had never been young.

"Yeah," he said, "I guess I do. I remember taking this shot after the Egyptians came across Suez. Tanks burning all over the desert, like fucking bonfires. Far as you could see, and they looked beautiful. Made a beautiful picture, all those burning tanks."

"Tim McCafferty, you sound like Tim Page."

"I don't think you should dismiss what he's just said so quickly," said Wilson. "There's something to that. War has a certain appeal to the senses—"

"Yeah," DelCorso interjected, "the sense of smell especially."

"I'm talking about sight, our stock-in-trade. There is something dramatic and appealing in the sight of tanks burning on a desert—"

"Sure there is, unless you're in one of the tanks."

"How about letting me finish, Nick? Why do you suppose pictures like that sell? Because people enjoy looking at them. You think a guy like Dunlop's committing a crime because his pictures are attractive. The fact is, you can't take the attractiveness out of war, which means you can't take the attractiveness out of war photographs."

"What the hell are we talking about all this for? I never think about it," said McCafferty, who was in Saigon on spec, selling to the highest bidder. "I just know a good shot when I see it and I take it and then sell it for every penny I can. The more pennies I get, the more chance I got of never going back to South fucking Boston. You want to talk philosophy, go ahead. I can't afford it."

"Hey McCafferty, I came out of the streets, same as you."

"I know that, Deecee. And I know that if it hadn't been for this kind of journalism, I'd still be on those streets."

"Where the hell do you think *I'd* be? On my yacht?"

"Gentlemen, please. The issue is not who qualifies as a working-class hero. The issue is whether or not you can take the glamour out of war."

"No, it isn't," Conklin said, his round, white face reddening. "The issue is whether or not our lives are bullshit."

"Conklin, what's got into you? That honey-wa slip something in your drink?"

"What got into Conklin was Baltimore," said McCafferty. "I never met a Catholic from Baltimore who wasn't fucked up."

"What got into me was that in the middle of all this bullshit, I started to miss my kids," Conklin said.

"Told you. Baltimore. He misses his kids."

"What's your missing your kids got to do with us?" Wilson asked.

"Yeah. My life isn't any mess. Wouldda been I hadn't gotten into journalism."

"I know, you got yourself out of the slums," said Conklin. "But look at yourself, McCafferty. Call me fucked up. Look at you. You've botched two marriages, you hardly ever see your kids, and you spend your nights with cheap chits like the one sitting on your lap."

"One sitting on your lap doesn't look like a princess to me."

"Didn't say she was. I botched my marriage, I hardly ever see my kids. And you, Wilson. Christ, you've gone through three of them."

"No, they went through me. That's why I do this. To help support my three exes in the style to which I stupidly accustomed them."

"Bullshit. You could make more doing something else. You're on the run, Wilson. Same as me. That's why we take on assignments like this. Keep moving so we don't have to stop and think how empty our lives are."

"Oh, for Christ's sake," said Wilson, absently rubbing Tuyet Hoa's narrow back. "You and DelCorso ought to team up. Him with his social-conscience rap and you with this empty-lives routine could take the fun out of an Irish wake."

Kissing Wilson's cheek, her long hair falling across his face like a veil, Tuyet Hoa said:

"Too much talk, Weirson. Soon curfew. You pay mama-san, then you me we go."

"In a moment, darling," said Wilson, brushing her hair aside.

"All right, Wilson," Conklin said. "You're so glib. What've we got in our lives?"

"McCafferty came close a minute ago. We've got journalism. We've got that and each other."

"Are you serious?"

"Like cancer."

"I was down before, now I'm really depressed. That's worse than having nothing."

"You're out of your tree, Conklin. I know what it's like to have nothing, and you believe me, having nothing's a lot worse than this."

"McCafferty, I've had it with the Oliver Twist horseshit."

"Sorry about that. You'd come up in Southie or the North End instead of Baltimore you wouldn't worry about having a full life. A plain old life would do."

"Listen, why don't you admit you've screwed yours up? We all have, except, maybe, Deecee."

"Oh?" said Wilson, raising his eyebrows, "and what makes DelCorso an exception?"

"He's still married to the same woman for one thing. How long have you and Margaret been together, Nick?"

"Seven years in August."

"There it is. That's got to be a record in this business. DelCorso has an actual personal life. When he gets off an assignment, he doesn't crawl into some empty hotel room or apartment. He goes to an honest-to-God home with a wife and kids in it."

"Listen to that shit. It's what they learn in Baltimore."

"Let's hear it from the horse's mouth now that we've heard from the horse's ass," Wilson said. "Tell us, Nick, if, as Conklin claims, we're on the run because our lives are empty, why do you run harder than any of us when yours is so full?"

DelCorso looked at his empty glass and wanted another double very badly. It made him nervous to be singled out in this way, especially when he recalled the quarrel with Margaret and how they made love on their last night together: she going through the motions but with her heart held in check, he trying to break her heart's restraints and growing more violent until, close to rape, he stopped himself.

"What do you say, Nick?"

"Get laid, Wilson."

"I intend to. But first I'd like my question answered."

"Kiss my ass."

"Why are you being so defensive?"

"So I don't get offensive and rearrange that face of yours."

"That's not much of an answer."

"What's your problem? Are you pissed because you're backing up for me?"

"What do I care? Unlike you, I'm not overly competitive."

"You don't have to be. Not with your money. What the hell, this is just a hobby to you."

"If I wanted a hobby, I would have started building model airplanes. All I want to know is why you're back in the trenches with us if you lead this idyllic personal life."

"My personal life isn't any of your goddamned business."

"I'm not asking for a description of what you and Margaret do in bed together. What I'm saying is this: ever since Cyprus, you've been leading as close to an ordinary life as any photographer is going to lead, and you were probably pulling down day rates that are equal to the weekly rate you're making now. But here you are in sweaty Saigon with all of us who are escaping our empty lives. I was just wondering why."

"You know why."

"I don't buy what you said this afternoon. Not completely. There's some truth to it, I guess, but I just don't buy that you're risking your ass for a noble cause. That sounds to me like the patriotic guff you hear from generals and colonels." Wilson's lips composed themselves into an odd smile, half sad and half knowing; a mournful smirk. "I recognize the signs, Nick."

"What signs?" DelCorso asked the question in his best

side-of-the-mouth, street-kid voice, but his sarcastic tone could not hide the beads of sweat erupting under his hairline. He felt like a suspect talking to a cop who doesn't believe his alibi.

"You know what I mean. Conklin's probably right. We're on the run, but so are you. I've been where you are. Been there three times."

For an instant, DelCorso felt as if his chair were toppling out from under him. He recovered his balance and cracked:

"Three times, huh? Then maybe you should go into marriage counseling."

"That would be like making an arsonist fire chief."

The remark broke the tension and everyone laughed. DelCorso, who didn't want to pursue the discussion any further, decided it was a good note on which to leave.

"There's still time to save yourself from the horrors of masturbation," Wilson said as DelCorso laid a wad of piaster notes on the table to pay his bar tab.

"We all better get on the move," said McCafferty. "We got to pay mama-san now if we're going to get these cunts out of here before curfew."

Wilson glanced at his watch.

"You're right. Gentlemen, start your engines. It's wick-dip time."

"See you," DelCorso said.

"Take it easy, Nick. Sorry if I started to hit too close to home."

"No problem," DelCorso lied.

7

EXCEPT FOR A FEW roving police patrols, the streets were empty as DelCorso walked back to the Continental. Five years ago they would have been jammed at this hour; and though he liked walking without being hassled every ten feet by a hooker, pusher, or pimp, he felt almost nostalgic for the times when each night in Saigon was a kind of Mardi Gras, amped up to such a degree that you couldn't step out your door without feeling you'd been plugged into a source of desperate energy that would trip every circuit breaker in your nervous system if you weren't careful. Life, however frantic and corrupt, was better than no life at all; the silence of these streets was not the silence of tranquillity but of exhaustion, of a burned-out city waiting for death. The big, white National Assembly Building had already taken on the ghostly look of a Roman ruin.

Two room boys—old men actually—were sleeping in the hall outside DelCorso's room. Stepping quietly between them, he opened the door and, when he switched on the light, saw a gecko lizard dart into a crack in the wall. He had left both the fan and the air-conditioner running, but the room still smelled of mildew and rot, the stench of the tropics, embedded in the stucco walls, in the terra-cotta tiles on the floor. The air clung to his skin like wet gauze.

Taking off his boots and his damp shirt, he lay down, lit a cigarette, and stared idly at his camera bag. It was on the dresser, beside the field equipment he'd bought yesterday in the Ben Thanh market: a helmet, flak jacket, web belt, the ammunition pouches in which he stored his film. The camera bag was khaki canvas, with his name and address stenciled in black. His address. Nick DelCorso had a fixed address, a home, wife, and children. He had it together. Why in hell had Conklin brought that up? DelCorso had wanted the conversation to stay where it was, on whether there was an attractiveness in war the starkest photograph could not efface. That the topic had changed abruptly was typical of journalistic shoptalk; newsmen had the attention span of six-year-olds. But Christ almighty, why had Conklin tried to portray him as a marital hero? Just the kind of thing Wilson would jump at; having failed three times, Wilson had concluded there was something wrong not with himself but with the institution of marriage. If he couldn't be happy, then no one could; any man who claimed to be happily married was kidding himself. Still, DelCorso could not deny that Wilson's probing had touched a nerve, making him feel the same discomfort he'd felt when Margaret asked him what was wrong. Nothing, he now said to himself. Nothing wrong with her or the marriage. The marriage was his emotional address, the point of reference in his gypsy life. If it hadn't been idyllic since her breakdown, it was still durable. Seven years was not a record, but, in the late twentieth century, it was nothing to be ashamed of. DelCorso chose to look at things optimistically. The stresses to which his marriage had been subject—his absences, Margaret's drinking, her father's efforts to break it up during its first year—were not signs that it was flawed but proof that it was sound. Wilson's suggestion that he had come to Saigon to escape was nonsense. Hell, if it was escapist adventure he was looking for, he could have taken a job for *National Geographic*. Gone up the Amazon. Photographed headhunters in New Guinea, Mongols in a yurt, bedouin on their camels. There was no good reason for him to be here other than the one he believed to be true: he was obliged to bear witness with his camera, to make people see the sort of horror he had seen this afternoon in the paddies outside Tan Son Nhut. To seize them by the throat and scream, *This is what we are doing to each other.*

He should not have allowed himself that thought; it conjured an image of a field strewn with small bodies, burned and dismembered, and with the image came fear for the safety of Danny and Angela. Something might happen to them while he was here. God would punish him for being away so much by taking them from him. Jesus, what a thought. Typical of his gothic, guilt-ridden Catholicism. The Jesuits had got hold of him at St. Ignatius, and true to their motto, had captured him for life. Looking at the ceiling, DelCorso tried to think more pleasant thoughts about home. He saw his first vision of Margaret in tennis whites, her long tanned legs stretching as she rose on tiptoe to serve. It was an image he could never forget, an image he would love always. He thought about the house on Willow Place. He had grown attached to it, even though maintaining it usually left his checking account empty at the end of each month. He liked its nineteenth-century solidity, its air of permanence. His work had made him acutely aware of how little endures in this world. Out of this awareness, a need had arisen in him to have something in his own life that would last, that would outlast him but bear his mark. The house had become the fulfillment of that need, although, at first, it was Margaret's idea to buy the place. She was fed up with cramped apartments; the house, in a bad state of repair, was a bargain at $50,000. DelCorso decided to do the renovations himself to save money. Because he wasn't good in the manual-skills department, he asked his father, a handyman and construction carpenter then on a seasonal layoff, to come in from Chicago. He was a big man, six-two, with the arms and shoulders that cannot be built through calisthenics or weight lifting but only through hard work. The principal attribute DelCorso inherited from his father wasn't physical strength but a sense of social responsibility: Frank DelCorso advocated the now almost extinct idea that a man owed it to society to turn in the best job he could. In his heart, he was a medieval craftsman forced to make a living in the modern building trades. He threw himself into the restoration of his son's new house with all the passion for care and quality that had been blocked by a lifetime of cutting corners to accommodate the greed of housing developers. The basic structural work was finished in a little over two months. When they were done, DelCorso's father asked:

"When'd you say this house was put up, Nick?"

"Eighteen fifty-seven."

"Over a century," Frank said, grasping a stud in his big,

knotty hand and bouncing on the floor. "Feel that, Nick? There's give but not a vibration. She's good for another century."

It was no exaggeration. Everything had been put together as true as the human eye and hand could make it. The way DelCorso felt, there was more of the endurance of art in the studs, beams, and joists of that house than in the best of his, or anyone's, photographs. He and Margaret had lived in it two years now, and he could not imagine himself returning to any place but it; certainly not to the sort of bleak, transient apartments where Conklin and Wilson hung their hats.

His mind was going into high-idle neutral. The doubles had not had the effect he'd hoped for. Trying to tire himself, DelCorso rose and started shadow boxing in front of the full-length mirror on the back of the closet door. Three jabs to the head, right to the heart, back to the head with a left hook. Because of his leg, he couldn't stay on his toes longer than a few seconds and had to throw the punches flat-footed. Bob, weave, feint. Jab. Jab. Cross. Jab. Right to the midsection. Jab. Hook off the jab. A tough one. Nessie Blumenthal had taught him how, keeping the right high to guard his face, shifting his weight on recovery and, without dropping his left shoulder, uncoiling the hook with all his 155 pounds behind it. His movements, clumsy and stiff at first, regained some of their old fluidity as his muscles loosened and his memory took him out of his hotel room back into Blumenthal's gym at Madison and Hamlin streets. He could smell it, a typical club fighter's hangout, its walls giving off the odors of sweat, cigar smoke, rubbing alcohol, leather, and canvas, all one stink really, the stink of boxers' dreams. DelCorso's was to fight his way out of the west-side Italian neighborhood called the Valley, the old First Ward, twenty phone lines running into the sandwich shops where the bookies took the bets and the loan sharks made threatening calls to delinquent customers—Six for five at noon Saturday or a friend's gonna use your knees as a strike zone, yeah—fight his way out of that bullshit and add his name to the roster of great Italian fighters: La Motta, Graziano, Basilio, Canzoneri, and the god of them all, Marciano. We have an announcement, ladies and gentlemen. In one minute, twenty seconds of the fourth round, the winner by a knockout and the new middleweight champion of the world, Nick DelCorso! Sure. What was the name of the black kid who ended that fantasy? Some spade name, Jackson, Jefferson, Washington, one of those Presidents. He was a little hungrier than DelCorso, a little meaner, a little more serious, and a lot faster, and halfway through the second round, he gave the future champion a nose job, then broke his jaw. A doctor told DelCorso that if he ever took another one on the chin, he'd end up eating baby food for the rest of his life.

With boxing closed as an avenue of escape, he got an inspiration to become a sports photographer. If he himself couldn't fight, he could take pictures of champions, travel around the country and the world, sit at ringside, get into dressing rooms—Hey, champ, how about one more of you with your manager? An uncle who made a side living photographing weddings and confirmations was responsible for this idea. He taught DelCorso the fundamentals, then helped him land a job in the *Sun Times* photo lab. A year of purgatory. Working with photographers but never getting a chance to use a camera himself. It was torment to see the prints of football games and prizefights, fires and murders, the usual amusements and mayhem of a big city, but not be able to participate in the excitement except vicariously. So he joined the army. Two jabs to the head, cross with the right, feint with the left, overhand right, Marciano's punch. DelCorso did not regret enlisting. The army got him out of the neighborhood. That was all he had ever wanted: to flee the smothering confines of that village within a city. He signed up for a four-year hitch in late 1962, a couple of months after his twentieth birthday. Infantry for the first year, until someone somewhere discovered he'd worked with a camera in civilian life and cut him orders transferring him to the Signal Corps' Photographer's School at Ft. Monmouth. Whoever that someone was, he'd made more of a difference in Del-Corso's life than the black kid who'd broken his jaw. All the difference, good as well as bad. Would he have eventually published in *Life*, *Newsweek*, and *The New York Times* if that anonymous officer hadn't looked at his records? Would he now have two good legs? He tried dancing on the balls of his feet, but, within seconds, pain shot up his left leg like a low-voltage shock. Shit. He went flat-footed again, popping jabs with crisp snorts. DelCorso stayed at it for ten minutes, building the tempo until sweat glistened on his body.

It was, he noticed with satisfaction, still a good, strong body, though he was at least ten pounds over his fighting weight. Suggestions of fat on the sides, a hint of flabbiness in his pectoral muscles. As he looked in the mirror, there came over DelCorso that fascination with himself he had experienced when he first saw his reflection as a small boy and realized he had an identity all his own. It was not a narcissistic fascination, but an awe at the turn his life had taken. His route out of the neighborhood could have been one of the two followed by most of his high school classmates: the tricky path of organized crime, or the dull, safe Interstate that led through a year or two of night school, a stint in the reserves or the National Guard, then back to school for a degree in, say, accounting, followed by a job and a move to the suburbs: tenement to split-level in a generation—the American dream. Either might have been his destiny, but he had been shunted onto a road where there were no lights or signs and, proving adept at handling dangerous curves in the dark, he'd ended up living a life he hadn't expected for himself. Street kid makes good, marries rich, beautiful woman, has glamorous career as free-lance photographer, name is entered in *Who's Who.* Curiously, DelCorso did not feel relief or satisfaction at having escaped his fate, but that sense of dislocation often experienced by people who head down a track other than the one life seems to have laid out for them. A momentary dizzy spell made his reflection appear slightly distorted. *Who's Who. DelCorso, Nicholas Lucien, photojournalist; b. Chgo., Oct. 16, 1942; s. Francis Anthony and Rose Marie (Maggio) D.; grad. St. Ignatius High School, Chgo., 1960; m. Margaret Delaney Fitzgerald, Aug. 21, 1968; children—Daniel Francis, Angela Rose. Staff photographer, Asso. Press, N.Y., 1967–68; self-employed as photojournalist in Vietnam, 1968; photo-corres. Life magazine, U.S., Biafra, 1968–70; free-lance photojournalist, Vietnam, Cambodia, N. Ireland, Europe, Middle East, 1970—Served U.S. Army, 1962–66; Vietnam. Decorated Bronze Star, Purple Heart. Recipient, Overseas Press Club Award, 1970; Asso. Press Award, 1972; UPI Award, 1973; Robert Capa gold medal, 1973. Address: c/o Northstar Photo Agency, 348 Madison Ave., N.Y., N.Y. 10017.* That's who he was according to *Who's Who,* but he wondered who he really was and what the hell he was doing, shadow boxing in the middle of the night in a hot hotel room in Saigon.

Working off the fat accumulated by months of commercial assignments, that's what. Lunches with art directors. Drinks with account executives, dinner with Goldie Hawn. Sweat it off. Jab. Jab. Right to the ribs. Work in close, you've got to get in close, DelCorso. Pound the midsection, then an uppercut, then a hook. He heard that Dunlop, fifty-one years old now, trained every day. If that fossil could do it, he could. All right, don't start thinking about Dunlop; but an image of the man, so clear it was almost an hallucination, appeared in the mirror. DelCorso, feeling the fury build within himself, snapped his punches harder and faster. He stopped when he came dangerously near putting his fist through the glass. Can't take pictures with a broken hand.

He showered after pacing the floor to cool down. Sprawled on the bed, all tensions purged, he fell asleep without turning off the lights.

8

STANDING BESIDE HIS DESK, a cup of stale coffee in one hand, Bolton stuck the last colored pin in his mural-size wall map of Vietnam. The pins and the symbols he'd drawn on the acetate cover were meant to do nothing more than help clarify the jumble of information Christensen had given him; but when he stepped back to gain a better perspective, the pattern formed by the dots, rectangles, and arrows appeared to him, a connoisseur of war, as beautiful and symmetrical as a work of art. The art was not his own, but that of a North Vietnamese general named Tranh Van Duc. Three arrows pointed toward Saigon, one to the northeast, representing the assault an NVA corps would make on the South's 18th Division at Xuan Loc. The second arrow, to the northwest, symbolized the attack another corps was to make against the 25th Division. The South Vietnamese would then have no choice but to commit their reserves to both battles. Once they did, two more Communist divisions, their positions marked by rectangles in the vast green smear near the Cambodian border, their route of advance by the third arrow, would smash through the ARVN 5th and barrel down the Binh Duong corridor into the city. Whatever was left of the ARVN forces would be cut off and masticated piecemeal. This plan, with its elegant and brutal simplicity, stirred Bolton's love of clearheaded professionalism. It would destroy the ARVN first, allowing the North to capture Saigon without costly, destructive street fighting. He didn't see how it could fail, even when he factored in the foul-ups that occur in all military campaigns. Hell, one look at the map and a green second lieutenant could see that the South had only one of two moves left: to concede, like a smart chess player when he knows he's beaten, or to put up a stiff fight that would merely postpone the inevitable.

Reflexively, Bolton's gaze shifted to the clock, which reminded him that he was a newsman, not an armchair general. Two-thirty A.M., time to open up shop. He sat in front of his typewriter, wrote the transmission code at the head of the page, and slugged the story "snap," IPS's lingo for an exclusive. As he roughed the first sentence of his lead, fatigue washed over him and something rare happened—his mind went blank. Not another word came to him. He looked at the clock again. No wonder he was tired. He had been up for nineteen hours, the last six with Christensen and two Vietnamese field agents so fresh from the bush they hadn't had time to clean their muddy boots. They and Christensen had given him everything: translations of captured documents, radio intercept logs, maps. To a reporter accustomed to digging for each factual nugget, it was like having a crate of bullion delivered to his doorstep. Bolton figured his mind had locked gears because he was suffering from an overload of information as well as exhaustion.

Trying to order his thoughts, he read the telex he'd sent to New York after he'd returned to the bureau:

120200 PROHALPRIN URGENT: SNAP UPCOMING. TOP SOURCES TOLD ME NNVVAA CMD ISSUED ORDER YESTERDAY TAKE SAIGON ASAP. COULD STORM CAPITAL WITHIN TWO WEEKS. SOUTH VIETS COULD NOT HOLD LONGER THAN 12 HOURS. HERE GOOD ONE: THIS INFO GIVEN AMBASSADOR BY SOURCES WHO URGED HE BEGIN EVAC U.S. CITIZENS NOW. AMB REFUSED. CLAIMS CURRENT LULL SIGNAL HANOI WANTS TALKS AND THAT EVAC WOULD PANIC SOUTH VIETS. RGDS BOLTON/SAIGON.

Below was the reply from Halprin, the day foreign editor:

121400 BOLTON RE YR 120200 SEND SNAP SOONEST. FYI KATY AND THE LADY QUOTING KISSINGER ALSO SAYING HE RCVD SIGNALS HANOI WANTS TALKS. BE SURE YR SOURCES. RGDS HALPRIN/CABLES/NY.

"Katy" and "The Lady" were IPS codes for the *Washington Post* and *The New York Times*.

Bolton took another sip of coffee, fidgeted for a while, batted out an unsatisfactory lead, ripped it up, and put a fresh sheet in the typewriter. His mind still wasn't working. Halprin. If that Nervous Nellie held true to form, he'd believe the idiotic pronouncements of officialdom before he believed his own man in the field. Bolton was especially irritated by the warning to be sure of his sources. Who the hell did Halprin think he was dealing with? Some punk like Grey, who didn't have the brains God gave a little yellow crayon? Be sure of your sources because Kissinger's received signals that Hanoi wants a powwow. Here it was, five minutes to midnight, and the American illusion mill was still spinning the wool of self-deception. Christensen was one of the best military intelligence men in the business; according to his information, Hanoi had committed all but two of its twenty divisions to the offensive—nearly 200,000 infantry supported by an armored division and 130-mm field guns. Against this, the ARVN could throw only four divisions, three of which couldn't whip the California National Guard. Christ on a crutch, if an ordinary man were as blind to reality as Kissinger, he'd be committed.

Bolton finished his coffee in one gulp, which created an instant eruption of his case of Ho Chi Minh's revenge. He ran into the bathroom, emptying himself in a great, noisy, liquid burst, then went back to his desk and took two Lomotil tablets from the bottle in the drawer. In five minutes, he wrote his lead and three paragraphs; it was as if clearing his bowels had cleared his mind. Figures. My DI in basic always said my brains were in my ass. Quickly, he edited his copy.

SAIGON (IPS)—THE NORTH VIETNAMESE HIGH COMMAND YESTERDAY ORDERED ITS ARMY TO ATTACK SAIGON AS QUICKLY AS POSSIBLE, ACCORDING TO RELIABLE WESTERN AND VIETNAMESE SOURCES. THE NORTH VIETNAMESE ARMY, WITH 18 RPT 18 DIVISIONS COMMITTED TO THE OFFENSIVE IN THE SOUTH, COULD BE IN POSITION TO STORM THE CAPITAL IN TWO WEEKS, THE SOURCES SAID. THEY ADDED THAT THE SOUTH VIETNAMESE COULD NOT RPT NOT HOLD OUT AGAINST A DETERMINED ASSAULT FOR LONGER THAN 12 RPT 12 HOURS. (MORE)

After penciling in a few changes to his lead and two of the following paragraphs, Bolton called in Dalman, the IPS correspondent who had earlier been trapped with the refugee column near Nha Trang.

"Get this to the operators and tell 'em to drop whatever they're doing. I want this punched immediately if not sooner."

Dalman glanced at the story and went out.

Bolton laughed silently as he wrote his next two paragraphs.

> IT WAS ALSO LEARNED THAT U.S. AMBASSADOR PERRY HUTTON WAS BRIEFED ON THE GRIM MILITARY SITUATION BY TOP INTELLIGENCE AIDES, WHO URGED HIM TO BEGIN AN IMMEDIATE EVACUATION OF THE 5,800 RPT 5,800 AMERICANS REMAINING IN VIETNAM. (MORE)
>
> ACCORDING TO THE SOURCES, HUTTON REFUSED BECAUSE HE SAID HE HAD RECEIVED SIGNALS THAT HANOI MAY BE WILLING TO NEGOTIATE FOR A POLITICAL SOLUTION. IN ADDITION, HUTTON WAS SAID TO HAVE ARGUED THAT EVACUATING AMERICANS NOW WOULD WEAKEN SOUTH VIETNAMESE MORALE, CREATE PANIC, AND MAKE THE FALL OF THE CAPITAL A CERTAINTY. (MORE)

"Dalman! Get back in here."

Dalman, who was about Grey's age, but taller, better built, and a lot less of a smart aleck, reappeared in the doorway.

"They're punching it, Harry."

"Damn well better be. Here. Get this to them."

Dalman took the page, pursing his lips in a way that let Bolton know he didn't like playing copyboy.

"One other thing. New York's going to want a comment from his excellency. Get on the hook and see if the ambassador has anything to say."

"It's three in the morning."

"I know what the fuck time it is. Get on the hook."

"Okay."

"I want to know why his excellency is going to risk six thousand American asses, including yours and mine, in the name of preserving South Vietnamese morale, which doesn't exist."

"Okay, Harry, okay."

The clock now read 3:10. A wealth of time. It was 3:10 in the afternoon in New York, leaving five to six hours before the morning newspapers locked up their final editions. With luck, he could make the late editions of a few of the afternoons.

As he worked, he pictured the story going out on the teletypes to IPS clients from Boston to L.A., the copy preceded by an editorial advisory. *Editors: the following story was obtained exclusively by IPS correspondent Harold W. Bolton, on assignment in Saigon.* It wasn't Watergate, a story that would rock the world, but it would by God send the editors of the other wire services running to the telex, firing rockets to their Saigon bureaus. *Bolton IPS quoting intelligence sources sez Reds planning to attack Saigon two weeks. ARVN cannot hold city longer than 12 hours. Hutton said to be ignoring advice begin immediate evac Americans in Viet. Can you match?* The good ones would do their damnedest to match, but in the predawn hours, with all their sources snug in bed, they didn't have much of a chance. Albury, the AP bureau chief, was his only serious threat; Albury was wired into Christensen, but Bolton had made the CIA agent swear on whatever is holy to a spook not to say a word to any other correspondents before eight in the morning. All alone, Bolton said to himself. IPS isn't playing catch-up anymore. The Horseman's in town.

Now, adrenaline overcoming his fatigue, his big, square fingers raced over the keyboard. With Dalman on the phone to the ambassador's residence, he had to run the copy to the teletype room himself, and was soon drenched in sweat. Stripping off his shirt, he began filing in one-paragraph takes.

ACCORDING TO THE SOURCES, THE TOTAL NUMBER OF TROOPS SOUTH VIETNAM CAN THROW INTO THE DEFENSE OF SAIGON IS 35,000 RPT 35,000. ALTHOUGH THIS INCLUDES THE CRACK AIRBORNE BRIGADE IN RESERVE, THE NVA ARE MASSING NINE OF THEIR DIVISIONS, 90,000 RPT 90,000 MEN, TO ATTACK THE CITY. (MORE)

WHEN THE AMBASSADOR WAS BRIEFED ON THE RAPIDLY DETERIORATING SITUATION AND TOLD OF HANOI'S CHANGE OF PLANS, HIS AIDES URGED THAT A LARGE TAMARIND TREE IN THE EMBASSY COMPOUND BE CUT DOWN TO CLEAR A LANDING ZONE FOR EVACUATION HELICOPTERS. U.S. MARINE GUARDS WERE STANDING BY WITH CHAIN SAWS, BUT HUTTON ORDERED THEM OFF, TELLING HIS AIDES THAT FELLING THE TREE WOULD SIGNAL AN AMERICAN PULLOUT AND DESTROY SOUTH VIETNAM'S WILL TO RESIST. (MORE)

Bolton chuckled when he read over the last paragraph. Too bad DelCorso hadn't been there to photograph the scene. The white-haired, aristocratic ambassador waving off a squad of marines armed with chain saws. The Ambassador and the Tamarind Tree: A Modern Fable.

"Harry," Dalman called from the outer office. "Hutton

wouldn't come to the phone, but I got hold of some flak from the press section."

"What'd he have to say?"

"Nothing that's suitable for family newspapers. When I told him what we had, he said Hutton would find the leak and plug it tighter than a nun's pussy. End quote."

"That's not the language of diplomacy."

Hunching over his typewriter, Bolton wrote:

INSERT A WHERE FITS: CONTACTED BY IPS, A SPOKESMAN FOR AMB. HUTTON SAID THE EMBASSY HAD NO COMMENT. END INSERT.

He worked hard for the next fifteen minutes to finish the story, frequently referring to the map. Fatigue setting in again, he paused to wipe his face with his shirt and check the clock. Three-forty. Not bad time for a thousand-word exclusive, although he'd been known to hammer out stories equally long in half the time. Then, almost dizzy, he finished his last paragraph.

He called Dalman in again.

"Take it away, amigo. Last graph. Whipped their tails on this one."

"About time for AP and UPI to get a few rockets."

"They'll look like Ft. McHenry. 'And the rockets' red glare,' " Bolton sang in his baritone, " 'let 'em know the Horseman was there.' " He slammed his palm against the desk. "This bureau is through playing catch-up. Goddamn, Dalman, do you know why Rome wasn't built in a day?"

"I'll bite."

"Because I wasn't in charge of that fucking detail."

Dalman laughed and went to the teletype room.

Rising from his swivel chair, its torn vinyl slick with the nervous sweat whose smell filled his nostrils, Bolton locked his hands overhead and stretched, his taut vertebrae cracking. He felt wonderful, tired as hell, but wonderful. Scoring beats like this was a real high, the best part of the wire-service business. That was why he had turned down a more lucrative offer from *Newsweek*. Hell, if he'd been working for them, this story would have been ancient history by the time it saw print. There would be no sense of victory. Bolton had always thrived on competition and the rush of winning, as a middle linebacker for the Citadel; as a door gunner, swooping into a hot landing zone and dueling with the enemy soldiers trying to blow him out of the sky; as a newsman, beating the competition because he had the balls to go where others wouldn't and the smarts to develop the right sources. He'd taken his knocks—a ligament torn in a game with South Carolina, a bullet wound in the shoulder, the wounds to his pride when competitors got a story ahead of him—but he usually came out on top because he hated losing more than anything else in life. The only loss he hadn't minded was Dorothy, his ex-wife, she of the unfulfillable needs and the round heels. Otherwise, he feared losing in the way some people fear a crippling disease or death itself. He'd seen what it had done to his father, who, through folly and bad luck, had lost the land that had been in the Bolton family since the Revolutionary War. John Bolton wasn't worth a damn after that, not as a father, a husband, or a man; it was as though he had lost his soul with those thousand acres of timber and pastureland in the southern Blue Ridge, and he took the traditional way out with a Smith and Wesson. The terror of becoming that way was what made his eldest son compete so fiercely at everything he did. The day you waited or rested was the day you lost.

The telex bell rang and Dalman called:

"Hey, Harry. Hong Kong wants you."

Hong Kong could mean only one thing: transmission problems. Bolton walked into the outer office, a circular scar on his shoulder puckering like a round, pink mouth with the swing of his arms. Sure enough, the message read:

120350 BOLTON: FIRST TWO TAKES 120250 SNAP GARBLED. RE-SEND PLS. COLLETTI/HK.

Son of a bitch. Two takes were nearly half his story. At only twenty-five words a minute, it would be a quarter of an hour before the old radio teletypes cleared the garbled copy. Give Hong Kong another ten minutes to relay it to New York by cable or satellite, New York another fifteen to edit it and put it out on the wire, and you were up to five P.M. Eastern time before it even got into the newsrooms. There went all chance of making the afternoons.

Tearing the message out of the telex, he bulled into the teletype room, divided from the rest of the office by a glass partition. Both operators were banging on the keyboards, unaware they were sending gibberish.

"Goddamnit!" Bolton roared. "What the hell is wrong?"

"Nothing wrong," said one of the men, a young Vietnamese with a Ringo Starr haircut.

"Look at this." He shoved the message in the operator's face.

Pausing to read it, the man then looked up at Bolton, 220 pounds of thinly controlled rage.

"Think maybe trouble atmospherics."

"I think maybe trouble is that you two Saigon cowboys don't know your scrawny asses from a slit trench. Goddamnit, a teletype operator who's got it together can tell when he's having trouble with transmission."

"Sorry, Harry, we resend."

"Yeah, and after every take, I want confirmation from Hong Kong that they've received okay."

There were suggestions of gray in the sky by the time Hong Kong sent its final confirmation: ALL RCVD OK. Bolton, light-headed from too much tension and too little sleep, his poisoned guts full of shooting pains, straggled back into his office to wait for the inevitable questions from the copy desk.

9

————

HE LAY DOWN on an army cot set against one wall beside a table littered with unwashed coffee cups. He was too wired to nap, and the cot's canvas smell brought a memory of the squadron tent camp near the Bien Hoa airstrip, the memory prompting him to look at the faded, stained photograph in his wallet. It showed him and Gillette in camouflage flight suits and crash helmets, the visors up. They were standing beside a Huey, Bolton with one arm resting on the downturned barrel of the door gun, Gillette with two fingers of one hand spread in a V, which was bisected by the middle finger of the other hand: his salute to victory. The photograph was too small to show the tattoo on Gillette's forearm, *Born to Lose*. And I guess you were, you crazed little Creole, Bolton thought as a movie camera in his mind projected footage of Gillette's helicopter burning in a jungle clearing like a gigantic railroad flare. Christ, they didn't find enough of him, the pilot, and the co-pilot to fill a willy-peter bag, and what they found looked like chunks of an incinerated shish kebob. Yeah, when you lost in war, brother, you lost it all.

Thinking of that day, Bolton felt the revulsion and the hurt all over again. The loss of Gillette was a wound that had never healed properly; a boyhood on an isolated mountain farm had not given Bolton much talent for making friends, and his belligerent personality didn't help. So he treasured the few friendships he had been able to establish. That was why he sometimes behaved protectively toward DelCorso, who was a lot like Gillette. Both were stocky and dark, both had a hotheaded courage that often lapsed into recklessness. Maybe some kind of karma was at work; he had met DelCorso the day after Gillette's death, the day he, Bolton, took an AK-47 round in the shoulder. Medevac into a hot landing zone. Stretcher-bearers loading a soldier with a shattered leg onto the chopper, a soldier strangely equipped with cameras instead of a rifle and bandoliers. The helicopter was lifting off when something knocked Bolton off his armored seat and spun him into a bulkhead. No pain at first, just the impact and then the warm wetness beneath the hole in his flak jacket. He and DelCorso ended up as wardmates in the hospital. Sure, karma. Lose one friend, gain another.

He studied the map again, but his admiration for General Duc's strategic artistry became marbled with remorse. The journalist in him gave way to the veteran, who realized that the North Vietnamese plans, if successful, would strip Gillette's death of even the illusion of meaning, a realization that filled him with anger and a sense of betrayal. He knew his anger had no rational basis—that those who died on the losing side died for nothing was a law of war—and he couldn't say by what or whom he felt betrayed. The emotions were there nonetheless. He struggled against them because he was a wire-service correspondent, an objective professional who could not allow his personal feelings to be affected by the events he covered any more than a professional soldier could allow himself to weep over his casualties.

Dalman stuck his head in the door.

"You awake, Harry?"

"Yeah."

"New York's on the twix."

Swinging his legs to the floor, Bolton went to the telex, where, in bold black letters, he saw the words:

YR COPY RCVD OK HERE. HAVE QUERIES. HALPRIN.

Sitting down, Bolton typed "GA," meaning "go ahead."

YOU SAY ARVN HAVE 35,000 TROOPS. WHEELER AT PENTAGON SAYS HIS SOURCES CLAIM 50,000. HOW COME?

You goddamned Nervous Nellie, you had to call Wheeler just to be sure, didn't you?

OTHER 15,000 GHOST SOLDIERS.

WHAT THAT?

Halprin, why did they make you foreign editor?

GHOST SOLDIERS NONEXISTENT TROOPS CARRIED ON ROLLS SO CMDRS CAN COLLECT THEIR PAY.

NEED GRAF EXPLAINING. WHEELER ALSO SEZ SOUTH HAS 5,000 ROTC CADETS TO DEFEND SAIGON. WHY YOU UNINCLUDED?

BECAUSE 5,000 SCHOOLBOYS NOT MUCH AGAINST 90,000 REGULARS.

Asshole.

NEED INSERT INCLUDING CADETS.

OK. ANYTHING ELSE?

REUTERS AND AFP HANOI SAY NORTH WANTS THIEU DOWNSTEP. INDICATE THIS PRECONDITION FOR TALKS, SUPPORTING KISSINGER THAT N. VIETS SEEKING POLITICAL NOT MILITARY SOLUTION.

WHAT IS QUERY?

YOU ABSOLUTELY SURE YR SOURCES?

How can you scream at a man on a telex?

OF COURSE SURE. NOW 0530 LOCAL. APPRECIATE YOU MOVE COPY SOONEST TO MAKE A.M. FINALS.

MOM PLS. DESK HAS QUERY. WHAT IS TAMARIND TREE?

For several seconds, Bolton stared at the question in disbelief.

BOLTON, ANSWER PLS. THIS COSTING MONEY.

TAMARIND TREE IS TREE THAT BEARS TAMARINDS, A PULPY FRUIT SIMILAR TO DESKMEN WHO ASK DUMB ASS QUESTIONS. ANYTHING ELSE, OR DOES DESK WANT TO KNOW MAKE OF CHAIN SAWS?

NTHG ELSE. DO NOT USE PROFANITY ON WIRE. BIBI HALPRIN/ NY.

The machine shut down with a whining whir that seemed to express Bolton's feelings.

The morning sun was ramming its heat through the window by the time he finished filing his inserts. Checking the world wire, which carried the copy by all IPS correspondents, he noticed that New York had yet to move his first paragraph. Filing early had turned out to be a strategic error; he should have waited until the morning papers were almost on deadline, leaving the Nervous Nellies no time to bite their nails and crosscheck his information with the Pentagon, the State Department, and Christ knew who else.

Now, in his knee and shoulder, in all the parts of him that had been broken or bruised, Bolton felt every minute of the twenty-two hours he'd been awake. The Geritol ads were right about turning thirty-five. Anyhow, he was damned if he was going to sit in this Turkish bath, waiting for New York to come up with more stalling questions.

"Dalman," he said, putting on his shirt. "I'm going to hit the sack. When Grey comes on, leave word with him that I'm in my room."

THE PHONE WOKE HIM out of a sleep that was akin to death.

"Harry," said the voice at the other end. "This is Grey."

"Grey? What the hell time is it?"

"One in the afternoon."

Bolton smacked his lips to rid his mouth of its dry, coppery taste.

"This had better be important, Grey."

"It is, and you'll blow a fuse when you hear it. Rocket from New York. It says, 'Late editions ayems carrying AP snap from Albury that NVA planning attack on Saigon in two weeks. Quotes intelligence sources that ARVN cannot hold city longer than twelve hours. Reports Hutton ignoring advice begin evacking Americans. Can you match?' "

Bolton stared down the length of his body to his feet, the toes burnished by a slat of light falling through the shutters.

"Grey, I hope to Christ Dalman and Vinnie put you up to this, because if they didn't, I'm going to kick your ass from here to the middle of next year."

"Nobody put me up to anything," Grey replied in the sincerest voice.

Dropping the receiver, Bolton dressed hurriedly and ran out of his room. Fast Eddie, parked on his go-cart near the entrance to the Continental, challenged him to a race, and Bolton yelled, *"Get the fuck out of my way,"* as he took off at a dead run across Lam Son Square and down Le Loi. At the building where the bureau had its offices, he didn't bother to wait for the lethargic elevator, but lunged up the four flights of stairs, nearly tore the door off its hinges and, breathing like an emphysema victim, checked the world wire. It hadn't carried a single paragraph of his story. Moving to the telex, he tapped out New York's number. When the answer-back came, he asked for Lucas, the overnight man on the foreign desk.

MOM PLS, the New York operator replied. Waiting, Bolton had to restrain himself from smashing the keyboard with his fists. The others in the office, Grey, Vincent, and Hoang, moved around him like members of a demolition squad around an unexploded bomb they didn't know how to defuse. Then the telex clattered.

LUCAS HERE.

LUCAS, WHAT THE HELL IS GOING ON?

CAN YOU MATCH AP?

THAT STORY MINE. FILED 0340 LOCAL. WHY IT UNMOVED?

DON'T KNOW. WILL CHECK AND CALL YOU BACK.

Half an hour later, after Bolton had driven his fist into a wall, kicked a desk, and threatened Grey with a slow and painful death if he so much as breathed too loudly, the telex rattled like a set of trick false teeth. It was Lucas's reply.

120150 BOLTON: FOUND YR COPY BOTTOM OF KILL SPIKE. FONED HALPRIN AND SOLVED MYSTERY. AFTER YOU FILED INSERTS, HALPRIN UPHELD STORY AND CALLED KISSINGER'S PRESS SECRETARY, WHO SAID YR SOURCES TOTALLY INACCURATE. STATE DEPT. HAS DEFINITE SIGNALS HANOI WILL TALK IF THIEU DOWNSTEPS. PRESS SECRETARY THEN FONED MCDANIELS AND ASKED HIM EMBARGO STORY BECAUSE IT COULD PANIC SOUTH VIETS AND WRECK CHANCES FOR NEGOTIATIONS. MCDANIELS KILLED STORY. BECAUSE OF KILL, HALPRIN DID NOT TELL ME YOU FILED WHEN I CAME ON.

Killed. Bolton was beyond feeling sick. Killed. Oh, he'd like to kill, all right. He wished he had the power to transform himself into pure energy and ride the telex signals back to New York, where he would rematerialize and strangle Halprin and McDaniels with a rusty coat hanger.

YOU STILL ON BOLTON?

STILL ON.

HALPRIN SEZ AS LONG AS AYEMS RUNNING AP, YOU SHOULD UPFRESHEN STORY AND SEND NEW LEAD. WE WILL USE KILLED COPY AS A-MATTER.

HE WANTS ME TO MATCH MY EXCLUSIVE IN OTHER WORDS.

AMOUNTS TO THAT. SORRY.

PLS ONPASS FOLLOWING MSG TO HALPRIN AND MCDANIELS. FUCK YOU BOTH AND THE HORSES YOU RODE IN ON. RGDS BOLTON/SAIGON.

10

IN HIS HOTEL ROOM, the early morning light grazing through the window, DelCorso began the ritual of preparing himself and his equipment for the critical instant when he would have to stand up under fire and shoot back with nothing but a camera.

He started by emptying the plastic and aluminum film cans from his camera bag and setting them in four rows on the dresser, the K-64 color in front, the high-speed Ektachrome behind them, then the Tri-X black-and-white, and, in the rear, the slower Plus-X. The arrangement looked like a battalion of squat toy soldiers on parade. He then set up his lens and film combinations by placing each of his four cameras beside its respective rank: the Leica M3D, fitted with a fast F1.4 Leitz, next to the K-64; the M5, with a 28-mm wide-angle next to the Ektachrome; a shock-proof, waterproof, fungus-proof, everything-proof Nikonos, useful in this climate, was matched with the Plus-X, and a 35-mm Nikon with the Tri-X.

Now, like a soldier practicing a blindfolded disassembly of his rifle, DelCorso loaded each camera with his eyes closed. Eyes still closed, he hung the M3D around his neck by its web strap, cocked the advance lever and, working the aperture ring with his left hand, the shutter selector with his right, made a lens and speed setting. F-eight at a sixtieth, he said to himself, then opened his eyes to check the scales. F-eight at a sixtieth. Closing his eyes again, he tried a second setting, a third, a fourth. Five-point-six at five hundredths. Eleven at one twenty-fifth. He practiced for half an hour, until he could make six consecutive settings with each camera without a mistake. If and when the shit hit the fan, Charlie wasn't going to cease fire so he could raise his head to see if he had the correct f-stop and shutter speed. He didn't go through this drill just to sharpen his proficiency but also to break down the inherent alienation between man and machine. That's all his cameras were: instruments, creations of applied optical physics. He loved the feel of them in his hands, but his most valuable equipment was in his head and heart, the camera devices that recorded not only the object but whatever was going on inside him when he pressed the button. For him, everything in a photograph came together just before the shutter was released. In that split second, he interpreted the meaning and felt the emotion of a scene, set his stops and speed, focused and composed simultaneously so that all the release did was duplicate on film the image fixed in his mind. If he performed these mental, emotional, and physical functions in coordination, his photograph would be complete and not need any manipulation afterward. To achieve this, he needed more than vision and manual dexterity; he had to be thinking clearly, his feelings had to be in harmony with those of the moment, his intimacy with his camera had to be such that his use of it at the decisive instant was reflex action, an immediate union of the tangible and intangible, of hand and eye, mind and heart.

Putting his cameras down, DelCorso opened the closet and took out a web pistol belt with two canteens, two ammunition pouches, and a medical corpsman's kit clipped to it. He loaded ten cans of K-64 in one pouch, ten of Ektachrome in the other. Another twenty rolls of black-and-white along with twenty spare rolls of color went into one of the kit's three waterproof compartments. Normally, he wouldn't carry so much film, but the battle at Xuan Loc was the first major action of the offensive since Danang had fallen and he intended to make the most of it. If he pulled this off, he'd probably get the cover, which would mean a thousand-dollar bonus. He cautioned himself against thinking about money as he placed his reserve camera, the Nikonos, in the kit's second compartment. The money was good when it came, but he couldn't allow himself to go after it.

Stuffing some first-aid gear, his painkillers, and water pu-
rification tablets in the third compartment, he stripped off his
shorts—in the bush, underwear turned your crotch into a mass
of inflamed lumps—wrapped an Ace bandage around his ankle
to give it support, then put on a pair of camouflaged trousers
and a fatigue jacket with deep side pockets, in one of which
he kept his light meter and caption book. DelCorso got into
his flak vest and hung his three remaining cameras from his
neck, adjusting the straps so they lay against his torso one
above the other. Buckling the pistol belt to his waist, he clomped
around the room tightening this, loosening that, snapping dry
shots with each camera until he felt comfortable. Finally, he
placed his only long lens, a 105-millimeter, in his trouser
pocket. You ain't ready now, Nicolò, you never will be.

He poured a cup of the coffee he'd ordered from room
service earlier. Lighting a cigarette, he thought, This is the
civilized way to go to war. *Café au lait from a silver pot.*
Outside, Lam Son Square was already smothered in traffic,
but DelCorso did not see the street and the endless flow of
cars and motorbikes; he saw the big Chinook cargo helicopter
he and Bolton would fly into Xuan Loc; he saw the chopper
and the rubber plantations around the city, where the 18th
Division had surprised everybody as well as themselves by
holding out for five days against an NVA corps. The Communists had backed off and proceeded to systematically pul-
verize the place with artillery. Fifteen hundred rounds a day,
one shell every minute. It was going to be a hot zone, maybe
the hottest in his experience. Damned Chinooks were so big
and lumbering, you could hit one blindfolded. His memory
played back a picture of a chopper he'd seen shot down during
Tet, the tracer rounds streaking up from the trees, the aircraft
bursting in midair like a miniature supernova. DelCorso's palms
started sweating while his belly did gymnastics. Fear, the fear
of war, the dread of violent death; and it was no less awful
now than it had been when he first felt it ten years before.
DelCorso took a deep drag from his cigarette, trying through
force of will to keep his terror from mastering him. That failing, he paced the room, wiggling his arms and rolling his neck
the way he used to before a fight. Shake it off, he said to
himself, shake it off. And when that didn't work, he did what
most fallen Catholics do in moments of crisis—resorted to
prayer. Crossing himself, he got down on his knees and recited
the prayer he used to say when the trainer was taping his

hands, fear and fury coalescing into an explosive ball in his gut.

"St. Michael the Archangel defend us in battle and be our safeguard against the wickedness and snares of the devil. May God rebuke Satan, we humbly pray, and by God's power may you, Prince of the Heavenly Hosts, cast him into hell with all the evil spirits who wander through the world seeking the ruin of souls."

The beautiful words began to calm him. "St. Michael the Archangel defend us in battle," he started a second time, but jumped to his feet at the loud knock on the door. Bolton would have died laughing if he'd seen him, mumbling like some altar boy.

"Harry," he said, keeping a tight rein on his voice, "it's open."

Bolton came in, a helmet under his arm, a flak jacket tossed over his shoulder in the style of a bullfighter's cape. Looking at DelCorso, he skewed his lips and nodded with mock admiration.

"I see by your outfit that you must be Nick DelCorso, combat cameraman," he said, a smile in his blue eyes. "Yes, kiddies, it *is* Nick DelCorso! Who else would have the panache to drink café au lait before plunging into the hell of battle?"

DelCorso picked up his helmet and held it, like a kettle, by its chin strap.

"Let's hit the bricks, Harry."

"Did you hear that, kiddies? 'Let's hit the bricks.' What laconic cool. You may remember from our last episode that our hero was about to photograph a Viet Cong Amazon who had defected to become the first one-titted centerfold in *Playboy*'s history. . . ."

His terror bursting like an abscess, DelCorso laughed.

"Horseman, thank Christ you're around."

"Saw it on your face the second I walked in. The creepie-crawlies."

"Didn't think it showed."

"They were on you like white on rice. No sweat. They hit me about three o'clock this morning. Realized I'm too tall for this crap. The round that goes over everybody's head gives me a third nostril."

Laughing again, more from the release of tension than at Bolton's joke, DelCorso got his key. The two men left the room.

"We've still got this all alone, if you're interested," Bolton said.

"I'm interested. The Arvin still going to fly that media circus into Xuan Loc on Friday?"

"If they haven't lost the place they will."

"Well, it looks like they'll hold. They've got the Airborne now."

Bolton pressed the button to the cage elevator.

"Yeah, right, the Airborne. So what? The Airborne's Saigon's last reserve and while they're stomping around in the rubber trees, Charlie's got six or seven divisions waiting to hit this town from the other side. Sorry, folks, all the Eighteenth's done is upset Charlie's timetable. Game plan remains the same. Suck in the reserves, pin 'em down, chew 'em up, then stroll into town. Need a chuckle? Read this. Got it from the home office last night."

Riding down to the lobby floor, DelCorso read the message.

201456 BOLTON: RE YR 192102 IF YOU CAN GET INTO XUAN LOC AHEAD OF PACK, GO. WE UNWANT THUMBSUCKER. WANT PLENTY OF BANG-BANG. GIVE US SIGHTS, SOUNDS, AND SMELLS OF BATTLEFIELD, QUOTES FROM 18TH CMDRS ON HOW THEY REPULSED REDS. FYI WHEELER FILED FOLLOWING YESTERDAY: + NO DOUBT ABOUT IT, + GEN. WHALEN SAID, BRIEFING NEWSMEN ON HIS RETURN FROM A FACT-FINDING MISSION TO VIETNAM, + THE ARVN TOOK A BEATING, BUT THE STAND THEY'VE MADE AT XUAN LOC SHOWS THEY'RE PULLING THEMSELVES TOGETHER, AND THEY'VE STILL GOT THE AIRBORNE IN RESERVE. THOSE LITTLE TIGERS WILL TURN SAIGON INTO ANOTHER STALINGRAD IF THE VC TRY TO TAKE IT. + KEEP HEAD DOWN, HARRY. RGDS/HALPRIN/CABLES/NY.

"Christ, Harry, what're they smoking back there?"

"I don't know, but whatever it is, I'm going to buy ten kilos if and when I ever get out of here. Bang-bang. Give 'em bang-bang. Well, fuck it, bang-bang's what they want, bang-bang's what they'll get. I'm lucky I've still got a job."

After the elevator let them off, they walked down a short flight of stairs to the lobby. Dunlop was there. Dressed for the field, his cameras, one with a lens half as long as a rocket launcher, crossed over his deep chest, he stood talking to one of his protégés, a lanky kid with a faint mustache. As DelCorso looked at Dunlop's thick, creased neck, tanned forearms, and rectangular head, there rose in him, as mysteriously and spontaneously as love, a self-multiplying hatred; his hatred for the older man bred hatred for himself for feeling hate, which bred further hatred for the man for making him feel it.

"You look all business, Nick," Dunlop said as DelCorso dropped off his key. The high voice, strangely feminine for such a bulky man, was full of artificial friendliness.

"Thought I'd earn what they're paying me."

Dunlop's lips sliced into a thin, angular smile.

"That shouldn't be hard with the rates you get."

"C'mon, Nick," Bolton said in an undertone, "let's go."

"What's that, P.X.?"

"Nothing."

"Goddamn right it was nothing." DelCorso stared into the eyes, which, set in a craggy face, looked like two blue rocks in the side of an extinct volcano. "You going out or just dressing the part?"

"What's that supposed to mean?"

"You going out, or are you sending in one of your stunt men, your dollar-a-day paparazzi, like that asshole standing next to you."

The thin young man took a step forward. DelCorso, all feisty street fighter, stood on the balls of his feet and let his hands fall loosely over the front of his thighs.

"The name's Lutter," the young man said. "Jim Lutter."

"Well, Jim Lutter, I don't think you want what I'd like to give you."

"He's staying right here, and I'll be out there. Hung Nam," Dunlop said, referring to the village between Saigon and Xuan Loc where the Viet Cong had set up a roadblock to stop supplies from reaching the provincial city.

"Don't take any chances, old man. With that lens you've got, you could shoot the story from the roof of the Caravelle."

"I'll be there, Nick," Dunlop repeated, the false cordiality gone out of his voice.

"Right. Just like your four-star buddies. Watching through high-powered lenses."

"For Christ's sake, let's shove off." Bolton took hold of DelCorso's arm and nearly dragged him outside. "You and that jerk ought to do everybody a favor and get this over with," he said as they walked toward the jeep. "Fight a duel or something."

"All right. I get to choose the weapons. A rubber hose for him, a sawed-off shotgun for me."

"You know, I read somewhere that a first-rate mind can

hold two contradictory ideas at the same time. If that's true, you're a genius."

"What're you talking about?"

They came to the jeep before Bolton could answer. Behind the wheel, Hoang said, *"Chao anh,"* and pulled the passenger's seat forward. Unbuckling his pistol belt, DelCorso climbed in the back and sat down beside a box of C rations.

"Where the hell is Wilson?" Bolton asked, setting his big frame into the front seat.

"He said if he wasn't here, he'd be at the Miramar."

"Miramar, Hoang."

Hoang nodded and pulled the jeep into Tu Do.

"All right, Harry, what was the genius bit supposed to mean?"

"How in the hell do you square all your high-flown social conscience with this vendetta you've got with Dunlop? What the hell are you trying to prove with this macho bullshit?"

"What macho bullshit?"

"That stuff about the long lens he's got. Like he's yellow because he doesn't want to get close enough to take some VC's portrait."

Bolton had to raise his voice above the noise of the traffic.

"Look, Harry," DelCorso said, leaning forward, "maybe I'm simpleminded, but I believe a camera has the power to change things for the better, and if I don't like that son of a bitch, it's because he's misused that power."

"What's that got to do with him being yellow?"

DelCorso, lighting a cigarette, tried to formulate a sensible answer.

"If you're going to tell the truth, you've got to get up close, not sit back with a lens that could take a picture of a gnat's ass at a thousand yards."

"Some speech, Nick."

"He's not a war photographer. He's a sellout, an entertainer, him and his Hollywood marines."

"All right, Nick. All right. Settle down."

But DelCorso, his blood molten, went on.

"Prove something. It's not macho, Harry. If I'm trying to prove anything, it's that I can shoot something straight and print it straight and still come out ahead."

Hoang parked in front of the Miramar. Wilson, with pouches under his eyes the size of hard-boiled eggs, was waiting at the door. He grunted a hello and got in, his cameras clattering.

"Mark, the way you look this morning, you couldn't get a part in a monster movie."

"Yeah, I'm almost as ugly as DelCorso." Wilson draped his flak jacket over the C rations and, stretching his long, thin legs, rested his back against the box. "Too much cheap brandy, too much Buddha Grass, and too much Tuyet Hoa."

"The snow bird."

"Snow blossom, you dumb wop."

"Can you see anything?"

"No, but I don't have to," Wilson said as Hoang drove down Nguyen Do Street, passing the presidential palace and the cool green expanse of the Tao Gen gardens before he turned onto Le Van Duyet. "Don't have to because there's nothing going on at Hung Nam. The ARVN shoot at the roadblock, the VC shoot back. *Ti-ti* story."

"Try and get something. The magazine closes day after tomorrow. They'll need something in case I don't get out of there on time."

"Let's hope that you get out. Personally I think you two *beaucoup dinky-dao* for going into Xuan Loc in a gook chopper."

"No balls, no blue chips," said Bolton.

"Right. That's what you're liable to end up with. Blue chips and no balls. Anyhow, better you than me. I've got responsibilities."

"Yeah, all that alimony for your three exes."

"To say nothing about supporting a fourth wife."

"If I were you, I'd stay clear of that."

"You're not me and I haven't. I love 'em all, eight to eighty, blind, crippled, and crazy."

"Nothing wrong with loving 'em. Just don't marry 'em."

"Too late. I already have."

"Have what?"

"Gotten married."

Bolton turned around, his face wearing an expression of total disbelief.

"I married Tuyet Hoa yesterday. I was going to save the announcement for later, but in conditions such as this, where the life of man is nasty, brutish, and short, now's as good a time as any."

"Who the hell is Tuyet Hoa?"

"A whore," DelCorso said.

"You're speaking of the woman I love, an honorable woman compelled by circumstances into a dishonorable profession."

"You married a whore?"

"It won't be the first time, and at least this one admits what she is."

"And you're telling us that we're *beaucoup* crazy?"

"Well, the truth is, I'm just sort of married to her."

"This has got to be good. Only Wilson can get sort of married. Let's hear it, Mark."

"All things are possible in Saigon. There's a black marketeer in Cho Lon selling marriage certificates for two-fifty U.S. All a girl has to do is find a Yank who's willing to buy one and put his name to it, and off she goes to the consulate for a visa as a dependent wife."

"And you . . ."

"Yup. I got to thinking what'll happen to Tuyet Hoa when Charlie opens up shop in Saigon. I pictured that lovely body hidden in some frumpy Mao suit. I saw her busting that lovely ass on a commune instead of using it the way it was meant to be. And I looked in the mirror and said, 'Wilson, you pretty man, you've got three Purple Hearts, it's time you earned a Good Conduct Medal.' So now, on paper, Tuyet Hoa is Tuyet Hoa Wilson, or Weirson as she would say. And she's going to live with me in Santa Barbara. You ought to understand that, Deecee. You're the advocate of monogamous marriage, right?"

DelCorso had tuned out the conversation. He was looking at the refugee settlements on the outskirts of the city, little cells of squalor that had metastasized over the years into one vast malignant sprawl.

"Earth calling Nick," Wilson said, cupping his hands over his mouth. "Earth calling Nick. Acknowledge please."

"What?" He liked Wilson, but there were moments when his flippancy made DelCorso want to cave in his skull with a two-by-four.

"Are you not an advocate of monogamous marriage?"

"Yeah. I wish you and Snow Blossom all the best."

"Just what the hell happens when this c— I mean, your sort of wife gets to the States?" asked Bolton.

"Either a quick sort of divorce or a life of conjugal bliss."

"Sort of."

"You never know."

DelCorso, who couldn't muster any interest in Wilson's latest sexual escapade, beyond wondering how he was capable of falling in love so frequently, continued to look at the panorama of misery outside. The jeep was moving fast, but not fast enough to outrun the smells boiling out of the settlements, the smells of mud and the rotten fish sauce called *nuocmaum*, of human and animal turds, wet thatch and woodsmoke. The promise of dawn must have mocked the multitudes in those crowded shacks, if, that is, any of them even bothered to pause and gaze at the wonder of sunrise. They probably didn't, but merely rose automatically from their bamboo beds, urinated and defecated, cooked their meager rice and then, in a state close to the sleep from which they'd just awakened—did what? What did they do, these peasants without villages, farmers with no fields to till? Got through the day until it was time to light the oil lamps, endure the mosquitoes, and get through the night. DelCorso watched a group of children, their bellies distended, their skin pocked with the oozing craters of impetigo, playing beside a canal in which women were washing clothes. The canal was the color of crankcase oil, streaked with green scum, and you could almost see the malaria, the typhoid, and dysentery breeding in it.

He wondered why it was supposed to be naïve to be outraged by such degradation and to want to change it. He knew Bolton's philosophy: war was not a moral evil to be eradicated, but a perennial disaster to be endured. Its banishment from human affairs would not occur until human nature underwent a reformation. DelCorso wasn't blind to the logic of this argument and was aware that the evidence was on Bolton's side. And yet, how could any reformation ever have a chance of taking place if, at certain times, some men did not make an appeal to what was best in human nature, to compassion, that capacity to share in the misfortune of others and be moved not only to avoid inflicting it but alleviate it?

Past the city, the hopeless torment of the slums gave way to the everyday poverty of rural villages. Heading up Highway 1 toward the helicopter base at Long Binh, DelCorso felt relieved by the sight of the rice paddies, their level green broken by the curvilinear roofs of Cao Dai pagodas. Fiery and clear, like a sheet of newly blown glass, the tropic light spread over the paddies and the rubber plantations, where it was broken into shafts that gave a golden-green color to the corridors between the straight rows of trees. It was not a landscape that lent itself to war photography; except in the wettest, grayest depths of the monsoon, it did not fit most picture editors' conception of a battleground as a somber place. Which was one of the reasons why Dunlop resorted to darkroom chemistry to create the right, the salable mood. Goddamn P.X. There he was again, interposed between DelCorso's eyes and the countryside, like a three-dimensional image projected on an invisible screen. It occurred to DelCorso that the feelings the man excited in him, though the polar opposite of passionate love, imitated the intensity of love; they obsessed him, seized his heart at unexpected moments, and tempted him to betray his own ideal self. For ever since the scene in the lobby, a compartment of his mind had been picturing a *Newsweek* cover with an exclusive on it and maybe one more double-trucked on the inside; and that same compartment enjoyed thinking about how the beat would make the old man squirm.

He could not expel these thoughts, but he had the discipline to seal them off so as to prevent their flooding his entire mental vessel. He concentrated on the landscape, imagining himself photographing this country in peacetime—an idea he'd entertained for several years. He would capture the way its shades of green changed with the time of day, the rice paddies darkening from near-yellow in the morning to emerald in the afternoon, the hills from jade to aquamarine. He saw images of the jungles full of primeval brilliance, not a sense of concealed menace; portraits of farmers whose expressions were open and relaxed, not cramped by fear; scenes of fields where twisted corpses did not lie. Photographing wars has not destroyed my faith in beauty, he thought, recalling the sight of white sheep sweeping over a grassy hill half a world away. That was only a little less than three weeks ago, but it already seemed like something that had happened in another lifetime. DelCorso tried to recapture the magic and wonder he'd felt then, but he could summon only the memory of the emotions, not the emotions themselves. It was impossible to do otherwise under these circumstances; for at the same time he was admiring the attractiveness of the countryside, he was also assessing it for potential dangers. The shaded avenues between the rubber trees made excellent fields of fire, that hill in the distance a good observation post for an artillery spotter, and that paddy dike, meandering like a muddy stream, was probably booby-trapped.

11

"DON'T THINK I'D LIKE FLYING those things in the best of times," Bolton said as they pulled into Long Binh.

His practiced eye critically examined the three Chinooks parked on the tarmac, but you did not have to be an aviation expert to see that those birds badly needed an overhaul. The patched fuselages and cracked windscreens inspired little confidence, especially in someone like DelCorso, who, despite the countless times he'd flown them, could never convince himself that helicopters were capable of flight.

"You wait, I find my cousin," said Hoang, parking beside a tin-roofed building against which four or five unarmed Vietnamese soldiers sat sipping tea and swatting flies.

"Who's his cousin?" asked Wilson.

"One of the pilots."

"I thought you thought Hoang was VC cadre."

"I know he is."

DelCorso looked around. Long Binh, once one of the largest American bases in Vietnam, had become a wasteland of derelict barracks, decomposing bunkers, and rusting barbed wire. He wondered if the Roman camps in Gaul and Britain had looked like this a decade after the legions called it quits.

Hoang came out with his aviator cousin, who affected an effete dash. He was garbed in a black flight suit set off by his squadron patch and a lavender scarf. A rakish bush hat covered his head, sunglasses his eyes, and he held his cigarette as though he'd learned how to smoke by watching Marlene Dietrich films. The fingernail of his extended pinky was very long, in Vietnamese society a symbol of the elite classes.

"Captain Midnight in drag," Wilson said. "Good luck with that character. He looks like he ought to be hustling tricks on Sunset Boulevard."

"That's probably what he'll be doing when the war's over," said Bolton.

Hoang made the introductions. His cousin, who spoke a passable French and English pidgin, explained he was taking a grave risk, flying two journalists into Xuan Loc without authorization. Bolton took the cue and an exchange was made. There was then the problem of flying them out, the pilot went on. His squadron's next mission wasn't scheduled until day after tomorrow and *c'est la guerre*, eh? Who could say what the situation would be in two days? *Beaucoup* VC around Xuan Loc and perhaps the landing zone would be very dangerous. Bolton, Hoang, and Hoang's cousin started arguing while DelCorso's belly did flips; if he didn't get out by tomorrow at the latest, his film wouldn't reach *Newsweek* before closing. It would have to wait till the next week's issue, by which time Dunlop and the media circus would have been ferried in on the government-approved expedition and taken enough shots of the battle to fill an album. Bolton gave in and came up with another wad of greenbacks, which the pilot zipped into a pocket of his flight suit.

"Very good," he said. "You will please be at the landing zone sixteen hundred today."

"We'll be there," Bolton said. "You will please be there, too. If you're not, my friend and I will walk out of there and when we find you, he'll take one leg and I'll take the other and we'll split you like a stick. *Toi hieu khoung!* Understand?"

"No sweat."

Bolton and DelCorso filled their pockets with C-ration tins just in case the pilot failed to keep his appointment.

"Okay, Mark, Hoang'll take you up to Hung Nam," Bolton said. "You can get a ride back with one of the herd covering that story."

"No sweat."

"Remember, you haven't seen us in case anybody asks."

"Don't worry. Well, keep your heads and asses down, God

speed and good luck, fair winds and a following sea, may the road rise up to meet you and assorted other clichés."

The two men walked across the gummy tarmac and boarded the Chinook. The crew chief was supervising the attachment of a cargo net to the underside of the aircraft. The door gunner, wearing a crash helmet with an opaque visor pulled down, his M-60 projecting like a stinger from his shoulder, looked like some kind of large, one-eyed, lethal wasp ready to defend its nest.

Déjà vu. The ear-numbing roar of the engines, the rush of the rotors sabering the air, the smells of grease and aviation fuel—all this was as familiar to DelCorso and Bolton as the sounds and smells of a commuter train are to men who have chosen a more sensible way to make a living. DelCorso wondered why he could not get used to this, why flying a helicopter in a war zone never failed to lay an egg of terror in his gut. St. Michael the Archangel defend us in battle, be our safeguard against anti-aircraft fire and engine failure and all the other things that can happen with these damn things, and I'll worry about the devil and my soul later.

They came down, contour-flying over the low hills, the cargo nets swinging just above the tops of the rubber and banana trees. DelCorso glimpsed the city through the hatch, a swath of rubble over which plumes of smoke rose as black as the smoke from a coal-fired generator. Then, the Chinook circling, he saw the ARVN firebase outside Xuan Loc—bunkers and gun pits and long-barreled 175s. The three choppers began hovering over the landing zone, but instead of flaring for a touchdown, lurched upward again, as though jerked by invisible winches. The LZ, a patch of raw earth, had become carpeted with people, hundreds of refugees who had been waiting in the shade of the banana groves and who'd rushed out as soon as the Chinooks made their approach. DelCorso took the Leitz off his Leica, snapped on the 105-millimeter, and started shooting as the helicopters made a tight turn that nearly pressed him against a bulkhead. They dropped quickly down, DelCorso's insides aching, as though he were riding an elevator that had slipped a cable.

The pilots held the aircraft high enough off the LZ to prevent anyone from grabbing hold of the landing gear, but low enough to make the rotors whip up a compressed tornado that drove the crowds back. Turning against the wind, the refugees retreated toward the trees, which were tossing and bending like those DelCorso had seen in newsreels of hurricanes. Then trees and people vanished in an eruption of yellow dust. Arms covering their faces, heads lowered, squads of Arvin came running toward the cloud to unload the nets. The crew chief lowered the aft ramp and started kicking out the cargo inside the aircraft. DelCorso heard a muted popping sound above the racket of the engine—small-arms fire. A line of Arvin were shooting over the heads of the refugees, who had regrouped and were again surging toward the helicopters, their figures obscured by the dust, the wind flattening their clothes against their bodies, blasting their straw hats off their heads, the hats sailing like cone-shaped Frisbees over the shuddering trees. The crowd came on with all the inexorable, mindless power of a mob, running over the line of soldiers, impelled by their desperation through the dust that lashed their faces. They were directly below in an instant, shouting appeals DelCorso could not hear for the pulsing rotors; hundreds of faces looking up, hundreds of hands clutching for the struts or the ropes of the cargo net. Emotions had to be in tune with those of the moment; the moment of exposure was the moment of truth, and the truth of this moment was utter and uncontrolled panic. He felt it; though he knew a Chinook could easily lift a truck, he was certain the desperate people beneath him would pull the chopper down, tip it over, and send it cartwheeling on the tips of blades until it exploded in a white magnesium flash. Aiming his wide-angle downward, he shot two or three frames, but knew they wouldn't show much. Nothing there to pull the confusion and fear together, no center to give it meaning. The crew chief tugged his shirt and, with frantic signals, told him and Bolton to get out through the aft ramp. Bolton clambered down to its edge, hesitated, then vanished into space. Behind him, DelCorso suddenly remembered his leg. His leg would never withstand the leap—twelve to fifteen feet at least.

He saw her in the same instant, and knew when he saw her that she was the emotional focus of the madness beneath him. She was standing almost directly under his legs, which were dangling over the lip of the ramp—if he had jumped he would have landed a couple of feet in front of her. Her open mouth exposing her teeth, blackened from chewing betel nut, her blouse torn, her silk trousers snugged around her thighs by the rotors' wind, her long loose hair blown back, she was standing in the whorls of dust and holding a small child overhead, her eyes turned upward with a look of maternal appeal.

Take it, take the child, forget me, take the child out of this. DelCorso focused the 105-millimeter on the eyes and pressed the shutter, arresting their expression and the child's legs, kicking just above her head. Knowing the depth of field would be too shallow with the longer lens at this setting—5.6—and wanting everything in the frame to be as clear as the woman and child—the frenzied masses surrounding her, the helicopter lifting off in the background, the dust coiling around the woman's body like a translucent tentacle—he stopped the lens all the way down and released the shutter again. He lowered the camera and was bringing the wide angle up to his eye when the crew chief shoved him out.

Instinctively, DelCorso folded his arms over his cameras, in the manner of a paratrooper holding his reserve chute, landed on the balls of his feet, managing to keep most of his weight on his right leg, and rolled the moment he hit the ground. Pain screamed up his left leg, but when he stood and tested it, he knew it hadn't been damaged.

"Glad you decided to join us," Bolton shouted. "What in the Jesus hell were you doing up there?"

"My goddamned job," DelCorso answered, angry that he hadn't been able to get at least one shot of the woman with the shorter lens. He looked for her now, but couldn't see her in the crowd, which was shambling back toward the sheltering groves to await its next chance. The Chinooks were well overhead, with a few civilians and Arvin deserters lying in their cargo nets like babies in the bundles of weird-looking storks.

He and Bolton started down a dirt track toward the firebase, about a kilometer away. A kilometer or so beyond that, North Vietnamese artillery struck Xuan Loc with the regularity of a loud metronome. Boom . . . boom . . . boom. Just as the reports said—about one shell a minute. A flight of gunships flitted over a distant ridgeline, the sound of their bursting rockets a series of muffled bangs, like garage doors slamming shut in rapid succession. A battery of ARVN 175s let go with an awesome crash. As soon as he heard these sounds, DelCorso sensed a quickening in his heartbeat, a heightening of awareness, an alertness somehow poignant. The midmorning light was almost piercing in its intensity. The green of the trees alongside the track, the heat shimmer rising off the ground like a transparent curtain, the sweat on the back of Bolton's neck—he saw everything in sharp detail, as though he were looking at the world through an invisible microscope. Del-

Corso had known this heightening dozens of times before, and he often wondered if it was one of the many cords that pulled him into places like this again and again. The threat of annihilation honed his senses and concentrated his mind, elevated him onto another, clearer plane of consciousness. Simply put, he seemed to work better when faced by the possibility of being killed at any second.

General Le Minh Khanh, commander of the 18th Division, was not happy to see two journalists at his firebase. General Khanh, who, with his wide forehead and coarse features, looked more like a Mongolian warlord than a Vietnamese, was in fact infuriated. No journalists were permitted in this area of operations until Friday. Bolton, gazing with contempt at the general's gleaming boots, polished shoulder holster, and starched uniform (they and the Huey helicopter parked outside his tent indicated that he was commuting to the front from his Saigon villa), wondered about this fixation with Friday. What was so special about Friday? Perhaps the Arvin wanted to make sure the story of their heroic defense made the Sunday papers; perhaps they needed a few extra days to make Xuan Loc secure enough to reduce the chances of a newsman getting killed—always an embarrassment. Whatever, General Khanh said he would see them on Friday; but now, he shouted over the bang of artillery outside his tent, they must return to Saigon. His personal pilot would fly them back in the Huey.

Time to play the trump card. Bolton drew from his pocket a pass signed by the 3rd Corps commander, Khanh's boss, authorizing Harold Winslow Bolton, correspondent for the International Press Service, and Nicholas Lucien DelCorso, *Newsweek* photographer, to visit Xuan Loc on this date. All cooperation and courtesies were to be accorded to these representatives of the American press. The general read the document carefully, then asked for their press cards, which he also scrutinized. Bolton, sweating from more than the heat, scanned the brutal face for signs of suspicion. He'd lost one exclusive to the timidity and stupidity of his editors; he didn't want to lose another over a piece of red tape.

With no change of expression, Khanh returned the press cards and folded the pass into his shirt pocket.

"Wait here," he said, walking out. "Do not take any photographs."

"Think he bought it?" DelCorso asked, sitting on a canvas chair.

"Don't know. Hoang is damned good. He's had a lot of practice forging I.D.s for his VC pals."

"It didn't look to me like he bought it."

"If he didn't, he's radioing corps headquarters for confirmation now. What the hell, worst that can happen is a fast trip back to Saigon. Anyhow, I'm here. Got my dateline. Maybe I can con a few quotes out of him before he ships us out and then wing the rest. Get a little background from the spooks at the embassy, toss in a little color—you know: 'As the big Chinook helicopter flew supplies into Xuan Loc, smoke was rising over the city, battered by constant shellfire from North Vietnamese gunners.' That kind of I-was-there horseshit."

"Bang-bang."

"Phoney bang-bang, but bang-bang nonetheless."

"I can't wing a photograph," DelCorso said.

"And I don't especially want to wing this story. I sure as hell don't want to come in here Friday with a gang of tourists. Those goddamned amateurs back there, Lizzie St. John and her TV boyfriend."

They waited nearly an hour. It was, in Bolton's phrase, hotter than nine kinds of hell. The air seemed to grow heavier by the minute; by late afternoon, unable to support its own weight, it would relieve itself in a biblical downpour. DelCorso busied himself by sneaking shots of the artillery pieces through the tent flap. He had the shutter at a two-fiftieth, to catch the muzzle flash of the huge 175s and 155s. It was absolutely the most banal, routine sort of war photograph anyone could take, but, for some reason, picture editors went for photos of heavy guns in action. Drama, he supposed. Bang-bang with a capital B.

Finally, a tall Vietnamese officer with a grin frozen on his face came in and introduced himself as Colonel Hiep. He asked the two men to follow him. Certain they were being escorted to the helicopter, Bolton asked the colonel a few questions about the fighting—one good quote would do—but all he would say was, "No problem, no sweat." Bolton wondered what he could make of that. *Assessing the situation in Xuan Loc, Colonel Hiep said*, "*No problem, no sweat.*" Not what you would call informative.

They were not taken to the helicopter, but to a small tent camp, pitched in a rubber grove near the edge of the firebase perimeter. Bolton was pleasantly surprised to see that General Khanh had bought the forgery and then some. In one tent, a large acetate-covered map stood on an easel, an enlisted flunky beside it, his rubber-tipped pointer ready to smack the map at the general's cue. An open fly-tent beyond it contained a dozen North Vietnamese prisoners, stripped to their green underwear, blindfolded, hands bound behind their backs. Close by, a few Arvin were putting the finishing touches to a display of captured weapons, a long, tidy rank of rifles, machine guns, and mortars. The prize of prizes hulked nearby—an enemy T-54 upon which a squad of South Vietnamese sat waiting to have their picture taken.

"Well," Bolton drawled, "we didn't teach 'em much how to fight this kind of war, but we sure showed 'em how to stage a briefing."

Colonel Hiep escorted them into the tent and invited them to sit in the chairs in front of the map. Khanh entered a few minutes later, wearing a ferocious scowl. The indomitable commander. It soon became evident that the general not only knew how to put on a slick, smooth briefing but also how to supply quotes guaranteed to see print. "This morning, the NVA made its sixth infantry attack on Xuan Loc, but the soldiers of my division resisted and repulsed them. . . ." "The enemy's tanks can no longer reach the city, we have destroyed all their tanks. Now the paratroopers are pursuing them and have pushed them two thousand meters back. . . ." "The enemy has tried to cut the road at Hung Nam, but we have opened the road. We have destroyed almost two enemy regiments." Bolton scribbled these fairy tales in his notebook. Then, careful not to ruffle the general's feathers, he suggested that the attacks may have been feints designed to pin down the Eighteenth and suck in the Airborne reserves. "No!" Khanh screeched. "The NVA have great valor but their valor cannot match the valor of my soldiers: if they send in three more divisions, I will knock them down! Our stand in Xuan Loc will give new confidence to the people of Saigon! No, they were not feints, they were large attacks and we killed many, we captured many weapons, we captured"—Khanh paused to glance at a crib sheet—"we captured forty-six AK-47 rifles, seventeen B-40 rocket launchers, twelve machine guns, six sixty-one-millimeter mortars . . ."

Right, Bolton thought. If you can't convince 'em with facts, numb 'em with statistics. Moments like this put Bolton's professionalism to the test. He did not feel like an observer of this sham, but part of the show. It was all he could do to stop himself from leaping up and shouting, *"Bullshit."*

"General, if you destroyed two regiments, how come you captured only forty-six rifles?" he asked tiredly, for it was a question he'd often asked in this war of body counts.

He'd asked it so often that he wrote the answer in his notebook before the general replied:

"The North Vietnamese are so short of weapons, they are sending their men into battle unarmed."

When Khanh was finished, he invited Bolton to interview whom he chose: Colonel Hiep, whose 40th Regiment had seen the hardest fighting; the soldiers who had captured the tank; the North Vietnamese prisoners, who would verify that they were being well treated. This Bolton did and, when he'd gotten it out of the way, he asked if he and DelCorso could have a look at the city. Khanh demurred; though the VC had been cleared from Xuan Loc, it was still dangerous—there was shelling. Bolton replied he had been under fire before and he very much wanted to visit the scene of the battle in which Khanh's valiant troops had won such a great victory. Flattered, the general agreed. Colonel Hiep would act as escort.

"No problem," Hiep said. "Shelling is *ti-ti.* No sweat. But where is your friend with the cameras?"

Bolton looked around. DelCorso, who had left the tent after photographing Khanh to take pictures of the T-54 and the captured weapons, was nowhere in sight. Overeager bastard just couldn't stay put.

12

DELCORSO WAS about a hundred yards into the rubber, lying behind a tree with his camera pointed at two Arvin soldiers who were beating a prisoner.

The pictures of the weapons display and the soldiers, striking conventional, heroic poses atop the captured tank, had been depressingly stock, the kind of junk that was destined for burial in a morgue file, the kind of junk the media circus would get on Friday. He needed to do a lot better. He'd been scouting around when he heard, a short distance off, a burst of rapid Vietnamese. Though he understood only a few words of the language, the familiar, staccato rhythm of the speaker's voice told him what was going on.

He followed a path through the rubber toward the sound. Seeing the three figures in a clearing ahead, he stalked to within range, then quietly lay down behind the tree. The POW had been stripped to his underwear, bound and blindfolded. He was sitting with his knees drawn up into his chest. One of the South Vietnamese soldiers, the one doing the questioning, squatted in front of him; the other stood off to the side, cradling a rifle. Light was falling through the leaves in thin, gray-green shafts that looked like transparent bars encaging the prisoner and his two captors. The interrogator asked a question; the POW mumbled an answer and was struck hard enough to snap his head backward so that it caught one of the beams of light. The same thing happened again. Given the nature of this war, given, DelCorso supposed, the nature of all wars, a photograph of a prisoner undergoing torture was also stock; and compared to some interrogations he'd witnessed, this one was mild, so far. It was the light that made the scene extraordinary, the barred light and the way the POW's face looked when that eerie radiance fell on it. Exalted, almost saintly—DelCorso could not define the quality in words; all he knew was that it was extraordinary and he needed something extraordinary on film. He also knew he could stop the torture, at least temporarily, by showing himself with his cameras or by making noise; so he was aware that he was making a choice as, his hands trembling from tension, he locked a 43-mm–86-mm zoom onto the Nikon, loaded with high-speed Tri-X, which would freeze the microsecond when the man's face caught the light. The soft click of the coupling bracket sounded as loud to him as a cracking branch. Then, extending the lens to its full focal length, he framed the three figures and waited with the nervousness of a hunter waiting for a deer to move into the cross hairs of a telescopic sight. The interrogator asked another question. The prisoner's muted answer was met with another slap, but DelCorso, overanxious, pushed the button too hard and moved the camera slightly, the photographer's equivalent of jerking a trigger. *C'mon, once more, c'mon.* Another question, another mumbled answer. *C'mon, c'mon.* As though in response to DelCorso's silent demand, the interrogator rose slightly on his haunches and smashed the prisoner with his fist. The man's head flew back, blood erupting from his nose and mouth, the dark blood and blindfold contrasting with his face, shining whitely in the ray of slanting light. DelCorso pressed the shutter, feeling in the fraction of a second it took for the mechanism to open and close as a hunter feels when he's made a clean kill—a mixture of thrill, pride, and remorse.

"Hey, DelCorso, where in the Jesus hell are you?"

Bolton's shout made the two South Vietnamese pause and glance around, wary and baffled; it had been years since they had heard an American voice in the bush. DelCorso got to his feet and went down the path without a sound, as though he were creeping away from two lovers he did not want to disturb. Of the emotions he had felt at the moment of the shutter's release only remorse remained; not remorse in the sense of sadness but in the older sense of repentance. He knew what he had done and had failed to do. More importantly, he knew why, and the knowledge of why made his cameras seem heavy around his neck, as heavy as anything he had ever carried. Walking down the path, he had an urge to open the Nikon and expose the last frame to the light. Light had created it, light would destroy it. But he knew that would not be an act of atonement. It would merely be destroying the evidence of his complicity. Those New Guinea tribesmen who believed they lost their souls when their photograph was taken were half right; what they didn't know was that the man behind the lens sometimes lost his.

"Where were you, behind enemy lines?" Bolton asked, coming up the path from the other direction.

"Just looking for targets of opportunity."

DelCorso flinched when the 175 battery fired a salvo.

"Hey, boy, you nervous in the service? That's outgoing."

"I know it's outgoing."

"Why're you so jumpy all of a sudden?"

"I'm not jumpy."

"Good. Colonel No Sweat's going to give us a guided tour of the city, where all the mail's incoming."

Colonel Hiep leading, they walked into Xuan Loc down an asphalt road. Moist and glimmering in the sun, the road looked like a polluted canal upon which floated empty canvas bandoliers, shell and cartridge casings, discarded helmets, spent flares, odd bits of barbed wire—the waste and junk of war. Refugees squatted in the drainage ditches, shielding their heads from the sun with the broad banana leaves. With the casualness of boys lobbing stones into a pond, the North Vietnamese gunners continued to drop shells into the north end of the city. They seemed to be using a Catholic church steeple as a registration mark. Though the shelling was not heavy, though he could see Arvin soldiers, tanks, and APCs dug into the edges of Xuan Loc, DelCorso felt alone and naked in his fall from grace. By the time he reached the center of town, where houses had been flattened as if by a wind of unimaginable power, their sheet-metal roofs twisted into fantastic shapes, his legs had grown reluctant and were threatening to stop moving altogether.

The colonel led them to his command post, a ruin of a building near a truck park that had been blasted into a heap of scrap metal. The air stank of burned tires. Two shells bumped into the street near the church, less than five hundred yards away. When they heard a weird moan, like the gulping of an ambulance siren, Colonel Hiep did a swan dive through the doorway of his CP, Bolton and DelCorso behind him, all three men landing in a pile just as the rocket exploded in the truck park. A metallic rain splattered against the walls and a huge piece of shrapnel spiked itself in the floor not six inches from DelCorso's feet.

"One-twenny-two rocket," said the colonel, smiling but a little abashed by his undignified dive for cover. "*Ti-ti*. No sweat."

He stood and unfolded a map on the table and began giving Bolton a history of the morning's battle. DelCorso dug the shrapnel out of the floor. It was still hot to the touch. Nothing *ti-ti* about that. His spooked state of mind inclined him to regard it as an omen, though he didn't know of what. Of death if he stayed here any longer? Or a warning to be careful of his motives and his actions in the future? It sometimes amazed him that he thought in this superstitious way, but a man whose livelihood required a constant confrontation with death needed some belief if he was to survive emotionally. Perhaps, too, he lacked a modern mind; he could not accept the rule of chance and the existence of the absurd. The world was full of signs and portents if you were open to them, and nothing happened without a reason. He put the shrapnel in his pocket for good luck and, while the colonel talked, took a few shots of the truck park, a panorama of devastation. Another shell burst near the church. Despite the safe distance, the noise made DelCorso's heart stop and he could no longer hold his camera steady.

"VC attack with twelve tanks this morning," he heard the colonel say. "We destroy two, others retreat, no sweat. Now I will show you."

After giving some orders to an aide, Colonel Hiep picked up a radioman and strolled through the rubble of the central marketplace with the nonchalance of a man who is either very brave or very stupid. They were well within the enemy artillery's cone of fire—the church was now only a block away at most—and each blast shook the tenuous hold DelCorso had on himself. The colonel, picking his way through a jungle of charred timbers, named the shells as they came in—one-twenty-two, one-oh-seven, one-thirty—as though he were an ornithologist identifying birdcalls.

They came out onto a street that ran past the bus and railroad stations, recognizable as such only by the blackened skeletons of the buses and the twisted rails, one of which was bent back on itself, like a U lying on its side. The destruction here was as bad as any DelCorso had ever seen and he'd seen his share. Almost nothing had been left standing except a few tree trunks and a few uprights of houses. Small fires crackled here and there. Homes and shops, the bus and railroad stations, furniture, cars, all looked as if they had been spewed out of a giant trash compactor and set afire. He saw nothing that resembled what it had once been except the frames of the buses, the bent rail, a few oil drums, and—he'd just spotted it out of the corner of his eye—a burned body lying in an alleyway. Circling around a shell crater, DelCorso stood over the corpse and saw that it was a woman's: the nubs of her breasts still showed, though she had been burned to cinder. She was lying on her back, her legs raised and bent at the knee, the shriveled stumps of her arms reaching upward, as though she were copulating with an invisible lover. The stench made his eyes water. He wanted to move back, but this was the only way to do it properly, up close. Collapse the distance because distant horror is not horror, collapse it not with the telescopic lenses or unusual camera angles but with the eye. DelCorso focused on the face, featureless except for the small round O of the mouth, out of which protruded the tip of a swollen, blistered tongue. Do you want the sights of the battlefield, readers of glossy news magazines, I'll give you one if the editors will print it. Do you want the face of war, here it is. This is the face of what was once a woman who might have made love or given birth in the position in which she's now lying, this was once a human being and now it is a lump of stinking ash unburied, and no one gives a damn. He took two or three frames. Concentrating as intently as an archer drawing a bow, he tried to force the rage and revulsion in his heart through the lens in the hope that those emotions would, through some mysterious process, permeate the final print.

He would have liked the stench to permeate it as well. Too bad some enterprising technician hadn't invented a filter that could suggest the unique stink of death. The sights, sounds, and smells of the battlefield. You want to do your bit to put an end to war, forget pictures and words, give them the stink. Bottle it and put it on the antiseptic desks in the Pentagon and Kremlin. Put it in the photograph so that when the readers of glossy news magazines open the page, it hits them, this special odor that is composed of the smells of wet garbage rotting in a hot sun, of the pus that leaks from skin ulcers, of the crotch of underwear unwashed for a week, of rotten eggs and sewer gas—that's the recipe.

"You see, we *can* beat them. You may take pictures if you wish."

DelCorso, whose concentration had put him almost in a trance, had no idea what Colonel Hiep was talking about.

"You see. There. T-54." Hiep pointed to the far end of the street, where in a grove of palm that looked as if they'd been chopped by a berserk lumberjack, an NVA tank lay on its side. "We hit with recoilless rifle. You may take picture."

DelCorso could have punched the man for breaking the strange spell that had bound him to the horror at his feet; he had lost himself and, in losing himself, had lost his fear. Now it was back, a cold lump just below his sternum. To satisfy Hiep, he photographed the tank. Even as he focused on it, he saw an afterimage of the woman's body, and her scorched, shrunken arms reaching out to embrace him.

"By the tank is the pocket VC occupy this morning," Hiep went on. "They try to take railroad station, but we fought them house-to-house. Come, I will show. I will show how we can beat them."

They went on up the street, which had been shelled so heavily they couldn't walk in a straight line for more than a yard or two. Limping, DelCorso almost wished he would fall in a crater and sprain his bad leg, so he would have an excuse for not going any farther; he pictured himself and the other three men encircled by the twin spheres of a VC forward observer's field glasses, and the FO calling into a radio, "Right one-hundred, fire for effect." He envied the squad of Arvin he saw hunkered down in an open sewer near the wreckage of the station's platform. One, his face the stunned, exhausted face of all soldiers who have been under fire too long, peered over the makeshift trench and stared with disbelief at his commanding officer, walking in the open with two Americans. The soldier ducked as a shell whooped over the church steeple, about half a block down an intersecting street. The blast went off a safe distance away, but DelCorso heard spent shrapnel falling with a hiss on the mounds of rubble. The coldness below his chest began to expand, like a balloon being pumped full of super-cooled oxygen. Superstition or not, he had no doubt now: some inner demon was telling him that his guardian gods, whose invisible armor he valued more than the flak jacket he wore, had withdrawn their protection; they required him to do something if he was to regain it. What, he didn't know. He gazed over the deathscape, looking with his eyes for a photograph, with another sense for some sign.

He saw neither. He saw only the flames licking up a serrated half-wall of the train station and the North Vietnamese dead, scattered here and there, some in positions the most limber contortionist could not duplicate. They hadn't been dead long enough to smell badly, but were beginning to bloat and turn yellow, a color that would quickly darken in the equatorial heat to green, then to blue, the bodies swelling to twice their normal size, and, finally, to black, when the puffed bellies and chests would collapse with gaseous eruptions. Looking at the corpses, DelCorso was fascinated by the ways in which they had died. One soldier, with dried blood trickling out of his nostrils, was sitting against a splintered telephone pole and looked so lifelike it would not have been surprising if he'd suddenly stood and walked off. Not three feet away, the body of another soldier gave no hope of miraculous resurrection. One leg had been blown off at the knee and something, probably shrapnel, had shredded the skin off his face except for a strip that ran diagonally across his skull like a bloody, twisted mask. Maybe, DelCorso thought, Margaret was right in saying that his attraction to the great Goya's sketches reflected some morbidity in his nature. On the other hand, was it morbid to be fascinated by the outward forms, the odors and processes of the greatest mystery? The mystery whose existence most people sought to deny with elaborate wakes and funerals—see, doesn't Grandma look beautiful all made up in her silk-lined coffin surrounded by sweet-scented flowers? Grandma isn't *dead*, she's just sleeping.

But DelCorso did not photograph the North Vietnamese. The burned body of the woman had made its mute statement, but a picture of the soldiers' corpses would be only a cliché and a gruesome one at that; horror for the sake of horror. He needed movement, but he, Bolton, Colonel Hiep, and the radioman were the only things moving in this place of obliteration. Even the soldiers in the sewage ditch, hunched down in their flak jackets, appeared lifeless. With their faces smudged, the uniforms plaster casts of dried mud, they were hardly distinguishable from the muck in which they sat, just as the corpses looked like part of the general wreckage. All right, that would make a good picture—devastation engulfing everything: houses, streets, and trees, the living and the dead. He backed up to compose the shot, centering on the body propped against the fallen telegraph pole, with the Arvin in the ditch on the left side of the frame, the collapsed train station on the right, the tank in the background. The vibrating rush of an outgoing shell made DelCorso flinch. Outgoing, he said to himself. Get a hold of yourself. He tried a second time, holding his breath to steady his aim, like a marksman before he squeezes off a round. Switching to the 28-millimeter, he backed up another twenty or thirty feet, the better to convey the impression of overwhelming wastage. DelCorso made one picture with the wide angle, then dropped quickly when he heard the screech of an incoming rocket. It struck within a hundred feet. Lying flat, he felt the shock wave pass above him. Shrapnel flew overhead with a short, sharp ring. There was some commotion in the trench and Colonel Hiep had stopped playing tour guide to take cover behind a concrete slab with Bolton and the radio operator.

DelCorso waited for a following round. When it didn't come, he stood; his hands started trembling so badly that he shoved them under his armpits, afraid someone would see them. Bolton, the colonel, and the radioman crawled out from behind the slab. Walking quickly, they started back down the street toward him.

"That last one was a little too close," Bolton said.

DelCorso, still unsteady, said nothing.

"I've got more than I can use. You?"

"What I've got'll do."

"Then let's get the hell out before it gets too dicey around here."

DelCorso turned and followed Bolton, who stopped suddenly and stood with the tense stillness of a bird dog on point.

"Swore I heard a tube." He meant a mortar.

DelCorso had not heard anything, but Bolton's ears could pick up sounds beyond the range of most people. The four men went a few steps farther, when Bolton yelled, "Hit it!" and lunged under a sheet-metal roof that was leaning against a wall. A shell crashed not twenty feet behind, its shrapnel clattering against the metal like a handful of nails flung by an unseen hand. DelCorso lay beside Bolton with his hands covering the back of his head. He hated mortars; you couldn't hear them coming until the last second, when it was often too late, and they burst with a sickening sound, a kind of throaty bark.

Another shell exploded somewhere near the train station.

"No sweat, colonel?" Bolton said.

"No sweat. Sixty mortar. *Ti-ti.*"

"Thought you said you'd pushed the bad guys back two thousand meters."

"Two thousand at least."

"Well, a sixty's *maximum* range is less than two thousand."

"Maybe infiltrator."

"Maybe those mortars are firing prep for infantry."

"No sweat."

After the third explosion they didn't need Bolton's hearing to know that one of the South Vietnamese soldiers in the trench had been hit. Gut or groin shot, DelCorso thought as the man's screams shrilled down the demolished street. Vietnamese normally suffered pain in stoic silence; only a hit in the belly or balls could make one cry out like that. Raising his head, DelCorso looked to see what had happened. Through a dirty, rent curtain of smoke, he made out two soldiers dragging a third by the arms. The smoke from another shell obscured them for a moment. When it cleared, he saw two men down and the third stumbling in his direction, holding the upper part of one arm. He recognized the picture immediately, but it was impossible to shoot from where he was.

"*You fucking crazy!*" Bolton shouted as DelCorso scrambled out from under the fallen roof and, genuflecting in the middle of the street, steadied the Leica by bracing his elbow on his knee, the mortars bursting no more than fifty to seventy-five yards from him. Afraid, but with a calm under the fear, DelCorso set the aperture and speed and took a color exposure. He switched to the black and white Nikon. Then, instead of waiting for the wounded man to stagger closer, he moved forward in a crouch, shrinking the distance between himself and the blasts. Too far and you don't have the picture, too close and you won't be alive to take it. That rule was often forgiving and left plenty of room to make mistakes, but under other circumstances, it offered no margin for error, requiring the balance, the judgment, and reactions of a motorcycle racer taking a sharp curve at sixty miles an hour.

DelCorso wasn't sure how many yards separated him from the soldier but figured he would have to get within ten to fifteen feet for the 35-millimeter to record the details he saw with his eyes. Crouched, he kept moving with the lens pointed at the man's face, adjusting the focus as the range closed, waiting for the right instant. It seemed he and his subject were coming toward each other with excruciating slowness, like two hard-hat divers walking the ocean floor. St. Michael the Archangel, defend us in battle. Another shell splashed into the ruins of the station. Be our safeguard against the wickedness and snares of the devil. Something cracked past Del-Corso's ear. Cast him into hell. Bolton was yelling. DelCorso couldn't hear what he was saying and didn't care. There was no time to explain that he wasn't taking this risk out of madness or foolish daring or mere ambition; he was taking it because it was demanded of him. Close. Capa's Law: If it isn't close it isn't true.

A fashion photographer had once told him that he made love to models with his camera. DelCorso wanted to make a kind of love to the soldier—to achieve a union with the man's terror and pain, to embrace with his lens the bleeding arm, to kiss with his lens the mouth that was ajar, like an exhausted athlete's, to penetrate the man's soul with his lens and see the panic that widened the eyes into a wild stare. The shock wave of an explosion plucked at DelCorso's shirt; when he heard a machine gun firing in the distance he recalled his own wounding ten years before: he did more than recall; he relived that moment at this moment, the frenzied emotions aroused by the sight of his blood, the growing weakness as it pumped out of him. Involuntary spasms rippled through his legs; each step was a conscious and deliberate effort, almost as though he had been hit again. A full concentration came in, maybe eighteen shells altogether. A brown cloud of high explosive and hot metal rose some distance behind the soldier, a cloud that appeared to be rolling down the street like a dust storm. The soldier's jaw dropped a little further—he might have been screaming—the eyes stretched into frantic circles, blood squirting through the fingers clasping the wound. *Now now now.* DelCorso tripped the shutter, the sense of cleansing release within him like orgasm. Then everything lost its slow-motion quality, and he tackled the injured man, pulling him behind the fragment of a wall just as the cloud roared past, ripping chunks out of the concrete.

The North Vietnamese walked the barrage down the street. The machine-gun fire had drawn closer, bullets going overhead with a rushing sound, as when a line of automobiles passes yours at high speed. Apparently, the Communists were attempting another probe of the Arvin forward positions: South Vietnamese guns had begun bombarding a hill not half a mile away. DelCorso, lying beside the wounded soldier, could see the gray smoke of the shells blooming amid the dark-green rubber trees. The air above him was full of hisses, shrieks, and moans; if he didn't know where he was, he would have thought he'd landed in an asylum for demented birds.

He looked at the soldier's upper right arm, meat and bone blown out of it, severed blood vessels like the wires of a radio that had been smashed open. From his medical kit, DelCorso took a bottle of hydrogen peroxide and emptied half of it in the wound. He cut off a piece of the soldier's sleeve, soaked it in antiseptic, stuffed it in the hole where the bicep used to be, and dressed it with a gauze compress. After crooking the arm in a makeshift sling, he fed the soldier an antibiotic and two Percodans. He felt pleased with his first-aid professionalism under fire, though he wasn't confident it would do much good if he didn't get the man to a medic. The soldier had lost a great deal of blood and his breathing was already a labored, shallow wheeze.

Hearing the clatter of an armored personnel carrier, DelCorso peered over the wall, which shellfire had carved into the appropriate shape of a tombstone. The mortar bombardment had lifted and the machine gun had stopped shooting, allowing him to raise his head without risk. Even if it had been firing, he would not have worried. He'd been offered a chance to redeem himself and had seized it simply by doing what he was meant to do—to tell the truth of a moment for the sake of truth and no other reason. He had no idea if the photograph would be published, nor did it matter. It was enough to know that he had been returned to the state of grace in which he felt, however foolishly, that nothing could hurt him.

Looking over the wall, he saw that all the mortar fire had done was rearrange some of the rubble and add two more bodies to the list. The APC had parked hull-down behind the station. Stretcher parties leaped out of it and started taking the wounded out of the trench. Others were dragging the two dead men by the heels. DelCorso shot several frames in black and white. It made a good picture: the litter-bearers carrying wounded to whom casualty tags had been tied like delivery slips, soldiers dragging corpses against a background of pulverized buildings and burned, broken trees.

With that photo taken, he put the camera down and bent over with the intention of carrying the soldier to the APC, but the man's eyes were still slits and pink bubbles frothed his lips. DelCorso felt for a pulse, then put his ear to the soldier's chest and heard the worst silence in the world. When he raised his head, he noticed the small puncture wounds, each no larger than a pencil point, on both sides of the chest. It must have been the last shell, just before he shoved the soldier behind the wall; slivers of shrapnel had entered the back and, ricocheting off bone, punctured both lungs. The man had drowned in his own blood. And DelCorso felt as if he were drowning or strangling or choking as he placed one arm under the soldier's knees, the other around his waist, and brought the corpse to the litter-bearers. They accepted it like a package.

Turning, he limped down the street. Bolton, the colonel, and the radio operator were squatting in a circle by the fallen roof. Blood from the soldier's arm wound had dried on the face of DelCorso's watch so that, when he raised his arm to signal Bolton that he was all right, he smelled a sweet, salty odor. The choked feeling still gripped his throat. Small wounds like that, he thought, while the sound of South Vietnamese artillery rolled off the hillside. A machine gun rattled rhythmically somewhere out in the rubber, and the swelling in DelCorso's throat grew until his windpipe felt narrow as a straw. Why this sorrow over the death of a man whose name he didn't know? Or was it sorrow for himself?

"You crazy bastard," Bolton chided, coming toward him.

DelCorso did not say anything.

"I got the shit shot out of me saving your ass once, I'm not going to do it again."

"No big-brother lectures, okay?"

DelCorso heard the tightness in his voice, the words distorted as they forced their way through the constriction below the root of his tongue.

"All right, no lectures. You okay?"

"Yeah," was all DelCorso could manage to say. He looked up at the bigger man, whose size and mustache, grayed with dust, made him feel childlike. At that moment, he wanted to cry as a child does, without restraint or embarrassment, but he forced his grief farther down his throat, all the way down into his gut, where it began to change into anger. "I just get sick of it, Harry. Sometimes I get so goddamned sick of it."

13

A BAND of home-defense militia—teen-age punks who'd been given carbines and the authority to patrol the streets they used to terrorize—stopped DelCorso and asked for his identification. Not about to give them an excuse to extort a few dollars or work him over for amusement, he politely showed his press card to the leader, a gaunt kid with flat dead eyes several decades older than the rest of his face.

"*Bao chi*—press?" the kid asked.

"*Bao chi.*"

The hoodlum pressed the muzzle of his carbine to Del-Corso's shirt pocket.

"You gimme one cig'rette."

"I'll do better." DelCorso dug six cigarettes out of the pack and passed them out. "There you go. One for each."

The thugs grinned with wolfish appreciation.

"Hokay. Very good. *Di-di*," the leader said, waving his carbine.

Assholes, DelCorso thought, walking to the PT&T Building, the only lighted building on the street. Inside, at one end of a cavernous room smelling of stale cigarette smoke, a telex operator was punching tapes, which a second operator inserted in another machine for transmission. Several newsmen, like passengers in a train station, sat around glancing at the clock or their watches as they waited for the operators to file their stories. A brief chill of paranoia passed through DelCorso when he saw that one of them was Dunlop's lackey, the scrawny kid named Lutter. Lutter pretended not to notice him as he handed his typewritten message to one of the operators, who logged it in and placed it at the bottom of a stack of raw copy as thick as the Manhattan Yellow Pages. DelCorso despaired; hours would pass before the message went out. He'd tried phoning New York with the information about his film shipment, but the connection was so bad no one could understand him. The *Newsweek* bureau was closed for the night, preventing him from using the telex there, and he didn't have the time to find Clayton, the bureau chief, to open the office. He didn't have the time to wait here, either; he had to process his black-and-whites and write his captions, send both on the wire, then bag his color film for shipment to the States on a refugee evacuation flight scheduled to leave Saigon in the early morning.

Looking around to make sure none of the correspondents saw him, he passed a ten-dollar bill to the telex operator. Without a change of expression, deft as a pickpocket, the man slipped the ten under his shirt and placed the message on top. Glancing now and then at Lutter, DelCorso smoked a cigarette while the tape chattered through the machine. After the message was sent, the operator gave him the carbon, which he checked for mistakes in transmission.

PROPIXDESK EXDELCORSO/SAIGON: HAVE EXCLUSIVES FIGHT-ING IN XUAN LOC. SEND BLACK AND WHITES W/CAPS VIA WIRE. FIVE COLOR ROLLS ON MATS FLT 714 RPT MATS FLT 714, ETA MACGUIRE AFB SEVEN PYEM RPT SEVEN PYEM YOUR TIME MONDAY.

Nervous about Lutter's presence, DelCorso kept the carbon. He walked out and had gone less than a block when an alarm sounded in his head and sent him back to the building.

His instincts, as usual, had been right. Off in a corner, Lutter was studying the tape and making notes. The holes in the ribbon were keyed to correspond with a letter or punctuation mark. Deciphering the code was a relatively easy art that had been mastered by some industrial spies in journalism. DelCorso hesitated for a moment in the doorway. A part of him wanted to let things ride—if Dunlop pulled strings to get into Xuan Loc before *Time* closed this week's issue, nothing would be lost except the story's exclusivity, which didn't mean much. The greater part of him, however, felt it meant everything; he had been through too much, taken too many risks to lose it this way.

"Hey, Lutter." DelCorso spun the younger man around by an arm that felt thin as a fishing rod. "Where'd you learn to read punch tapes? Columbia Journalism School?"

"What the hell are you talking about?"

"*This.*" DelCorso snatched the tape and notebook, a glance at which told him that Lutter had deciphered the first sentence. "Outside, you skinny prick. We'll talk more about it outside."

"Look, man, I don't know what your problem is—"

"Outside, or I'll deck you right here."

Though he didn't look very bright, Lutter was bright enough to know when he was in danger of serious physical harm.

"Okay, what the hell were you up to?" DelCorso said when they were on the street.

"Listen, I don't have to tell you a goddamned thing."

The bony physique, the faint, ill-kempt mustache, the nasal voice, grated DelCorso's nerves.

"Yeah, you do, because I'll punch your lights out if you don't."

"Man, you're full of negative energy, you know that?"

"What were you up to in there?"

"Sending a couple of service messages. Okay? Fucking service messages. The telex over at the bureau is down, so Dunlop sent me over here to send a couple of service messages."

"What were you doing reading that tape?"

"I wasn't reading the tape. Who the hell reads tapes?"

"Lutter."

DelCorso lightly slapped Lutter's sunken cheek with the notebook.

"Okay, okay. I saw you slip the operator a bill and I was, you know, wondering. Curious, I mean I wanted to know, hey, you know."

"Yeah, I know. And I know you'd best keep what you know to yourself."

"Now look, man, I told you, okay? I was just curious."

"Just keep it to yourself."

"Hey, what're you? Some Mafia hood with this keep-your-mouth-shut bullshit? Fuck you, you guinea bastard, I don't have to put up with this."

Lutter wasn't so bright after all. He never saw the punch that caught him between the legs. Howling and cupping his groin in his hands, he fell to his knees.

His outcry brought the band of deputized delinquents running down the street. DelCorso, picturing himself wasting hours in a police station, cursed his temper. Then he had an inspiration: the exclusive would have ironclad protection if Lutter spent the night behind bars.

The militia, as DelCorso figured they would, recognized him as the *bao chi* who had been generous with cigarettes and immediately took his side. The kid with the old, dead eyes—he couldn't have been more than seventeen or eighteen—asked what had happened. Affecting an injured, innocent look, DelCorso pointed at Lutter, still on his knees and moaning.

"*Beaucoup dinky-dao.*" DelCorso said.

"*Dinky-dao!*"

"*Beaucoup, beaucoup.*"

In more pidgin and sign language, rolling his eyes crazily, DelCorso explained that Lutter had assaulted him, forcing him to defend himself. Mimicking the motions of a man popping a pill, he suggested that the wasted-looking American was on drugs, which excited the militia's interest. Lutter had the appearance of one of those young hash-heads or opium eaters who drifted through Saigon, the last stop on the Kabul-Nepal-Indochina trail; lacking the protection of press or other official credentials, they were prime targets for predators like this mob, who now had a license to steal.

"What the hell are you doing?" Lutter shouted. Two of the adolescents pinioned his arms, a third rifled his pockets, and a fourth took off his shoes, tearing off the heels to look for a stash. "You goddamned gooks, what're you doing? *He* hit *me*, for Chrissakes."

Motioning with the carbine, the leader told him to keep quiet.

"You dumb fucking gook! He hit me!"

Lutter freed one of his arms, apparently meaning to point at DelCorso; instead, whipping out like a string in a high wind, the arm smacked the head of the boy searching his shoes. That was all the gang needed. Finding no drugs to take off Lutter, they decided to amuse themselves by exercising their auxiliary police powers. They jerked him to his bare feet and slammed him against a wall, pinning him while one of their number ran to fetch a gray police jeep, parked at the end of the block.

"Bao chi! I'm bao chi! Give me my shoes! Bao chi."

"No bao chi. Beaucoup dinky-dao," the leader said with great authority.

"DelCorso, you son of a bitch."

Lutter tried to lunge forward, but one of the militia shoved him back with the butt end of a carbine.

"Good luck. If you're not out by tomorrow, I'll let the embassy know."

"You lousy son of a bitch!"

DelCorso was about to laugh at the success of his little scam, but there was something about the way Lutter's face looked at that moment, the way it looked sidelighted by a streetlamp, the cheeks hollow, the eyes angry and frightened, the crooked teeth clenched, that inspired not laughter but uneasiness.

HE SAW the face again in the blackness of the lab. He was alone, having given Bolton's labmen a few dollars to get drunk, get laid, get whatever they wanted so long as they got out; he didn't trust them with his film. DelCorso usually loved the darkroom, where an event as miraculous as birth happened. He often imagined the circular developing tank, which he was now agitating in his hand, as a kind of womb, the silver-bromide crystals on the film as eggs fertilized by light, then united by the salts of the developing solution into clusters, the clusters drawn into strands, the strands into a living image of pure silver. Also like birth, the process required great care and concentration on the part of the midwife; one major mistake would abort whatever truth had been conceived in the burst of exposure. But he could not concentrate, thinking about Lutter. Having been the victim of a few dirty tricks, he knew they were as common in journalism as they were in politics. Protecting an exclusive was generally considered an act of professional self-defense that allowed otherwise unacceptable behavior; but even those expanded limits did not include groin-chopping a man and then engineering his arrest by a goon squad. The incident now struck DelCorso as sordid and stupid, a manifestation of the part of him that still lived in the alleys and gutters the rest of him had left behind long ago.

He rinsed the film in the stop bath, then poured fixer into the tank to freeze the image, and waited four minutes. The timer went off with an irritating ring. He shot a jet of hypo-eliminator into the tank to reduce the washing time, then unwound the reel, hung it from a clip, sponged it dry, and glassed the negatives in the amber glow of the safelights. This should have been a pleasurable moment for him, the moment when the latent image was made manifest in tones of metallic silver. The roll, which included the shot he'd taken during the mortar attack, appeared to have turned out—he would know when he printed the positive—but he felt no anticipation while he examined the frames under the magnifying glass, only his stomach doing nervous acrobatics. His imagination concocted scenes of the awful things that might be happening to Lutter. Saigon jails weren't known for their comforts any more than the Saigon police were known for impeccable conduct.

DelCorso's Jesuit Catholicism assailed him. Leaving the film in the drying closet, he went to the phone in the outer room and called the *Time* bureau. No one answered. He then dialed the home number of the embassy's P and C—the press and culture attaché.

"Hello?"

"Mike, this is Nick, Nick DelCorso."

"Yeah, Nick. What can I do for you after working hours?"

"I was just over at PT&T and saw some home-defense boys hauling off a *Time* stringer. Thought I'd let you know."

"What's his name?"

"Jim Lutter. Young guy, twenty-one or -two. He strings for Dunlop. They picked him up in front of PT&T and were hauling him away to a police jeep last I saw."

"When'd this happen?"

"Maybe an hour ago."

"Shit, I was just on my way to Le Van Binh to eat Szechuan. All right, if it's one of Dunlop's crew, I guess I'd better see what I can do to get his ass out. Thanks."

DelCorso hung up and returned to the lab with his mind and conscience somewhat clearer, though not as clear as he would have liked. Maybe Lutter already had a few broken bones, and if he did, Dunlop would go way over the speed limit to get even.

Trying to put Lutter in the back of his mind, he switched off the safelights to process the remaining rolls. Retest the solution temperature, load the film onto the reel, the reel into the tank, agitate five out of every thirty seconds for seven and a half minutes, hyponeutralize. In the darkness, whose quiet was broken only by the whir of the air-conditioner, the exacting routine of development gradually soothed him. By the time the strips had dried and he began making the prints, Lutter was out of his thoughts entirely. Examining his first contact sheet under a magnifying glass, a prickling sensation passed through his hands: the single frame of the wounded soldier looked like one of the best photographs he'd ever taken. When he laid the negative on a sheet of newspaper, he handled it as if it were made of some volatile explosive. He could barely read the type through the highlights, which meant the negative had normal contrast. Centering it in the carrier, he held it at an angle under the enlarger lens to inspect it for dust, then locked the carrier under the lamp housing, set the aperture on the enlarger lens, and turned off the room lights.

Under the glow of the safelights, yellow and diffused, he made a test print by covering four-fifths of the printing paper with a piece of cardboard, which exposed the last fifth. He had the timer set for five seconds. Sliding the cardboard, he exposed the next fifth for the same interval, thus increasing the first section's exposure to ten seconds, then the next fifth for another five seconds, until he had a picture with five bands varying in tone from bright gray to deep black. The method wasn't unique. Nearly all photographers follow this procedure to judge which exposure time produces the correct density and contrast. It was DelCorso's method of judgment that distinguished him from a photographer like Dunlop, for whom the correct density and contrast were those that conformed to a preconceived idea or mood. The camera doesn't lie, but there are plenty of photographers who do. DelCorso remembered Dunlop's picture of marines loading their dead aboard a helicopter at Con Thien; it had been taken at noon, but Dunlop altered reality by developing the print at fifteen seconds to make the time of day appear to be dusk, which created a haunting, elegiac effect. The only effect DelCorso sought was a duplication of the moment as it had actually occurred: the brightness of the sky, skin tones, and shadows had to be as close as he could make them to the way they were at the instant of the shutter's release. If those surface facts were accurate, the underlying emotional truth would be revealed naturally; there would be no need to fog unacceptable details with a flashing pen or use a burning tool to deepen shadows and instill a mystery that existed only in the photographer's imagination. After all, the purpose of news photography is to make a record, not poetry.

He groped for the switches, flicked on the lights, and saw immediately that the print needed a five-second exposure. Except for the soldier's face, which had printed too dark, probably because of some flaw on the negative, the highlights and shadows at five seconds most closely matched those of the image in the eye of his memory. Holding that image, he again darkened the lights, laid a fresh sheet of contrast paper on the easel, and pushed the timer button for the final print. Concentrating on the skin tones of the picture in his mind, he dodged the soldier's face by moving his finger over it for a second or two. That was as much manipulation as he would allow himself.

When the timer went off, he immersed the sheet in the developing tray and waited, agitating the print gently with a pair of tongs. The dark tones came up first: blood hemorrhaged onto the wet paper, forming an irregular shape around the as yet invisible fingers; the uniform appeared, then two black dots—the pupils of the soldier's eyes; the fingers filled in around the blood spot; in the background, the exploding shell showed as a vague, grayish cloud flecked with the black of the rocks and debris it was spraying in all directions; finally— the brightest points in the picture—the whites of the eyes formed ovals around the pupils. After a minute, the photograph was complete.

DelCorso washed it and blotted it dry. Looking at it in the uncompromising glare of the room lights made him draw in a breath. The eyes were the focus of the photograph, their terror and panic pulling the viewer's eyes toward them. The soldier's head and torso were pitched slightly forward, almost as if he were about to lunge off the print into three-dimensional reality. The mouth was open from sudden shock, open in a silent cry. Behind the figure, the burst of the shell had been arrested by the fast film and the fast shutter speed at which DelCorso had shot the picture; he could sense the violence of the explosion by the ripples in the soldier's shirt and by the blurred, black specks flying out from the edges of the gray cloud. God almighty, without realizing it at the time, he had taken the exposure at the instant the slivers of shrapnel had pierced the man's lungs like miniature spears. DelCorso knew it from the expression in the soldier's eyes, eyes that screamed, "I'm hit and I'm dying, *I'm dying.*" DelCorso also knew the picture was more than the best war photograph he had ever taken; it was among the very best anyone had. Unless he'd lost all ability to judge his own work, he thought it was as good as the best of them all, Capa's Spanish Civil War picture, "Death of a Loyalist Soldier."

He sat on a stool and lit a cigarette, trying, unsuccessfully, to keep his imagination from launching itself into the deep reaches of fantasy. Editors all over the world would bid for this picture after it ran in *Newsweek.* He saw it in the histories that would one day be written about Vietnam and in books with titles like *War Photography: Crimea to the Present.* "A classic of the genre . . . Mr. DelCorso's photograph is among the most remarkable ever taken of combat. . . ." He allowed himself to dream briefly of winning a Pulitzer and to wonder if the photo's distribution would make him rich. Eddie Adams's shot of a Vietnamese general executing a Viet Cong had earned more than a hundred thousand dollars. With a hundred big ones he could pay off the mortgage, buy new equipment for his lab, and perhaps have enough left over to take Margaret to Italy; she had always wanted to return to Florence.

Bringing himself down from this trip, he looked at the photograph again to make sure he wasn't, in his overwrought, exhausted state, imagining it better than it was. Some niggling critic could probably find fault with it, but DelCorso liked the starkness of its contrast—all blacks and whites, with no intermediary shades to soften the awfulness of what was happening. The position of the soldier's body, bent forward above the waist, the legs knock-kneed, had a jerky spastic quality with none of the balletic grace of Capa's falling Loyalist, which had suggested that violent death could be dignified. The eyes were the most exceptional aspect, reminiscent of the bug-eyed terror of the figures in Goya's sketches; the eyes obviated the necessity for an explanatory caption because they said everything—this is what it's like to be mortally wounded, this is what it's like to feel your own death and there is nothing dignified about it, nothing to redeem it, nothing to mitigate it.

The second glance convinced DelCorso that his first impression had been accurate and that his fantasies had not been so fantastic after all. He had a solid reputation as one of the best in his field, but this photograph would catapult him into more select ranks. It would make his name, as "Death of a Loyalist Soldier" had made Capa, as "Yankee-Papa 13" had made Burrows, and "Requiem at Toko-Ri," a picture of dead marines in the North Korean snows, had made Dunlop.

Abruptly, DelCorso's conscience soured the idyll. If the photograph brought him prizes, money, and fame, wouldn't he be capitalizing on a man's death? He crushed his cigarette, annoyed with this puritanical minister who lived inside his head, this relentless moralist who would not allow him even to dream without guilt. All right, yes, I'll be capitalizing on a man's death, he replied to his conscience. But I wasn't thinking about Pulitzers and hundred-dollar bills when I took the picture. And haven't I given that nameless soldier something? Maybe not immortality, but a kind of extended life? Besides, I paid my dues by risking my own neck, I've earned whatever this image brings me. How's that, conscience? Get off your pulpit and leave me alone, I've got work to do.

He set about doing it. After he'd finished the remaining rolls, he slipped the negatives into their protective sleeves and took the prints to the newsroom for transmission. Walking into the racket of typewriters and teletype machines after the silence of the darkroom made him feel like a diver resurfacing from the depths. Apparently, a story was breaking; the door to Bolton's office was shut and all three of his staff were intently hacking out copy. Finding the only spare typewriter, DelCorso sat down to caption his prints, a chore he hated because he didn't have much talent for writing and the captions had to be fairly long—miniature news stories. Who, what, when, where, why. The first photograph was the one of the woman's burned body. What the hell was there to say about it? Who: no one knows; what: a charred female corpse; when: April 20, 1975; where: Xuan Loc, South Vietnam; why—answer that question and your name will go down in history. "Burned body of a Vietnamese woman lying in the streets of Xuan Loc," DelCorso typed on the caption sheet. "Hundreds of civilians have been killed or wounded in the intense fighting for the strategic city forty miles northeast of Saigon." Gazing out the window, watching the tracer rounds that looked like red claw marks on the inky skin of the sky, he tried to think of something else to say. His conscience got back on its pulpit, making him question if he ought to send the picture at all. Vietnam had given birth to a school of horror photographers who churned out ever more grotesque images, not to make an indictment of war but to make money by pandering to a corrupted public's demand for shock and sensation. They were pornographers of violence. Even cameramen with the best intentions occasionally fell into the trap, and DelCorso wondered if that's what he had done with this picture.

He looked at it carefully, but trying to judge whether its gruesomeness was unjustified was like trying to distinguish between the erotic and the obscene. By what standards could the judgment be made? What made the fine but critical difference? In the end, it was the photographer's motives and emotions that guided the movements of his hands, dictating at which angle the picture was shot, which details were focused on and which omitted so that his feelings as well as his purpose were revealed in the print. If he was titillated by the horror, the final image would be titillating and nothing more. Recalling his own emotions at the time, his anger and disgust, DelCorso decided to send the picture through; if some readers chose to see in this woman's fate only the fascination of the grotesque, that was their problem.

An hour passed before he finished the final caption, pasted it to the print, and handed the stack to the teletype operator. A peculiar feeling, relief mixed with a sense of loss, came over him when the photo of the mortally wounded soldier went out over the radio wire.

He knocked on Bolton's door, smiling at the sign, *That Which Is Not Prohibited Is Mandatory*.

"Fuck off, Grey, unless it's important," came the voice from inside.

"It's Nick."

"Private DelCorso may enter."

Inside, the Horseman sat hunched over his typewriter, his big hands masking the keyboard, his back and shoulders flaring out a foot on either side of the small typing chair. Under his desk, tagged and addressed, was the red and white *Newsweek* bag with DelCorso's color film.

"I sent twenty-five prints. That's eight hundred-odd bucks I owe you. I can pay you when Clayton gives me my allowance or set it up so the magazine pays your guys in New York."

Bolton shrugged without looking up. "Whatever."

DelCorso poured himself a cup of the worst coffee east of the International Date Line.

"Listen, if it's okay, I'd like to borrow Hoang to run my color stuff out to the airport."

"Okay by me, but what's wrong with *Newsweek*'s couriers?"

"The bureau's closed."

"Closed? Shit, I ought to go to work for one of those weeklies. It's like semiretirement. Yeah, go ahead and use Hoang. Hope your pix get you a herogram. Already got mine."

Bolton paused to hand DelCorso a message from the IPS New York office:

200930 BOLTON: 202030 XUAN LOC EYEWITNESSER GREAT BANG-BANG. ALL PLEASED HERE AND SEND CONGRATS. RGDS HALPRIN/CABLES/NY.

"You and me, amigo, we got the biggest exclusive of this offensive so far."

"I guess."

"You *guess*. Where the hell have you been?"

"Playing happy old printmaker in the darkroom."

"So you didn't hear. Xuan Loc's in the process of going down the tubes. We got out just in time. Charlie hit it with two full divisions tonight. Remember Colonel No Sweat? His regiment got overrun—"

"Holy shit."

"Yeah, I'll bet that's what he said when he saw two divisions coming at him. The other two regiments are being turned into ground round even as we speak. The bad guys, meanwhile, are sending another division on an end run around the city. Looks like they're moving on the airfield at Bien Hoa. They take that and there won't be anything between us and the yellow hordes but palm trees."

Bolton clasped his hands over the back of his head and looked at the wall map, in which the colored pins had been moved to correspond to the movements of the NVA divisions.

"But that isn't the only big news tonight. It looks like Thieu is going to step down tomorrow, and this gaggle of washed-up generals, washed-up politicians, disgruntled priests, weirdo Buddhist monks, and bitchy intellectuals are going to form a coalition government to do—guess what?"

"Negotiate with the North Vietnamese."

"Right. Hutton, naturally, has given them his blessing. Hopes they'll come up with a plan to end the bloodshed, blah, blah. Which means he's still not making plans to evacuate Americans when the crunch comes because he doesn't believe the crunch is going to come. Better yet, the members of this coalition are arguing about who's going to be president. Like the crew of the *Titanic* arguing about who's going to take the helm. Anyhow, the bureau got another herogram out of all this. Vinnie got the Thieu story, bless his opium eater's heart, and we beat AP on it by fifteen minutes, UPI by ten. Big deal. All I wanted to do after what we went through today was file the story, have a decent meal, get drunk, and get laid as cheaply as possible. Instead, I've got to write this garbage."

He pointed to the type-blackened page in his Underwood.

"The Horseman's unlucky enough to have one of these coalition members for a source, a Catholic priest. He called me with their peace plan. Another exclusive. The trouble is, I've got to take it seriously. I mean, listen to this. 'Among the offers the proposed coalition government will make to Hanoi are that: both sides agree to an immediate cease-fire in place; South Vietnamese forces will not attack North Vietnamese troops now in South Vietnam.' Like that one? Hanoi will really jump on that. Christ on a crutch, South Vietnam doesn't have anything to attack with. Oh, Lord, why do I do this?"

"It's better than working for a living."

"No, seriously."

"You always said you're a pro. This is what you do better than anything else and better than anyone else, so you do it."

"Something must have happened to my brain housing group this afternoon, because professionalism doesn't seem like enough anymore. I nearly got turned into corned-beef hash today and what do I end up with? 'Great bang-bang. All pleased here and send congrats.' I nearly get killed and what do I end up feeling? Happy that my bureau beat AP by fifteen minutes. What does that amount to? About as much as a popcorn's fart. Harry the Horseman comes within a hair of being sent home to Mama in an eight-by-eleven manila envelope and instead of getting a chance to have a few drinks to settle his nerves, has to write a story about a government that's proposing not to attack with an army it doesn't have in the first place. Another exclusive that's just going to wrap fish or wipe somebody's ass in an outhouse the day after it runs."

"Harry, what put you in this state?"

"Those mortars. Don't ask me why. I've been through a lot worse, but the mortars did it."

DelCorso studied his friend's face for a couple of moments. He noticed, seemingly for the first time, that the lines on Bolton's forehead and the crow's-feet at the corners of his eyes, which used to appear only when he laughed or squinted, were now permanently etched into his skin.

"What it is, Nick, is that for the first time, I'm wondering if I want to spend the rest of my life risking my life to beat AP by fifteen minutes. Or even by ten minutes."

"What else would you do?"

"Hell if I know. The trouble with this war-correspondent business is that it burns you out for anything else. Like trying to go home to a dumpy wife after you've spent a week with the best whore in Las Vegas."

"You'll pull out of this," DelCorso said. He wanted to change the subject, which had reawakened his fears for his own future. What would he do if he didn't have at least a conflict a year to cover? With one or two exceptions, he knew of no war photographer who had been able to cope with peace.

"Yeah, I'll pull out. When do you need Hoang?"

"In an hour or so. The plane doesn't take off until six, but I figure customs will be easier to deal with at night. The word is, some of them are charging up to two-fifty to let film through. In green."

"Sure in green. The little people know which way the wind is blowing even if the big ones don't. Hoang can help you there. He knows most of those thieves. He'll get you bargain rates."

HOANG DID INDEED. The bribes amounted to only a hundred dollars, which would ensure that the film got on the plane. It made good business sense; if a customs official got a reputation for losing film, he would lose his illicit income. DelCorso was nevertheless worried as he and Hoang drove back from the airport through the hot, sewage-stinking tyranny of Cho Lon. The plane might crash. It might be delayed en route. The pilot might lose the bag. A dozen disasters could happen. DelCorso had lost film only once in his career, but he'd never forgotten it: risk and effort totally wasted.

With the streets empty, he made it back to the Continental in no time. In his room, after evicting a rat that had been nibbling on a tin of C-ration crackers he'd left open, he placed another call to *Newsweek* to confirm that they'd received the telex and the black-and-whites. He lay down to wait for the call to go through. Only then did he realize how tired he was.

The gauge of his exhaustion was the degree of throbbing in his injured leg, which now felt as if it were being stabbed by a thousand hot needles. He washed down a Percodan with a jolt of brandy and stretched out on the bed. All that he had seen and experienced in the past eighteen hours, more than most men do in a lifetime, crushed him into a deep sleep.

The phone woke him up.

"Mistuh DelCorso? Your call to USA," the operator said.

"All right," DelCorso replied drowsily. "When I'm through, hold the line open. I have another call."

"Hokay. Will hold line open. Here is New York now."

This time the connection was better. The picture desk confirmed receiving the message; a courier would be standing by at MacGuire; the black-and-whites had arrived in good shape; everyone was excited by them; as far as was known, *Time* had nothing to match them.

After the magazine rang off, he had the operator call his home number; feelings of anticipation, of a lover's excitement flooded him. *Home*. He was calling home.

"Hello?"

It was Angela. DelCorso pictured her, as dark-eyed and dark-haired as he, but without his coarse features. She had Margaret's nose and cheekbones, thank God.

"Angie? Can you hear me? It's Daddy."

"Daddy!"

"How are you?"

"Daddy! Mama, it's Daddy! Daddy's on the phone!"

The small, exuberant voice filled him with affection and longing.

"Angie, how are you?"

"Is that *really* you, Daddy?"

"Sure it's me. I'm calling all the way from Saigon."

"Where's that?"

"Far 'way. How are you?"

"I'm mad at Danny. I built a pretty house with the Lego blocks and Danny ran it over with his dump truck."

"Where's Danny now?"

"With Eddie. He's spending the day at Eddie's. He's going to sleep over at Eddie's because Eddie slept over here."

"That's nice," DelCorso said, though he didn't think so; he wanted desperately to hear his son's voice. He was also confused. Who was Eddie? He didn't want to ask, afraid of revealing that his contact with his children was so episodic that he didn't know the names of their friends. "But you tell Danny that the next time he knocks your Legos down, I'll give it to him."

"Are you coming home?"

"Of course I am. Soon."

"Wanna talk to Mama?"

"Put her on. I love you, Angela Rose."

"I know," she answered coyly.

Waiting for Margaret to come to the phone, he felt a less pleasant anticipation, having no idea what her mood might be. He was grateful to hear her answer in the voice he recalled from their courting days—clear, cheerful, upbeat to the point that you wondered if she really was as happy as she sounded or merely pretending.

"This connection's incredible, Nick. Like you're next door. I got your telegrams."

"Good. It's been almost impossible to get through on the phone. Whole place is falling apart."

"It sounds awful on the news."

Oh, Maggie, Maggie Fitzgerald, my red-haired beauty, I love you, I miss you desperately because it is awful, worse than you imagine, a man died in my arms today and I'm so sick of this and I wish I were making love to you now, kneeling between those long legs of yours and inside you, on a cool, clean bed where there is no pain or fear of death.

"It's not so bad. I'll be all right."

"You always are, but you know how I feel. I wish you wouldn't do this."

"How're you doing?"

"Oh, fine. I went to a wonderful luncheon and fashion show the other day."

"You're all right, then?"

She knew the question was code for another and answered: "Nick, it's delightful hearing from you, so don't spoil things by bringing that up again. I took Michelle out for drinks after the show, and all I had was a Perrier."

"Michelle?"

"Eddie's mother."

"Who the hell is Eddie?"

"Michelle's son."

"Very funny."

"Michelle Landry."

"Who's she?" Jesus, don't I know anybody in my family's life?

"She lives nearby."

"Where?"

"On Warren."

DelCorso's stomach flipped. Warren was a frontier street, bordering the old, Italian section that cut off the Heights from the slums. He had visions of Danny and Eddie surrounded by wolf packs of Puerto Rican gangs.

"I hope this Michelle watches them. That's a tough neighborhood."

"She does. And she has an Italian landlady who keeps an eye on things. How did you know Danny's with Eddie?"

"Angie told me." DelCorso sensed that the conversation, such as it was, was coming to an end. "Be sure to tell Danny I called and that I'm thinking about him."

"All right. Do you miss me, Nick?"

"Of course I do."

"I miss you. We all do." There was a faint ring in the background. "Ah! That was the timer," Margaret said with an urgency in her voice. "I've got to get my quiche out of the oven. I love you."

"Love you."

He hung up, his feelings of affection and warmth replaced by depression and a vague anger. There was so much he'd wanted to say to her, so many blocked emotions he'd wanted to express, and all they'd ended up talking about was some kid named Eddie and quiche. Actually, it wasn't the conversation that bothered him so much as the truth the conversation revealed—that they did not live in separate worlds but in separate galaxies: while he watched a man die in his arms, she baked a quiche. Or broiled one. Or whatever the hell you did to a quiche.

14

——

THE NEIGHBORHOOD near the National Police headquarters reminded Dunlop of a Philippine fishing village he had photographed after it had been hit by a typhoon. The shacks and shanties in this slum had looked impermanent to begin with, so their transformation into sad, scattered little sticks struck him as no great tragedy and not worth a single frame. The faces of the people, blank, uncomprehending, stunned by the capricious force that had shattered their homes and torn the lives out of their relatives and friends, made better subjects for his camera. The Viet Cong rockets had been aimed at the police headquarters, but salvo after salvo of the inaccurate shells had struck this quarter instead. Dunlop could imagine what it had been like for these people, hiding under their flimsy beds while the rockets came down on them, howling and hissing and ripping the night apart. He had just finished photographing an entire family lying dead on the narrow staircase of a concrete building, one of the few structures still standing. He could see, by the positions of the corpses, how they had sought shelter in the stairway, how the parents had thrown themselves over their two youngest children—a futile gesture because a shell had burst within ten feet of the doorway and the shrapnel had found the two small bodies anyway.

The other photographers in town would probably be surprised if they knew he was here. He was aware that they saw him as a man insensitive to the sufferings of war's civilian victims: the old lion who specialized in frontline heroics, who could not have cared less about what happened to those caught between clashing armies. He resented this image even as he admitted the truth in it: he was attracted to the front. Yes, modern war was total; yes, it butchered civilians, turned decent women into whores, wrecked economies, destroyed societies, bred corruption; but the front remained the epicenter of armed human conflict, the place where the nature of war and the nature of men at war could be seen in all their various tones and contrasts. The fashionable trend among younger photographers to dwell on the other aspects of warfare, whether it was Philip Jones Griffiths wringing his hands over napalm victims in Vietnam or Don McCullin taking portraits of starving mothers in Biafra or Nick DelCorso focusing on American soldiers looting temples in Cambodia, reflected, in Dunlop's view, a philosophical cowardice. Such photographs made an easy appeal to the emotions, but evaded the essential truth, a truth most clearly manifested in combat, that war is a state of irreconcilable contradictions. That it brought out the best and worst in men was no less true for being a cliché. Nor were the best and the worst separate and distinct. They were intertwined, symbiotic, interdependent, two faces of the same being.

He loved war because it was the earthly reenactment of the original battle between the forces of light and darkness. It was the stage upon which all aspects of human nature revealed themselves boldly, the laboratory in which the full range of human emotion could be examined, the book wherein was writ the fundamental truth that no good is possible without evil, no mercy without cruelty, no heroism without cowardice, no hope without despair. That each of these required for its existence the existence of its adversary opposite was a mystery, which was why Dunlop found war eternally mysterious and never tried to present it as anything else. The new breed, who seemed to think of themselves as social workers righting the world's wrongs with their cameras, had never read Rilke. They did not realize that devils and angels are spiritual Siamese twins suckling off the same umbilical cord. If anyone ever succeeded in exorcising from man's soul the demons that drove him to war, the angels in him would be put to flight as well, and the world would be populated by a race of ironed-out creatures beside whom those chanting monks of the East, who confused a hunger-induced apathy with serenity, would appear full of fire and vitality.

Dunlop found it curious that none of the social workers had showed up to record the wanton destruction of this slum quarter. If it had been caused by American bombs or shells, they would have arrived in battalions, Nikons and Leicaflexes clicking away to present yet another Western atrocity. They seemed, these young men, to be selective in their compassion for war's innocent victims, eager to condemn their own civilization, ready to forgive any band of terrorists so long as it included the word *liberation* in whatever name it gave itself.

He checked himself from becoming too indignant; his own reasons for being there were more accidental than professional. He had personal business with Colonel Vinh and thought he might as well take a few photographs while he was in the neighborhood. Dunlop walked through the mud and the ashes of burned huts and climbed into his jeep, ordering the driver to take him to police headquarters.

Inside, the faded walls expelled the stale breath of French colonial bureaucracy. In every room, beneath a lethargic fan, some slave was sitting behind a desk piled high with ledgers, files, and dossiers. Dunlop felt as if he were inside some drab fantasy world. Xuan Loc had fallen, the airfield at Bien Hoa was under shellfire, the army struggling to keep the roads open to the delta and to Vung Tau, the last seaport still in South Vietnamese hands, but the clerks and administrators in this building continued to perform their daily rituals—as though they and the bureaucracy they served would go on forever.

He had to wait for Vinh, which irritated him. At this stage of his career, Paul Xavier Dunlop was willing to wait for presidents and prime ministers, but not for middle-level police officials of a collapsing country. Sitting in the small anteroom, which smelled of the strong Gaulois cigarettes Vinh smoked, Dunlop had nothing to read and nothing to do except stare at the late afternoon sunlight that fell through the jalousied window to form a row of bright hash marks on the floor. He sat and stared and stewed about DelCorso, toward whom he now felt such intense animosity that the mere thought of his name filled Dunlop's stomach with an acidic bile. The bile rose at the recollection of the insult the younger man had thrown at him a week before, insinuating that he'd lost his courage, at the humiliating message he'd received from *Time* three days ago, DELCORSO EXCLUSIVES FROM XUAN LOC ON NEWSWEEK COVER, DOUBLE TRUCKED INSIDE WITH TEXT, and the thought of what DelCorso had done to Lutter.

Not that Dunlop held any affection for Lutter, a talentless gypsy looking for someone to open doors for him. Nevertheless, Lutter worked for him, so Dunlop felt obliged to send a message: no one, DelCorso most of all, was going to get away with such behavior toward one of his stringers. The incident typified everything he despised about the new generation: they pretended to a high morality but behaved as if everything were permitted. In Dunlop's mind, DelCorso was the embodiment of these arrogant young men. He disliked the way DelCorso spoke, with that sneering, nasal Chicago accent, the way he walked, trying to compensate for his limp with a quick, loose, street fighter's strut; he couldn't bear the hypocrisy that allowed DelCorso to preach photographic sermons against violence but to behave violently himself, to lay claim to compassion and then to publish a photo of a castrated soldier with no consideration whatever of the effect such a picture would have on the man's family; he hated his irreverence, which was not healthy journalistic skepticism, but nihilistic contempt for the values Dunlop believed in, the values that help a civilization defend itself against its enemies: loyalty to country, courage, the nobility of sacrifice, endurance in the face of overwhelming odds. He had seen these virtues in the volcanic ash of Iwo Jima, in the snows of the Chosin Reservoir, in the murky trenches of Khe Sahn. With his camera, he had sought to portray the qualities by which men at war affirm their humanity in the midst of war's degradation. And what did DelCorso focus on? The degradation; he photographed the looting and atrocity that is committed by a small, sick percentage of every army and tried to present such actions as typical of the American fighting man. For this, DelCorso had been praised while, increasingly, Dunlop had been criticized for glorifying war. Dunlop knew, even as he fought off such attacks on his work, that they would not have stung if they hadn't contained an element of truth, if he hadn't felt a failing in his coverage of Vietnam, if he hadn't realized, within his innermost self, that he had avoided seeing certain truths about the war because he found them unacceptable.

His sense of failure had never been stronger than now, as he sat gazing at the diagonals of light on the floor. A copy of this week's *Newsweek* had been air-expressed to him, arriving just this morning. Dunlop was secure enough in his reputation not to be troubled by having been scooped. All photojournalists pursued exclusives, but he'd won and lost enough of them to know they were valued only by editors concerned about outselling the competition, and even then their importance was passing. He was, however, deeply disturbed by DelCorso's photographs, which reminded him of the thing he most disliked about the younger man—his talent. In this case, his genius. There was no other word for it. The picture of the mortally wounded Arvin soldier, which took up an entire page, was the most striking Dunlop had ever seen: all the agony, the sadness and hopelessness of this defeated country seemed compressed into that one image. He had looked at it for a solid half-hour, examining it from different angles, from a distance and close up, and hadn't been able to find a thing wrong with it. Oh, it could have been darkened here, lightened there, but the photograph was basically as complete as anyone could make it. This recognition made Dunlop angry. That photograph struck at the very heart of Dunlop's art, for it was his conviction that the negative image was raw material refined into art by painstaking work that required the vision of an artist and the precision of a scientist. How many hours had he spent cloistered in the lab, how many reams of paper had he used up trying to create the right mood, the correct texture, the proper balance of contrast and tone? Added up, the hours would equal years; piled up, the paper would possibly reach the roof of a high building. And yet, the best of his work did not match the pictures he'd seen this morning, and that seemed cruelly unfair, because he knew DelCorso's method of printing was simply to follow the manufacturer's directions, like some storefront hack who specializes in bar mitzvahs and weddings. How he was able to produce the work he had merely by tripping the shutter baffled Dunlop. Luck? No, DelCorso's performances were too consistent. He had a special gift, Dunlop had to admit, but it rankled that it had been bestowed on such an insolent, half-educated, disloyal son of a bitch.

He looked at his watch. Twenty minutes. He had never had to wait this long for someone of Vinh's stature, and the closed door to Vinh's office, behind which he could hear muted voices, struck him as an insult; it was as though even Vinh realized he had been outdone and was no longer worth immediate attention. Dunlop knew this to be a foolish thought; the colonel did not care who had outdone whom, or who ranked where in the journalistic pecking order. Outside of a small professional circle, no one cared. Nevertheless, Dunlop could not help feeling diminished as he looked at the closed door.

The bright rectangles had advanced a little farther across the floor. Closing his eyes against the light, Dunlop saw again DelCorso's Arvin soldier, felt again the sting he'd suffered when he saw DelCorso's photographs this morning and could no longer deny that his own talent had failed him. He had ceased to grow, he didn't know why—perhaps because of his inability to overcome his reliance on the formulas that had brought him success in the past.

Two air-force officers came out of Vinh's office and walked past Dunlop without looking at him.

"Paul, my friend, please come in," Vinh said in French.

He was slightly paunchier than the last time Dunlop had seen him, but his European mannerisms, acquired when he was a student in France, were still in place. Vinh was one of those colonial-era counterfeits whose attempts to imitate the ways of the ruler evoked in Dunlop an admixture of pity and loathing.

"I've kept you waiting, for which my apologies."

Dunlop sat down without being asked. His glance wandered from Vinh's puffy face to the patch of clean wall directly behind the desk.

"Ah, yes, that," the police officer said, turning in his seat. "President Thieu's picture used to be there. So now we have a new president, but"—Vinh gave a Gallic shrug and a sardonic laugh—"what is the use of putting up his photograph? In a week's time it will have to come down, and I have no pictures of the politburo in Hanoi."

"A week with luck."

"Certainly. Already they are shelling Bien Hoa, and the rocket attack last night . . . would you like some tea, Paul?"

"No."

"Very well," Vinh said, lighting a Gaulois that smelled like burning manure. "So. You are here about this young man, this Monsieur—"

"Lutter."

"Yes, Monsieur Lutter. He works for you, not so?"

"He does," Dunlop responded in English. "He's also accredited with *Time* magazine and with the Ministry of Information."

Opening a drawer, Vinh pulled out a file. Dunlop saw the protest he had written under *Time's* letterhead after Lutter's release from jail.

"Yes, we discovered that later on. The men who arrested him, they were told by another American journalist that your Monsieur Lutter was not with the press. The militia, they were told he was one of those, how do you say in English? A vagrant. A drug addict."

"Nevertheless, that gave your men no right—"

"Paul, I understand, and you're right. It was a mistake, no? These are difficult times. There is so much strain on everyone, and many of the people, they feel the Americans have abandoned them, so perhaps sometimes they take their anger out on Americans. But this Lutter, he did not suffer serious injury, not so?"

"A few bruises. An uncomfortable time in jail."

Vinh shrugged again.

"So, some bruises, some discomfort. What is that? And what can I offer you but the same I offered the man at your embassy? An apology. I apologize to you for the treatment Monsieur Lutter received. I will personally apologize to him if you wish."

"That won't be necessary."

Vinh narrowed his eyes until they resembled two pencil lines drawn on either side of his small nose.

"So. What is it you wish?"

"It's about the journalist who was responsible for Mr. Lutter's arrest."

"Yes?"

"His name is Nicholas DelCorso. I was surprised to see him in the country because he was expelled and blacklisted in 1970 and refused entry two years later. I thought blacklists were permanent."

"Usually."

"I was wondering why he was allowed entry this time."

"Perhaps he paid someone some money. More likely it was a mistake. In times like these we cannot keep track of all who come and go."

"You should have kept track of this one."

"This isn't my responsibility. Shouldn't you address this problem to the Ministry of Information or the Interior Ministry?"

"Perhaps," Dunlop said, unwilling to admit that he had

lost his high-level contacts in both ministries in the recent change in government. "But I thought it might be more effective if I discussed it with you. Surely you have a dossier on him."

"I'm sure we do. But let us speak directly because really, Paul, I am very busy. You wish for me to help have this man expelled from the country again, this is what I owe you for the unfortunate business of Monsieur Lutter. Not so?"

"In a word, yes."

"May I ask why?"

"Well, as you know, I've always supported the war, one of the few journalists to do so." Dunlop paused to give weight and validity to his words. "At this critical stage, I believe it would be detrimental to allow this man to continue working in this country, detrimental to South Vietnam."

Vinh's cynical smile said he did not believe a word of it but was willing to accept the lie as an appropriate mask for the truth. Then, rising and opening the door to a closet in which half a dozen suitcases and a small trunk were stacked, he said:

"Regard this. The belongings of my family. The two officers you saw leaving just now, they are the brothers of my wife. Both are helicopter pilots. We know an American evacuation fleet is assembling off the coast. When the time comes, my family will gather here, the brothers of my wife will fly a helicopter to this place and take us to one of the American carriers. You see, don't you?"

"Yes, of course."

"To have this man expelled again would be no great matter in better circumstances. It would require certain formalities, certain procedures, which could take some few days. But I haven't the time. I am very busy ensuring for the safety of my family."

And, Dunlop thought, the safety of whatever's in those suitcases besides clothes.

"Now, I don't know why this man falsely accused your Monsieur Lutter. I don't know why you are so eager for his expulsion. Possibly a woman is involved, possibly money, possibly some other thing. Further, I don't care why. Further, what is the sense of expelling him now? We'll all be expelled in a week at most. There are alternatives to expulsion which would be less trouble and take not so much time."

"I know."

"I'm certain we have a dossier on this man. His photograph would be in it. I need only have the dossier pulled, make a phone call to someone who will come here and look at the photograph, and so forth."

"No. I don't want that."

"Then what?" Vinh asked with another shrug.

"I would want . . . well, certainly I would want more control . . ." Dunlop felt sordid; even with a legitimate excuse for it, this sort of thing was beneath him.

"Ah! I understand. You would not want things to go too far. You would wish to hold the dog's leash, not so?"

"That says it well."

"Very good. Then I can be of some help." Vinh wrote a name and phone number on a piece of scrap paper, which he handed to Dunlop. "I'll tell this man you'll be calling him. He's efficient, will do whatever you want, no more, no less, a well-trained dog so to speak. I suggest you phone him once you have decided what it is you wish to do."

15

"OH, WHO, who can cheer up this morbid soul," Wilson said, cutting into his medaillons of veal. "I got into this business expecting boon companions, comrades cheerful in the face of adversity, jolly buccaneers of the working press, and what do I end up with? This." He pointed his fork at Conklin, whose face wore a somber expression and whose shirt, unbuttoned in the heat, revealed a round, white belly shellacked with sweat. "This is what I get, a displaced suburban father dreaming of picket fences and little ones on his lap."

"Wilson, if you'd had children, you'd feel the same way."

"I made many mistakes in my marriages. Propagating this pathetic race wasn't one of them."

"Sandra and I were good Catholics. Four in five years."

"Fucking Baltimore. You hadn't come up in Baltimore, you would have done what the U.S. should have done here long ago. Pulled out."

"McCafferty, don't start with your Boston-slum-kid rap. As far as you go, Wilson, I hope you knock up that whore of yours. I'd like to see you changing diapers."

"Tuyet Hoa may indeed get knocked up, but not by me, at least for now. She is safely on her way to the land of the free, to Santa Barbara, where she'll probably take up her old trade among the West Coast affluent."

"Goddamnit, I don't want to stay in this suckhole. What a bullshit way to make a living."

"Then do something else and knock off your crying, Conklin," said McCafferty, who, having inhaled rather than eaten his meal, was now gulping a glass of brandy. "I'm sticking. Be a helluva story. I'd like to photograph the first North Vietnamese tank to come rolling down Tu Do Street."

"And then I'll photograph what's left of you. Look, you're staying because you want to. I was ordered to. Fucking ordered, like the army."

"That's what you get for being a wire-service wage ape."

"So what're you two guys going to do?"

"Play it by ear," Wilson answered.

"I'm birding out with the evacuation, if the ambassador ever orders one," DelCorso said. "That'll be as big a story as the North Vietnamese takeover. And—hate to say this to you, Conklin—but I miss Maggie and the kids. Been gone from her a month, nearly six weeks from the kids."

"Another suburban father," Wilson said wearily.

"Yeah, but he lives with his kids. I get to see mine once a year for a month, when school lets out. Which is soon—they get out in May. And Christ, there's no telling how long I'll be stuck here after the Reds run up the flag. They're not going to let us take a few shots and fly home. I could end up here for months. Goddamned AP. I oughta quit."

"Right. And while you're looking for another job, you'll miss a couple of child-support payments and here comes the sheriff. Face it, Conklin. You're trapped. You've got mouths to feed."

"You're all heart, you handsome prick."

They were eating in the Continental's open-air courtyard, where the tables were drawn in a rough circle and covered by thatch roofs supported on bamboo poles. With small trees potted here and there, the place resembled a miniature rural hamlet, and the rats that scurried occasionally across the floor to pick up some scrap added unwanted authenticity to the village atmosphere. The tables were crowded, mostly with sweating journalists laughing and talking a little too loudly because they could hear, above their own voices, above the clatter of plates and glasses, the rumble of artillery in the distance. For the past week, they had been measuring the progress of the war by that sound, which grew louder each night. It was loud enough tonight that everyone had an ear cocked for the fitful sibilance of an incoming shell.

At a small table on a veranda separated from the courtyard by a low wall, Dunlop sipped a chilled white wine and picked indifferently at a rather poor poached snapper. He hadn't phoned Vinh's well-trained dog; he'd had second thoughts: even to consider taking such action made him as disgusted with himself as an otherwise reasonable husband who begins to think about killing his wife. But now, the sound of DelCorso's voice grating across the courtyard, the sight of him sitting with his friends, obviously pleased with his little coup, gave Dunlop second thoughts about his second thoughts. He could have borne sharing center stage with someone like Larry Burrows, but he was damned if he would do it with an ex—juvenile delinquent who would have wound up tightening bolts on an assembly line if it hadn't been for his undeserved gift with a camera.

"I am all heart," Wilson was saying to Conklin. "I'm concerned about this funk you're in. I feel obligated to pull you out of it."

"Why?"

"Because you're a depressing dinner companion."

The volume of conversation in the courtyard lowered a couple of increments when the volume of shellfire on the city's perimeter rose. For several moments, under the thatch awnings, the dining journalists grew as tense as South Sea islanders listening to the rumbling of an oncoming typhoon.

"One-thirties," McCafferty said, as though naming the caliber of the guns would somehow diminish the menace in their low, throaty growling.

"Maximum range of sixteen-point-two miles," DelCorso offered. "If we figure they're five miles behind the infantry, we've got a hundred thousand North Viets about ten miles from where we're sitting."

"Which means," said Wilson, "we might *all* be here when the Reds raise the flag whether we like it or not. That ought to cheer you up, Frank. You'll have lots of company."

"I wonder what it'll be like when they come roaring in here."

"Won't be anything like Baltimore."

"I mean, Tim, I wonder what they'll do when they see a hundred Yank newsmen. Some of those guys have been fighting Americans for ten years. All it would take to get our shit blown away would be one pissed-off NVA grunt with a machine gun, right? Their army's got to have at least one Lieutenant Calley in it."

"Frank, you get any more depressing I'm likely to shoot you myself."

"Fuck it, Wilson. Getting wasted is a real possibility. Or they could toss us into a concentration camp."

Wilson sliced off another bite of veal.

"In that case, Conklin, you're lucky to have Nick and me as friends. The golden guinea and I know what to do in a Commie prison camp. Right, Nick?"

"Escape-and-evasion school," DelCorso said smiling. Though no less nervous than anyone else, he was in a rare, mellow mood thanks to the wine he'd drunk with dinner, the herogram he'd received from *Newsweek*, and the message from his agent telling him that several clients had paid top dollar for the photographs the magazine hadn't used.

"E-and-E." Wilson chewed his meat slowly. "See, Frank, Nick at one time *was* a prisoner of the Communists. And I, now hear this, I, the product of California capitalism, I ran, I was the boss, the head honcho, the El Supremo of the camp, a Red's Red, the evil Captain Woo. In other words, Nick and I have had lots of experience on both sides of the barbed-wire fence."

"What the hell are you talking about?"

"Our brief acting career."

"What acting career?"

"At one time, Nick portrayed a prisoner of war and I the commissar of the camp."

"This is one I haven't heard," said McCafferty, now working on another brandy. Tiny blood vessels curled from the rims of his pupils, like frayed red threads from gray buttons. "Deecee an actor?"

"Yeah. I was brilliant. With the right breaks, I could have been another Al Pacino."

"With the right breaks you couldn't have been another Lou Costello, even if you had a sense of humor," Wilson said.

"I wasn't bad. I just got into the part a little too much."

"Let's hear it, for Christ's sake," Conklin demanded.

"It was when the army sent us on temporary duty to photographers' school," Wilson explained. "We had guardian angels because after we finished the course the army wanted us to learn to do training films. We were sent to the Army Pictorial Center in Manhattan. Best time we ever had in the service. Right in the core of the Big Apple, on Thirty-fifth, in the old Paramount studios. A weird place. They had a gondola Rudolph Valentino rode in, the moat where Tarzan wrestled alligators, the volcano Maureen O'Hara got tossed into when she was sacrificed in that movie, what the hell was that movie, Nick?"

"Don't remember."

"Anyway, it was there, Maureen O'Hara's volcano. Our instructors were these actors and directors from the forties, people I thought had died and gone to heaven. We had a couple of old TV people thrown in. We were taught some of the ropes by the guys who'd played Captain Midnight and Tom Corbett, Space Cadet."

"Who?" McCafferty asked.

"Having been a deprived child, I suppose you didn't have a TV in your family."

"I didn't have a family. Forget TV."

"You are then unfamiliar with the infancy of American television, Captain Midnight and Tom Corbett, Space Cadet, were early television heroes. Captain Midnight was a pilot who fought for truth, justice, and the American way."

"I liked Tom Corbett," said Conklin. "A lot of times I didn't do my homework so I could watch Tom Corbett."

"Don't reminisce about your childhood, Frank. You'll start thinking about your kids again and depress everybody. I'll continue. The tale of the infamous Captain Woo. That's who I was for three months of my service career. It's obvious why I got the part. My face is irresistible. This is how Deecee got the part. We were doing special effects for training films on tank warfare. We had these big Mitchell cameras on dollies, thirty-two grand apiece. In one scene, Nick was supposed to get a shot of a tank gun firing a round. We did it with mirrors. The gun faced this big mirror, and he was supposed to shoot the film into the mirror. Well, he was a little late lowering the camera into position. The guy in the tank fired off a blank powder charge that nearly blew his head off and blew the camera to shit. End of Nick DelCorso's film-making career. He got transferred to the Fifth Corps Escape-and-Evasion School. Our job was to show guys how to evade capture and how to follow the code of conduct if they ended up in POW camps. We had a road show, traveled all over the country to different bases. I was cast as Captain Woo, the boss of the Communist prison. Talk about good duty. I was living in motels, letting my hair grow long, dressing in civilian clothes except when I got into my Captain Woo suit, and all the pussy any man could hope for. What I did was to get up on stage with Nick and three other GIs who played the prisoners. I'd call them Yankee Dogs, pawns of the capitalist monopolists of Wall Street, lackeys of the puppet regime, the standard revolutionary clichés.

"We had our act down so well that we were sent abroad for a month. Yes, gentlemen, Mark Wilson and Nick DelCorso played on the stages of Europe . . . well, Turkey, really, we toured the American bases in Turkey. One of the skits we did was about this hip GI played by Deecee who scammed his way through prison camp in Korea. He'd found marijuana growing wild in the place and just stayed high for two years. The Reds thought he was crazy and left him alone. So, to give our act a little authenticity, we thought we'd score some hash in Istanbul. Our child of the streets nailed a quarter of a kilo, and in our next performance Nick toked himself up. You know the saying, Reality is for people who can't handle drugs? That's Nick, at least as far as hash goes. I went into my Yankee Dog routine and Nick went nuts on me. Jumped me and grabbed me around the throat and screamed, 'You dirty Commie motherfucker.' As you both know, Deecee can get awfully serious about things. A couple of guys in the audience had to pull him off me. Our CO was RA but no dummy. He came on stage and took one look at Nick's eyes and knew. Nick tried to cop an alibi, but it didn't do any good. He could have gotten six months' stockade and a BCD, but our CO liked him. He sent him to Vietnam as a combat photographer with the Airborne. I took thirty days' leave, went to France, photographed the Le Mans race, and sold the pictures under a pseudonym. Nick's never forgiven me for that stroke of luck."

"*Te absolvo*," DelCorso said, making the sign of the cross over Wilson's forehead.

"Thank you, Father."

"*That's* the story?" Conklin asked.

"Yes," Wilson said. "Don't you see the point?"

"No."

"If it looks like we can't get out on time and we're going to have permanent reservations at the Hanoi Hilton, Nick and I are going to hoard enough Cambodian Red and Buddha Grass

for all of us. Then all we do is stay high, act crazy, and we'll
be returned to our loved ones before Christmas."

Dunlop felt his stomach turn over. He had drunk one too
many whiskeys before eating, and the alcohol was making it
difficult for him to control his emotions. He pushed his plate
away. From across the veranda he could hear raucous laughter
and fragments of conversation about Korean prison camps. He
saw DelCorso smiling at something Wilson was telling him,
heard again the laughter, a blurred mention of Korea, and
suddenly he once more saw the emaciated wretches who had
come out of those camps in 1953. DelCorso and those other
three could not have been more than ten years old then. What
right did they have to speak so lightly of men who had endured
so much? Feeling disgraced by sitting in the same room with
the younger men, Dunlop signed his bill and rose to leave. As
he stood, the whiskey and wine in his system sent a throbbing
rush of blood to his head. A burst of sudden, passionate anger
propelled him across the courtyard toward DelCorso's table.

"What the hell do you know about Korea?" he said, his
high voice quavering. "What the hell do you know?"

He did not look at Wilson, but at DelCorso, who, taken
unaware by the outburst, glanced up without saying anything.

"You at a loss for words for a change, DelCorso? Let me
hear it. What the hell do you know about Korea?"

Again, DelCorso said nothing. Never having seen Dunlop
in a state like this, he had no idea how to react to it. Then,
looking at the redness in the other man's eyes, he realized
Dunlop was a little drunk, a realization that gave him a sense
of cold calm, like a boxer in control of a fight.

"C'mon, you tell *me* all about Korea, you know so much
about it."

"What'd you want to know, P.X.?" Wilson asked. "Land
area, population density, gross national product?"

"I'm talking to him. Let's hear it, DelCorso. What do you
know about the Korean War?"

"I don't know what bug got into you, P.X., but I think you
ought to take two aspirins and go to bed."

"Quiet, Wilson, I want to hear from DelCorso."

DelCorso backed his chair away from the table, thinking,
If it's a fight the old bastard wants, he'll get one. I'll come off
the chair, feint a left to the head, and give him a right in the
solar plexus.

"I want to hear from you, DelCorso. You're an expert on

Korea. You get one exclusive, you get a cover, and it makes you an expert."

"It makes me somebody who whipped your fucking ass."

Now it was Dunlop's turn to remain silent. He'd noticed DelCorso had unhooked his heels from the rung of the chair and had his hands on his lap, ready to swing. The idea of this confrontation becoming physical appalled him. It was already embarrassing: several people at nearby tables had stopped talking and were looking at him. He was making a fool of himself. His blood began to cool and he wondered how he could get out of this demeaning situation without losing any more face than he already had.

"You didn't whip anything unless you count what you did to my stringer."

"Your stringer isn't good for anything except peeking over transoms."

"And those exclusives of yours aren't good for anything except lining birdcages. Birdshit, DelCorso. Those pictures are catching birdshit right now."

"That a fact, P.X? You want to know what that means to me? It means birdshit to me, coming from you."

"You listen." Dunlop pointed at the tuft of hair that made DelCorso's eyebrows a solid black line across his forehead. "You listen. I was number one in this business before you got into it, and I'll be number one after you're out of it."

What a ridiculous thing to say, Dunlop thought. I've got to get out of this.

Unable to think of a more dignified way to extricate himself, he merely turned abruptly and walked away, feeling as though all eyes in the courtyard were on him. Their looks, real or imagined, stirred his anger anew; if it had not been for DelCorso, he would not have lost the reins to his temper and degraded himself.

"That was something," DelCorso said, watching the older man pass through the lobby entrance. "It looks like I got to him for a change."

"It's safe to say," Wilson remarked lightly, "that you struck a responsive chord."

16

THE SHRIEK OF THE JETS pierced Bolton's eardrums like a
high C from an electric guitar blasted through a thousand-
watt amplifier, a noise so loud it was felt rather than heard;
it seemed to make his skin ripple. He threw himself out of
bed and low-crawled toward the door, the building quaking,
the air outside shredded by the most intense small-arms fire
he had ever heard. The windows and the mirror on the dresser
vibrated from distant explosions. Reaching up, he opened the
door and rolled out into the corridor, where he would at least
be safe from flying glass.

Several other newsmen had taken shelter in the hall. The
terrifying noises had stripped them of the mask of cynical
nonchalance war correspondents usually wear to conceal their
true feelings, if they have any. Crouched down, cringing at
the sounds, they did not look very tough or very brave now,
but like confused, frightened children. Bolton would have felt
contemptuous of them if he hadn't been just as confused and
frightened.

"Hey, Harry, what in the hell's going on?" Purcell shouted
from several doors down.

"A serious conflict of views," Bolton shouted back.

Another plane screamed overhead, and the small arms rose

in volume until it sounded like all the carbines, rifles, and machine guns in Saigon firing at once.

"Street fighting, Harry," Purcell said, trying to tuck his head in the hollow formed by his hunched shoulders. "North Viets must have broken through."

That sounded plausible—since the fall of Xuan Loc a week ago, the Communists had pushed to within ten miles of the capital—but the tremors rocking the hotel's ancient walls could only have been caused by heavy bombs. *Bombs.* Holy Christ. Bolton ran down to the lobby, which was packed with more confused newsmen, all speculating about what was happening but unwilling to risk their necks to find out. The girl from *Rolling Stone* was there, looking dazed. The amateur brigade, Bolton thought. Lizzie St. John, harlot to British aristocracy, stood by the front desk snapping pictures of the people whom the gunfire had driven off the street—a mob of hysterical kids and a few members of the Saigon freak show, Fast Eddie on his go-cart, The Crab with his question mark legs and arms, and Needle Tracks, trembling from fear or withdrawal or both.

"Eddie, did you see anything?"

"Yes, Ha-ree. Two plane. South Vietnam plane. No MIG. Maybe coup."

"It's a little late in the day for a coup."

Bolton heaved open the door, which resembled the gate to a Norman castle, and went outside. It was eerie to see the streets empty in daylight. Except for a few policemen running across Lam Son Square and a TV camera crew, also running, there was no one. He caught up with the cameraman, who said they had seen two South Vietnamese A-37s dropping bombs on the presidential palace; it was definitely a coup. But the column of black smoke Bolton saw rising in the distance was too far away to be the palace. Tan Son Nhut, the last airfield in government hands, had to be the target. Bolton headed for the bureau, the bursts of machine-gun fire adding a quickness to his step.

At the office, he found Vinnie in his usual stupor, Dalman on the phone, and Grey, dressed in a helmet and flak jacket, frantically pounding a typewriter. Grey's lead was already on the outgoing wire:

281640 EXGREY FLASH URGENT: SAIGON—HEAVY STREET FIGHTING BROKE OUT IN CENTRAL SAIGON MONDAY AS

NORTH VIETNAMESE COMMANDOS SMASHED THROUGH THE
CITY'S CRUMBLING DEFENSES. MORE.

Glancing over Grey's shoulder, Bolton saw there was more
all right; more nonsense. He pulled the sheet out of the typewriter and tossed it on the floor.

"Grey, you could fuck up a two-car funeral."

His small face half hidden by the helmet, Grey looked up
with a perplexed expression.

"Put a kill on that story. Now."

"Harry, that's the word, they've broken through, they're
in the streets—"

"I just *walked* here, jerk-off. I didn't see a single Communist on the streets. I didn't even see a liberal. *Now kill that
story before I shove your helmet up your sorry ass.*"

Bolton then turned to Dalman.

"What the hell are you doing?"

"Checking out this rumor about a coup," Dalman said,
cupping his hand over the phone.

"Jesus Christ. Look out the window, Dalman. They're
bombing Tan Son Nhut. Goddamnit, Grey's putting a story
that NVA commandos are going berserk in the streets and
you're working on one that says, no, it's a coup. Can't I leave
this bureau for five minutes without it turning into a Chinese
fire drill?"

"I was checking out a rumor."

"Hang up, Dalman. Say bye-bye to whoever you're talking
to and hang it the fuck up."

Dalman hung up.

"All right. Now the two of you listen. You too, Vinnie, if
you're receiving signals in whatever solar system you're in.
You guys can have a beer, have a cup of coffee, play circle
jerk, but don't touch a phone, don't touch a typewriter, don't
do a goddamn thing until I find out what the hell's going on."

Bolton went into his office. Amateurs. I'm surrounded by
amateurs. He fell into his chair and phoned Christensen at
the CIA's headquarters on the embassy's sixth floor. The line
was busy. He put the phone down and gazed idly at the wall,
bare except for the map, on which the pins now formed a
dense circle around Saigon. He could not hear any more gunfire
and the rumble of bombs had been replaced by a series of
smaller detonations—either shells or secondary explosions.
There was a mournful tone of finality to each muffled thud.

Looking at the map, filled with the weird names of places that had become as familiar to him as the names of the towns near his home (he still thought of Bryson City, North Carolina, as his home, though he hadn't been there in years), Bolton realized he was going to miss Vietnam. He would miss its good and bad smells, its green paddy lands, slow brown rivers, and dark hills, the whole landscape in which the union of beauty and danger created a peculiar charm. He had complained about this country often enough and sometimes hated it more than any place on earth, but this alien land would always claim a part of him, for he had come to manhood here. "We've only one virginity to lose," he recited silently from the Kipling poem, "and where we lost it, there our hearts will be."

Bolton, who was suspicious of the softer emotions and who never allowed his own to get out of control, checked himself from sinking any further into this melancholy nostalgia. He dialed Christensen's number again, and, after several more tries, got through.

Nestling the phone between his ear and shoulder, he took notes on his typewriter. Christensen confirmed that it had been an air raid: two captured South Vietnamese planes, flying under government radar, had taken off from the old ARVN airbase at Phan Rang and dropped five-hundred-pounders on the airfield. The Communists were following up their first air raid of the war with a rocket attack on the runways, making a fixed-wing evacuation of Americans and South Vietnamese refugees impossible.

"If we ever get out of here," Christensen said, "it's going to be on choppers. And Lord help us if Charlie starts popping missiles at those things."

"I don't think the Lord gives a damn one way or the other. Okay, Dave. I've got to get this out."

"Call me back in an hour or so, Harry. Think I may have another feather for your war bonnet."

Bolton, stifling his curiosity—it was like struggling to close an overstuffed suitcase—hung up and wrote two takes on the airfield attack. Walking out to the teletype room, he could see, through the window, a flickering light that colored the clouds over Tan Son Nhut. Dalman speculated that the rockets had blown up an ARVN ammo dump.

"Check it out," Bolton said, returning to his office to wait for the hour to pass. Half of it had gone by when one of the

17

"FOR CHRIST'S SAKE, Deecee, let's pack it in," Wilson said. "We're losing light."

"We've got an hour," DelCorso replied, elbowing and shouldering his way through the mass of humanity that was pouring down Highway 1 with the mindless power of a river in full flood.

"An hour for what? How many shots of refugees do we need?"

"As many as it'll take until I get the ones I want."

"Well, you've got an hour to get them with me along. Then I'm splitting."

"I'll get them," DelCorso said, raising his voice to make himself heard above the noises of bawling infants, the crack of gunshots, the creak of oxcarts, the roar and sputter of trucks and Lambretta buses; above the cattle with their mournful lows, above the herdsmen with their wild yells, above the old women with their high-pitched wails.

DelCorso and Wilson walked along the shoulder of the highway, climbing a gentle rise, DelCorso driven by the sort of headlong determination that, in soldiers, produces dead heroes. The two men were about ten miles from Saigon, unaware of the attack on the airfield. Topping the rise, they were about to cross the bridge over the Dong Hai River when a monsoon cloud, bloated with rain, opened up, drenching them in seconds. They ducked into a thatch-roofed shack at the foot of the bridge and waited for the downpour to pass. Both needed the breather; they had been walking for an hour, scorched one moment, soaked the next, walking through the countless thousands of refugees and retreating soldiers. DelCorso's neck ached from the weight of his cameras, but he was resolved to stick it out until the last second of the last available light.

"This is really nuts, you know that, Nick?" Wilson brushed a length of wet, dark hair from his eyes. "What the hell kind of shot are you looking for?"

"I'll know it when I see it. What's bothering you, Mark? You upset because you lost the crease in your designer jeans?"

"Under normal circumstances, I'd have a witty retort to that. These being abnormal circumstances, I'll just say, Fuck you."

A shell ripped over them and burst in a tree line several hundred yards off the highway. Wilson, trying to conceal his nervousness, fumbled in his pocket for a dry cigarette.

"I know what it is. You've gotten cautious now that you're a married man again."

"Ditto the fuck you. Listen you Italian troll, I know what's bothering *you*, and that's what's really nuts. Film gets lost sometimes."

"I'd like to believe that's what happened to it."

"Your paranoid imagination is in high gear again."

"Look, for whatever reason the film didn't get to New York, it didn't get there, and that makes me look like shit."

"All right, do what you have to do. Mark Wilson stays here, nice and dry in this little grass shack. If you're not back in forty-five minutes, I'm hiking back to the jeep and heading for Saigon, where I'll report you missing in action."

"Thanks."

"Anything for a pal."

When the rain let up, DelCorso climbed onto the road. From the middle of the bridge, for as far as he could see in either direction, the highway was covered by an ever-moving tide of people, vehicles, and livestock, packed so thick hardly a square foot of blacktop was visible. Brightly painted Lambrettas with arms, legs, and torsos sticking out the windows. Army trucks crammed with wounded. Dun-colored carts groaning on wooden wheels under mounds of trunks, suitcases, furniture, and bundles of clothing. Gray water buffalo whose shiny black horns swayed from side to side. Spotted hides of cattle. The bobbing masses of conical straw hats, cork sun helmets, print blouses, and white-and-blue cotton shirts speckled with the camouflage helmets and green ponchos of soldiers who had quit fighting. And faces, tens of thousands of them, some slack with exhaustion, some shriveled by fear, some whose expressions betrayed no emotion at all. Once in a while, in attempts to stem the relentless flow, attempts so futile as to be ridiculous, a squad of military police would fire their M-16s into the air; but the great column, fleeing the North Vietnamese advance, kept moving, toppling over the oil drums that had been filled with dirt and stacked as tank barricades, moving toward Saigon and away from the rumbling horizon, where pillars of smoke rose under the roof of the pewter-colored sky.

DelCorso, sitting on the guardrail, aimed his 105-millimeter down the length of the road. He took a few shots, though one look through the viewfinder told him no photograph could suggest the awesome scale of this migration, the immeasurable misery of it, the sense of defeat that was almost tangible. Below, the muddy Dong Hai flowed quietly, the current forming white-flecked Vs around the concrete pilings of the bridge.

Paranoid imagination. Maybe Wilson was right. DelCorso wanted to believe it was only his imagination. The steady solemn scrape of sandals and boots on the asphalt, the heads of the people, bowed against the rain, gave the column the appearance of a massive religious procession and made him aware that the loss of a few rolls of film was less than insignificant; but because the mind cannot always translate its understandings into the language of the heart, this awareness did not cool the anger he felt when he thought about the missing film nor diminish the certainty that its disappearance had not been accidental. The shots had been routine, nothing like those he'd made at Xuan Loc the week before; still, a week's work had been shot to hell, another day wasted trying to trace the shipment. This in addition to the loss of the negatives, each one a potential sale, and the damage—minimal, but damage nonetheless—to his reputation as a photographer who always delivered. DelCorso swung off the guardrail and crossed the bridge, driven by his anger through the surge of flesh and bone crossing it from the opposite direction.

A flight of F-5s, four swift darts piercing the clouds, unloaded their bombs on a ridge perhaps three miles away, and the asphalt vibrated underfoot. A herd of water buffalo, excited by the explosions, bellowed, raised their heads, and slashed the air with their curved horns. *Eeeeeah, eeeeeyah!* the herdsmen cried, smacking the muscular haunches to prevent the animals from stampeding. DelCorso got a picture of the scene, but it wasn't what he wanted. What kind of shot *do* you want? I'll know it when I see it. Faces, faces, faces. There were too many faces and too much suffering in them to elicit any emotional response from him other than the numbed awe one feels when witnessing a colossal natural disaster. A face. He needed a face if he was to make sense out of this; a face like the one of the man kneeling before the firing squad in Goya's *Third of May, 1808,* the eyes reflecting a terror that was the terror of all of war's victims; yes, he had to find in the masses shambling past a single face whose expression stood as a metaphor for the misery of all, and their endurance of misery, for there was affirmation in the blind will of these people to go on and beauty in the affirmation. After all the destruction he'd recorded in the past month, DelCorso wanted at least one photograph that would speak, however faintly, of the power of man's spirit to survive.

He shoved ahead, toward the junction of Highway 1 and Route 15, where another column of refugees met this one in a confused, jostling confluence. The noise of the trucks and buses, of motor bikes and clanging bicycle bells, of the countless feet stomping against the asphalt was deafening; still, he was able to hear, overhead, a sound as of a knife slicing through a taut canvas awning. The shell burst near a South Vietnamese bunker guarding the bridge. Panic rippled through the column, but the crowds were so dense that no one could move faster than a slow walk; and the sense of a repressed mass hysteria seeking an outlet, the press of bodies, and the thick, humid air made DelCorso claustrophobic. Like a stadium gate-crasher, he bulled a path to the shoulder of the road, where he slid down the embankment, jumped over a culvert, and walked toward the junction by way of a paddy dike. The junction had become his objective: if he didn't get any decent shots by the time he reached it, he would rejoin Wilson.

Another shell struck the bunker overlooking the riverbank five hundred yards behind him. He passed four South Vietnamese soldiers serenely butchering a cow's leg. Farther on, he photographed an army truck, its front end mired in the culvert. The back was full of wounded and dead: dazed faces, mud-spattered uniforms, bandaged legs, blindfolded eyes, a corpse lying beside the rear wheels, one stiffened arm raised with a rigid finger pointing at the sky as though in accusation. The multitudes on the highway tramped by without looking. A third shell crashed into the riverbank. The rain started to fall again.

Recrossing the culvert, DelCorso climbed the embankment back onto the road just short of the junction. A small boy of perhaps eight, with skin ulcers on his face and an oversize sun helmet on his head, was shuffling along, crying. Losing light. Had to get something. A face. This kid's face. Too sentimental perhaps, too obvious, but it was better than nothing. Holding his light meter near the boy's blistered cheeks, DelCorso took a reading. Eleven at a sixtieth. Still good light but it was fading. Another twenty to thirty minutes and he'd have to shoot close to wide-open. Walking backward, or, rather, allowing the moving wall of humanity to push him backward, he shot the boy with the 28-millimeter. Even with the extra-wide angle, the range was too close to get much else in the frame, to capture some sense of the vast, suffering organism of which the child was but one small cell. Shoving against the people behind him, elbowing them like a basketball player roughing it up under the boards, he managed to increase the distance a few feet and tripped the shutter again. Then, looking at the boy's face through the viewfinder, one word filled his mind. *Danny!* This kid could be Danny. Overcome by a rush of fatherly protectiveness, he wanted to scoop the child into his arms and find his parents. Impossible in this mess. The kid ran up to him, the small hands grasping his belt. Sorry, he thought, prying the fingers loose. Sorry, sorry, I've got work to do. The child whimpered, then broke into a full-throated bawl that lanced DelCorso's heart. *Danny!* Sorry, little one. I hope they find you, I hope you live. Closing his ears to the boy's cries, he turned his back and went on.

He became aware of a change in the column's movements as a man wading a deep stream becomes aware of a shift in the undercurrent: it was something felt rather than seen. He moved on until he came to an oval-shaped open spot in the crowds. Ripped off at the thigh, slightly bent at the knees, swollen in the damp heat, a leg lay in the middle of this clear space; the whole great mass of people and vehicles were parting into two files and flowing around the torn limb as a river flows around a rock. It was glanced at, sometimes with disgust, sometimes with indifference, sometimes with morbid fascination; but all took care not to step too close to it, as if to do so would be to invite death upon themselves. Or were they avoiding it out of respect for the dead? Or out of a superstitious awe of a place where someone has been killed or wounded? DelCorso didn't know. He did know that the severed leg somehow gave meaning to the chaos around him. It was grisly—the great Goya would have loved it—but he was moved by the humanity of the vast multitude's refusal to touch or draw near it. These thousands who, fighting for their very existence, toppled tank barricades, defied shells and the gunfire of military police, would not tread upon the shattered limb of one of their own. Whatever their reason, it struck him as a peculiarly human act, a gesture affirming the endurance of man's spirit in the most extreme circumstances. A small, more cynical corner of his mind wondered if it really was that, or if he had merely chosen to see it that way; maybe these people were just too lazy or squeamish to move the limb and bury it. That possibility stirred loose a whole snake's nest of questions about reality and the photographer's perception of reality, questions for which DelCorso had no time.

Moving to the roadside, he composed his picture. After three exposures, he realized the angle was wrong; shooting from ground level, he wasn't able to communicate the size of the column, nor the inexorable flow that could not be stemmed or diverted by barricades and shellfire, but was turned by a fragment of human flesh. A mahogany tree a few yards off the road offered a platform. DelCorso checked his light meter: still f-eleven, but to maintain the correct exposure at that aperture, he had to slow the shutter to a fifteenth of a second, which could be too slow to freeze the movement of the crowd. He opened the lens to eight, increased the speed to a sixtieth, and gazed at the tree again. If he could get up there quickly enough, he could stop down to, say, sixteen to increase the depth of field; that would underexpose the negative, but he could compensate by souping up the development, which he did not regard as illegitimate manipulation under these circumstances. The only problem with pushing the development would be graininess, the very graininess and obscurity he sought to keep out of his work. What the hell, can't have it both ways, and it would make a helluva shot if he could get it.

Thinking in his eagerness that he was agile enough to make the climb before the light failed, DelCorso slung his cameras over his back to prevent crushing them against the tree, then shinnied up to the fork of the first branch, which was almost as thick as the trunk. The camera straps cinched around his throat, nearly gagging him. Avoiding prominent trees is to battlefield survival what two plus two equals four is to arithmetic; artillery spotters use them as reference points for directing fire. DelCorso, however, had judged that the mahogany was close enough to the road to be a safe perch; the North Vietnamese were unlikely to tarnish their image as liberators by shelling refugees. He questioned this judgment when, pulling himself into the fork, two shells zipped directly above him, their rushing sound so loud that he ducked his head. The rounds exploded in a paddy about a hundred yards short of the riverbank, mud and water flying up and out in a fountain of smoke. Big stuff. One-thirties. Too late now, he felt committed to this attempt. Straddling the branch, his cameras banging against each other, he inched out until he had a clear view. Even from fifteen or twenty feet above the ground, he could see no beginning or end to the procession. Looking at the immense column reaching to the horizon, where pillars of smoke leaned in the wind, aroused in him the same breathless arrest inspired by the sight of a volcano erupting or a great storm at sea. The spell lasted only a couple of seconds, broken as he recognized what a fool he had been to try this, to overestimate his physical capacities, thinking himself some kind of limber Tarzan and not a thirty-two-year-old man with a bad leg, and forgetting the elementary rule that light fades more quickly in the tropics than in the northern latitudes. He had wanted a photograph that would duplicate what his eyes saw—a somber spectacle resembling a nineteenth-century battle panorama, the confusion given emotional coherence by the macabre tragedy of the severed leg. But in the time it had taken him to make the climb and set up, he had lost two f-stops: down to four now, which meant that everything from the middle distance on would be hopelessly out of focus. Underexposing by stopping down would be equally hopeless; he could come down only two stops at most, which would still leave the background blurred. If he tried it down another stop, the development would have to be pushed to such a point that the print would be a fog of grain. DelCorso had of course known these fundamentals before he scrambled up the tree; he simply believed he was quick enough to beat the clock, the unalterable rhythms of light and darkness. Fucking impulsive idiot. What the hell are you doing, up here in a tree, pursuing the impossible? The question was rhetorical: he knew the answer all too well.

He clambered down, scraping his shins and hands on the bark. Hobbling toward the shack where Wilson waited, his lower left leg such a mass of pain that he felt as if he were walking on the bare bone of his arch, DelCorso was favored by his gods with a little vignette that saved his efforts from total fruitlessness. A convoy of three deuce-and-a-halfs, horns braying, was plowing through the foot traffic. Shell-shocked deserters and seriously wounded packed the first two trucks; the third, loaded with a cargo of dead men, their rubber ponchos for winding sheets, was towing a 4.2-inch mortar. Thirty or forty soldiers, some with their weapons, some without, shambled behind like a bedraggled funeral cortege. The convoy slowed down at the bridge, where the highway narrowed. A crone whose body was bent into an L under a bundle of clothes as big as she feebly waved to the driver of the lead truck. He signaled her to climb aboard, but she could barely move with the great weight on her back, and walking without sandals had so torn and bloodied her feet that they stuck to the asphalt. Then the bundle rolled off her back and broke open, shirts, trousers, and rags scattering in the wind like programs at a football stadium. The convoy bumped and jerked across the bridge while the old woman tried to gather up the clothes. Focusing on her with the Leitz, which he had wide open, DelCorso snapped a picture of her when she gave up, throwing her arms in the air and letting out a cry of despair that showed rows of teeth dyed the color of clotted blood by betel nut. It was as good an image as he had made all day.

Congratulations, Nicolò, maker of good images, you've earned another dollar off someone else's misfortune. Would it always be this way? he wondered, going toward the shriveled figure. Would he spend the rest of his career capturing instants of human suffering and then, assailed by guilt, try to salve his conscience with some charitable gesture? Rach Giang and the dead in the hut, the dead lying around the well, was he still trying to atone for Rach Giang?

The crone protested when he lifted her in his arms and carried her toward the trucks. Her tongue flapped between the reddened teeth, making unintelligible sounds, her feet kicked weakly, her hands flapped like broken bird wings at the bits of clothing, which were being trampled underfoot or picked up and examined by other refugees as if they were articles at a rummage sale. DelCorso carried the woman along, and though she weighed next to nothing, he was relieved when he propped her in the back of the last truck; his legs could barely support his own weight. Leaving the old woman safe aboard with the dead, he limped to the shack.

Wilson wasn't there. Wilson, DelCorso saw, was about a quarter of a mile down the road, his tall, slim figure distinct amid the swarms of Vietnamese. So the movie star meant it when he said he wouldn't wait longer than forty-five minutes. Probably has some new dolly in Saigon he's just got to see before the VC bring down the final curtain. The hell with it, I'll catch up. Resting his back against a bamboo pole, DelCorso removed his boot and massaged his leg. At moments like this, he almost wished they had amputated the damn thing, given him a brand-new, indestructible fiber-glass prosthetic device, immune to pain. For the lump of throbbing meat with which they had left him, a needle would do nicely now, a kiss from Mother Morphine, she who takes away the aches of the body and soul. Second choice would be a few good hits off an opium pipe, but all he had were his Percodans. He took one from his medic's kit, broke it in half, and washed it down with sickeningly warm canteen water. Half a tab would get him through the three-mile walk to the jeep without dulling his alertness.

Wilson's figure was just visible through the twilight as DelCorso started down the highway, sticking to the shoulder so he could take cover quickly in case something happened. Bands of refugees and deserters were drifting off into the paddies and building makeshift shelters out of ponchos, plastic slickers, and tarpaulins. Despite the wet weather, a few had managed to light small cooking fires, which winked in the semidarkness. DelCorso's ears picked up the vibrating whisper of another shell, but there was a pitch to the sound that registered a warning. *SHORT ROUND!* Rolling down the embankment, he lay with his hands over his head. The shell whooped into a paddy no more than a hundred yards ahead and, from the sound of it, only a few yards off the road. Its twin burst a little farther down, another shell farther still. Not short rounds, he thought. Walking them alongside the highway, searching fire. Searching for what? *The convoy.* A miserable target but a legitimate one in military terms. Sure, the convoy. Some North Vietnamese spotter was getting in his last shots before the light failed him. We must all do our work while there is light to do it.

Three or four hundred yards down the road, half a dozen of the 130-millimeters exploded one after the other. The medley of creaking car wheels, sputtering engines, and shuffling feet had turned into a cacophony of shouts, screams, and squeals, of crunching metal and a hideous bellowing. Rising, DelCorso staggered forward. He saw a ball of flame at the bottom of the embankment ahead. It was one of the convoy trucks, blown off the road and burning—the truck in which he had put the old woman. The big mortar's barrel was clearly visible in the firelight. So were an overturned oxcart, the silhouettes of people, pigs, cattle, and water buffalo helter-skelter, and—the source of the bellowing—a buffalo whose hind legs had been smashed. It was crawling forward on its forelegs and slamming its jaw against the berm of the paddy dike in spasms of agony until a soldier shot it to death with an M-16. The stench of burning flesh assaulted DelCorso's nose as he drew closer to the impact zone. Wounded and dead seemed to be scattered everywhere, wounded and dead people, dead dogs, dead pigs, wounded pigs squealing, a bicycle bent in half as if by some strongman, its rider lying near it, dead.

The smell more than he could bear, DelCorso climbed toward the highway to catch up with Wilson. He thought he saw him, in the glare of the firelight, sitting against the embankment a short distance away. Three Vietnamese soldiers were standing beside him. "Mark," DelCorso called, "Mark." One of the soldiers shone a flashlight in his eyes, temporarily blinding him.

"You Ahmericun?" asked the soldier.

"Yeah, American. Turn that damn thing off," DelCorso answered in English. Damned Arvin. They'd had an enemy spotter dropping shells on them a few minutes ago and they turn on a flashlight.

"*Lai dai, lai dai*—come here," the soldier said urgently.

DelCorso, shielding his eyes with a hand, stumbled toward them.

He heard Wilson making an odd guttural sound. The soldier turned the light away from DelCorso's face. When his eyes readjusted to the darkness, he sucked in a breath. "Oh, Christ Jesus."

In the flashlight's beam, the side of Wilson's face showed

as one swollen, purple lump. Glistening, a mound of pale blue and greenish intestine bulged through his muddy shirt. His cameras were missing—the Arvin had probably helped themselves—but one of the straps still hung from Wilson's neck, rather like a priest's scapular.

"Christ, Christ Jesus," DelCorso repeated, seeing that Wilson had been slit open from navel to sternum.

"I . . . ugh . . . ugh," Wilson said in a hoarse whisper. "Ugh . . . I." He raised a hand and seemed to point at the slick, foul-smelling mess oozing through the ragged incision, which did not look as though it had been made by shrapnel; nor could DelCorso explain the bruises, unless they had been caused by concussion.

"Mark," he said, kneeling beside the eviscerated form, "don't talk."

Wilson appeared to nod, a look of animal panic on his once exquisite face.

"It's me, Nick. It's Nick."

"Nuh . . . Nuh-ick . . . ugh . . . see?"

"Stop talking," DelCorso said, trying to constrict his nasal passages against the stink.

"Nuh-ick. . . . See?"

Though only semiconscious, Wilson braced his hands and somehow managed to sit more upright. The panic in his face mounted when he looked at the coiled heap forcing its way out of him like some monstrous infant.

"Nuh-ick! That—that's me! Nuh-ick!"

Gently, DelCorso pressed Wilson back down on the embankment, on the wet and sparkling grass.

"Don't talk or move. Be easy, Mark."

Struggling to contain his own growing panic, he turned to the soldiers.

"*Bac-si*—doctor. *Bac-si. Maulen!*"

"*Bac-si?*" answered the one holding the flashlight. *Bac-si* no good." He pointed the light at Wilson and said, "*Ba muoi lam, sau lam,*" a slang Vietnamese phrase that meant, in this case, that Wilson was hopeless.

"No! *Khoung, khoung!*" DelCorso exclaimed, springing to his feet. "I've seen men live with gut wounds as bad as this."

The soldiers looked at him blankly.

"You find *bac-si.* Now, damn you. *Maulen,* quickly."

"*Bac-si* no here. *Bac-si di-di Saygone.*"

"Bullshit." DelCorso grabbed the man by the shirt collar

and shook him. "You find *bac-si. Anh hieu khoung!* Or did you three little pricks do this? Maybe you tried to steal his cameras and then beat the hell out of him and knifed him. Is that it, you murdering little pricks?"

Though he did not understand DelCorso's words, the soldier got his meaning and shouted back at him in rapid Vietnamese, gesturing toward the rice paddies. The other two joined in. Out of their babble, DelCorso heard one word repeated several times, a word he did not understand. Behind him, Wilson continued to rasp, "Nuh-ick, That's me! Nuh-ick." The rain came down steadily, but without enough force to dampen the flames of the burning truck. The flames leapt and fell, leapt and fell. The soldiers kept repeating that one word, gesturing at the rice paddies, where DelCorso saw nothing except the shapes of a few water buffalo, hulking in the darkness.

"*Toi khoung hieu,*" he said angrily. "I want *bac-si, bac-si.*"

In an exasperated voice, the soldier with the flashlight spoke the word again, pointing at Wilson with one hand, and with the other casting the beam on the buffalo, stomping in the mud a hundred or so feet away.

"*Anh hieu khoung!*" asked the soldier. "*Fini. Bac-si* no good."

Looking at the animals pawing the earth with their hooves, tossing their horned heads, DelCorso saw what the soldier was driving at, and all the anger and desperation, all the fight and spirit drained out of him at once.

"*Anh hieu khoung!*" the soldier said again. "You now un-nastan'?"

DelCorso nodded. Turning, he knelt down, and to make sure he had understood correctly, gently pressed his fingers against Wilson's rib cage. The ribs gave way easily, forcing a short sharp cry of pain from Wilson's throat. "Nuh-ick! Damn . . . ugh . . . I'm . . ." *Michael the Archangel defend us in battle when you can but when you can't grant us a dignified death a warrior's death from shell or bullet and not a death such as this.* Taking his hand from the ribs, he pressed Wilson's left thigh, feeling solid bone beneath the muscle; but the right one was mush, mush clear through. Wilson screamed again. *Fini* for sure. He had not only been disemboweled, but half the bones in his body had been fractured or crushed into powder. *You thought it was glamorous, Mark. Do you think it's glamorous now?* DelCorso asked silently. Then he whispered in the blue-black lump of Wilson's ear:

"Mark, can you hear me?"

"Ugh-lee, Nuh-ick." The words were barely discernible through the swollen lips. "Ugh-lee."

"Yeah, ugly Nick." DelCorso wanted to cry but could not allow himself the luxury of tears. "Can you understand what I'm saying?"

He could not tell if the movement of Wilson's head was a nod or just a nervous reaction to pain.

"Mark, if you understand me . . . if I hadn't stayed so long . . . if I'd got back just a few minutes earlier, maybe this wouldn't have happened."

"Ugh-lee . . . Nuh-ick."

"Yeah, ugly Nick."

"I'm . . . ughlee, I am."

"No, you're not. You're still one good-looking son of a bitch. Did you hear me? You're still a good-looking son of a bitch, and if I hadn't stayed so long, maybe . . ." Something other than tears was trying to escape from DelCorso's throat. With great effort he held it back.

"Inside . . . ughlee . . . ughlee!"

"Damn it, Mark. I'm sorry. God almighty I am. Forgive me."

"Ugh-lee!"

Perhaps Wilson's pain had opened the valves of his adrenal glands, perhaps that entity called the life force, invisible yet as real as any physical organ, was making a final effort before it expired. Whatever its name or sources, some power gave the shattered man strength to rise onto the knee of his good leg and from his knee into a one-legged half-crouch. It gave him the strength to do that and to cry out in the tone of a man who has made an astounding self-discovery:

"I'm . . . ughlee inside!"

Obeying the inflexible law of gravity, Wilson's intestines and stomach, which resembled a spinach-colored wineskin, spilled out of him, pulling in their train liver, kidneys, and spleen. Wilson collapsed back onto one knee, snatched at a length of viscera in an attempt to put it back. Wilson was trying to put himself back into himself. DelCorso instinctively grabbed the slick mass, but it slipped through his hands like warm pudding.

Then Wilson pitched forward. DelCorso quickly rolled him over and cradled the battered head in his lap.

"Mark?" The thing rose higher in DelCorso's throat. Wilson's eyes were wide and white and did not blink against the rain, and his shirt sagged in the cavity where his middle had been. "Mark?"

The thing that was not a sob but some other expression of emotion rose higher still, choking DelCorso, higher and higher until it burst out of him. Cradling Wilson's head, cradling and rocking on his knees in the mud and wet grass, he heard himself howling like an incoming shell.

18

HE REGAINED his self-control rather quickly. In exchange for helping carry Wilson's body to the jeep, DelCorso offered the soldiers a ride into Saigon. Two hours later, he dropped them off on Tu Do Street, then drove to the American embassy. There, a surprisingly cooperative duty officer took down the pertinent information, then dispatched two marine guards to take care of the corpse, which had been tied to the hood of the jeep with the Arvins' web belts. The marines zipped Wilson into an olive-drab body-bag and put him in an ambulance in the embassy compound. DelCorso watched and, seeing in his memory an image of Wilson's insides spilling out, had an urge to howl again. He suppressed it and climbed into the jeep, ordering the driver to take him to the IPS bureau, where he would have his film processed. *I'm all ugly inside*, he thought. At least Wilson had remained true to his nature: vain unto the grave.

Exhausted, DelCorso slumped in the seat and stared with dulled vision down Le Loi Boulevard. The darkened windows of the buildings watched over the vacant street. Metal shutters and the intricate hatchwork of security grates covered the entrances to bars and shops and movie theaters advertising martial-arts epics. The trees diffused the glow of the street-lamps, which gave the only light save for the distant flicker of the exploding fuel depots and ammunition dumps near the airfield. Tan Son Nhut, DelCorso had learned from the duty officer, was closed for good, which relieved the necessity of shipping his film by plane. He would transmit black-and-whites by wire and find some other means to send the Ektachrome. If the color shots arrived late, who cared? *Newsweek* magazine would survive to publish another day and Nicholas DelCorso would survive to take more photographs.

He had always survived and had always looked upon his emergence from whatever maelstrom into which he'd cast himself as a sign that he remained under the blessing of his gods. He wasn't so sure about that now. He certainly did not feel blessed, although, to shuck off the burden of guilt, he tried to persuade himself that he had not returned to Wilson on time because his personal deities had not intended him to; if he had, he, too, would have fallen under the horns and crushing hooves. As for Wilson, the dice had rolled the wrong way. It was as simple and awful as that. Or was it? Guilt weighed upon DelCorso, especially when he raised his hand to light a cigarette and caught the reek of Wilson's innards. He had wiped the blood from his hands, but the smell clung to his skin as unforgiven sin clings to the soul. He could not wipe it off any more than he could deny his guilt with notions about gods, destiny, and fateful dice.

To keep his thoughts and emotions under control, he immersed himself in the practicalities of his trade. He went up to the lab and worked hard for nearly an hour, developing and printing his film. As always, the amber twilight and womblike silence of the darkroom tranquilized him. When the prints were ready, he was as reluctant to leave as a man lying under a warm quilt on a cold morning is reluctant to get out of bed. He wanted to remain forever in the dim quiet where events were governed by predictable chemical reactions, where a man could correct his mistakes, where, in general, things made sense.

Seeking to maintain his calm, he did not write his captions in the clattering newsroom, but in a small spare room sometimes used by the special correspondents who filed through IPS. Its one window faced northward, looking over the crazy geometry of apartment blocks, shantytown, pagodas, temples, and churches that was intermittently lighted by the flashes on the horizon. The rockets falling on the airfield created a muffled, arrhythmic drumbeat, reminding DelCorso that he was a citizen of a world where very little was predictable and even less made sense.

The captions finished, he went into the newsroom and gave them to the teletype operator. As usual, the place was noisy; as usual, Vincent was sitting at the rearmost desk in an opium daze; as usual, Bolton's office door was closed, but DelCorso sensed a change in the atmosphere. It wasn't anything he could put his finger on; nor did he have the inclination to find out, because he had one last unpleasant duty to perform. Picking up a phone, he called Clayton at the *Newsweek* bureau.

"*Gored by a water buffalo?*" Clayton shouted.

"You heard me."

"Gored by a fucking water buffalo?"

"How many times do I have to tell you?"

"Nobody gets killed by a water buffalo."

"Wilson did."

"What the hell was he doing, playing matador?"

DelCorso explained the circumstances.

"Jesus Christ," Clayton complained in his Georgia drawl. "I've got this week's cover story to file, I've got a list of queries from New York as long as a Wall Street ticker tape, I've got to make sure our Vietnamese stringers get on the evacuation if there ever is one, and now I've got to deal with this. All kinds of crap about getting the body back, life insurance hassles—"

"It's lonely at the top, Clayton."

"Screw you. All right, where's his body?"

"At the embassy."

"What're they going to do with it?"

"How the fuck do I know?"

"Shit. Okay, I'll call and find out." Clayton paused, then said with great indignation, "Gored by a water buffalo. Christ almighty, I can't say that."

"What do you mean, you can't say that?"

"I can't say that a photographer on assignment for *Newsweek* was gored to death by a goddamned water buffalo."

"Don't say it then."

"You got any suggestions for alternatives?"

"Clayton, what're you talking about?"

"Maybe you didn't get the word, but for your information,

an AP man was wounded in the attack on the airfield and
some other wire-service guy named Grey was killed. New
York wants me to do a few graphs on those guys for the media
section. You can bet your last pair of clean skivvies that they'll
want a few more on Wilson. How in the hell am I going to
say that this Grey was killed by a shell while *Newsweek*'s
man was gored by a water buffalo? It'll sound ridiculous. War
photographers aren't supposed to die that way."

"Pass that on to Wilson. Maybe he'll try to do better next
time."

"All right, wise-ass. Listen, you were there, so you tell me
if it would be factual to say that Wilson was killed while the
Viet Cong were shelling a retreating South Vietnamese convoy
on Highway One."

"That's factual."

"Then that's what I'm going to say."

"Mark Wilson not only dies heroically, but factually."

"There it is."

"*Ciao.*"

"Hang on. In the laundry list of questions I got from New
York is a query if you'll stay on after the North Vietnamese
take over for an extra five hundred a week. You got an answer?"

"Yeah, but it isn't printable in a family magazine." DelCorso
slammed down the phone.

"I guess it's been a bad night for the fourth estate. Grey
bought it, too."

DelCorso turned and looked at Vincent's face, its skin so
spare that you needed little imagination to picture the skull
beneath.

"Clayton told me on the phone. I thought something was
wrong when I walked in here."

"Nobody's in mourning if that's what you thought. Grey
was a jerk. It's him." Vincent languidly gestured at Bolton's
door, behind which a typewriter was clacking. "I think Harry's
gone *ti-ti dinky-dao.*"

"Everybody who's spent more than three days in this shithole is a little crazy. Fact is, anybody who spent any time here
and who isn't a little crazy has got to be a whole lot crazy."

"Maybe." Vincent shrugged, his gaunt, knobby shoulders
rising above the tops of his ears so that he resembled a buzzard
with folded wings. "A little crazy or a lot crazy, I've got a

feeling that whatever Harry's writing in there, it's going to wreck his career, at least as far as IPS is concerned. I think he's wrecked it already."

"What makes you say that?"

"You know how he is about beats and exclusives. He got another one tonight. Found out the ambassador is still twiddling his thumbs about an evacuation, so the spooks, the chargé d'affaires, the consulate, just about everybody in the embassy except the cleaning ladies are organizing the whole thing themselves, sort of a palace revolt. When the balloon goes up, they'll move everybody out of here whether Hutton says 'go' or not. Pretty good story."

"Sure."

"Bolton gave it all to *The New York Times*."

"That doesn't sound like the Horseman."

"He handed it to the *Times* like a Christmas present."

"Doesn't sound like him at all, but it isn't going to wreck his career unless somebody at the *Times* tells your New York office how they got the story."

"Right. This is what's going to wreck his career."

Vincent took a clipboard from a hook on the wall behind him. It was filled with copies of messages and filed stories.

"We got this message from New York after we'd telexed them about Grey," he said, flipping to the correct page and handing the clipboard to DelCorso. The copy read:

281015 BOLTON: HAVE JUST LEARNED AP'S EDWARDS ONLY WOUNDED IN SAME ATTACK GREY KILLED IN. FILE ASAP BANG-BANG WITH PLENTY OF COLOR FROM GREY'S NOTES IF YOU CAN. GREY'S HOMETOWN PAPER, HAMMOND TIMES, REQUESTS 400 WD. OBIT. WHAT KIND OF REPORTER WAS HE, HOW WAS HE KILLED. REACTION OF OTHER NEWSMEN TO HIS DEATH, ETC. RGDS/HALPRIN/CABLES/NY.

"Harry was still working on the evacuation story," Vincent went on, "but when he saw that, he put it down and gave it all to the *Times*. Then he filed the stuff underneath."

DelCorso turned the page and couldn't help smiling when he saw that the Horseman had not gone a little crazy, but, rather, a little sane.

282235 HALPRIN: HAVE ONPASSED TO GREY THAT EDWARDS ONLY WOUNDED AND CONGRATULATED HIM. REQUEST AUTHORIZATION TO GIVE GREY FIVE HUNDRED DOLLAR BONUS

FOR GETTING KILLED. NOW SENDING BANG-BANG WITH PLENTY OF COLOR. OBIT FOR HAMMOND TIMES UPCOMING. GOD BLESS YOU ALL. BOLTON/SAIGON.

Below was Bolton's story.

282242 ATTACK EXBOLTON FOR GREY (DECEASED): SAIGON—MAGENTA! NORTH VIETNAMESE FORCES POUNDED SAIGON'S TAN SON NHUT AIRBASE LATE MONDAY WITH ARTILLERY AND ROCKETS RED GLARE GREEN YELLOW BLUE. THE ATTACK RENDERED THE RUNWAYS USELESS, THUS CLOSING SOUTH VIETNAM'S LAST REMAINING AIRFIELD. A FIXED WING EVACUATION OF THE 900 AMERICANS REMAINING IN THE COUNTRY HAS BEEN RULED OUT, SAID A U.S. EMBASSY SPOKESMAN, PAINTING A GLOOMY SOMBER PICTURE OF THE SITUATION. (MORE)

THE ENEMY SHELLS WHINED OUT OF THE DARK BLACK CHARCOAL SABLE PITCHY INKY SOOTY SKY SHORTLY AFTER A GORGEOUS SUNSET SENT ITS VARIEGATED LIGHT OVER THIS PIEBALD CITY. AMMUNITION AND FUEL DUMPS WENT UP IN SCARLET CINNABAR AND VERMILION FLAMES. AN AMERICAN NEWSMAN, WILLIAM R. GREY SLATY SILVER NEUTRAL COLORLESS, 23, WAS KILLED WHILE COVERING THE BOMBARDMENT. GREY'S DEATH MADE OTHER JOURNALISTS IN SAIGON SAD AND COBALT LAPIS LAZULI SAPPHIRE TURQUOISE BLUE. (MORE)

IN CENTRAL SAIGON, THE GARISH BRILLIANT BRIGHT VIVID INTENSELY GAUDY FIRES OVER THE AIRFIELD COULD BE CLEARLY SEEN. AS THE SHELLS CONTINUED TO FALL IN GLARING FLARING EXPLOSIONS, THE NORTH VIETNAMESE SAFFRON LEMON AMBER YELLOW HORDES WERE MASSING FOR A FINAL ASSAULT ON THIS BELEAGUERED CAPITAL. IF THE U.S. IS UNABLE TO LAND HELICOPTERS HERE, AMERICANS AND THOUSANDS OF VIETNAMESE WILL BE MAROONED CRIMSONED CARMINED INCARNADINED BY THE BRICK BEET RUBY REDS. ENDS/BOLTON/SAIGON.

"They'll shitcan him for that," Vincent said when Del-Corso placed the clipboard on the desk. "I don't care what kind of track record he's got, they'll shitcan him."

"He's got a Pulitzer. That's like having a guaranteed annual income."

"The news business is a tight little world. Once McDaniels puts out the word, Harry'll be lucky if he gets a job on the copy desk of the *Arizona Republic*."

"Vinnie, I need some O."

"So do I."

"You look like you've had your share."

"Hours ago. It's worn off. Bye-bye buzz. If you want some,

you can get it at the Palace. They bring it up with room service."

"I want it now. I was with Wilson when he got killed. His guts spilled out of him like groceries out of a shopping bag. Know what I mean?"

"Yeah. You see something like that and deferred gratification doesn't make much sense anymore."

"The only thing I've seen today that makes any sense is the story Harry filed."

"I've got some—Vinnie's emergency rations. But we can't smoke in here. If Bolton caught a whiff, he'd go bananas."

"Maybe a pipe or two would do him good."

"I wouldn't bother him, not when he's in this weird a mood. Anyway, he doesn't use the stuff."

"Where, then?"

"Sometimes, when I can't get out of here, I use the bathroom in the photo lab. Bolton never goes in there."

DelCorso sat on the edge of the rust-streaked bathtub while Vincent, on the floor with his scrawny legs folded under him, lighted a tablet used to heat C rations, and dropped it into a perforated ration tin. Over this makeshift stove he cooked a brown gumball, twirling the opium on a needle until it bubbled and softened.

"Laotian," he said, tamping the bead into a pipe, which he passed over the flame with the bowl upside down. "The best."

DelCorso inhaled deeply, the sweetish smell stirring in him the sort of anticipation a man feels before making love to a beautiful woman. He handed the pipe back to Vincent, who smoked it out with one long, expert drag.

"Primo Laotian. Graham Greene introduced me to this stuff. *The* Graham Greene. Bet you didn't know that me and Graham Greene were running buddies."

DelCorso, his lungs and throat burning, shook his head.

"I knew him. Met him on my first visit to this place, in 'fifty-four. I was a young snotnose stringing for UPI."

"What was he like?"

"Okay. We used to go to one of those old-time *fumeries* in Cho Lon, you know, clean mattresses to lay on, nice furniture, kind of like a class whorehouse." Vincent took a hit off the second pipe, his hollow cheeks collapsing in on themselves. "Yeah, he was okay. Guess he was a little crazy in his way, but like you said"—he passed the pipe to DelCorso—

you've got to be real crazy if you've been here and aren't a little crazy."

After the third pipe, a warm drowsiness crept into Del-Corso. His blood turned to honey and his eyes fixed on a fly exploring a crack in the wall tiles. He reached out to touch it, to touch, not to crush it, but his arm moved as if a weight were tied to his wrist. The fly vanished, then reappeared on the door.

"I think you would have liked Graham Greene, Nick. He was as different from you as any man could be, but you're similar in a way. You're restless the way he was."

"Restless," DelCorso repeated like a child who has just learned a new word. He drew twice on a fourth pipe; in the small, airless room, the opium surged through him with a rush at once exciting and languorous, like a sensual woman's caress. "Restless. Me and Graham Greene."

"Restless in the same way. Some guys keep moving because they're curious. They've got to see the other side of the hill. Some guys like variety, but Greene, he was always on the move because he was miserable inside. Guess he's settled down now that he's an old man, but back then, he was afraid of what he might do if he ever stopped moving. Or maybe he was afraid he'd have to face something about himself he didn't want to face. He was always covering wars, too. It was like wars and traveling were a drug to him."

"Drug," echoed DelCorso.

"Yeah. I think you're a little that way, Nick. I'll bet if you ever settled down and went to work every day like ninety-nine point nine percent of the guys in the world, you'd be so damned depressed you'd feel like killing yourself."

"Maybe." DelCorso paused to look at the fly, a black speck on the white door. "Maybe I would, but"—he paused again; he was having difficulty enunciating—"but I think something will kill me first. Yeah, that's what'll happen. *Zap. Adios*, Nick, *adios*, *muchacho*, ah-dee-fucking-os."

"Stay in this racket and something will."

"A little more, Vinnie, a leetle more, *por favor*."

"How much are you going to do?"

"Only done four."

"Look, four pipes is to me what a soup cracker is to a glutton. When you're not used to primo stuff like this, too much'll make you sick."

"I want enough."

"Enough for what? You tell Dr. Vinnie where you want to go and he'll prescribe the dosage that will get you there."

If the opium had made DelCorso's speech turgid, it had the opposite effect on his mind, flooding it with the acute clarity of winter sunlight. *I want to be purified*, he thought. *I want enough to cleanse the guilt I feel for Wilson's death, the guilt I feel for putting the old woman on the truck the shells blew off the road.* Somehow, though, he could not translate the thought into words. All he said was:

"Wilson."

Vincent was cooking another gumball over the blue, acrid-smelling flame.

"I've got you. You want enough to stop the bad visions."

DelCorso nodded, aware that he had a stupidly benign smile on his face. The fly vanished again, shooting off at a sharp angle to light on the plastic shower curtain that felt like silk against DelCorso's skin.

"One more should do it," Vincent said. "One more and it's *adios* to bad visions."

"Ah-dee-fucking-os."

MUCH AS HE HATED to lose, Bolton looked forward to losing his job. He had never felt more free than he did tonight, hammering the nails into the coffin of his career. Once New York saw the obituary he was writing for the *Hammond Times*, they would have no choice but to fire him. This wasn't the professional way to go about things. A professional would submit a dignified resignation, but Bolton did not want to resign, because the International Press Service did not deserve dignity and because, on a more practical level, there were financial advantages to being fired. As for his professionalism, he had begun to wonder if, like the skill of the few good officers he had known in Vietnam, officers who had adroitly led their brigades and battalions to no end whatever, it was a professionalism enlisted in the service of idiocy. Give us bang-bang with plenty of color from Grey's notes if you can. Sweet Jesus, Grey and his notes had been splattered from one end of the airfield to the other.

He finished penciling in the corrections to the obituary and brought it into the transmission room. There, he saw a service message from Hong Kong on the incoming wire.

BOLTON: 282142 ATTACK GARBLED. RESEND PLS. Y. CHEN/HK.

What's wrong Mr. Y. Chen? Don't you recognize a color story when you see one? Laughing to himself, Bolton sent a reply.

Y. CHEN: 282142 ATTACK UNGARBLED. SEND AS IS. BOLTON/ SAIGON.

Standing over the teletypes, he watched the lines of his obituary click-clacking over the wires. If it was a bit sophomoric, it was at least the most honest story he had ever written.

292401 GREY OBIT SPECIAL TO HAMMOND TIMES EXBOLTON: SAIGON—INTERNATIONAL PRESS SERVICE CORRESPONDENT WILLIAM REYNOLDS GREY, A NATIVE OF HAMMOND, INDIANA, WAS BLOWN TO PIECES MONDAY NIGHT (SAIGON TIME) DURING A VIET CONG ROCKET ATTACK ON TAN SON NHUT AIRBASE. ANOTHER AMERICAN CORRESPONDENT, MICHAEL EDWARDS, WAS MERELY WOUNDED, PROVING ONCE AGAIN THAT IPS CAN BEAT AP ANY DAY OF THE WEEK.

GREY, 23, DIED IN PURSUIT OF BANG-BANG, WHICH IS CURRENT JOURNALISTIC ARGOT FOR WAR DISPATCHES THAT ATTEMPT TO CAPTURE THE IMMEDIACY, TO SAY NOTHING OF THE SUPERFICIALITY, OF TELEVISION. TOTALLY UNINFORMATIVE, BANG-BANG STORIES SATISFY A JADED PUBLIC'S APPETITE FOR VICARIOUS BLOODSHED AND THUS HELP TO SELL NEWSPAPERS. FOR HIS HEROIC ATTEMPT TO BRING THE SIGHTS, SOUNDS, AND SMELLS OF THE BATTLEFIELD TO THE AMERICAN BREAKFAST TABLE, GREY WAS POSTHUMOUSLY AWARDED A FIVE HUNDRED DOLLAR BONUS BY ACTING SAIGON BUREAU CHIEF, H. W. BOLTON.

BORN IN HAMMOND ON JUNE 26, 1951, GREY WAS A 1972 GRADUATE OF THE NORTHWESTERN UNIVERSITY SCHOOL OF JOURNALISM, ALTHOUGH YOU WOULD NEVER KNOW IT BY THE QUALITY OF HIS WORK. REGARDED AS INCOMPETENT BY HIS COLLEAGUES, HE WAS ALSO KNOWN FOR HIS ARROGANCE, SMART MOUTH, AND GENERAL UNWILLINGNESS TO DO WHAT HE WAS TOLD. THE EMOTIONS OF HIS FELLOW NEWSMEN UPON LEARNING OF HIS DEATH WERE BEST SUMMED UP BY VETERAN IPS REPORTER AND NOTED OPIUM ADDICT RICHARD VINCENT:

+I WON'T MISS THE LITTLE BASTARD. HE WASN'T WORTH THE POWDER IT TOOK TO BLOW HIM TO HELL. + ENDS/BOLTON/SAIGON.

That would do it, surely that would. He would be sacked before dawn. What kind of life was this anyway, hopping on airplanes to record strange people's wars? Already, Bolton had a new existence planned for himself: he would return to his Carolina mountains, build a cabin, find an undemanding job on a local newspaper, and in his spare time fulfill the fantasy almost universal among journalists—write a book. He had no theme or subject in mind—a book, that's all, any book, something that would endure beyond the next deadline. This seductive vision had given rise to his pecuniary motives for trying to force IPS to fire him. It was company policy to give severance pay as well as travel and moving expenses to any correspondent who was let go; if he quit, he or his new employer would have to foot the bills. With a hundred dollars in his savings account and an apartment full of belongings to ship, Bolton could not afford to take a walk.

He looked around for Vincent, who was supposed to be handling routine night-shift stories. Finding him gone, Bolton went to look for him in the spare room, then caught a familiar sweet smell coming from the bathroom down the hall. Goddamned doper, goddamned opium-smoking, opium-eating drug addict. He was about to drag Vincent out when he thought, Why should I? Why bother? The show was coming to an end anyway. *La guerre est finie*, and Harry Bolton was as good as *fini* with IPS. Let Vinnie smoke himself into stoned heaven. Lighthearted, feeling the liberation of the recently unemployed, Bolton returned to the newsroom, where he cracked open the bottle of I. W. Harper in his desk and toasted his new freedom.

Half an hour later, pleasantly drunk, he checked the teletypes for the message he expected from New York. What he found instead were transmissions of his two stories, as they appeared on the world wire.

SAIGON—NORTH VIETNAMESE FORCES POUNDED SAIGON'S TAN SON NHUT AIRBASE LATE MONDAY WITH ARTILLERY AND ROCKETS, CLOSING SOUTH VIETNAM'S LAST REMAINING AIRFIELD AND RULING OUT A FIXED WING EVACUATION OF THE 900 AMERICANS REMAINING IN THE COUNTRY.

THE ENEMY SHELLS WHINED OUT OF THE NIGHT SKY SHORTLY AFTER SUNSET, SETTING FUEL AND AMMUNITION DUMPS AFLAME. THE FIRES COULD BE CLEARLY SEEN IN CEN-

TRAL SAIGON. AS THE SHELLS CONTINUED TO FALL, THE
NORTH VIETNAMESE MASSED FOR A FINAL ASSAULT ON THE
CAPITAL. IF THE U.S. IS UNABLE TO LAND HELICOPTERS HERE,
AMERICANS AND THOUSANDS OF VIETNAMESE MAY BE
STRANDED. ENDS/BOLTON/SAIGON.

The obituary appeared farther down.

SAIGON—INTERNATIONAL PRESS SERVICE CORRESPOND-
ENT WILLIAM REYNOLDS GREY, A NATIVE OF HAMMOND, IN-
DIANA, WAS KILLED MONDAY NIGHT (SAIGON TIME) DURING
A NORTH VIETNAMESE ROCKET ATTACK ON TAN SON NHUT
AIRBASE THAT ALSO WOUNDED ANOTHER AMERICAN NEWS-
MAN.

GREY, 23, DIED WHILE COVERING THE INTENSE SHELLING.
HE WAS KNOWN AMONG HIS COLLEAGUES AS AN AGGRESSIVE
YOUNG REPORTER, WILLING TO TAKE GREAT RISKS IN PUR-
SUIT OF A STORY.

BORN IN HAMMOND ON JUNE 26, 1951, GREY WAS A 1972
GRADUATE OF THE NORTHWESTERN UNIVERSITY SCHOOL OF
JOURNALISM. HE JOINED IPS THE FOLLOWING YEAR AS A RE-
PORTER FOR THE CHICAGO BUREAU. HE WAS LATER TRANS-
FERRED TO SAIGON, WHERE HE REPORTED ON THE RELEASE
OF AMERICAN PRISONERS OF WAR. HIS DEATH WAS MOURNED
BY THE SAIGON PRESS CORPS, WHOSE FEELINGS WERE SUMMED
UP BY A VETERAN CORRESPONDENT IN THIS WAY:

+HE WASN'T WITH US VERY LONG, BUT WE'LL MISS HIM. +
ENDS/BOLTON/SAIGON.

They can't do this to me. Bolton karate-chopped the teletype. *They can't do this to me.*

"They can't do this to me!" he exclaimed to no one in
particular. "I'm not going to live this way." He turned his gaze
on the teletype operator with the Beatle haircut. "You hear
that, Ringo? I won't let them do this to me. I'm not going to
spend the rest of my life risking my ass and getting people
killed just to beat AP by five minutes. Goddamnit, Ringo,
listen to me."

"I listen," said Ringo Starr, his hands flying over the keyboard.

"I'm not going to let them get away with this. If Harry
Bolton wants to get fired, Harry Bolton will by God get fired."

"I listen."

"They're going to fire me and pay my way back to the
States and I'm going to live in the Great Smoky Mountains

and write a book and if I ever see another deadline again, I'll poke its eyes out and break its legs and run it over with my four-wheel-drive jeep."

"I listen."

"Goddamn right you do."

He dropped his 220 pounds onto the chair in front of the telex and punched the keys for New York's call number. The machine answered:

IPS NY GA.

BOLTON FOR HALPRIN URGENT.

MOM PLS.

While he waited, he tried to think of what he would say to the foreign editor, but his whiskey-fogged brain refused to function.

HALPRIN HERE GA.

Go ahead, Bolton thought, go ahead, ga ga GA.

YOU SEE STORIES SLUGGED ATTACK AND GREY OBIT?

YES. EDITED MYSELF.

YOU CAN'T DO THIS TO ME.

YES, I CAN. I FIGURED OUT WHAT YOU TRYING TO DO, BUT I WON'T LET YOU. YOU TOO GOOD TO LOSE. ALSO, YR TRAVEL AND MOVING ALLOWANCE WOULD COME OUT OF MY BUDGET, BUT I HAVE STRICT INSTRUCTIONS DOWNHOLD EXPENSES.

I WANT OUT.

WILL SUBMIT TOMORROW REQUEST TO GIVE YOU FIFTY DOLLAR A WEEK RAISE.

WOULDN'T STAY FOR FIVE THOUSAND A WEEK. I WANT OUT.

IF YOU WANT OUT, YOU HAVE TO QUIT.

FYI, YOU WILL SEE TOMORROW'S EDITIONS NYT EXCLUSIVE
ON U.S. EVACUATION PLANS. I GAVE STORY TO TIMES. WILL
NOT RPT NOT MATCH IT, WILL NOT RPT NOT FILE ANOTHER
WORD.

ARE YOU SAYING YOU QUITTING?

AM ON STRIKE. WHAT YOU GOING TO DO ABOUT IT?

NOTHING.

YOU CAN'T DO NOTHING.

YES I CAN

Bolton pictured a pine-and-cedar cabin with a wooded
mountain rising above it. He saw himself inside the cabin, the
pages of a manuscript piled high beside his typewriter, sunlight leaning through a window. He would work, say, three
days a week for some rural local; on the other days, he would
write until late afternoon, catch the evening rise on the White-
water or the Horsepasture River, and, at night, sit on his deck
listening to hounds running coon in the dark hollows.

ALL RIGHT. I QUIT.

AS BUREAU CHIEF ON EXECUTIVE PAYROLL, YOU REQUIRED
SUBMIT RESIGNATION.

RESIGNATION FOLLOWS: UPSTICK JOB ASSWARDS.

UNACCEPT YOUR RESIGNATION.

YOU CAN'T SANDBAG ME. I'M NOT FILING ANOTHER WORD
FOR YOU. I'M THROUGH, FINISHED, DONE WITH IT.

SLEEP ON IT.

NO.

THINK IT OVER.

NO.

HOW DOES A HUNDRED A WEEK SOUND?

LIKE SHIT.

DO NOT USE PROFANITY ON WIRE.

FUCK YOU.

YOU'LL FEEL BETTER IN MORNING.

I FEEL FINE NOW.

LOOK FORWARD TO YOUR NEXT FILE.

THERE WON'T BE ANY. BIBI.

WE'LL SEE. BIBI.

Bolton shut the machine off and, going back to the I. W. Harper in his office, muttered to himself, "I'm through, all done, a free man, BIBI, bye-bye." He sat on his cot, savoring the whiskey and wondering why, now that he had quit, the feeling of liberation had deserted him. It would come back. Give it time. He took three pulls from the bottle. The feeling would return and, just as soon as he could get out of Saigon, he would be on his way to a new life in the Carolinas. He looked outside at the black and red horizon and took another drink. Then, lying down, he listened with the ear of his imagination to hounds running coon in the woods.

19

HE DREAMED about them, baying above the hypnotic buzz of summer locust. They fell silent in his dream morning, which dawned with rhomboids of sunlight shining through the trees onto a pool whose still surface was dimpled by feeding bream and on whose bottom brown trout lay with their jaws into the current and their tail fins fanning.

Bolton's eyes opened to another kind of sun, harsh with the white light of the tropics. Dalman was shaking him by the ankle.

"Reveille, Harry."

Bolton sat up, his skull electrified with pain. On his desk, the I. W. Harper stood two-thirds empty. The window beside the desk framed a portrait of war: smoke and curtains of flame rose and fell over Tan Son Nhut. Bolton heard explosions and the staccato of not-so-distant small-arms fire.

"Time on deck," he said.

"Nine-thirty. Christensen's on the phone."

"My tongue feels like the Chinese army marched over it in stocking feet. Coffee on?"

Dalman filled a cup from the aluminum pot and gave it to Bolton with the mixture of solicitousness and disgust the sober reserve for the severely hung over.

"Lord," Bolton said, rubbing his forehead. "This one is a

gold-medal beauty, this is the Olympic champion of hang-
overs."

"Christensen's on the phone."

"I heard you the first time. What's going on?"

"The bad guys are still shelling the airfield, they've knocked
out every foot of runway, they shot down a South Vietnamese
C-119 with a surface-to-air missile about fifteen minutes ago,
and they've got infantry trying to take the Newport bridge."

Bolton would have jumped to his feet if he had been capable
of it.

"Newport? Christ, that's only three miles from here." Bolton moved toward the phone, then remembered that he had
resigned. "Wait a minute. *You* talk to Christensen. You're
acting bureau chief now."

Dalman looked at him uncomprehendingly.

"You heard me," Bolton said, pushing the lighted button
and handing the receiver to Dalman. "I quit last night. You're
numero uno now."

Hesitant, Dalman put the phone to his ear and said:

"Dave? This is Dalman. . . . I don't know what's going on,
but Harry says he's quit. . . . I'm acting bureau chief now. I'm
supposed to talk to you."

Dalman stood nodding silently for a few moments, then
held the phone out to Bolton.

"He said he's talking to you or no one. It's important."

"What the hell. Talking to him can't do any harm."

"Harry, what's this bullshit about you quitting?" Christensen asked in the tone of a father speaking to a teen-age son
who has just announced that he's getting married.

"It's not bullshit. I'm through with it. I'm going to North
Carolina to write a book."

"Say again?"

"I'm going to North Carolina to write a book."

"I've been here a long time. I've seen this before. The
Australians used to call it 'going troppo.' "

"I haven't gone troppo. I am going to North Carolina to
write a book. Whatever you've got will interest me in a personal, not a professional sense."

"Harry, Saigon is surrounded by two hundred thousand
North Vietnamese. They're shelling the airport. They've captured Vung Tau. Every road, canal, and river out of here is
ambushed. Forget North Carolina—you couldn't get to Cho
Lon right now."

"We'll see."

"Under these circumstances, your saying you quit is a little like one of Custer's troopers telling him in the middle of the Battle of the Little Big Horn, 'Excuse me, general, may I have my discharge papers? My enlistment just expired and I'm going home to write my memoirs.' "

"Funny, funny. What've you got that's so important?"

"A beat, Harry, a helluva beat."

"What is it?" Bolton asked, unable to overcome his instinctive curiosity. At the word *beat*, his heart rate had quickened involuntarily.

"The evacuation is going to get under way in about an hour."

"About time." Bolton's voice registered false nonchalance and repressed excitement.

"It's all over, Harry. The longest war in American history and the only one we've lost."

"How much of a beat do you figure?"

"You'll have a good hour on the competition, and I'll give you background none of them will get for at least a day, if you're interested."

"In a personal sense. We'll be going out on choppers, right?"

"No other choice. Sixty-one Marine CH-46s and 53s will use Tan Son Nhut as a landing zone. The Marines and Air America are sending about twenty Hueys to the embassy. The birds will be lifting off the carriers around ten."

"How many do you figure to evacuate?"

Goddamnit, he could not stop himself from asking questions, each one of which was like a shot of whiskey to someone who has taken the pledge.

"About nine hundred Americans and six thousand Vietnamese," Christensen answered. "That's the official number. Unofficially, it'll be four or five times that. This is going to be the biggest military evacuation since Dunkirk."

"That poetry?"

"Fact."

"How big?"

Without wanting to, Bolton picked up a pencil and started making notes.

"I already told you—eighty-one helicopters. A marine battalion will provide landing-zone security, with two more standing by on shipboard in case things get sticky. Navy and marine Phantoms are going to fly cover and flak suppression if that's needed. Most of the Seventh Fleet is out there and a shitload of merchant ships—forty-five ships altogether."

"You expecting flak?"

"Don't know about the North Vietnamese, although the choppers are going to carry decoy flares in case they fire any heat-seeking missiles. Tell you the truth, we're just as likely to catch ground fire from the South Vietnamese. They're not going to be happy to see us leaving them in the lurch."

Bolton scribbled his notes quickly. A nice touch: North and South Vietnamese joining forces to shoot down American helicopters. Against his will, his mind began to compose a lead. *Americans began withdrawing from the longest war in U.S. history Tuesday morning. . . .*

"Hutton fiddled while Rome burned right to the last second," Christensen continued. "Earlier this morning he told the White House that everything was all right and to cancel the evacuation, and they did. So a few of us went over his head, gave Washington the facts, and they changed their minds in fifteen minutes."

"What does he want, to go down with the ship?" *Americans began fleeing the longest war in U.S. history Tuesday morning in a fleet . . . no, not "fleet" . . . in an armada of eighty-one helicopters while a marine battalion guarded the landing zones and fighter planes roared overhead to protect the evacuation.* Not bad, not bad at all.

"If it was up to Hutton, he'd play Gordon of Khartoum, blasting the wogs with his forty-five until they dropped him. But we'll drag him out of here kicking and screaming if we have to. We probably won't have to because of his schnauzers."

"His schnauzers?"

"He's worried about his pet schnauzers. He already sent some flunky over to his residence to pick up the schnauzers and make sure they get on a helicopter. Where the schnauzers go, Hutton goes."

"Jesus Christ." Bolton wrote the tidbit about the ambassador's dogs in his notebook. The end of America's longest war, the largest military evacuation since Dunkirk, an ambassador who was behaving like some mad imperial proconsul, an hour's beat on the competition—this story was an embarrassment of riches.

"I'm calling you on a secure phone, Harry, so all of this is on deep background."

"I've got you. No attribution beyond 'informed sources.' "

"Right, although I don't have to worry about you. You're going to North Carolina to play author."

"Are you sure this is on?" Bolton asked, ignoring the sarcasm. "I don't want to put out a lead and then have to kill it."

"How can you put out a lead if you've quit to write books in North Carolina?"

"Call it my valedictory story."

"The evacuation is on. It's bye-bye everybody. But if I were you, I'd tune in to the embassy channel on your CB radio and not file a word until you hear someone say, 'Whiskey Six, this is Dragon Airborne Control, Dragon has crossed India Papa.' If the answer is, 'Dragon Control, this is Whiskey Six, the temperature in Saigon is one hundred and five degrees and rising,' that means the first wave of choppers have crossed the coastline and have been given the green light to come into the landing zones."

Christensen hung up. For several seconds, Bolton stared at his typewriter, its black keyboard evoking in him the desire and repulsion an invitingly full bottle evokes in a reformed alcoholic. Theoretically, the reformed drunk could take a sip and put the bottle aside; theoretically, Bolton could write this piece and go ahead with his plan to quit. Theoretically.

As he stared at the typewriter, the words to the second paragraph arranged themselves in his mind, then the third and fourth. He did not struggle for them; they came to him like an inspiration and began to kick and thump inside his brain, demanding to be written. Journalism. He was married to her for better or worse, and even the vision of writing books in a woodland cabin was not attractive enough to seduce him into leaving the bitch.

"God damn you," Bolton mumbled, not knowing whom or what he was addressing. He put paper in the Underwood, typed the timegroup, slug, and pounded out the story, seemingly as quickly as a telex. When he had finished, he swallowed a ten-milligram Dexadrine with his coffee to overcome his hangover. Nothing like a good breakfast before a long day. Turning his citizens-band radio to the proper channel, he listened to exchanges of encoded gibberish until he heard a crisp voice command. "All stations, all stations, this is Dragon Airborne Control, please clear this frequency unless you have emergency traffic." During the static-filled pause, punctuated with faint "Rogers," Bolton's heart drummed rapidly, the Dexadrine opening his sweat glands. Then: "Whiskey Six, this is Dragon Airborne Control . . . This is Whiskey Six over . . . Whiskey Six, Dragon Airborne Control has crossed India Papa, over . . . Roger, roger, Dragon Control, this is Whiskey Six, the temperature in Saigon is one hundred and five degrees and rising . . . Roger that, Whiskey Six, we're coming in."

"That's it!" Bolton exclaimed, bounding into the transmission room with his copy. "That is it!"

Dalman looked out the window as a flight of Phantoms whistled overhead.

"That's it, Dalman. The evacuation, the big bug-out. Bye-bye everybody."

"Well, holy shit."

"Holy, holy, holy." The strong coffee and speed had kicked Bolton into overdrive. "I want you to get out to Tan Son Nhut and let me know how it looks there. I'm going to roust Vinnie and send him to the embassy—they're going to be landing helicopters on the roof, so that should be some scene. Listen, before you take off for the airfield, get one of those free-lance photogs we've got stringing for us. I want pictures of Hutton making his exit."

"Where're you going to be, Harry? On the first helicopter to North Carolina?"

"North Carolina." Bolton's excitement subsided for a moment, and he spoke the name of his native state in the way a man speaks the name of a former mistress he thought he had loved. "Nothing has happened in North Carolina since the Civil War. Harry the Horseman doesn't belong in one of the most boring states in the Union."

"I could have told you that going in."

"Get to work, Dalman. We've got an hour's beat on the competition and I'm not going to lose it."

DELCORSO WOKE UP from his opium dreams to the howl of jets. Doors were slamming and people running down the hall outside his room. Rising, he opened the window and looked up. Exhaust trails smudged the monsoon sky like streaks of tar on a great slate shingle; formations of helicopters speckled the low clouds. Three floors below, a TV crew lumbered across Lam Son Square with their cameras and sound equipment. Turning his head to look down the length of Tu Do Street, he watched the helicopters, descending toward Tan Son Nhut, disappear into a tower of smoke whose top had been drawn into a huge black anvil.

Trying to shake off the opium grogginess, he dressed and got his equipment ready. He did not need to make any calls to know it was ending and, realizing he might have to make a quick, unplanned exit from the city, he tossed his passport, shaving kit, and a change of underwear into his camera bag before slinging it over his shoulder and going outside. It was so humid he began sweating immediately. The red and yellow Vietnamese flag on the National Assembly Building clung to its pole like a wet sheet. A policeman sat with an odd calmness on a folding chair under a tree in front of the building, and a plainclothesman was leaning against the tree, his revolver bulging under his white shirt.

The sounds of rocket and small-arms fire came from all directions on the outskirts of the city. Helicopters were putting down near the embassy, a few blocks away on Thong Nai Street, the noise of their rotors priming DelCorso's adrenaline pump. Across the way, photographers and TV crews were lined up like ranks of old-fashioned infantry on the rooftop balcony of the Caravelle Hotel. He would start there: like most magazines, *Newsweek* preferred a few overviews and aerial shots to establish a story. As he was crossing the street, the plainclothesman cut diagonally across the front of the Assembly Building and fell in step beside him.

"Hey, hey you," the man said.

DelCorso kept walking.

"Hey you, you American?"

"Yeah, American."

"All American *di-di* now?"

"Guess so."

"You *di-di*? Where you go now?" The man tugged at DelCorso's sleeve.

"Up there. Caravelle."

"Now all time curfew. You must not be on street."

"I'm press. *Bao chi.*"

The man's fingers tightened around DelCorso's upper arm with a wrestler's strength.

"You *bao chi*, I see ID card."

Trouble was written all over him in capital letters. He was DelCorso's height, tall for a Vietnamese. His neck formed a thick wedge above his shoulders, his face looked as if he'd spent several years as a journeyman sparring partner, and he had two fistfuls of knuckles that had not been broken because someone had stepped on them.

"*Here.*"

DelCorso took out his press card, which the man studied with great care.

"Okay?" DelCorso asked.

"Hokay. I see passport."

"Look . . ."

"*Passport.*"

No nonsense in those eyes and a suggestion in the movement of his body that he would use the revolver if he had to. A thug taking advantage of the situation, DelCorso decided. He'll pretend to check my passport, then ask me to open the bag to see if I have anything worth ripping off.

"My passport's in my room. In the Caravelle," DelCorso lied.

"You no stay Caravelle. You stay Palace. I see you come from Palace."

"I meant the Palace," DelCorso replied, his heart thrumming at the recognition that he was not a target of opportunity for a strong-arm robbery. The man had been watching him.

"You go Palace. Find passport. I wait in lobby."

"Sure," DelCorso said, aware of the necessity of keeping his temper under control in dealing with this character.

He was following DelCorso back to the hotel when Vincent and Hoang, rounding the corner in a jeep, spoiled whatever game he was up to. The jeep braked to a halt at the curb and Vincent called out:

"Hey, Nick, we're headed for the embassy if you need a lift."

"Yeah," DelCorso said, breaking into a run. "Yeah, hang on."

When the jeep pulled away, he saw the Vietnamese cut across the boulevard behind the National Assembly, heading in the direction of the embassy.

"Who was that dude?" Vincent asked.

"Hell if I know. Some gorilla looking for trouble."

"Yeah, all the bad actors are coming out of the woodwork now. Get what they can before Charlie starts throwing them in concentration camps."

"I was heading for the top of the Caravelle."

"The Caravelle? What the hell's going on at the Caravelle?

That primo Laotian must have put you in Lotus Land. Big story at the moment is at the embassy. Half of Saigon is trying to climb the walls to get aboard the choppers."

"I've been in Lotus Land all right. How about a fill?"

"We've got the mess at the embassy. Choppers have just landed the marine ground-security force at Tan Son Nhut. Most of the evacuees are going to be bused out there, thousands of 'em. The word Bolton got, this is supposed to be the biggest military evacuation since Dunkirk."

"So the Horseman didn't get fired."

Vincent laughed. "He sure tried hard enough . . ." A low-flying helicopter drowned out his voice. ". . . It's a long story. I'll leave it to him to tell you if you two ever get out of here."

"You staying?"

Vincent nodded.

"Fifteen years, Nick, and I was in and out of here for six years before that. Saw the French go, now I'm watching us go. This place . . . well, shit, I just can't leave it."

"You're crazy, Vinnie."

"You know what you said about being here and being crazy."

Hoang parked the jeep half a block from the embassy. With its narrow windows, set like firing loops in its concrete façade, its iron gates, and its high wall topped with barbed wire and surrounded by a shoving, shouting horde, it resembled a fortress under siege. Marine guards in battle dress stood atop the wall smashing rifle butts against the hands of Vietnamese trying to boost themselves over. As a silver Air America helicopter set its skids on the roof, a file of embassy staffers, running in a crouch, scrambled aboard with all the dignity of commuters leaping onto a train at the last moment. Thousands of desperate faces on the street looked up when the aircraft rose in a rapid, nose-down climb, another helicopter landing right behind it.

"Great exit for the U.S. of A., isn't it?" Vincent shouted. "Shit, the French pulled it off with more class than this. Peace with honor, that's what this was supposed to be."

It was a rioting crowd at a rock concert, it was a stadium full of football fans rushing onto the field, it was a panicked audience fleeing a theater fire—DelCorso did not know how to describe the masses crushing themselves against the thick walls, leaping and clutching for handholds, crying out when their flesh was bitten by the barbed wire, climbing on each other's backs to form human pyramids that swayed and toppled under the smashing rifle butts and slashing bayonets of the marines.

DelCorso waded in, trying to reach the wall. He wanted to photograph the crowd from above to suggest people struggling to escape from a pit; then he would shoot along the length of the wall, getting in the barbed wire and the marines, massive and menacing looking in their helmets and flak vests. The final image of the war: marines clubbing the people for whom the war had been waged just so a handful of foreign-service officers, embassy secretaries, and newsmen could escape safely.

Someone shoved DelCorso from the side; someone else elbowed his ribs; an elderly man clung to the back of his shirt. Then half a dozen people in front of him fell backward, almost knocking him down. The point of a shoe jabbed his bad ankle, sending a shock of pain up his leg. He had always tried to bring some dignity to a profession not known for dignity, but this melee was forcing him to behave like some savage paparazzo. He bulled his way through the mob with his powerful shoulders, shoved, pulled and pushed people out of his way; and, for his efforts, gained only a few yards and a torn camera strap. Finally, within fifteen yards of the wall, the bodies fused into a solid mass and he could make no headway whatever. In an effort to get something on film, he held his camera over his head, as he had while covering campus riots during his apprenticeship with AP, and took several frames without looking through the viewfinder. This was to photography what randomly spraying a tree line with an automatic rifle was to marksmanship: fire away and hope you hit something.

Clawing his way back to the edges of the crowd, his leg aching—he wondered how many more years it could withstand this kind of punishment—he crossed to the far side of the street. He did not see Vincent. Nearby, a television crew were busily filming looters stripping an embassy car. DelCorso climbed onto the hood of another car and brought the wall up close with a long lens; close, that is, in visual terms; emotionally, he felt distant. *Snap.* A father holding his small son in the air, apparently pleading with a marine to take the child. *Snap.* A man and a woman, boosted by a knot of other people, heaving themselves to the top of the wall before the marines can club them down. *Snap.* The man and woman balance themselves to jump to the other side, then fall into the barbed wire, in whose coils they writhe and twist. *Snap.* Their clothes shred, dark blood spots mottle the man's shirt and the woman's white silk trousers, then they quit struggling and lie still, like the dead on a perimeter wire after an attack. The marines leave them there. *Snap.* Another helicopter lands on the roof, takes on its passengers, and flies off. *Snap snap snap.* If a photographer had been present when the Romans withdrew from Britain, what would that have looked like? When Napoleon retreated from Moscow, the British from Kabul. Did the finales of those imperial adventures appear in reality as they did in the paintings of artists who had never witnessed them, full of somber drama? Or like this—full of shabby cruelty? *Snap.* The man and the woman lie bleeding in the wire's steel thorns. *Snap.* The marines' rifle butts rise and fall. *Snap.* The helicopters land and take off with the regularity of shuttle buses.

He was panning for another shot when a familiar, blocky figure dressed in a khaki bush jacket appeared in his lens. Atop the wall, moving cautiously along its narrow width, Dunlop was photographing the anarchy of faces and uplifted arms beneath him. Then DelCorso watched him aim his Leica at the two people tangled in the wire as a marine freed them with cutters and, holding them under the arms, dropped them like sacks back into the chaos below. How in the hell did P.X. get up there? From the other side, from inside the embassy compound, dummy. The side gate. Too much opium last night, DelCorso thought, climbing down from the car. Why didn't you think of that, the side goddamned gate?

Walking toward the gate, he encountered more looters. Soldiers, policemen, and civilians were tearing the upholstery out of a line of embassy cars, ripping out engine parts, removing tires with the efficiency of pit crews. There was, amid the general panic, delight in the freedom to commit vandalism without fear of consequences. All things were permitted now— a kind of Mardi Gras before the endless Communist Lent. A couple of white mice, as Saigon's traffic cops were called for the color of their uniforms, sat at curbside guarding a treasure of carburetors, batteries, spark plugs, radiator caps, fan belts, and rearview mirrors. The shot too good to pass up, DelCorso exposed a frame, then moved off a few feet to get a different angle. His 35-millimeter brought into focus a policeman's carbine, pointed directly at him. The cop was yelling at him in Vietnamese.

"He say you shoot picture, he shoot you," someone behind him translated.

Turning, DelCorso was startled to see the muscular man in the white shirt, grinning with all the humor of an anaconda.

"You no shoot picture. You go by hospital Gia Dinh Street. Assembly place for Americans. You *di-di*. Now Vietnamese very angry at Americans."

"That Vietnamese is," DelCorso said, gesturing at the cop. He studied the man's wide, scarred face to determine what he was and what he wanted. There wasn't a clue—just the reptilian grin and the coiled, destructive energy in the tightly muscled body.

"Yes, he angry," the Vietnamese was saying. "Americans leave him to VC. VC will be very hard on policemen. You must *di-di*."

"Right. That's what I'm doing."

DelCorso moved on down the street toward the side gate. When he got into the fringes of the crowd, out of view of the camera crews and other newsmen, the Vietnamese came up behind him and, grabbing his elbow, spun him around.

"I say you *di-di*!" he commanded. "Hospital Gia Dinh Street. You no shoot picture, you unnastan' me?"

"Get this, motherfucker—hit it. *You di-di.* You understand me? *Di-di* your ugly fucking face out of mine."

"You go by hospital Gia Dinh Street. Assembly place for Americans. Bus take you Tan Son Nhut. You no shoot picture."

"You're *beaucoup dinky-dao*. Get the fuck out of here."

DelCorso turned to walk away as a helicopter, hovering for a landing, threw its shadow over the street, its rotors whipping dust and papers and debris into the jostling mass of people. The man seized DelCorso's arm again, jerking him backward. His temper snapping, DelCorso pivoted on the balls of his feet, raised his right to protect his chin and popped a left at the potato of a nose, realizing in that instant it was absolutely the stupidest thing he could do, the very reaction that had been expected from him. Before he could pull the punch, it landed squarely. The Vietnamese countered with an expert front kick that struck DelCorso's bad leg like a club. Then a spinning back kick, delivered with a dancer's grace to his chest, doubled him over. The wind taken out of him, drawing in his elbows to guard his midsection, bringing up both fists to shield his face, DelCorso saw, over the rim of his knuckles, the butt end of the man's pistol just before it cracked into his forehead, knocking him unconscious.

EVERYONE STANDING in the aisle would have fallen if there had been room to fall when the driver abruptly stopped the bus halfway down the empty street, then jerked it into reverse.

"What the hell are you doing?" asked Bolton, seated behind the young, very nervous marine.

"Backin' it up," the marine said, his eyes on the rearview mirror. "I'm backin' up the bus, sir."

"*Why* are you backing up? Tan Son Nhut's the other way."

"It's a one-way street and I was goin' the wrong way."

Having ferried marines into combat, Bolton was acquainted with their mindless discipline and understood why this reason made perfect sense to the driver; but the other correspondents, or "evacuees" as they were now called, hooted, hollered, and banged their fists against the windows, covered with wire mesh against grenades or whatever else might be thrown at them.

"Hey, jughead," one newsman said, an undertone of hysteria in his voice, "you expect a medal for obeying the traffic laws in a combat zone?"

The lance corporal said nothing, but continued to back up until he reached the intersection, where he turned and went down the next block, one way in the opposite direction. His passengers whistled and applauded in derision. To listen to them, you would have thought them a high school football team on their way to an out-of-town game, but Bolton recognized their sarcastic raucousness as a mask for their fear. They were packed in the bus like tuna in a net; it would take only one disgruntled Arvin to toss a grenade under the wheels and send them all home in rubber bags.

The driver, following the route his detachment commander had given him at the assembly area, steered the bus down one street after another, passing each evacuation point to see if any stragglers had been left behind by the previous lifts.

"Look, marine," Bolton said, leaning over the back of the driver's seat, "if you're going to keep this up, why not go all the way and start announcing points of interest?"

"Sir?"

"We don't need a tour of Saigon. Just get us to the airfield."

"Sir, my orders were to check each evacuation point and pick up any stragglers."

"I'm a civilian. You don't have to 'sir' me. What're you going to do if you find fifty people waiting? Shove 'em in the luggage compartment? There isn't enough room in this thing for a chihuahua."

"I understand, sir, but . . ."

"Never mind." Bolton slumped back into his seat. "You've got your orders. Go ahead, take us around. Stop if you see a McDonald's. I'd like a Big Mac and an order of fries."

Tired from the day's hectic filing and from the residue of his hangover, on a shaky downslide from the Dexadrine high, Bolton shut his eyes. He had been in tight situations before, and on a scale of one to ten, he rated this a five at worst; he was reasonably confident they would reach the airfield, board the helicopters, and fly out intact. Shifting his body into a more comfortable position, he folded his arms across his chest. As he did so, the message in his front shirt pocket made a crumpling noise. Bolton didn't know why he'd saved it; a memento perhaps, the last herogram he would ever receive in Saigon. Opening his eyes, he took it out and read it with a wry smile.

292330 BOLTON: 291045 EVAC BEAT AP AND UPI FORTY FIVE MINUTES. ALL PLEASED HERE AND SEND CONGRATS. SAIGON BUREAU TO DALMAN TO COVER SOUTH VIET SURRENDER. BOLTON OUT TO COVER EVAC AND RETURN BEIRUT ASAPEST. CHRISTIAN MOSLEM FIGHTING ESCALATED INTO RELIGIOUS CIVIL WAR. RGDS/LUCAS/CABLES/NY.

A forty-five-minute beat. The Horseman had again ridden ahead of the rest of the herd. He was too damned good for his own good, doomed to this life by his professionalism and love of winning. And a fine life it was, wandering from one conflict to the next. If he ever did write a book, maybe he would entitle it *Bolton's Guide to the World's War Zones*. Yes, a fine life; at least he was never bothered by insurance salesmen calling to find out if he had adequate coverage.

He folded the message into his pocket and looked through the mesh at the passing city, vacant, shuttered, devoid of life. Saigon. The old whore had turned her last trick. Saigon, soon to be rechristened, according to Viet Cong broadcasts, Ho Chi

Minh City, was to be reformed and turned into a dull Socialist mother; the Paris of the Orient would become Moscow with palm trees.

A nostalgia edged with bitterness gripped Bolton. He had first glimpsed this city in the same way: through the wire-mesh windows of a military bus on a gray, humid afternoon. He was a young, ignorant soldier then—if not as young and ignorant as the driver of this bus, young and ignorant enough to believe that life was on the square, that officers knew what they were doing and therefore deserved respect, that the war was an adventure, and that he would compensate for his expulsion from the Citadel by becoming a comic-book war hero, flying into hot landing zones behind a blazing machine gun and winning medals while his former class-mates crammed for finals and escorted snobbish Charleston belles to tea dances. Oh, those girls. They hadn't thought much of Harry Bolton, not those ladies who pretended to such refined behavior in public but who would suck the bend out of a river if that's what it took to land a Citadel cadet for a husband—provided he had the right background and a respectable bank balance. But Bolton came from the western mountains, an up-country boy with no English or French Huguenot in his blood lines, and no money in his checking account. Back then, Saigon promised him the chance to show those stuck-up bitches just what an up-country boy could do. The old whore fulfilled her promise. She gave him his chance and he'd shown what an up-country boy could do: an up-country boy could take a bullet through the shoulder.

The bus had passed the Ministry of Social Welfare Building, circled the green patch of Kennedy Park, and was slowing down as it neared the brick, spired Saigon Cathedral, the last evacuation point on the route. The driver accelerated when he saw no one except a legless cripple, pushing himself down the sidewalk on what looked like a child's go-cart.

"Hold it, marine," Bolton ordered. "Hold it up."

"Sir?"

"Hold it up, I said. That Vietnamese back there is one of your stragglers."

"You sure?"

"He used to work for me," Bolton said; it was not com-pletely a lie, but an extreme expansion of the truth: eleven years ago, Bolton's squadron had flown Fast Eddie's battalion into the Battle of Tam Ky, where Eddie lost his legs and Bolton received his baptism of fire.

"All right," the driver said, throwing the shift into reverse. The marine guard posted at the front door with an M-16 asked what was going on.

"This guy says that Vietnamese back there near the church is an evacuee, a straggler. Says he used to work for him."

"Fuck, we ain't got no room for no one," said the guard, who was no less jumpy than the driver.

"What the hell, he ain't got no legs, so there's only half of him we got to get aboard."

"Okay, but we ain't puttin' that whatever the fuck it is he's ridin' on, we ain't puttin' that on."

A number of correspondents who heard this exchange now hooted at Bolton, complaining he was risking their lives for no good reason. When the bus stopped in front of the cathedral, he stood, so tall his head missed the roof by only a couple of inches, and shouldered a path to the door.

"No good reason?" he sneered at his colleagues. "Listen, he was a *trung-si*, a sergeant, in the Eleventh Rangers and the half of him that's left is a better reason than all your sorry asses put together."

Actually, he did not know why, on the impulse of the moment, he had decided to rescue Fast Eddie. It was the kind of boy-scout gesture DelCorso would make. Perhaps it had been Bolton's nostalgic mood: the old amputee represented a connection to his past, of which he wanted to salvage something.

"Everybody by the door back up," the driver commanded. "Back it up. I can't open the door."

There was a movement of bodies on the steps, Bolton fighting to stay in front. When the door folded open with a hydraulic hiss, he poked his head out and called:

"Hey, Fast Eddie, hey, *trung-si*."

Eddie, who had been propelling himself on the flats of his hands, raised them to allow the go-cart to glide on momentum. He looked toward the bus.

"*Trung-si*, it's me, Harry."

"Ha-ree! Ha-ree! You take me?"

"Yeah. C'mon, *lai dai. Maulen.*"

Fast Eddie's hands began to pump again.

"You said this guy used to work for you," said the marine guard. "You holding his papers?"

The question caught Bolton by surprise.

"What papers?"

"His evac papers. We ain't pickin' up every Vietnamese we see on the street, just the ones who worked for us over here or some other American outfit, and they gotta have the papers to prove it."

The marine, who was close to Bolton's size and who, in his flak jacket, looked as big as a football player in full equipment, stood barring the door, his rifle held at high port. Fast Eddie waited on the sidewalk, the cathedral behind him.

"Hey you, Ha-ree, you take me, you me we go."

"Yeah, Eddie, show your papers to this soldier," Bolton said, stalling for time until he could think of some plausible excuse for Eddie's lack of documents. But nothing came to him.

"Ha-ree. No unnastan'."

"Your papers, Eddie."

The guard's boyish face aged with a look of suspicion.

"All right, mister, you stay on the fuckin' bus." Then to the driver: "Bowlen, I'm going to check this gook out. Close the doors just in case."

"For Chrissake," Bolton said, "what do you think he's going to do? Pitch a grenade in here?"

By this time, the other passengers were nearly rioting, stomping their feet on the floor, cursing the marines and Bolton all at once. Through the door's dirty windows, Bolton saw the marine talking to Fast Eddie, on whose face the only expression was total bewilderment. Then the marine pounded on the glass and the driver opened the door.

"Mister," the guard shouted above the chorus of catcalls, "he hasn't got jackshit on him. Now if you don't have papers on him, he stays and we go."

"Listen, you sound like some East European border guard with this where-are-his-papers horseshit. I'll vouch that he's a certified, authorized grade-fucking-A U.S.-government-approved evacuee. Just get him on the bus."

"You listen," answered the marine, all crew cut, muscular authority. "I can put him on the bus, but they'll check him out at Tan Son Nhut, and if he don't pass muster, they'll leave him there. So you got your choice. Leave him here or leave him there."

The boom of artillery at the edges of the city was clearly audible; everyone aboard was chanting, "Let's go! Let's go!

Let's go!" Bolton was aware that Fast Eddie's fate depended on his wit, his ability to think quickly on his feet, but for once in his life, Bolton had nothing to say. A feeling of grief surged through him with such a sudden rush it was as though someone had injected a powerful depressant into his bloodstream.

"All right," he said, his voice a little unsteady, "leave him here."

"Door's clear, Bowlen," the guard said. "Shove off."

To the grateful cheers of the panicky passengers, the doors closed. As the bus lurched forward, knocking him against the dashboard, Bolton caught only a brief glimpse of Fast Eddie's trunk, perched atop the go-cart.

"That Vietnamese dude some sort of friend of yours?" said the guard, standing beside him with his rifle slung.

"Sort of. I was with a chopper squadron here. We flew his outfit into Tam Ky."

"Where?"

"Tam Ky," Bolton repeated, forgetting that this war had gone on so long that the young marine had neither heard of the place nor knew that a battle had once been fought there. "Maybe I thought that because we flew him into that hellhole back then, we owed it to him to fly him out now. Just trying to do something for him."

"I would have liked to help you out, but if you was in the service, you know how it is when they give you the word."

"Yeah. There never was a damned thing we could do for these people anyway."

PART TWO

—

1976

20

OPENING HIS EYES to the light obliquing through the french doors of the bedroom, DelCorso saw that Margaret, a habitual early riser, had already gone downstairs to make breakfast. She had fluffed her pillows and smoothed the cover sheet on her side of the queen-size bed, as though to remove any signs that she had been lying beside him only a short time ago; but her scent lingered where she had lain. DelCorso drew in the faint female musk, along with the Sunday-morning aromas of brewing coffee and frying bacon, and heard Danny and Angela playing with their blocks in the room across the hall. Rolling onto his back, he centered himself on the bed and stretched, his fingertips touching the headboard, his legs out over the edge of the mattress. The healthy flex of his muscles, the smells, the spring sunlight brightening the ocher walls of the room, and the sound of his children's voices inspired in him a feeling of domestic contentment. Wife, children, house: the furniture of his emotional address was in place.

Only one thing disturbed his tranquillity: the organ that gives a man moments of ecstasy at the price of years of regret stood under the bedsheet like a pole under a partially folded circus tent. He had had an erotic dream just before waking up. Consciousness had erased its details, but now, with Margaret's scent in his nostrils, he had a waking fantasy of taking her in his arms and making love to her all morning with crazed abandon. He might have tried if it had not been for Fiona, whose presence in the house, of which he was reminded by the shower hissing in the spare bathroom down the hall, prevented him from running downstairs naked with an erection. The children added another restraint. Also, he noticed that the electronic clock on Margaret's dresser was flashing eight-thirty. In half an hour, she would begin dressing the children for Sunday school and herself for ten o'clock mass at St. Charles. Even if the obstacles of Fiona, the children, and a mass schedule had not existed, he doubted that he and Margaret would have wound up uttering wild orgasmic cries amid tangled sheets. Except for her occasional lapses with alcohol, she was moderate in her behavior, a moderation that extended into the bedroom. She was tender and willing enough, but preferred wading in the gentle shallows of love and lacked whatever it took, courage or recklessness, to cast herself into the dark tides of passion.

DelCorso reached under the sheet and touched himself. It was the kind of erection he produced regularly when he was nineteen, but now not more often than once a month, the kind Bolton called a "blue head." He wrapped his fingers around it—it was thick, like the rest of him—and when, for the hell of it, he measured it by placing the heel of his hand at the base of his penis, the palm laid against the shaft, he was pleased to note that his hard-on extended beyond the tip of his middle finger. Close to seven inches and his beautiful wife just downstairs and he unable to do a thing, what a waste. Rejecting masturbation as a ridiculous outlet for a married man, DelCorso tried to soften the rigid tissue in his hand by thinking about the two dull but lucrative assignments he'd completed this month. One was a corporate-annual-report job for Simpson Electronics, the other a publicity campaign for Alcan Oil on the Gulf Coast; but the memory of the photographs he'd taken of microchips and minicircuits, of offshore rigs and cracking-plant gas fires flaring into purple Louisiana dusks could not efface from his mind visions of Margaret's dark red hair bursting like a sunrise on the pillow, her mouth parted, her eyes closed, her legs wrapped around his, white against olive. It was the lingering perfume of her body that breathed life into this erotic image and kept his penis pointed at the light fixture straight over head, pulling his bikini underwear so tight that his testicles ached.

"Danny! You took all the blue Lego blocks!" Angela's voice pierced the bedroom door.

"I did not."

"Did so."

"You used 'em all."

"Did not. There were a whole bunch more of blue blocks and you took them."

"You're crazy, Angie. Y'know that? You're nuts." Except for its soprano register, Danny's voice was an imitation of his father's, its inflections and intonations those of a street-bred wise guy.

"Am not crazy. Am not, am not. I built *four* blue houses for my village yesterday and now I can build only three. You *took* some of the blue blocks."

"You call that a village?"

"Is so a village."

"That's a crazy village. Crazy Angie's village."

"You stop saying I'm crazy."

"You are crazy."

"Where'd you put the blue Legos? I want the rest of the blue Legos to finish my village."

"I buried 'em in the blue-Lego-block cemetery."

Suddenly, DelCorso's heart began beating so fast that, looking down at his chest, he could see arteries squiggling like small snakes beneath his skin.

"If you don't tell me where you put them, I'm going to tell Mommy you *stole* them."

" 'I'm gonna tell Mommy, I'm gonna tell Mommy.' G'wan, g'wan and tell Mommy."

"All right for you."

DelCorso, his heart now pumping rapidly enough to give him fears of a coronary, heard a door open and Angela shout:

"Mommy! Mommy!"

There was no response from the kitchen. Village. DelCorso lay on his back taking deep breaths. In through the nose, out through the mouth, in and out. His problem with lust had been solved, his anxiety having shrunk his erection as quickly as an ice-cold shower. Village. Rach Giang. Crazy village. God, he hadn't had one of these attacks in—how long was it now? At least two years. Its sudden, unanticipated onset after all

this time was startling in itself, like a cancer victim's redis-
covery of a tumor that was supposed to have been surgically
removed. In through the nose, out through the mouth. In and
out. *Village.*

"MOMMY!"

DelCorso lunged out of bed, opened the door of his bedroom, and stood before his daughter, unmindful of his near-
nudity.

"Damn it, Angela, don't scream like that."

Agitated as he was, DelCorso could not help but feel a
spontaneous love at the sight of her small figure, standing in
a cotton nightdress at the head of the stairs, her hair, like his,
all midnight waves, her eyes, like his, burnt umber.

"Daddy! You're in your underpants!"

"That's right, Angela Rose, and I'll lay a strap over *your*
underpants if you scream like that again."

"Danny *stole* my blue Legos," his daughter said, a fire
burning under her earth-brown eyes. She had his temper as
well as his coloring, and he knew she would be trouble when
she grew older.

"All right. Danny."

"Yes, Dad," answered Danny from the children's bedroom.

"C'mon out here."

Danny, who was tall for his age—he looked closer to nine
than to seven—and who had his mother's hair and fair skin,
stood in the doorway, his pale eyes looking in suppressed
amusement at his father, dressed only in a pair of skin-tight
blue underwear.

"Did you take your sister's Lego blocks?"

"She's crazy, Dad. Her and her crazy village."

Village.

"Did you take those damn blocks?"

"Yeah, okay, I took 'em."

"What do you mean, 'yeah'?"

"I mean, yes, Dad."

"That's better. Okay. It's quarter to nine. The two of you
forget about the Legos and get dressed for Sunday school and
mass."

"*Yuck.*" Danny screwed his freckled face into a grimace.
To look at the kid you'd never believe there was Italian blood
in him. Face like a map of Ireland. "Yucky Sunday school.
Why do I have to go to Sunday school?"

"Because you'll be making your first communion."

"Sunday school's boring."

"I know," said DelCorso, remembering from his childhood the interminable hours memorizing the Baltimore catechism. "But you've got to go if you're going to make your first communion."

"Did you make your first communion?"

"Sure I did."

"How come you don't go to mass, then?"

"That's my business. Now get dressed, the both of you."

"Mommy doesn't want us to get dressed before breakfast," said Angela, as if she were instructing a new stepfather on the routines and rhythms of a household strange to him. "She's afraid we'll spill stuff on our clothes."

"Go to breakfast, then. Just don't fight. Understand? I've been on the road a month, it's Sunday morning, and I want it quiet."

"Okay, Dad."

He went back into the room, closing the door behind him. Settling the dispute between his children had calmed him, but he remained shocked by the unexpected attack of nerves. Village. Angela's mere utterance of the word had recomposed the mental image of Margaret: her face became the face of another woman with parted lips and eyes closed, closed forever, one of three dozen corpses littering the rubble of Rach Giang.

"Danny, Angela. Breakfast," Margaret trilled from downstairs.

"Coming," Angela answered.

"And tell your father."

His son and daughter thudded down the stairs, Angela calling, "Breakfast, Daddy, breakfast."

THE CHILDREN HAD RETURNED to their room to dress. Margaret was feeding the scraps from the breakfast dishes to the growling disposal and DelCorso puffed on a cigarette over his third cup of coffee. He had not recaptured his earlier tranquillity.

"I woke up this morning as horny as a goat," he said, affecting a bantering tone utterly out of tune with his inner turbulence. He had become fairly expert at this form of vocal masquerading because Margaret, though a champion when it came to social chitchat, was not a woman with whom one could hold serious conversations easily. She tended to avoid them, probably out of the same caution that made her withdraw from the drop-offs of sexual passion.

"That isn't news, Nick. That's how you wake up every morning."

"I mean really horny. I wanted to lock the kids in their room, tell Fiona to take a hike, and screw your brains out all morning."

Margaret said nothing. With a glance at the clock hanging on the wall beside the refrigerator, she scraped a plate, transferred it to the dishwasher, then picked up another and scraped it, the disposal snarling like a dog with a metal larynx.

"You interested in hearing the details?"

"I've been your wife nearly eight years, Nick, but I still like to be courted."

"You weren't there to court. You were down here."

"I mean I would be interested in the details if you had said you wanted to make love to me all morning. Somehow the idea of having my brains screwed out doesn't excite me."

DelCorso snuffed his cigarette, simultaneously annoyed by her propriety and ashamed of himself for speaking to her as if she were some cheap number he'd picked up in a bar.

"Okay, m'lady, I wanted to make love to you all morning."

"We did last night."

"Does that mean we've used up our allotment for the week?"

"Of course not," Margaret assured him as she checked the clock again. Nine twenty-five. DelCorso knew by her movements, which now evidenced a jerky, nervous tension, that she was running late. She attended the ten o'clock mass without fail; it was part of the unaltering household schedule she maintained because she was an organized woman by nature and because, he supposed, it helped her cope with his continual absences.

The last plate was scraped and the intermittent roar of the disposal replaced by the hum of the dishwasher. Without missing a step, Margaret wet a cloth under the faucet and started to wipe the table.

"Hey, Maggie, if we can't make love, do you think we could at least *talk*?"

"We are talking."

"I mean talk talk." Finishing his coffee, DelCorso stood

and dropped the cup and saucer in the sink, allowing the clatter to italicize his irritation. "You know, sit down and talk. Just the two of us. You're polishing this place up like you're expecting a photographer from the home and design section of the *Times* to show up any second."

"You know I hate to come back from church to a mess," she said, now giving the tiled countertop a once-over.

"Fiona can do it. That's what she's paid for."

"Sunday's her day off."

"Then I'll do it while you and the kids are at mass."

Margaret's oval mouth formed one of her queenly smiles. Then she kissed him on the forehead.

"Thanks for the offer."

"You don't believe I'd do it," he said, stretching himself to his full height. In the inch-and-a-half Scandinavian clogs she was wearing, she stood a little over his five-ten, and it bothered him that she'd been able to kiss him above the eyebrows without raising her chin.

"I *know* you wouldn't. My Italian macho man hasn't washed a dish or wiped a table in his life."

"I could start."

"Not doing the dishes isn't one of your flaws."

"What are my flaws?"

"They're not worth mentioning."

"Mention one anyway."

"All right. The street kid in you, the one who makes you say things like 'I'd like to screw your brains out,' that sort of coarseness. But it isn't important enough to mention."

"But you've thought about it."

"Oh, for God's sake." Margaret looked at the clock as if she were expecting a bomb to go off. "I love you, Nick, and I love you for what you are."

"Maybe that's what I wanted to talk about, Maggie," he said, dropping the bantering tone. "Not about going to bed."

"What, then?"

"About what I am."

"What you are? You're my husband and a photographer and a very good one."

"Husband or photographer?" he asked, already backing away from a direct confession. What was the use anyway? Margaret was wriggling like a woman who has to go to the bathroom urgently but is continuing a conversation out of politeness.

"Both," she answered, again kissing his forehead. "Nick, I've got to get moving. We can talk when I get back."

"Sure."

THE BELL AT ST. CHARLES WAS tolling ten, reminding DelCorso of Sundays in the Valley. He wandered through the empty house in search of something that would hold his attention so he could keep the memory of Rach Giang at bay.

From the kitchen, where the sun glanced off the glazed counter tiles, he sauntered into the dining room, in whose curtained half-light he admired the symmetry of the round, inlaid walnut table, the credenza, and the breakfront with its tidy display of china. He merely glanced at the parlor, which Margaret had furnished in French Empire, bumblebee motifs sewn into the chaise longue on which she read at night, a room so elegantly formal he could not stand to be in it for longer than five minutes. His mind was diverted for a while in the small library, adjacent to the parlor, but he did not feel much more comfortable there. For one thing, almost all of the books were Margaret's—except for military histories and books about photography, DelCorso read very little; for another, Margaret's choice and arrangement of the furniture created in miniature a copy of her father's library in Marblehead. DelCorso wondered at times if she had done this because she believed all men, like Thomas Fitzgerald, had a taste for leather, wood, and brass or because she wanted to impress the old man on the rare occasions when he visited. Maybe the room was meant to make a statement to him: this library is very much like yours, Father, and Nick is not as different as you thought; *I did not make a mistake marrying him.*

But when DelCorso sat on the Chesterfield couch, his eyes roving over the shelves and the wall where his major awards hung in simple black frames, his thoughts took a Calvinistic bent. The room and everything in it spoke of success and respectability. He was inclined to think that he would not be the winner of prestigious awards, the owner of this house, the husband of a beautiful, well-born woman, the father of two healthy children for whom he could afford the luxury of a governess if the world had not forgiven him. Therefore, it wasn't necessary to make a confession to Margaret and hope for her forgiveness; it would be as senseless as admitting to an affair long since over. *I love you for what you are.* True, she did not fully know him for what he was; he had never shared with her the secret he knew about himself. And yet, a woman as good as she would instinctively have sensed a stain on his soul and, sensing it, would have been unable to love him. So her love and acceptance, like the house, the prizes, and his money, was another sign that he had been absolved.

On the other hand, Margaret was naïve. She was a virgin when DelCorso married her, in mind as well as body. She knew as much about the world as a young woman raised under her privileged circumstances could be expected to know— next to nothing. Nor had she ever shown much eagerness to overcome her ignorance; she seemed to recognize intuitively that she hadn't been prepared to deal with the age into which she'd been born and that her survival depended on the main- tenance of an environment from which the pollutants of real- ity would be filtered out. The first time DelCorso saw her, she was playing tennis on the courts at Columbia University, she and another graduate assistant: two girls in whites vol- leying a ball while radicals occupying buildings on the other end of campus cried revolution and tear-gas canisters exploded and skulls bled under the swat of police batons.

DelCorso, who had been covering the sit-in turned riot, watched them through the high Cyclone fence enclosing the courts. He could hear the urgent, pulsating cries of police and ambulance sirens near the quadrangle, but the two women, a tall redhead and a shorter brunette, went on with their game as though heaven had lowered an invisible, soundproof bubble over them.

Standing with one foot slightly behind the other, graceful in her height, the redhead reached into the pocket of her skirt, then, rising on her toes with the fluid ease of a ballet dancer, tossed a second ball into the air and drove it over the net, her body bending forward on the follow-through so that her skirt rose to give a teasing glimpse of her white panties.

When her partner's return struck the net, the redhead smiled as DelCorso had never seen a woman smile before, a burst of white between her lips. White teeth, white skin, white blouse, white skirt, white panties, white tennis shoes and socks. The whiteness of a nun's summer habit. He was fascinated not only by her pristine beauty but by her ability to play with such calm concentration that the sit-in might as well have been taking place on a campus in North Dakota. In his cap- tivation, he forgot he was on deadline, he forgot the smell of

21

DELCORSO POPPED OUT of the chair. One of his fits of
restlessness had seized him, a foot-itching, feverish need to
go somewhere. It disturbed him; usually, a month or more at
home had to pass before he started feeling this way, but here
he was, back less than seventy-two hours, and ready to hop
on a train, plane, or bus. His disquiet had something to do
with his reverie about Margaret, though he could not quite
put his finger on it. Something *was* wrong, not so much with
her as with—with what? With this whole setup, he thought,
gazing around the library; but he wasn't able to put his finger
on that either. He only knew that the house had suddenly
taken on an alien quality, as though he were a visitor or in-
truder.

Unable to sit still, he continued his aimless house tour,
trying to expurgate the feeling that he did not belong here. He
wandered through the children's room, where he caught sight
of the village Angela had built of Lego blocks, white walls
under blue roofs. One of the houses—was his imagination
working overtime?—resembled a pagoda, like the pagoda B
Company, in its violent ecstasy, had blown to powder with
satchel charges. *Village.*

Stepping across the hall, its oak floors gleaming like the
varnished deck of a yacht, he entered the bathroom and uri-

nated. Mrs. Watkins, the cleaning lady, had been in on Friday, and the toilet bowl, sink, and bathtub sparkled. Somehow, the antiseptic fixtures heightened his sense of being in a strange place. On an impulse, he opened the medicine chest to check Margaret's Valium. The label said the prescription had been filled on February 15, six weeks ago, and the bottle was nearly full, a good sign. Full bottles of Valium and full bottles of vodka meant a happy Margaret. The more-or-less normal life he'd been leading the past year had been the key to her contentment. His only news assignments had been safe outings—a two-week jaunt with the Carter campaign and a week at a refugee center in California, covering the arrival of Vietnamese boat people. Although he'd been away a good deal, Margaret could look upon herself as essentially no different from the wife of a traveling businessman.

Which, DelCorso reflected as he passed into the master bedroom, is exactly what I've been the past year. A highly paid peddler of commercial pictures. That was one of the things troubling him. He had no prejudices against commerce or making money; with gasoline prices up, an increase in his property taxes, and his son attending St. Paul's, whose annual tuition looked like the price sticker on a Lincoln Mark IV, he needed to salt away as much as he could.

Was that the sole source of his unrest? DelCorso wanted to lie down and reflect on this question, but Margaret, the domestic wonder woman, had made the bed in the five minutes she had to spare between dressing and leaving for mass; and she'd made it so perfectly a drill sergeant would have awarded her a meritorious promotion. It did not invite DelCorso to lie down, it repelled him in the way a freshly shampooed carpet repels one from walking on it with dirty shoes. Christ, I ought to mess this place up just to prove it's a home and not a museum. Tear the bed apart, take a bath and leave a ring in the tub, fill the ashtrays with cigarette butts, spill coffee on the kitchen table. All this excessive neatness and order—somehow it felt like death.

He sat in the chair and scanned the room, whose dark, heavy furniture looked as though it belonged in the hacienda of a Spanish grandee. That's me, Don Nicholas, lord of the manor. All right, Don Nicholas, just what is bothering you? Three days ago, driving up to New Orleans from Morgan City, you were so excited about flying home to New York after a month of motel rooms and solitary meals that you turned down an invitation from Alcan's PR director for a weekend in the French Quarter. Now you're restless again and everything in this house irritates you. Just what the hell is eating you?

His inner voices were mute. He could not relax in this overly tidy house, and therefore couldn't concentrate. The only thing to do was to leave for a while, take a walk and clear his head.

It was balmy for early April, buds appearing on the trees. Low clouds raced on a southerly wind, which smelled faintly of the sea, and the wind and the light Sunday traffic gave the air a clarity it might have had before the invention of the automobile. DelCorso walked down Willow Place, headed for the bridge.

In a cul-de-sac near the promenade, two teen-age boys played roller hockey, using garbage-can lids as goal markers. He paused to watch them, but the noise of the skates got on his nerves, and the boys' quick turns and stops reminded him too much of an agility he had lost forever. Strolling along the promenade, the river below him, he gazed across to Manhattan, which resembled an enormous barge carrying a cargo of gigantic boxes.

After crossing the Brooklyn Bridge, whose sweeping guys and buttresses always moved him, he walked to Mulberry Street, nearly empty on this late Sunday morning. Little Italy—its resemblance to the Valley made him feel at home. In the shadows of the tenements, down the treeless sidewalks, he passed Lombardi's restaurant and the D & G Bakery and Rocky's, the lunch joint where he sometimes ate with the firemen from Engine Company Fifty-five. L. J. Latona, the mortician, was closed. Death takes a holiday. At the Italian men's club across the way, a club very much like the one DelCorso's grandfather had belonged to, old men were playing cards while an espresso machine hissed and gave off its wonderful aroma. From Mulberry, he turned onto Broome, where the fire station was squeezed between Italian groceries and Chinese laundries, and the smells of lettuce and fruit clinging to the empty crates outside reminded DelCorso that he hadn't eaten. By the time he reached Grand and Mott, the cheeses and salamis hanging in the barred windows of Dipolo's made his mouth water.

Near his loft, he popped three quarters into a newspaper box and scanned the headlines. OPEC CONSIDERING NEW OIL-PRICE HIKE . . . CARTER PLEDGES EMPHASIS ON HUMAN RIGHTS IF ELECTED . . . PATTY HEARST TO APPEAL CONVICTION . . . FIGHTING CONTINUES IN BEIRUT . . . MOSLEMS, CHRISTIANS BATTLE SECOND DAY FOR HOLIDAY INN . . . GNP SLOWS TO 4.5 PERCENT IN FIRST QUARTER . . . CITY'S PLANS FOR BICENTENNIAL NEAR COMPLETION . . . THAI PRIME MINISTER MAY LOSE SEAT IN NEW ELECTIONS . . .

He had not kept up with the news the last few days of his trip. Lugging the *Times* under his arm, he went to the loft.

It was in a gloomy building at Spring and Greene, an old warehouse whose freight elevators had been bricked up and whose floors had been converted into trendy apartments for well-heeled bohemians or into studios for artists and photographers. DelCorso's occupied half of the top floor; a painter had the other half, where the windows admitted the northern light.

He put a small espresso pot on the hot plate. When it had brewed, he poured the strong coffee into a demitasse, added sugar and a slice of lemon from the refrigerator, then sat in his swivel desk chair, leaning back against one of the file cabinets that held his negatives and transparencies. The cabinets stood flush against the wall dividing the darkroom from the rest of the studio, which looked like the lair of a shady private detective. Smoking a cigarette and savoring the coffee, DelCorso flipped through the slides from his last two assignments. He had a notion to index and file them, not because it was a job needing immediate attention but because it might help him resist the temptation to read the story about the war in Beirut. Shouldn't have bought the damned paper. The hell with it, I don't feel like indexing transparencies, most boring part about this business.

As he read the story, he felt a prickling in his skin and a warm, rushing sensation in his head. He recognized these as the physical symptoms of his compulsion to be where the action is, to walk along the edge, to escape the everyday by throwing himself into conditions of extremes. He wondered if Vincent had been right about him; maybe he was incapable of going to work and then home like most men. Action junkie. Action junkies were hooked on the pursuit of an intensity of emotion they could find only in conditions of violence or danger. It was a common addiction among war photographers and correspondents; like an addiction to heroin or cocaine, the habit required ever-increasing dosages for its satisfaction, and its consequences were catastrophic: you got killed or you burned out. Poor old Sean Flynn. He'd called himself a photographer, but he'd only been playing a role out of one of his father's movies, taking risks for the sake of risk, ending up among the missing in Cambodia. Or Tom Payton, who couldn't get enough of it until it gave him more than he could handle. Payton overdosed. The last DelCorso heard, he was working as a house painter somewhere on the West Coast, a plate in his skull and the rest of him held together with pins and skin grafts.

DelCorso refilled his cup, adding another two spoonfuls of sugar to take the edge off his hunger. He rebelled against the thought that Flynn and Payton's habit afflicted him, not only because its consequences were awful, but because it would eventually make his work no better than theirs. They had got up close, and yet their photographs lacked the truth proximity was supposed to bring. A sense of connection, of reciprocity, of shared suffering was missing. Their pictures were little more than daredevil stunts. Look, Ma, no hands.

He rummaged through the paper, glancing at the sports page—the Yankees had won an exhibition game, Ali was to fight Jimmy Young later in the month—then at the back pages of the first section—a gas-station owner in Utah claimed to be one of the heirs to the Howard Hughes fortune—but nothing held his interest. The Lebanese story, accompanied by a wire-service photo showing Palestinian guerrillas firing from a barricade, kept drawing his eyes; and though the picture was routine, bulletin-board photography, the smoke, the bullet-eaten walls in the background, and the postures of the guerrillas, leaning forward against the recoil of their AK-47s, again brought the tingling to his skin, the feverish rush to his brain. Why in the hell *did* he want to go there if he couldn't make a good case for action addiction? Try boredom. He could make a good case for boredom. Today was Sunday, a day that had oppressed him for as long as he could remember. The drab predictability of ordinary life was intensified on Sunday, with its domestic obligations, its set routines of church and family gatherings. Sundays made him feel trapped. He'd felt trapped all this year: there was no way he could convince himself that photographing microchips and oil refineries was interesting, satisfying, or important except in the sense that corporate assignments made him rich: after taking off his agency's forty percent, he'd earned eight thousand off the Alcan assignment alone. Eight grand for ten days' work. He hadn't made that much in a year when he started with AP. He felt almost nostalgic for the hungry, ambitious kid he'd been then. The kid who'd fallen in love at first sight with a tall redhead in spotless whites.

Maggie. A portrait he'd taken of her hung on the brick wall behind his desk. He was hungry no more, thanks to her. Did he need to earn eight thousand in ten days? Yes and no. He did because she needed him to. Early in the marriage, she'd discovered that marrying down incurred certain liabilities she was unwilling or unable to accept. He recalled the time shortly after Danny was born. It was DelCorso's second year of freelancing. He was doing well for a novice, but the couple were living in a small walk-up on East Seventy-fourth, half a block off Third Avenue. He'd come home one afternoon to find Margaret nestled in a chair beside a half-emptied pitcher of vodka martinis. Danny was crying in his crib, the apartment in total disarray, dust rags scattered here and there, the vacuum cleaner, still plugged in, standing silent watch in the middle of the living room, an unpacked bag of groceries sitting on the kitchen table. Maggie was reading *The New Yorker* while she drank. What was wrong? She looked up, or, rather, seemed to look down from the heights to which her vodka-fueled rocket had powered her. Nothing, she replied in a tone that said just the opposite. What the hell was the matter? he insisted. It took a while to get it out of her and then it flooded out. The apartment was too small, the neighborhood seedy; she had to lug groceries and laundry up two flights of stairs, she couldn't seem to keep up with everything, with the cleaning and cooking and caring for the baby. She felt like a drudge, and was not going to allow herself to turn into some dumpy hausfrau; so she'd taken the afternoon off to read and have a few drinks. DelCorso, angry at first, was tempted to give her a son-of-the-working-class speech, praising his mother, who cooked, cleaned, and raised four sons in an apartment only one room larger than this one, lugged groceries up *three* flights of stairs, did laundry in an old Maytag, the kind with a hand-cranked wringer, took on part-time jobs to help make ends meet, bagging groceries in a market, waitressing in a short-order joint frequented by beat cops, numbers runners, and bookies, and never, as DelCorso recalled, took an afternoon off to read and get blitzed on vodka martinis. But before he could speak a word of this, Margaret started crying; his heart went out to her. He knew she was trying hard to be the Perfect Traditional Wife and was simply finding herself not up to it. And, when he thought about it, he did not want her to turn into some dumpy hausfrau, either. Looking at her, sitting in that drab, cramped apartment, he felt guilty, as if he'd harnessed a thoroughbred to a plow.

In the end, they entered into an unspoken agreement that day: in exchange for allowing him the freedom to pursue his nomadic career, he would slave to earn the money required to create a world in which she would remain contented and beautiful forever, a world easy, convenient, and manageable. There was a subclause in the contract, its print so fine DelCorso could hardly read it at the time: this world was to be made emotionally as well as physically manageable. Human and mechanical servants would take the drudgery out of Margaret's life; a protective atmosphere of order would save her from having to deal with those facts about modern existence she found disgusting. The last quarter of the twentieth century, with its confusing voices, its nasty little wars, its social upheavals, its morbid self-consciousness, liberties, shoddiness, opportunities, and temptations, was to be locked out. In spirit and appearance, the DelCorso household was to be a replica of the households of 1950s television dramas, with Margaret adding just the right touch of style. He wanted it that way and she wanted it that way, and so far, they had pulled it off. DelCorso, however, had lately grown more and more conscious of an artificiality permeating their way of life, a certain lack of synchronicity between it and their times. If some couples they knew had gone too far in one direction, following every new trend, however silly, latching on to every new idea, however absurd, he and Margaret had gone too far in the other. Their home was something of a museum, their marriage something of a period piece. He was also aware that keeping it that way was extracting a high emotional price, forcing a kind of tension; it was as though he and Margaret were on an Interstate in a handsome antique automobile, all the while glancing in the rearview mirror for the turbo-charged eighteen-wheeler that would smash into them at seventy miles an hour.

No smoking diesel on the horizon yet. DelCorso could see how well he and Margaret were upholding their bargain by glancing at the portrait, taken only a few months ago. If any over-thirty wrinkles creased her skin, he would need an electron microscope to find them. It was the museum's chief exhibit, the preservation of Margaret's beauty. Photographing wars has not destroyed my faith in beauty, he thought, his eyes shifting to a blow-up of a flock of sheep flooding over a barren Irish hill. The photograph had turned out as he'd wanted it, Maggie had turned out as he had wanted, her looks and innocence intact. Her innocence: she wore it like a suit of armor and DelCorso kept the metal bright. He saw in that mirror a reflection of his own innocence, an image of himself untarnished by the guilt of his filthy little secret; and if that image was merely an illusion, well, he'd dealt with enough gritty realities to know that illusions were sometimes necessary to get through the day without cracking up.

Village.

DelCorso stood and paced the room, the wooden floors creaking underfoot. He stopped to stare out the dusty window, down at Caselmo's Gallery across Greene Street, one of the slick, track-lighted art galleries that had sprung up after the paint-and-brush set discovered this part of Little Italy and renamed it Soho. Turning, he looked at the row of file cabinets, all but one marked with job and assignment numbers, dates, subject index numbers, record codes, numbers, numbers. Margaret. With her organizational talents, she had set up this filing system for him. His own had been a mess, and for this alone, he felt he owed her a great deal, enough to make him dislike himself for the unkind thoughts he occasionally had about her. The green cabinets stood in a rank, seemingly looking back at him. Prints, negatives, transparencies, and contact proofs. DelCorso's Gallery. His eyes fell on the unmarked drawer in which he stored the evidence of his secret. It was, so to speak, a wing of the gallery closed to the public. No one but he had ever seen the pictures in there. No one ever would. Illusions were necessary sometimes; at other times it was necessary to stare the monster in the face, without the benefit of a mental filter to soften its ugly features. Unlocking the cabinet, he opened the drawer. The prints were stuffed in several manila envelopes under a stack of old tax returns, letters, caption carbons, and marketing lists. He had taken the pictures ten years ago, April 1966, the day he first saw the monster get loose. He hadn't looked at them for a long time. Stare the monster in the face to remind yourself of its existence, to remind yourself that men are capable of almost anything when the cage is open and that you, as a member of humankind, are no less likely to turn the key when the beast wants out. He kept the prints as another kind of reminder: that in the photography of war, it wasn't courage that counted, though courage was needed; it wasn't closeness, though you had to be close to arrest the truth; and it wasn't the lens, the angle, or technique. The critical difference was made by purpose in the photographer's mind, the purpose above all.

DelCorso opened one of the envelopes and held a print up to the light. Its tones fading, its contrasts growing less distinct, it could be mistaken for a still life when looked at from a distance. He had intended it to look like a still life. He had, like any still-life photographer, arranged his subject. By chance, half the bodies had fallen in a rough semicircle around the village well. DelCorso persuaded two marines to drag more corpses from elsewhere to complete the circle; then he climbed a low mound and framed the scene from above; in the print, the well appeared as the center of a flower, the dead as its tattered petals. Most of the other photos recorded events that needed no staging. One print froze the grins of three paratroopers having a good time over a Viet Cong whose legs had been sheared off above the knees. The trunk lay on its side, a burning cigarette stuck to the lips of the face with its white, staring eyes.

DelCorso went on with his private show: The interior of a hut just beginning to burn, smoke fingering between the bamboo poles to touch the body of a guerrilla, identifiable as a VC by his webbed cartridge belt; the others were civilians, seven, eight, or nine of them—it was difficult to tell how many—men, women, and children shredded by automatic-rifle fire, limbs promiscuously tangled. Look the monster in the face. DelCorso forced himself to go on, through more pictures of bodies and bits of bodies and flaming huts, of the demolished pagoda, a chubby, shrapnel-chipped buddha knocked from its altar, its stone eyes gazing benignly at a soldier who, with a knife drawn, was doing something to a corpse.

Sweating, his hands like a drunk's in need of a shot, DelCorso flipped through the entire collection, and some of the photographs had a reality so overwhelming the great Goya would not have been able to stomach them. Some made DelCorso feel the way he had when he was twelve and found a packet of pornography in a trash can: shocked, ashamed, fascinated. Seeing something he was not meant to see and yet had.

He replaced the envelopes in the file and locked the cabinet, hiding the key in a desk drawer. If, through some darkroom sorcery, he was able to blend all those images of massacre and atrocity into one mural-size montage, the impression would be of a scene in a world of fire and death ruled by chaos, where men obeyed the voice that urged them to go beyond their reason. But he would never publish the pictures in any form. He would never show them to anyone because they made no indictment and no appeal to reason. The purpose, the purpose above all. What purpose did he have when he went into Rach Giang with B Company? None that he could recall. He had been swept up in the tide of hysteria that carried the paratroopers into a condition so far beyond the ordinary it seemed nothing could ever recall them; they were totally free to do as they wished, and the experience had been strangely exhilarating. DelCorso had gone in, pressing his shutter button as unthinkingly as the soldiers pulled their triggers, aiming his lens as indiscriminately as they did their rifles. He'd shot the butchered family moments after they'd been cut down. Almost literally shot them. Some were still alive when he ran into the hut; they died in the time it took him to adjust his setting to the dim light and compose the picture, so that, when he exposed the frame, it was as though he had murdered them with his camera. He felt no remorse at that moment, only a cruel satisfaction in the bloodshed, and that cruelty was in the photographs. None of them cried out, *This is what happens and we must try to avoid its happening again*; they said, rather, *This is inevitable*, and in stating it was inevitable, conferred a legitimacy upon it.

Two nights later, in his tent at division headquarters, he heard his gods speak to him for the first time. The division psychiatrist later explained these voices as auditory hallucinations caused by a religious hysteria resulting from a post-traumatic reaction. Medical gobbledygook. DelCorso had heard them after he'd awakened from his nightmare and, soaking wet, his heart drumming, his lungs paralyzed, sprung up in his cot, tearing at the mosquito net because he thought he was suffocating. They spoke to him as the ancient gods had spoken to ancient men, directly, without the intercession of clergy, and told him he had incurred a debt too heavy to be paid all at once. He would have to reduce it in installments, he would have to use his talents to make the indictment he had failed to make in Rach Giang. That was the assignment his gods had given him on a sultry, flare-lit night in Vietnam a decade ago. He had heard them, and no matter what the psychiatrist had said, DelCorso knew their voices were not imaginary; they were no less real or more unreal than the voice of the God worshiped in cathedrals, mosques, and temples.

The phone was as loud and startling as a fire alarm. DelCorso, feeling dizzy, stared at it as it rang again. Who the hell would be calling him here on a Sunday? He picked it up on the third ring.

"Nick . . ."

"It's you," he said distractedly.

"Who did you think it was?"

Something was the matter; Margaret's voice had its scolding schoolmarm tone.

"I didn't know."

"I figured you'd be there. It's one-thirty."

DelCorso paused. Half his mind was still ten years in the past and ten thousand miles away, and he couldn't grasp the significance of this chronological information.

"Yeah, you're right," he said, looking at his watch. "One-thirty."

"We'll wait if you can get a cab back."

Christ, he'd forgotten. Margaret's household bureaucracy scheduled Sunday dinners for one.

"I'm sorry, Maggie. It slipped my mind. Don't fly off the handle."

"I don't fly off handles. I'm just annoyed, that's all. It seems to me—"

"It seems to you that a man who spends so much time on the road could at least have the courtesy to be on time for Sunday dinner with the family. I know the speech, Maggie, and I don't need to hear it today. I'm sorry, all right?"

"Do you think you could be here in twenty minutes? I'm keeping everything warm in the oven."

"If I can get a cab."

22

―――――

DALMAN WAS HANGING OVER the balcony like a seasick passenger. After he'd spilled his breakfast onto the street, six floors below, a tremor of dry heaves shook his body. Less than a mile away, the Moslems and Christians were finishing the first movement of their daily concert of death, the wild scherzos of automatic-rifle fire building to a blazing finale that fell off quickly to a coda of dynamite blasts. Another spasm wracked Dalman, who made a sound like water trying to force its way through a clogged pipe. Poor son of a bitch. IPS had rewarded him for holding the fort in Saigon by assigning him to the Paris bureau after the Communists expelled him from Vietnam. He'd grown soft covering nothing more dangerous than the French parliament and going to bed each night assured that the next morning would bring no terrifying surprises. Also, Bolton thought, he'd grown stupid as well.

"Hey," he called through the shattered window, "if you don't get sniped out there, you'll get dinged by a stray round. You gotta puke, puke in the head."

Dalman, his rounded face a dingy green so that his eyes resembled gray chips in a plate of weathered copper, walked back in. He held his head stiffly to avoid looking at Nabil, whose body made even Bolton a little queasy.

"God, Harry. Goddamnit, even Nam—"

"Yeah, everybody says that. Even Nam wasn't like this. Nothing anywhere was ever like this. This one's unique, but you'd better get used to it. You've got to do ninety days, same as the others. If you're still alive and sane at the end of it, you'll go back to gay Paree."

"I want out *now*."

"It's only your first day on the job. I need another white man in this bureau, Dalman, and you're it for the next three months. You'll get used to it."

"How in the hell can anyone get used to something like that?" He cocked his head in the direction of Nabil's corpse, slumped against a wall in a thick pool of blood that was speckled with shards of broken glass. "Christ, I was talking to the kid yesterday."

"What the Looney Tunes did to him is standard operating procedure for both sides when they capture a sniper. One side does it in the name of Jesus and the other in the name of Muhammad."

"Jesus and Muhammad, Jesus and Muhammad," Dalman said, as if the repetition of those two sacred names would help him comprehend the horror. "Jesus and Muhammad."

"Go in the head and clean up. This place smells bad enough without you walking around with puke on your shirt."

"Last year I heard Vinnie call you a first-class asshole. He was being kind."

"Quit whining."

While Dalman washed up, Bolton assessed the damage to the bureau office: three windows shot out, two teletypes smashed, a few chairs broken, a few hundred Lebanese pounds stolen from the petty-cash fund. All in all, it wasn't bad. When he'd heard the office had been hit, he'd expected a total shambles: the vicious excesses of the Looney Tunes were legend even in Beirut, where vicious excesses had become commonplace. Perhaps they'd gone easy so as not to lose the protection Bolton paid them to keep the office in operation. Perhaps they had simply expended their savagery on Nabil and hadn't had enough left to thoroughly trash the office. Bolton looked at the wreckage of what had been one of his night-shift teletype operators and wished Raymond would return and get the body out of here. The salty smell of blood and the musk of urine—the odors of new death—permeated the room.

Dalman came out of the bathroom, water stains on the front of his blue, military-style shirt. Why did all these young

correspondents doll themselves up to look like British officers? Bolton wondered. He sat on the edge of the desk, un-
folding a large street map of Beirut, down the center of which
he had drawn an irregular green line.

"Grab that chair over there and I'll give you a fill," he said.
"And a few tips on how to get through this alive."

"You're fucking kidding."

"No, I'm not kidding."

"You expect me to sit here and get a fill-in from you with
that mess over there?"

"Raymond'll be up in a few minutes and get rid of it."

"And while we're waiting for him, you're just going to sit
there and give me a *fill*? What in the hell's happened to you?"

Bolton, his palms flat on the desk, took a few deep breaths
to restrain himself from flinging Dalman into the chair. Outside, the second movement was just beginning, AK-47s firing
short bursts allegro, rocket-propelled grenades providing per-
cussion.

"Hear that? That's what's happened to me. I've been covering this butchery since day one. It'll be a year in May. You're
a college boy, Dalman. Ever read Thomas Hobbes?"

"*Leviathan?*"

"Right. What we have in Beirut is the Hobbesian state of
nature, or something damn close to it. Every man fighting
every other man. To give you some idea what it's like, imagine
taking the meanest street gangs in Chicago, Detroit, and New
York, then releasing all the murderers and rapists from all the
maximum-security prisons, then all the violent psychotics
from the lunatic asylums, arm the whole bunch with AKs,
RPGs, and machine guns and give 'em free rein to have at it.
That's what it's like here. When the Christians aren't fighting
the Moslems, they're fighting each other; when the Lebanese
Moslems and the Palestinians aren't fighting the Christians,
they're fighting each other. Sometimes one Palestinian faction
will join the Lebanese to fight another Palestinian faction. A
lot of times, we've got maybe half a dozen wars going on here
at once. Listen, Dalman, when civilization as we know it
comes to an end—and it's going to—when all the glue comes
unstuck and all the bars are down and everybody's got a license
to kill whoever the fuck he feels like killing, the whole world's
going to look like Beirut. That's what's happened to me. I've
been covering a dress rehearsal for the collapse of modern
civilization."

Dalman did not respond and Bolton paused, looking past the younger man to the apartment building across the street. Shrapnel and bullets had flayed off almost every inch of the yellow paint, leaving only a gray, pocked surface that resembled a distant photograph of a dead planet.

"Yeah, a preview of coming attractions, that's what this is. I saw blood running in the gutters when the Christians took Karatina. I was at a Phalangist barricade one night when this dumb punk, sixteen or seventeen, a dumb punk like Nabil over there, sneaked up behind one of the militiamen and for a joke, shoved an AK in the guy's back and yelled *rat-a-tat-tat*. The guy was wired real tight and he whipped around and cut the punk in half with half a clip, and then went out of his mind because it turned out the punk was his kid brother. So it doesn't bother me when a yo-yo like Nabil decides to play sniper and gets caught at it."

"Harry, I hope to Christ I never get to the point where something like that doesn't bother me."

"You'd better, unless you want to lose your breakfast every morning. Or lose your mind."

"I'd rather lose that than whatever you've lost."

Bolton got to his feet, his control slipping. He poked a finger in Dalman's chest, conscious of his intimidating size.

"Fuck you and fuck that. You're starting to whine like that jerk Grey."

"Grey. Yeah, Grey. I don't intend to end up like Grey."

"You don't sit down and listen and you will."

Dalman's face again turned the color of old copper when, to avoid the hard blue stare of Bolton's eyes, he inadvertently gazed at Nabil's corpse.

"Won't do it," he said. "Won't sit in this room with that in here."

"Remember Bolton's Law." He pointed to the sign on his office door: *That Which Is Not Prohibited Is Mandatory.*

"Screw that, Herr Stürmvonführer. I'm not sitting here unless that mess is dragged out of here."

"You want to do the honors?"

Dalman made no reply.

"Didn't think so. All right, Dalman. All fucking right. I'll do it. I don't want you barfing again."

Squatting beside the body, Bolton saw what a sham he'd staged for Dalman's benefit, acting like a hardened homicide detective with a boiler-plate stomach. His gut started to contract and expand, pumping a bilious fluid into his throat. Even by Lebanese standards, this was an elaborate job of mutilation, a truly baroque monstrosity. Bolton stood, and, taking hold of Nabil's trousers, which had been pulled down and tied around his ankles, dragged the horror into the hall. He slammed the door on it, fighting the wave of sickness welling up within him.

"Happy now, Dalman, or do you want me to mop up, too?"

Through force of will, Bolton closed the valve in his throat. To keep it shut, he avoided looking at the blood, in which the hatchet and the ice picks the Moslems had used looked like heraldic symbols on a dark red shield. He again sat on the edge of the desk. Dalman pulled up a chair, pretending to concentrate on the map, but Bolton could tell by his complexion, now the color of pea soup, that his mind was still on the devastated Nabil.

"Are you going to upchuck again?"

"Nothing left," Dalman said, shaking his head.

"Okay, then. Lesson number one. See the green line? That's The Green Line, the border between the Christian and Moslem sectors. We're in the Moslem half of the city. If you have to cover something on the Christian side, you have to cross the line, and my only advice to you is, get across it as quickly as possible. It's a no-man's-land, and snipers from both sides will shoot at anything moving across it. Men, women, kids, dogs, cats, cars.

"Lesson number two—on the Christian side, you've got two militias, the Phalangists and Chamounists. The Phalangists are called *kataeb*. On the Moslem side, you've got the Looney Tunes—the Mourabitoun. They're also called the Nasserites because they say they believe in Nasser's pan-Arab socialism, but they don't believe in anything except hash smuggling, extortion, and murder, and you've just seen what they're capable of. Then you've got at least half a dozen other left-wing militias, each one of them armed, paid, and supported by a faction from the Palestinian Liberation Organization, or by some Arab country. The Looney Tunes are backed by Arafat's Fatah, the Communist militia by the Popular Front for the Liberation of Palestine, the Workers Party militia by the Popular Democratic Front for the Liberation of Palestine. The Popular Front for the Liberation of Palestine–General Command is supported by Syria, the Arab Liberation Front by Iraq, Junblatt's Socialists by Syrians also. Then you've got the

Syrian National Socialists—Arab Nazis who're fighting on the left-wing side and supported by a right-wing monarchy in Jordan. Got all that?"

"My brain hurts."

"Yeah? Well, get this. Each of these factions issues its own press pass. You come up to a barricade or roadblock and some thug asks you for your pass, you had better show the right one. You slip up and hand a Palestinian pass to a Phalangist, bend over and kiss your ass good-bye. Give it the same kiss if you do the opposite. I can guess what you're thinking. It's what every guy thinks when he gets here. I'll put my Christian passes in my right pocket and my Moslem passes in the left and I won't get in trouble. Wrong. You've got to show the right Moslem pass to the right Moslem faction. Guy from *Time* a few weeks ago drove up to a PFLP roadblock and accidentally showed them a PDFLP pass, but he figured, what the hell, they're on the same side. What he didn't know was that the PDFLP and the PFLP had started one of their intramural wars that morning, so he got locked up in a windowless cell overnight and worked over with rifle butts before they let him go. And he was lucky."

"Send me back to Paris, Harry, no shit."

"No chance. Raymond's got your passes. We've got the factional initials written in the corner in English so you know which one you're showing. On to lesson four. That racket you hear in the background is the big story right now. The great battle for the Holiday Inn. It's one of the tallest buildings in town, thirty-three stories, so it's to urban warfare what the high ground is to war in the bush. But that isn't why it's a big story. It's a big story because the editors at home think the Holiday Inn is a symbol Americans can identify with. The Phalangists have snipers and mortars on the roof. They've got a machine-gun nest in the rooftop restaurant. Our Moslem friends, meanwhile, are in the Phoenicia Hotel next door. They're using it as a kind of firebase to keep the Christians under siege. There it is, Dalman. They're killing each other for a Holiday Inn."

"I was doing real well in Paris."

"You'll be back in three months, *inshallah*. That means 'God willing' in Arabic. You'll be saying that a lot before you leave here."

The door opened and Raymond appeared with four raggedly dressed men who appeared beyond fighting age. Two were carrying sheets of plywood and, at Raymond's instructions, set to boarding up the windows. The other two were told to wrap Nabil's body in a tarp and haul it away.

"Very bad, very bad," said Raymond, trilling the r. He went into the kitchen and heated a pot of aromatic coffee while the workmen nailed the plywood to the windows, the sound of their hammers reduced to a tacking by a crescendo of rifle, machine-gun, and rocket fire. "Very bad," Raymond repeated, coming out and seating himself in the other unbroken chair. He was a black-haired, middle-aged man of medium height, casually but impeccably dressed in loafers, cream-colored trousers, and a tight-fitting shirt unbuttoned to his chest. Before the war, a gold crucifix affixed to a gold chain gleamed in the curling hair beneath his throat, but he'd quit wearing it because, in this sector, jewelry like that could get a man a bullet in the head. He was the bureau's office manager, translator, contact man, and all-around fixer. It was Raymond who'd negotiated with the Looney Tunes for protection payments the bureau could afford, Raymond who could talk his way through any roadblock, Raymond who'd procured a generator to keep the teletypes running when the electricity was knocked out. Now the plywood.

"You're indispensable," Bolton said. "Where'd you get the wood?"

"Friends," Raymond replied. He liked to maintain an aura of mystery.

"When they're through with the windows, be sure they clean the floor."

"But of course," said Raymond, gazing at the emblem of blood. The shooting diminished to a few random bursts, then rapidly built to a stuttering chorus. "Very bad."

"Bad?" said Dalman, who was cringing in his chair, his twenty-five-year-old face pinched into the creases and wrinkles of a man twice his age. "Bad? That sounds like the Tet offensive out there."

"I didn't mean that." Raymond took a sip of the coffee, its chicory smell blunting the other odor. "That is bad, yes, but this with Nabil is very bad. It was excess. They're savages, these Moslems. They should be put in zoos."

"Knock it off, Raymond. The Jesus Christ brigades haven't behaved like cub scouts."

"They've never done anything this bad, Harry. Only Moslems could do this that was done to Nabil."

"All right. I won't argue religion with you. You get hold of his family?"

"Yes. Those two men are putting his body in the trunk of my car. This afternoon, when I go to my house, if I am not killed before I get there, his brothers will take it. Already, each has vowed to kill ten Moslems, but when they see what was done, they will do more than just kill. Nabil has six brothers, and some will succeed in killing ten and putting out the eyes of ten, and then the brothers of the Moslems who are so killed will vow to do the same to ten Christians and so on. Is that not the story of this war, Harry? Ten thousand families taking revenge on ten thousand other families?"

"That's about it. Fact is, that *is* it. Another good lesson for you, Dalman. This war is one big family feud, it's the Hatfields and the McCoys raised to the thousandth power, only you can't write that. You can't write it because the editors in New York can't understand it. To them, it's Right versus Left, rich versus poor, the cross versus the crescent. That makes sense to them. A blood feud on a national scale doesn't."

"Yeah, right," said Dalman in the voice of one whose mental circuits are on overload.

Raymond emptied his cup and lit a cigarette with a gold Dunhill that complemented the gold Rolex banding his wrist. The watch shone in the morning light.

"This has been very bad, and I will be sure to tell the others not to use this office for their private vendettas."

"Or their public ones," said Bolton, folding the map and replacing it in a file cabinet. 'We've got three operators left, and three stringers, and if just one of them pulls a stunt like Nabil, the Looney Tunes'll blow this place to hell with us in it."

"It won't happen. Nabil, I think, was an unusual case."

Bolton slammed the cabinet drawer shut.

"Bullshit. Everybody here's as nuts as he was. They ought to put a hundred-foot wall around this city and declare it a home for the incurably insane."

Raymond shrugged.

"An unusual case, and yet a very Lebanese story."

"All right, let's hear it. Maybe there's a lesson in it you could pass on to the others."

"A lesson? What happened to Nabil is lesson enough. No, there is no lesson for anyone except, perhaps, for Mr. Dalman."

"I've had enough lessons for one day. School's out. . . ."

"This lesson, Mr. Dalman—"

"It's Martin."

"Martin. This lesson, Martin, may help you understand the situation you're dealing with." Crossing his legs, Raymond balanced an ashtray on one knee. He spoke in the way of the world-weary Levantine, a tone of sad cynicism. "In addition to his six brothers, Nabil had three sisters, and one of these sisters, the eldest, was not the best sort of girl, something of a *putain*, eh?"

"I think I know the end already," Bolton said.

"So, this *putain*, she, how do you say it, developed a passion for a young man." Raymond paused to drag on the cigarette, then delicately flicked the ash into the tray. "A Moslem boy."

"I knew I knew the end."

"The young man developed an equal passion for her, and why not? Lillian—that was her name—Lillian was a beautiful woman, and the Moslem women, well, they are so confined that fucking them is like fucking a nun, not so? Of course, in this situation, the meeting of this boy and Lillian had to be very secret, and the secrecy and the danger intensified the passion. The more the war kept them apart, the more they loved each other, or imagined they did."

"Romeo and Juliet go to war."

"Yes, yes, Harry. Like Romeo and Juliet. I confess I cannot imagine some Moslem pig who has probably had it up the ass from another Moslem pig as a Romeo, but let us call them Romeo and Juliet. One can imagine how difficult this love was, the arrangements that had to be made, the rendezvous—"

"Quit wallowing in it, Raymond."

"One must appreciate all the circumstances, Harry, but I will come to the inevitable. The lovers are discovered. More, Lillian is discovered to be pregnant. A *putain*, yes, but a Christian woman with Moslem seed in her belly, perhaps the seed of one who has killed many Christians. The affair is discovered by Nabil, but the Moslem boy has vanished, escaped. He leaves the *putain* with his seed in her belly, but what is her family to do? They could say she was raped, but there would always be the chance the truth would be found out. Abortion is out of the question. The doctors in Beirut are far too busy with the wounded, and besides, the faith prohibits it. The family would be in utter disgrace were the secret learned, in disgrace and great danger, for to have a daughter pregnant by a Moslem at this time—unthinkable. The *putain* has already disgraced them with her recklessness, and endangered them and so . . . and so . . . what to do before all is found out, what to do to punish her for this abomination?" Raymond held for a few counts to heighten the drama. Then his eyelids, like partially draw . shades, closed halfway over his black pupils. "What to do was what to do was done. She was killed, of course."

"*Killed?*"

"Executed by her family."

"God almighty."

"Nabil killed her."

"I don't want to hear any more."

The gleam of Raymond's Rolex was dulled as the last sheet of plywood went up, and the shield on the floor appeared almost black in the dimness.

"He killed her on the instructions of his father, who is a big man in the Phalangist party. It was done at night and in such a way to make it appear Moslems killed her. Thus, not only was the secret kept, not only was the family honor preserved, but much sympathy befell the family. Thus was the father's standing in the party enhanced—the poor man's daughter was murdered by Moslems. But more than this, being Lebanese, the family of Lillian have convinced *themselves* she was murdered by Moslems. This lie is easier to accept and also helps to feed their hatred of Moslems."

"And that's why Nabil came up here with a rifle last night?"

Again, Raymond shrugged.

"Who can say? Perhaps, to justify murdering his own sister, he had to convince himself it was the work of the Moslems, and out of this false conviction, came here to shoot Moslems. Perhaps he was driven mad by what he had done and came on what you would call a suicide mission. We only know he fired through the window into the building across the street and that some of his bullets killed a small child. Then the Mourabitoun . . . well, you know the rest."

"Like I said, throw a hundred-foot wall around the place," Bolton remarked, "and declare it an asylum. Or better yet, get a hundred cargo helicopters to drop a giant net on this place, scoop everyone up, and dump 'em into the Mediterranean."

"That's not the lesson for Martin. I see he is a young man, a young American who has been living in Paris. I know America, I lived in New York three years. I know Paris as well. I know the West, and in the West today, a woman may fuck whom she chooses without serious consequences, or if she suffers them, she can have them removed. In the West, if one is done an injustice, one can appeal to the law. If one is accused, one goes before a judge who will not be too severe. But here? Here there is only vengeance and blood and the law of the Kalashnikov. A woman of one faith has an affair with a man of another and is made pregnant. What is that? A story as old as mankind. It is no great thing except here. Here, not only do actions have consequences, Martin, small actions have very grave consequences."

"What he means is, Welcome to the Middle East."

23

"WELCOME. *'AHLAN WASHLAN'* is how the Arabs say it." Lifting, Raymond's eyelids appeared to pull his lips into a sardonic smile. "Welcome, welcome."

"Now I'm getting language lessons," said Dalman, whose complexion was slowly improving; it had gone from green to putty.

"How about giving me a lesson in the art of cumshawing?" Bolton said. "I need two new teletypes."

"Difficult," was Raymond's only comment as he contemplated the machines, both total losses.

"Getting a generator was difficult."

"They're easier to come by than teletypes. I will talk to Sarkashian," Raymond said, referring to his Armenian partner. Sarkashian was a fence for the Phalangists, the most thorough and best organized looters of the war, with a warehouse full of furniture, TV sets, radios, tape components, typewriters, auto parts, liquor, cigarettes, clothes, telephones—a huge illicit shopping center in a city where it was a feat to buy a loaf of bread.

"Okay, talk to him. Meantime, we'll have to file from the Commodore's telex. The bill for that'll give Old Downhold a seizure."

"I passed by the Commodore on my way here. These were in your box."

Raymond pulled two small envelopes from his back pocket. Bolton opened them as he might notices of back rent; if there was anything he didn't need this morning, it was a query from New York. He prepared himself for the usual nonsense, but the first message was unexpectedly sane—it almost disappointed him.

170300 BOLTON: UNABLE CONTACT YOU VIA WIRE. ANYTHING WRONG? RADIO SERVICE WANTS SOONEST ROSER HOLIDAY INN BATTLE. RGDS/LUCAS/CABLES/NY.

The second, however, lived up to standard.

170935 BOLTON: MCDANIELS WANTS TO KNOW IF YOU CAN DO ROSER FROM INSIDE HOLIDAY INN, THEN GIVE US 800 WDS BANG-BANG FOR WIRE. ALL CLIENTS EAGER FOR AS MUCH AS WE CAN GIVE THEM THIS STORY. GREAT BEAT IF YOU CAN GET IT. REPLY ASAPEST. RGDS/HALPRIN/CABLES/NY.

Bolton folded the messages into paper airplanes, which he sailed across the room to make perfect landings in Dalman's lap.

"Read 'em and weep, amigo. Recess is over. You're going to get another lesson." Then to Raymond. "Those two ragheads you hired are sitting with their hammer and nails up their asses. Get 'em to clean up this mess."

"Yes, of course."

Without moving from his chair, Raymond ordered the workmen to start their next project. They took brushes, a bucket, and cleaning fluid from the broom closet and began to scrub the last remnants of Nabil from the floor. Dalman's face lightened from putty to the pallor of a cocktail-lounge piano player, then took on a normal hue as the ammonia smell of the fluid smothered the other odors.

"What the hell is a roser?" he asked after reading the messages.

"You know about the radio service IPS started this year to compete with AP's and UPI's?"

"Heard about it is all. We don't have it in Paris."

"We've got it here. Spend half my time on it. Perfect bureau for it. Plenty of noise and action. The radio stuff's my job, but you might as well learn it in case I get dinged."

"You're supposed to be indestructible."

"Yeah, like the *Titanic* was supposed to be unsinkable."

"So what's a roser?"

"A roser is the radio equivalent of bang-bang, an on-scene report, the purpose of which is to give our listening audience a few thrills while they're driving home on the expressway. Here, I'll show you the exciting recording studio of IPS radio news, Beirut bureau."

Bolton led Dalman to another room, where he opened the door to what had once been a large storage closet. Inside, white acoustic tiles had been attached to the ceiling and walls. A chair was pushed under a shelf on which three cassette recorders sat beside a telephone and headset. A Sanyo tape deck with two small, pentagon-shaped speakers took up a second shelf.

"This is it. Not exactly a broadcast nerve center, but it serves its purpose, and not just for recording radio spots." Bolton turned his eyes toward the ceiling, which wasn't much more than six inches above his head. "Sometimes I get away from it all in here. When this fucked-up war gets to be too much, and that's about five times a day, I like to sit in here with a bottle of I. W. Harper and get buzzed and look at the designs in the soundproof tiles. Look at them, Dalman. See those holes? They're different sizes and if you get a little loaded or a little high and you look at them long enough, you can see anything you want. Faces. Trees. Clouds. Dragons. Houses. Sometimes I see a house in the mountains in North Carolina."

"Hey, Harry."

"Yeah, I know. I'm drifting off the point. Well, I've gotten a little drifty in this war."

"A roser."

"Right. It's show-and-tell time. I'll show you how to do a roser. I'll do the one New York wants, on-scene at the momentous battle of the Holiday Inn. I will begin my demonstration with this fundamental axiom: the primary obligation of a war correspondent is to stay alive. I used to believe that his duty was to go farthest fastest and get the story ahead of everyone else, but Beirut has changed all that because he who goes farthest fastest here isn't likely to come back. Twelve newsmen have died in this war so far, a few more were carried out of here on stretchers. Stay alive—that's obligation numero uno. Rosers, like bang-bang, make it difficult to fulfill this obligation. They make it *more* difficult because you know as well as I do that you can wing bang-bang, but it's damned hard to wing the actual sound of gunfire. I will now show you that trick. That's the title of this demonstration—winging a roser."

Grinning at Dalman's baffled expression, Bolton plugged a hand microphone into one of the cassette players, then brought it onto the balcony. Quickly checking rooftops and windows for snipers, he crouched low, wrapped the cord around the railing, and lowered the mike like a fishing hook. It hung in midair, about ten feet below. In the hotel district, an automatic rifle was drum-tapping. Bolton punched the Record button, then motioned Dalman to get back inside.

Closing the balcony door, he said, "No need to stay out there and run the risk of getting sniped." Bolton, gesturing to Raymond and the workmen to keep still, looked at his watch. "We'll give it three minutes."

The single rifle kept drum-tapping. Another joined in, then several more. A heavy machine gun added its basso notes.

"That's better," Bolton whispered.

Three sharp explosions followed one another by split-second intervals.

"RPGs. Good."

The rifle, rocket, and machine-gun fire built steadily into a solid sheet of noise, like a monsoon rain beating against a tin roof.

"Terrific. Couldn't have ordered better sound than that."

After running the tape recorder another thirty seconds, Bolton dashed outside, retrieved the microphone, and, with the quickness of a thief, sprang back into the office, the recorder under his arm.

"We've got the background music, amigo. Next step is to write the script for the voice-over."

"Script for the voice-over?"

"Yeah, the script for the voice-over." Bolton sat down and rolled a sandwich of typing and carbon paper into his Underwood.

"Voice-over? That sounds like . . ."

"Like what?"

"Hollywood," Dalman said tentatively.

"You learn quick. That's what broadcast journalism is. Show biz. Wait'll you hear Harry Bolton's radio voice."

Fifteen minutes later, Bolton had his script written.

"Hey, Raymond, are you in good voice today?"

"Always," replied Raymond, brewing another Turkish coffee in the kitchen. Bolton wondered if the enormous coffee consumption in the Middle East contributed to the instability of the region—all that caffeine hyping up nervous systems, all that sweetener upsetting blood-sugar levels.

"Look this over. We're going to do a roser in a few minutes."

Raymond, sipping from a demitasse, walked out and took the carbon Bolton handed him.

"What part do I play today?"

"A Palestinian guerrilla fighting a *jihad* for Allah and the Holiday Inn."

Lighting another cigarette with his trim Dunhill, Raymond sat down to study the script. Bolton read it aloud, taking both his and Raymond's parts while timing it with a stopwatch. The tattered workmen, on their hands and knees, continued to scrub the bloodstain, which now looked like a puddle of rusty water.

"Two minutes forty-five seconds with the pauses," Bolton said. "That's about right. Rosers run from a minimum of one minute to a max of five. Got that, Dalman?"

Dalman stood silently for a moment. He reminded Bolton of a slow student trying to comprehend a complex experiment.

"Harry, how the hell can you *script* a story like that?"

"No speeches on journalistic ethics. The name of this game is survival. Follow me. We've got to modify the sound. That nondirectional mike I hung outside doesn't pick up too well. The fire-fight'll sound like it's taking place in the next country if we don't magnify it."

Bolton returned to the recording room, ejected the tape from the cassette player, inserted it into the holder of the deck, whose volume knob he turned to maximum, locked a fresh tape into the player, then hooked the microphone into a metal clip on the wall above the shelf.

"This is how you do it. See those speakers? Raymond cumshawed them from the Phalangists. They're Bose, just about the best there is, dynamite amplifier system, less than two percent harmonic distortion, woofers set backwards so the sound refracts off the walls." Bolton locked the door. "You ready? I don't want you to move or bump anything. I don't even want you to breathe hard."

With the door shut and the two men inside, the cubicle was stifling. Bolton put the cassette player on record, allowing the tape to run for ten seconds. This done, he punched play-back on the Sanyo. In the enclosed space, the din blasting through the speakers so startled Dalman he hopped backward into the door. Bolton stopped both machines.

"Goddamnit, I told you not to move."

"Christ almighty," Dalman whined, "that sounded like World War Three."

"I want it to sound like World War Three. The whole secret to this is noise. Bang-bang. Just do what the hell I tell you. You want to learn how to wing a roser, do what I tell you. It might save your worthless ass someday. You ready for a second try?"

"Yeah, all right. This is the goofiest shit I've ever seen."

"For sure they don't teach it at the University of Missouri journalism school. That's where you went to J-school, isn't it? Missouri?"

Dalman nodded.

"Listen to Professor Bolton and forget what they taught you. Those J-school jerk-offs can't teach you how to save your ass. Stand by."

For the next three minutes, the cubicle trembled to the stammer of AK-47s, the buzz and thud of RPGs, the guard-dog bark of heavy machine guns. Calm under this replicated fire, Bolton checked the recording level, the counter on the tape deck, and his stopwatch. He made notes on his script—"45 sec, MG fire . . . 75 sec, explosion, 98 sec, explosion . . ." By the time the tape ran out, sweat was dripping from under Dalman's long, blown-dry hair like raindrops from under a thatch eave.

"You nervous in the service, boy?"

"Do you like torturing people? Put a man in this room long enough with that racket and you'll shell-shock him."

"Everybody in this scumhole is shell-shocked to one degree or another. All right, *amigo*, we now have our background master. Let's see how it turned out." Bolton popped the original tape out of the deck, replacing it with the one in the cassette player.

"Hey-hey, number one," he shouted over the cracks and booms. "Hear that? That's those Bose speakers. Refracts the sound in all directions, whips the sound waves off the walls like racquet balls. The mike picks up the echo. Makes one AK sound like two or three."

Dalman slumped with relief when the tape was turned off.

"Next step is the voice-over. I plug this cord into this jack and pipe the background from the tape deck into the cassette player. Now I put a clean cassette into the player, plug the headset in so I can hear the firing and key my voice to what's going on. Then my voice and the bang-bang goes onto the tape in the cassette, which I'll then feed to New York. Okay, we are ready to roll. Listen, it's absolutely essential you don't make a sound while I'm recording. You got to sneeze or fart, do it now. Do you have to sneeze or fart?"

"No."

"Good. Don't move, either."

Opening the door, Bolton summoned Raymond, who entered with his copy of the script.

"Know your lines, Ramon Novarro?"

"I only have three. Of course I know them."

"All right. No farting, no sneezing, no rustling of papers, no movement."

With three grown men in the tiny space, it was almost impossible to move. Wriggling his arms, Bolton pressed REC on the cassette recorder and held the mike close to his mouth.

"This is Harry Bolton in Beirut with a two-minute-forty-five-second roser on the battle of the Holiday Inn. Suggested lead-in: Heavy fighting in the Lebanese civil war continued Monday, as Christians and Moslems battled for the third straight day for control of Beirut's Holiday Inn. Left-wing Moslems are trying to dislodge rightist snipers, who Friday afternoon occupied the roof of the building, one of the city's tallest. IPS correspondent Harry Bolton has an on-scene report from the embattled hotel . . ."

Bolton counted to ten by thousands, then pushed STOP.

"That, Dalman, is how you start all rosers and spots. With a suggested lead-in. The announcers in New York need it because they generally don't know what's going on anywhere, so you have to clue 'em in. They do the lead-in, you do the rest." Bolton paused for a second. "Hate to do this to you, gents, but I forgot to do my push-ups. Let me out."

Raymond, the smallest of the three, reached behind his back to open the door. Bolton maneuvered into the hall outside, dropped to his stomach, and started pumping out three-count push-ups.

"One-two-three-one, one-two-three-two . . ."

"*What* in the hell is he doing now?" Dalman asked.

"Push-ups," said Raymond.

"No shit."

"He does them before a roser to make him sound out of breath. If he sounds out of the breath, it helps the realism."

". . . one-two-three-forty-eight . . . forty-nine . . . fifty."

Bolton got to his feet, his chest rising and falling, the swollen blood vessels in his arms like lateral roots under a thin crust of soil. Again, the three men shoehorned themselves into the white chamber. Bolton, after taking a few deep breaths to regain some of his wind, clamped the headset over his ears and pressed PLAY on the Sanyo, REC on the cassette. The microphone held a few inches from his lips, he spoke in his radio voice, a voice not his own, its mountain accents planed into the flatness of midwestern speech and coated with a dramatic overtone as artificial as the flavoring in frozen orange juice.

". . . the fighting for the thirty-three-story hotel is fierce . . . guerrillas from the Popular Front for the Liberation of Palestine are pouring fire into the top floor, where Phalangist snipers are holed up. . . . There are more snipers on the roof . . . now and then we can see them . . . we're behind a Moslem barricade near the Holiday Inn . . . the guerrillas are raking the hotel with automatic-weapon fire . . . wait . . . they're bringing up a rocket launcher . . ."

Bolton held a forefinger in the air to cue Raymond; when the finger dropped like a miniature railroad-crossing gate, the Lebanese hollered in Arabic, "*Abu Rashid, fire your RPG, the third window from the left!*"

"That was a guerrilla commander ordering his men to fire a rocket-propelled grenade at a Phalangist position . . . you just heard it go off . . . the explosion has torn a hole into the wall, smoke is billowing out of a window on the top floor . . ."

Bolton's finger dropped again.

"*Another, Abu Rashid, a little more to the left!*"

"The Moslems just fired another rocket . . . a direct hit through a window . . . But we're still taking sniper fire from the roof . . ."

"*You, with the machine gun, the roof!*"

". . . now the leftists are spraying the roof with machine-gun fire ... I can see the bullets ricocheting off the concrete ... I doubt if they're hitting anyone, but they're keeping the snipers' heads down ..." Bolton exhaled sharply into the mike. "This is some of the most intense fire I've experienced ... the Moslems succeeded in surrounding the hotel yesterday ... they're firing into the Holiday Inn from the Phoenicia across the street and from barricades like this one ... if Christian militiamen are unable to break through Moslem roadblocks with supplies and ammunition, it's difficult to believe their men can hold out much longer in the besieged hotel. ... This is Harry Bolton for IPS radio news in Beirut."

Bolton put a five-second tail on the tape before turning the machines off.

"Good work, Raymond. You get any better at this, I'll have to start paying you residuals."

Raymond waved his hand as if to say it was nothing.

"Now I will pay those men. They are waiting."

The cubicle was so warm the air from the hall felt frigid when Raymond opened the door; blotches of sweat printed a floral pattern on Dalman's military shirt.

"Let's hear what my electronic sorcery hath wrought," Bolton said.

The tape was nearly perfect—Bolton considered it one of his best. Smiling the smile of a successful con-artist, he leaned the back of his chair against a wall, his legs outstretched; they nearly reached to the other side of the room, where Dalman stood with his arms folded across his chest.

"Sheer artistry. What do you think?"

Dalman's shoulders rose in a noncommittal shrug.

"C'mon, Dalman."

"You really want to know?"

"Yeah."

"I think what you just did sucks." Dalman's voice was small and hesitant.

"Continue."

"I look up to you ..."

"You should. I'm the best there is."

"That's what I thought, but seeing you pull off a scam like this—"

"Disillusions you. Makes you wonder if there are any heroes left. Makes you want to sing, Where are you, Joe Di-Maggio?"

"Something like that."

"I can tell you where Joe DiMaggio is. He's peddling coffee makers on television."

"And you're peddling lies on the radio. Lies and coward-ice." Dalman's voice shrunk almost to inaudibility on the last word, and he appeared to be bracing himself for abrupt dental surgery. Bolton, however, listened with equanimity. He hadn't heard anything he hadn't told himself more than once.

"Congratulations, Dalman. Including you, I've had three guys in here on three-month stints, and you're the only one who wasn't chicken to give it to me straight."

"You asked for it, but I'll tell you right now—if I'm told to do one of these on-sceners, I'm not going to fake it."

"Thought you didn't want to end up like Grey."

"I don't, but I'm not going to peddle lies."

"It's your ass. I've showed you how to lessen your chances of getting killed over here. Done my job on that score. As far as cowardice goes, I'll tell you this—I couldn't wing a story like this if I hadn't done it for real at least once. Thing is, I don't have to prove anything anymore. I've proved myself more times than you could count with an IBM computer. Came to me a while ago, three, four months after I'd gotten back here from Saigon. Came to me one morning while I was shaving, no shit. I looked in the mirror and remembered that I had a Purple Heart and a Silver Star and a George Polk Award— journalism's Medal of Honor—that I'd done it and done it and done it and didn't *have* to anymore. Talk about St. Paul's conversion. Hit me like that, lightning out of heaven and this big booming voice saying, 'Harry Bolton, you no longer have to play Ernest Hemingway.' Felt like somebody'd taken a ten-ton truck off my back."

"I didn't say you were a coward, Harry."

"I don't give a damn. That's the important thing—I don't give a damn if you or anyone thinks I'm the bravest dude to come down the pike since Audie Murphy or if I'm as yellow as a urine sample from a guy with kidney stones. Don't give a holler in hell about it. As far as lying goes, the story on that tape is no different than it would have been if I'd actually gone out and got shot at. I know the formula and I know there isn't an essential falsehood in that story. So what if I wasn't there?"

Dalman remained silent. Bolton could see the question in the younger man's eyes: Did you lead me into speaking my mind just so you could make this speech?

"It doesn't make any difference if I was there," he went on. "I don't believe in journalism-school idealism, but for the sake of argument, let's say the public in a democracy has a right to know the facts. Let's say good journalism appeals to the intellect by presenting the facts accurately. But which facts? Does the public have a *right* to hear actual gunfire? Do they have a *right* to read stories full of blood and gore and bang-bang? Does any of that make them better informed? Hell no. It excites them is all. It makes a difference to them only in that sense. It makes a difference to McDaniels because it helps him peddle his news-broadcast service to radio stations, and the stations buy this garbage because they know that out there on the freeway some fat-assed tax attorney is going to get a little tickle in his crotch when he hears *rat-a-tat-tat* on his AM. For two or three minutes, he escapes his crummy little world. What this on-scene bullshit appeals to is the sensations, not the intellect. And fifty percent of what I do and what all war correspondents do is this bullshit. It's Fleet Street penny-press I-was-there heroics all gussied up to look or sound like useful information. It's just some correspondent proving to the world what a ballsy guy he is and his network or newspaper or wire service proving what hot shits they are for employing him. The public has a right to the facts, it doesn't have a right to ask me or you to risk our lives just to make *their* lives more interesting. Listen, you don't want to wing one of those rosers, don't. Go put your ass on the line so the attorney can have his vicarious thrill before he goes off to make more money in a day than you'll make in a month."

"Harry, if you get any hotter under the collar, you won't have to worry about getting shot. You'll die of a heart attack."

"That's a lot cleaner."

"What're you going to do about that second query? Wing that too?"

"Nope. You don't wing stories like that. They create too much attention and make it too easy to get caught. If you do those, you gotta do 'em on the square." Bolton shifted his weight and tapped the shelf with a pencil as if he were sending a message in code. "As far as that story goes, I'd as soon not do it. The hotel's surrounded. It's damned near impossible to get in, and if you manage that, it would be damned near impossible to get out. But I know I'm going to end up giving it a try because McDaniels won't let up until I do. Besides, you can make book that every news hawk in this town has been asked if he can get in, and if one of them makes it, I'll be getting a rocket every five minutes."

"If the place is surrounded, how the hell are you going to pull it off?"

"C'mon, Dalman. The Horseman is still the best there is. I've already got an idea that'll get me in and out of there with a minimum of risk."

24

———

THE CRACK OF STEVE MCQUEEN'S RIFLE alarmed him out of his sleep. Sitting up, his joints stiff from lying with nothing but a blanket between him and the concrete, he heard the ejected cartridge ring against the pavement and wished he were waking up beside the woman he had loved for twenty-five years. His watch read six in the morning, dawn of his second day trapped in Ashrafiyah. It would be eleven P.M. in New York. Whatever Arlene was doing at this hour, reading, watching television, or sleeping, he longed to be with her; and this longing, as much as the aches in his body, made him wonder if he was pushing himself beyond his limits. Too old, cried his sore joints, too old; but something in him rose up against the dictates of his physical self. When he couldn't walk anymore, when his eyes went bad—then he would be too old. He stood, his back guarded by the apartment building, and worked his muscles loose.

Steve McQueen's rifle cracked again. The sniper was seated on a folding chair, of the sort used in school cafeterias, his 7-mm Remington magnum bench-rested on a sandbag atop the wall enclosing the building's parking lot. Smoking, the second shell casing arced out of the chamber and clattered on the asphalt, whose cratered black was still marked by the yellow lines designating parking spaces—reminders of a nor-

mality that seemed lost forever. "Up one, right one," Mc-
Queen's spotter, squinting through a twenty-power, tripod-
mounted range scope, said in French. McQueen, wearing a
green baseball cap turned backward and a green stocking cap
over his face, eyeholes cut out of it, adjusted the windage and
elevation on his three-by-nine Bushnell. Nestling his cheek
against the Remington's stock, decorated on both sides with
a painted image of Our Lady of Mt. Lebanon, he took a breath,
exhaled some of it, and squeezed the trigger expertly. The
report of the rifle double-echoed off the walls, the echo hissing
over the rooftops below like a wind through dry leaves. The
spotter, peering with an astronomer's concentration, joined
his thumb and forefinger to signal that McQueen was on target, the S in a sign over a mattress factory that said SLEEP WELL.

The sniper took the rifle from his shoulder and slipped the
loop sling from his arm. Then he got off the chair and sat with
his back against the wall, lifting the mask over his mouth to
light a cigarette. He was ready, all sighted in for the day's
work; now he could relax. His *nom de guerre* had been tagged
on him because, the other Phalangists said, he bore a resemblance to the movie actor. Dunlop would have to take their
word for it; he'd seen nothing of the man's face except his
thin lips and his eyes—two blue-gray metal disks that reflected light but gave off no warmth whatever. Perfect sniper's
eyes. The *kataeb* claimed he was one of their best, he had
shot Moslems as far away as eight hundred meters. Dunlop
would have to take their word on that as well; so far, he hadn't
seen McQueen kill anybody of any faith, though he didn't
doubt he was capable of blowing heads apart at great distances.

Dunlop thought about photographing him now. The early
morning light in Lebanon was perfect. There was no other
light in the world quite like it—a gold transparency gilding
the high outcrops of the mountains to the west and painting
the rooftops of the city the color of freshly cut oak. He remembered the first time he'd seen it, long ago, when it fell
on Beirut like a benediction. Now it seemed only the afterglow
of a vanished grace, a radiance that mocked the rubble and
the tormented people cowering under the broken roofs, as the
light of heaven was said to torment the damned by showing
them all they had lost beyond regaining.

But it remained extraordinary light for his work. Dunlop
focused his Leica. Steve McQueen, finished with his cigarette,
had drawn his mask back over his mouth. Of the sniper's face,

Dunlop saw only the metallic eyes, cauterized of all emotion. Then they betrayed a faint amusement as McQueen, looking at the camera, forked two fingers into a victory sign and held the rifle with the butt resting on his thigh, the Virgin's white, beatific face framed by the burnished wood of the stock. Dunlop tried to see in the image in his viewfinder some measure of the redemptive qualities he'd always discovered in the worst of wars: a hint of courage, of endurance, of duty, but all he saw was a masked killer. His inner censor checked him from pressing the shutter. Why glorify this assassin by taking his picture? He pretended to expose a frame, lowered the camera, and smiled to conceal his hatred of the man. He caught a ripple of movement beneath the olive-drab mask—Steve McQueen was probably smiling back. He thought he was on film, immortalized. Smile and watch the birdie.

Dunlop sat down, depressed. Another photograph untaken. In the past two weeks, he'd used only two rolls, and he'd exposed those merely to justify the money *Time* had spent to send him here. The power that had restrained him from photographing the truths about Vietnam he'd found unacceptable now hamstrung him entirely; for he found this whole conflict unacceptable. Four days ago, he'd seen a captured Phalangist tied to the bumper of a jeep and dragged through the streets of a Moslem quarter, where the people shot the Christian to shreds, hacked the shreds into bits, then trampled the bits into the concrete until nothing was left behind the jeep except a few rags and lengths of twisted meat.

Dunlop felt dirty as well as depressed. A shave and a bath would help to restore his morale, but the Commodore, though only a few miles from here, might as well have been in the Amazon. To get to it, he'd have to cross The Green Line, a feat as easy as crossing the Himalayas under these conditions. He and McCafferty had tried it day before yesterday, and were forced back by sniper and mortar fire from both sides. Their driver, a Maronite from Ashrafiyah, had sped up a street to this spot, a dead-end in every sense of the term. A few yards from the parking-lot wall, a hill fell steeply to the Beirut River, across which lay the Moslem neighborhood of Nabaa. A tall, heavyset Phalangist, whose name was George and who appeared in nominal charge of Steve McQueen and several other gunmen, assured the two photographers that he would look after them. They were Christians and Westerners and the Phalange, after all, was fighting for the West and for Christ. He also assured them they would be escorted across the line as soon as the next cease-fire went into effect; there was a cease-fire at the end of every month so the banks could reopen and the leaders of the various factions draw money to pay their militias. The cease-fire could come at any hour, he'd said. But it hadn't come night before last, or yesterday, or last night. What with McQueen zeroing in this morning and, in the distance, the sound of the fighting for the Holiday Inn, it didn't look as if it would come today. Listening to the battle noises coming from the hotel district, Dunlop felt like a captive, a prisoner of this mad butchery they called a war.

Across from him, wrapped in blankets, the driver and McCafferty were still sleeping. It was bad enough to be trapped up here, but almost intolerable to be trapped with that moron. McCafferty was the quintessence of the new breed of atrocity-monger spawned in the swamps of Vietnam. It offended Dunlop's sense of personal dignity to be in the man's presence. He'd won his third Pulitzer this month, the most a single photographer had won in the history of the award, and it seemed to him he deserved a better companion than a half-witted thug on assignment for a pulp magazine. Beirut, however, was so dangerous that journalists had to run in packs or pairs to survive, and you couldn't always choose your company.

A bullet, snapping overhead, chiseled a piece of concrete out of a house across the street.

"Hoo-hoo," said Steve McQueen, looking up.

A second round struck only inches from the first.

"Hoo-hoo."

A third sent dust flying just under the second.

"Hoo-*hoo*."

"A tight group," a voice behind Dunlop said in English.

George emerged from the apartment building, red-eyed and unshaven. He was dressed in green army trousers and a dirty undershirt, over which he wore a shooting vest adorned with colorful patches: New York Rod and Gun Club; Winner, State Skeet Championships, 1969; National Rifle Association, Life Member; 3d Place, U.S. National Pistol Matches, 1972. A naturalized American citizen, George had returned to his native Beirut to enlist his skill with firearms in the fight for Christ and the Maronite rite.

A fourth round figure-eighted one of the other bullet holes.

"Hoo-hoo."

The fifth bullet struck in the center of the pattern formed

by the previous four so that hardly an inch of the building's russet paint showed between the chips.

"Hoo-hoo-hoo."

"Yes, a very tight group. That fellow can't be Moslem."

"Why not?"

"Because Moslems can't shoot that well. They haven't the mentality for it."

Dunlop scrutinized George's face, dusty with a three-day growth of beard.

"What about the cease-fire?"

"Just now I received a call from Phalange headquarters. It went into effect twenty minutes ago."

"It doesn't sound like it."

"A Lebanese cease-fire," George said with a shrug. "A cease-fire here is like a screen door on a submarine. You would like some breakfast?"

"I would like to get the hell out of here."

"You will. By this evening you will be in your room at the Commodore."

Dunlop tried not to let this promise raise his hopes too high.

"I will see you and your friend are given something to eat."

"He's not my friend."

"Colleague."

"Not that, either."

"Whatever he is, he will be hungry, Mr. Dunlop. Certainly he sleeps well."

"He saw the sign your boy was shooting at."

After George had gone inside, the spotter, crouching behind his range scope, jabbered something in Arabic and pointed. Rising to a squat, an alertness in the predatory eyes encircled by the holes in his mask, Steve McQueen settled himself onto the chair. Cautiously lifting his head until only the top of it showed above the wall, he cinched the loop sling around his bicep, rested the rifle on the sandbag, and nuzzled his cheek into the face of Our Lady of Mt. Lebanon, his sighting eye about an inch from the Bushnell. The spotter asked him a question. From under the mask came a muffled "*La*—no." Pointing to the left of the sign, the spotter spoke again in rapid Arabic, ending the sentence with another question. The fingers of his right hand moving as though he were fine-tuning a dial, Steve McQueen turned the adjustment ring on the Bushnell, bringing the scope to full magnification. Then he pivoted the rifle barrel an inch or two to one side.

The rifle crashed and the spotter, switching to French, said, "Low and to the right, low and to the right." McQueen grunted in disgust, ejecting the shell with a rearward flick of the bolt, smoke slithering out of the chamber and tinging the air with the smell of sulfur. Dunlop could not see the Moslem sniper—only an asymmetrical checkwork of rooftops, walls holed by rockets, blast marks streaking out from the rims of the holes like rays from black suns, a traffic light faithfully signaling at a deserted intersection, the Sleep Well sign, and, left of it, the strange domesticity of laundry hung out to dry on a balcony. McQueen slid the bolt home, aimed, and fired again. The spotter shook his head, speaking in an incomprehensible gumbo of Arabic and bad French.

The second shot awoke McCafferty.

"Open for business early again, are they?" McCafferty's voice was still husky with sleep. The South Boston accent, the thick, truncated cone of a neck, the broad face, the eyes, small, stupid, but cunning—all of this raised a tide of loathing in Dunlop.

"What's going on, P.X.? Same old shit?"

"Have a look for yourself."

In an ape's crouch, McCafferty moved to the wall, raising his wide head like a periscope.

"McQueen's shooting at a Moslem sniper."

"Don't see a sniper. Don't see a fucking thing."

Nevertheless McCafferty trained his camera on McQueen, and the whirring and clicking of the motor drive seemed to prod the marksman into making greater efforts. He fired off five rounds rapid-fire, working the bolt with perfect rhythm.

"This kind of trash is right up your alley, isn't it, Mc-Cafferty? You and the rag you're working for."

"Wouldn't call it a rag. It's a magazine."

"Do you call that pulp trash a magazine?"

"That's what it is, asshole. A magazine."

"*Mercenary* isn't a magazine," Dunlop said with a sneer. "It's a war comic for middle-age gun nuts with fantasies of high adventure."

Anger shone in McCafferty's dull gray eyes, then faded, as if, like some dumb animal, he'd instantly forgotten what had made him angry.

"The money's right."

"For guys like you, the money's always right, even when it's wrong."

"Not all of us can get the plums, P.X."

"Not all of you are good enough."

"Trouble with you is you're a fucking snob."

"If I am, I've got reason to be."

The street delinquent's malice in McCafferty gathered in his eyes, which had shrunk to a pair of pinholes.

"I thought that thumping DelCorso gave you a year ago knocked the stick out of your ass."

"He's lucky he's still working in this business."

"Tell me something, since you and me are trapped up here, makes us sort of pals, doesn't it? So pal to pal, you really do that in Saigon? Hire some goon to take his film and give him one in the head?"

"You and I aren't pals," said Dunlop, wrinkling his nose against McCafferty's smell, the stale stench of a factory worker's unwashed shirt.

"That doesn't answer my question."

"I wouldn't dignify it with an answer."

"That's what politicians say when they got something to hide."

McCafferty's smile, revealing a wall of uneven teeth, was at once vicious and idiotic.

"Listen. DelCorso's lucky I didn't sue him for every dime he's got."

"Heard you wanted to. Some kind of legal problem because he thumped you aboard ship on the high seas."

"I could have hauled his ass into court in the ship's home port. I didn't think it was worth the trouble."

Why am I bothering to explain myself to this bum? Dunlop asked himself.

"Yeah," McCafferty said, the last letter in the word rolling into an r. "It's what your kind does when they get thumped. They sue. Where I come from, you get thumped, you thump back."

"Nowhere is where you come from."

"Fucking-A right, P.X. And I'm never going back."

The sun bulged over the rim of the Lebanons, varnishing the mountain slopes to a dark blond and slanting into Steve McQueen's field of vision. He turned his hat around, pulling the bill down low to shade his eyes. His shot racketed between the buildings, like a hunter's in a box canyon. There was another exchange of conversation between him and the spotter; apparently he'd missed again. The Moslem sniper appeared to have gone to ground. McQueen propped his Remington against the wall and took another smoke break. A few mortar shells burst in Ain Roummaneh, a Christian suburb to the south, the sound of the explosions amplified by the narrow streets. Then George came out and announced that breakfast was ready.

They ate in the apartment building's lobby, a gimcrack, fifties-modern place with fake marble floors, mosaic-tiled pillars, an elevator whose tinny doors had been painted brass, and expanses of windows. The glass had been shot out long ago and replaced by walls of sandbags, which made the room dim as a cellar. George invited Dunlop and McCafferty to sit at a blanket on the floor, around which half a dozen young *kataeb* were wolfing down fried eggs, olives, pitah bread, and strong tea. They were brimming with masculine good fellowship, a merry mob wearing a rummage-sale assortment of quasi-military uniforms and gold crucifixes. Garish images of tormented Christs and haloed madonnas made their Kalashnikovs and M-16s look like icons. Dunlop thought it would make a good picture—the gunmen's picnic—but there was an unwholesome quality about them, an air of banditry, that inhibited him.

"*Sabalkhair*, my friend," said Haddad, a kid whom McCafferty had befriended.

"Saba your hairy ass, too."

"Today maybe I will help get for you your picture."

"Maybe, if you shoot at something besides windows. We don't want pictures of broken windows."

"No windows today." Haddad sopped up egg yolk with a piece of pitah, shoveled it into his mouth, then licked the tips of fingers. "No windows. Maybe I will go into Nabaa, very close, close enough to kill a Moslem with this." He drew from his holster a chrome-plated .44 magnum. *Boom-boom.* "A forty-four, this is the gun of Clint Eastwood in *Dirty Harry*."

"You get that close, I won't be with you," said McCafferty.

Dunlop sensed a bond between the two—one street thug relating to another—and wondered, What am I doing here, eating with this filth?

"Ya, with this gun, I can shoot through a car. *Boom-boom*. I can shoot through doors. *Boom-boom*. Like dirty Harry. *Boom-boom*."

He waved the huge revolver in the air until George admonished him to put it away.

"A crazy boy," George said by way of apology. "Most of them are crazy boys."

Dunlop, picking at an olive, said nothing, although he fully agreed with George's assessment. It was best not to say anything that might cause offense; these people were his ticket out of here.

"All of this is craziness. You see Haddad's magnum? He bought it from a Palestinian during a cease-fire. All craziness. I don't like it. I don't like killing people."

"Then what are you doing here?"

George chewed thoughtfully. "Not to kill anyone. I've killed no one this whole time. I'm a match shooter, what marksmen call a paper puncher. I've come here to train. I trained Steve McQueen. Before me, he could hit nothing. Now, at eight hundred meters . . ." George snapped his fingers. "But I? I've killed no one."

"It amounts to the same thing, doesn't it?" Dunlop put the question softly, but his attempt at civility was undermined by McCafferty, who said:

"Yeah. What's the fucking difference, Georgie Boy?"

"The difference is I have killed no one myself."

McCafferty grabbed a handful of olives as if they were peanuts and, popping one into his mouth, spit the stone into his hand.

"Well, that makes you a true Christian."

"It's necessary for we Christians to fight, so it is necessary for me to train others to fight and to shoot well."

"Sure it's necessary. You Christians got all the gravy in this country and the Moslems, from what I hear, don't have a pot to piss in, so you've got to fight to hold on to what you got."

"Propaganda. You've been listening to their propaganda. They're fanatics, those *fedayeen*. Communists. Our fight is against communism."

"Fuck. Everybody says that. Over in Cambodia the fucking Communists are fighting against communism."

"If we don't fight them, perhaps you'll have to someday."

"What're you telling me? This is a crusade? Onward Christian soldiers?"

"Yes. Like a crusade." George's voice rose and anger purpled his face. "A crusade, yes!"

"Cool your jets, George. I'm not speaking for the Moslems. Who's right or wrong—that never made a damn bit of difference to me."

The ringing of the telephone prevented McCafferty from doing any more damage. George picked it up behind what had once been the concierge's desk. Nodding, he spoke in short, guttural phrases. Overhearing him, two of the *kataeb* fell into what sounded like a quarrel, but Dunlop couldn't tell if they were arguing with each other or with George, who held up a hand in a signal for them to be quiet. He spoke some more into the phone, then hung up and delivered a few words to his militiamen, all of whom began arguing. He listened patiently to whatever they were saying until a Moslem machine gun took a few bites out of one of the sandbag walls and resolved the dispute. Everyone went sprawling, Dunlop, McCafferty, and George diving for cover behind the concierge's desk. When the bursts of fire let up, the *kataeb* ran outside, took up positions behind the wall of the parking lot, and loosed deluges of lead, the spent casings chiming as they struck the concrete, the Moslem bullets thudding into the sandbags or ringing off the face of the building.

"George, what in the hell is going on?"

"It was party headquarters on the phone. They said all the leaders of all the parties agreed to a cease-fire, but, as you can hear, none of the fighters agreed with their agreement."

"Nothing like democracy," said McCafferty.

"It's just the craziness again." George seemed genuinely embarrassed, like a host whose guests have behaved badly. "It will blow over. . . . There. . . . You see? Already the firing is not so much."

The shooting had died down, but the relative quiet did not diminish Dunlop's feeling that he was locked in the closed wing of an asylum.

"Perhaps you would like to go to the roof."

"What's on the roof?"

"It's safe there. It's safer there than here because it is difficult for the Moslems to fire that high accurately. Also, you could take pictures from the roof. Then, when things settle down, I will give you two men to get you through our side of The Green Line."

"What the hell. Maybe we can see who Steve McQueen's shooting at from up there."

With that, McCafferty fetched Haddad, who reappeared with an M-16A1 that had a high-powered Leupold telescopic sight bracketed to its carrying handle.

The electricity out, they had to climb nine flights of stairs to the roof. Though he didn't smoke or drink and worked out regularly, Dunlop felt every one of his fifty-two years when they reached the top. The paunchy George was gasping, but McCafferty and Haddad were not breathing hard, which made Dunlop despise them all the more. A double layer of sandbags raised the wall around the roof to about the height of an average-size man's chin; in the two corners facing Nabaa, the bags were piled four or five high, with firing loops and horseshoe-shaped parapets upon which rifles or machine guns could be rested. In a far corner, shielded by a crescent of more sandbags, an 81-mm mortar, like a silver sewer pipe, leaned against its bipods. At street level below, Steve McQueen's rifle banged again. From the direction of the Holiday Inn came a sound as of a fire in a dry pine forest.

"All right, Haddad, we'll see if you can get the sniper Stevie Boy's shooting at. Let's set up over there."

McCafferty pointed to one of the triangular bunkers. Haddad rested his rifle on the parapet. Beside him, McCafferty readied his motor-driven Nikon with a 400-mm lens. In a half squat, Haddad moved the barrel right to left, left to right.

"See anything?"

"No." Haddad, obviously enjoying his status as a kind of photographer's assistant—from the side, Dunlop could see him smiling with the warmth of a shark—fiddled with the scope. McQueen's rifle sounded again and Haddad said:

"Wait . . . yes, yes, I see . . . very far . . . too far, I think."

"Give it a try."

Legs bent, shoulder into the butt, Haddad aimed. McCafferty tripped the shutter, the motor drive whining and clicking as the rifle went off.

It was all Dunlop could do to restrain himself from seizing the camera and rifle and flinging both to the street below.

"You nail him?"

"I don't think so. It's very far for an M-16. The sniper is

on a balcony, and there are clothes drying on the balcony. . . . He is hiding behind the clothes . . . ."

"Give it another try if you see him again."

It would be wonderful, Dunlop thought, it would be very wonderful if that machine gun the Moslems have over there blew these two to hell. And thinking this, he saw McCafferty's broad skull halved by a bullet, the pale animal eyes locked in death's stare, and Haddad's sharklike grin frozen in death's smile. *Scum*.

"Why are you not taking pictures?" George asked him. "Please do so."

He sounded as though he would be disappointed if Dunlop didn't take a photograph. He also appeared nervous and distracted, unsure of what to do with these journalists whom chance had thrown under his wing.

"There isn't a damn thing to take a picture of."

"But there is everything. From here you can see everything."

Everything. Everything of what? There was Ashrafiyah below them, once a neighborhood that resembled New Orleans's French Quarter. The scroll iron of its balconies now hung over the streets like mangled vines, the streets themselves were shell-pitted junkyards for bombed-out automobiles, the pastel-shaded houses fire-blackened. Downtown lay beyond, the part of the city that had been hardest hit by the plastiquers, who had blasted the *souks* and the stone, Ottoman-era buildings into heaps that looked like the unexcavated ruins of a vanished civilization. Beyond that, across The Green Line, West Beirut, its forests of apartment blocks cut down, mounds of brick, concrete, and twisted reinforcement rods piled as high as snow after a blizzard. He hadn't seen a city obliterated like this since World War Two and Korea; the remarkable thing was, it hadn't been done by aircraft, artillery, and naval gunfire, but with mortars, small arms, and plastique bombs. Nor had it been done by a foreign invader; the Beirutis had done this to themselves, so that the wastage of this city seemed less an act of war and more an act of mad, mass vandalism. They had destroyed their own house and the thoroughness of the destruction spoke of a delight in destruction and of some fiendish impulse toward self-annihilation Dunlop could neither comprehend nor accept.

"Perhaps then," George said abruptly, "you would take my picture."

"Your picture?"

"Yes. By the mortar. I will give you the address of my relatives in New York. You could send the pictures to them, if it's not too much trouble."

Dunlop didn't know whether to laugh or throw down his camera bag in despair. A three-time Pulitzer winner was being asked to take a snapshot, like a tourist. Well, why not? Throughout this assignment he'd felt like a tourist on a trip through a Disneyland of violence. Why not? Might as well accommodate the bastard; maybe then he'll get us out of here.

At his direction, George moved over to the mortar, the upper part of his body showing above the sandbags, one hand resting on the muzzle. Straightening the colorfully patched vest, he attempted a warlike expression, but looked nevertheless like an overweight grocer. Simultaneously amused and disgusted, Dunlop took shots.

"If you have a pen, I'll write their address."

Dunlop got a ballpoint and notebook from his camera bag. While George, laying the paper on a sandbag, carefully printed the address, Steve McQueen's rifle cracked twice and Haddad echoed with two rounds of his own.

"Anything?" McCafferty asked.

"It is too far."

"Please mail the photographs to them," said George, handing the paper to Dunlop, who stuck it in a pocket where he knew he would forget it.

He then moved to the bunker opposite McCafferty's, taking a pair of field glasses from his back to look for the sniper who was proving so elusive to Haddad and Steve McQueen's marksmanship. Focusing the binoculars on the balcony, which he judged to be at least five or six hundred yards off, he saw only the laundry hanging from the lines: shirts, jeans, underwear, and bed linen, banners proclaiming the invincibility of the mundane. He caught some sort of movement on the balcony, but the sniper, wearing a checkered *kaffiyeh*, was difficult to make out against the varicolored wash, fluttering in the breeze. A puff of concrete dust blew out of the foot of the balcony as McQueen and Haddad's rifles crashed almost in unison. The figure appeared to be crouching behind the balcony, a solid slab of cement; his arm reached up and tugged a pair of jeans off the line; then he vanished into the doorway, an instant before another of McQueen's rounds chipped the wall.

Dunlop cleaned the binoculars with lens tissue. He had no intention of attempting what McCafferty was trying to do, but his curiosity was up. This was a strange sniper, more intent on bringing in wash than he was on shooting. Bringing the field glasses to his eyes, he again saw the figure, bent low, head moving from side to side, like a hunted animal, the arm rising, this time to snatch a pillowcase. Now it wasn't curiosity that held Dunlop, but awe at the cruelty and cowardice of what he was witnessing.

25

THE FIGURE WAS a stout woman wearing some sort of patterned housedress; what had appeared as a *kaffiyeh* was actually a kerchief, tied loosely around her head. A woman taking in her wash, not knowing that with each shirt, each pillowcase, each pair of jeans she successfully retrieved, she became a clearer target.

Maybe Haddad and McQueen were deliberately shooting wide of the mark, amusing themselves until the cease-fire took hold. This possibility consoled Dunlop for a moment or two, until he recognized it as an illusion created by the filter he carried in his head, the one that automatically subdued reality's ultraviolet. Another round made dust spurt from the wall above the doorway. The woman dropped down and crawled inside with her prize, the pillowcase.

She stayed inside for a couple of minutes, reappearing on her hands and knees, a feral alertness in the movements of her head. Clutching a corner of the bedsheet, she yanked one end of it free. Steve McQueen did not fire; nine floors below, he could not see her behind the balcony. Haddad could, however. He let off a round, but the M-16, inaccurate at ranges greater than three hundred yards, didn't come close. As the woman pulled the other end of the bedsheet free, it snapped and shook, like a sail being lowered with a fouled halyard.

McQueen must have spotted the odd movement, for his rifle racketed again across the rooftops, the bullet digging another chunk out of the balcony. The bedsheet came down and the woman scrambled inside, looking, on all fours, like some round little animal ducking into its burrow.

Dunlop watched, fascinated not only by the snipers' murderous persistence but by the woman's determination as well. Was it determination or an incredible stupidity? Or was it defiance? Or Moslem fatalism, this carrying on with everyday chores at the risk of her life? Dunlop put the field glasses aside and picked up a 500-mm mirror lens, resting it on the sandbags as Haddad and McQueen did their rifles.

Possibly he could shoot a sequence, although he wasn't very good at sequence photography. He would make a record of this repulsive vignette. Snipers trying to kill a Moslem washerwoman—a microcosm of this war. Setting the shutter at a thousandth, he turned the focus ring until he had a clear image of the balcony and the dark gap of the doorway behind it. The woman crawled out once more, her figure much smaller than it had appeared through the powerful binoculars. On a print, she would be nearly indistinguishable from the shirts and dresses hanging on the lines. Dunlop screwed on a tele-extender, which brought the image twice as close. The double would fuzz the negative, but he could etch in the details in the lab.

There was a blur of movement. The woman, with a quickness belied by her squat frame, stood, snared a few more bits of clothing, and disappeared. Haddad fired three rapid shots, McCafferty's motor drive whirring. Then the roar of the Remington.

Dunlop exposed a few frames, steadying the sensitive mirror lens on the sandbags. With a shorter camera, he moved across the roof in what would have looked like a cat burglar's crouch ten years ago, but now appeared more like an old man's stoop. Leaning over the edge, he framed an overhead view of Steve McQueen and the spotter. Interesting perspective. The top of the green baseball cap, the slim length of the Remington's barrel, the black hair massed atop the spotter's head, which, behind the range scope, resembled from this angle a large, dark apple on the end of a squat stick. What would he call this one? "The Sniper and His Squire"? As he brought the elements of the picture together, his finger crooked over the shutter button—and stayed there, paralyzed, like the trigger finger of a soldier who cannot fire his rifle at the enemy. Dunlop had seen instances of that in Korea, and had wondered what restrained those men, conscience or fear. He wondered now if it was conscience or fear restraining him. Moving back to the bunker, casting a sidelong glance at McCafferty, he ruled in favor of conscience—conscience not only in the ethical sense but also in the sense of good taste; and in both senses, photographing snipers attempting to kill a housewife was the equivalent of photographing a rapist in the act. If he went through with the sequence, its logical climax would be the woman's death. That is what he would have to hope for, the same as McCafferty. *Her death.* God almighty, for the last few minutes he had lost himself in this lunacy, becoming no different from McCafferty. Worse. With the shorter lens, McCafferty couldn't see that the target was an unarmed woman.

Now Dunlop felt himself again, but he was not entirely comfortable. Good taste. All of his photographs had been in good taste, and he had always taken pride in his ability to keep himself and his work out of the swill; yet, at this particular moment, his conscience, his censoring refinement, bothered him. They were liabilities here; a hunch told him that Vietnam, for all its brutishness, would be the last conflict in his lifetime to offer instants of bravery, of self-sacrifice, of magnanimity. From now on, most wars would probably be like this one, devoid of all the qualities that had made armed conflict bearable, even sometimes attractive. If battle had once been an endeavor that brought out the best and the worst in men, it now brought out only the worst, and though he could accept pure human evil as an idea, he could not bring himself to express it in his work. But if, a hundred years from now, his photographs were to be the first chosen to illustrate the history books and his name be to the wars of this century what Brady's and Fenton's had been to the wars of the last, then he would have to learn how to breathe in this new disgusting environment. The trouble was, he did not believe he could. Gazing out over the waste of what had once been one of the brightest cities on earth, he was struck by the realization that only the McCaffertys and DelCorsos had lungs for it.

He was more than struck by it; it set a match to the tinder of resentments and jealousies inside him. The fire leapt into a blaze of hatred. He would have seized McCafferty by the throat if the same reserve that checked him from taking certain photographs did not also repel him from physical confrontations. He wasn't afraid of being hurt—a strong man, he could withstand punishment—he simply recoiled at the very idea of touching anyone violently, or being touched. It still embarrassed him to recall the brawl with DelCorso aboard the *Denver*, DelCorso coming at him with flying fists, one punch knocking Dunlop to the deck, then the disgusting intimacy of a wrestling match when DelCorso pounced on him, slugging wildly until someone pulled him off.

Rising, his stiff joints again reminding him of age, he went over to George, who was sitting by the mortar pit, munching on a loaf of pitah.

"So you found something to photograph?"

"Yes," Dunlop said, squatting on his haunches in front of the militia commander. His professional code prohibited intervening in events he was meant to record, but this situation demanded he do something. "Do you know what your men are shooting at?"

"Moslems, of course."

"A woman, an unarmed woman."

Dunlop's voice quavered from the intensity of his anger, a river with more sources than just an outraged conscience.

"A woman," George said, as though referring to a species of game animal.

"She's trying to take her laundry off a balcony."

One side of George's face bulged as he stuffed half the loaf in his mouth.

"She's very foolish for doing that. Typical Moslem mentality. If there was a war in your hometown, would you cut your lawn in the middle of the fighting?"

"She doesn't deserve to be shot for being a fool. Put a stop to it."

"What?"

"You heard me."

A hardness shellacked the naturally soft expression in George's oval brown eyes.

"I take orders from party headquarters, not from you."

"Put a stop to it."

"I will not. I cannot. Moslems are Moslems. Two days ago they killed two of our women very near here. They opened fire on a house with an anti-aircraft gun. They butchered them with an anti-aircraft gun."

"How long did you live in the States?"

"Seven years. . . . But don't appeal to me as one American to another. I'm a Middle Easterner in my heart."

"If *Time* magazine publishes photographs of your men trying to kill a defenseless woman, it won't do the party any good, it won't do the Christian cause any good."

McQueen's rifle made its sharp crack. They could hear the rush of the outgoing bullet, like an expulsion of breath.

"I'm not an officer, this isn't a regular army. It's a militia. What control I have over my men I have because they respect me. If I order them not to fire at Moslems, I'll lose their respect."

"The party and the Christians will lose respect if such photographs appear in the magazine. I don't like to publish photographs like that, I don't even like to take them, but I will if I have to."

"Then take them. Go ahead. Take them." George's voice took on an unstable excitement. "Take them, and if you mean to make propaganda for the Communists, I'll confiscate your film."

"If you do, that will be written in the magazine and do even more harm to the party's image."

Dunlop looked directly into the brown eyes. The hardness in them had cracked like spar varnish in severe sunlight. Yes, George was merely the nominal commander of a band of gunmen who called themselves a militia, but that did not make him immune to the almost universal desire for a good press.

"You're putting me in a difficult position."

"You've put yourself in it."

"I couldn't do what you're asking."

"All right, have it your way." Dunlop stood and pointed to the camera with the mirror lens. "That's a five-hundred-millimeter with an attachment that doubles its focal length. I could photograph moon craters with it. I sure as hell can get a clear picture of her. It'll look wonderful in the magazine. The whole goddamned world can see it—this is what the brave anti-Communist Phalangists are doing—sniping at housewives during a cease-fire."

"You're a man of great integrity, Mr. Dunlop."

He said nothing.

"Also I admire the courage of your convictions. If you tried this sort of blackmail with Moslems, they would do far worse than confiscate your film."

"Confiscate it, then. Either that or you put a stop to what's going on."

"I can't confiscate it You're right. It would harm the party's image if I did that and it were printed in your magazine. We need the support of the West. The party would come down on me. All the same, I cannot order my men to stop firing. That's the position you've put me in."

"Frankly, it surprises me that you'd allow this to go on."

"Does it? The only thing that surprises me is that my men haven't been able to hit that idiot of a woman." George looked up, and Dunlop would have sworn the hardness in the dark eyes had liquefied into sorrow. "They don't shoot as well as I'd thought. You will wait here, Mr. Dunlop."

"Wait?" Dunlop asked, feeling suddenly less sure of himself, for he saw that the sheen in George's eyes was not sorrow, though sorrow was one of its elements; it was, rather, the gleam of what George called the craziness, the madness that seemed to infect all the people of this city in varying degrees, a madness that lacked even the twisted logic of ordinary insanity.

"Yes, wait. Wait here. I will solve this dilemma you have put me in." He commanded Haddad to cease fire. "*Malesh*," George replied to Haddad's protests, holding his palms in a calming gesture. "*Malesh*—it's all right."

Dunlop's certitude returned. His efforts were succeeding after all. Haddad laid down his rifle, scowling contemptuously at George.

"Once again, Mr. Dunlop, wait here. Wait till I call for you," George instructed, opening the door to the landing.

McCafferty, who was sitting with one leg tucked under the other and the cable release on his lap, stuck his tongue into a corner of his mouth and cocked his head to the side.

"You got a clue about what's going on, P.X.?"

"This shit's going to stop, then we'll be getting out of here."

"I'm not all that hot about getting out. Haven't got a decent picture yet. Why in the fuck did he tell Haddad to hold fire?"

"I told him to. They've been trying to kill a woman in case you hadn't noticed, an unarmed woman."

"No shit. And you told him. You're a regular boy-fucking-scout, P.X."

The Remington fired again. The scowl on his face fading, Haddad turned around and positioned himself behind the M-

16. Without shooting, he looked through the scope and exclaimed:

"Ya! Ya! Ma-caff-a-ty! "

"Ya, what?"

Haddad gestured at the camera.

"*Shuay, shuay*—wait. Now McCaffaty now."

"Got something, do we?"

"Now . . . now."

As McCafferty released the shutter, the motor drive's rapid
clicks like a film sprung loose from a sprocket on a motion
camera, the Remington's echoes once more rebounded off the
buildings. Dunlop took several quick strides to the edge of the
roof, while Haddad shouted, "Good, good, very good!" Looking
below, his stomach slid down a wave of revulsion and incom-
prehension. The craziness. The madness without madness's
logic. He heard George calling to him from below. Opening
the door to the landing, he ran clumsily down the nine flights
of stairs, bursting out the front door in time to see Steve
McQueen, who had taken over as spotter, giving George a
congratulatory pat on the back.

"Hoo-hoo," he said through the mask. "Hoo-*hoo*."

George, ejecting the cartridge, propped the rifle against the
wall. Turning in the chair, he faced Dunlop, who now saw in
the lacquered brilliance of his eyes brushstrokes of a shared
guilt, such as might be painted in the eyes of a criminal when
he looks at his accomplice.

"Mr. Dunlop." George's lips skewed into an enigmatic
smile.

"What in the goddamned hell . . . I thought you said you
didn't . . ."

"Didn't like it? I don't. I like it even less now, but it was
necessary. You put me in a dilemma."

Dunlop looked at him silently.

"You may take my picture with this rifle if you wish, and
you may say, you may tell all the world what I, George Saman,
have done. You may say to all the world that only I among
these men had the skill to do it. I won't take your film. I won't
censor you because you're a man of integrity and I know you
will also tell all the world that I was forced to do it. So I would
not have to order my men *not* to do it. Forced by a meddling
American. Do you have so much integrity that you will say
that? I think not, Mr. Dunlop."

He said nothing. From his bag he took out the field glasses, centering them on the balcony. He saw only the small gray craters the bullets had made in the concrete and a clothesline drooping like a severed tendril over the balcony. She must have had it in hand and torn it from its hook when she fell.

"You can't see her from here," George continued. "You might try the roof. From there, perhaps, you can see her and take photographs if you wish, but I don't think you'll wish to."

The wave in Dunlop's stomach dipped again, then rose, crested with a bile that filled his throat.

26

DELCORSO HAD REACHED that stage of anger in which almost anything anyone said or did struck him as a personal insult.

"If that bitch walks past me again, I'll trip her. Maybe that'll get her attention," he said, meaning the cocktail waitress who had just failed to acknowledge his signal for the third time.

"It definitely would, but I don't think it would get you a drink." Kaplan spoke in a tone at once indulgent and remonstrative. "Not a damned thing I've said to you in the past half-hour has sunk in. Now you want to trip the waitress."

"I want a goddamned drink. She acts like I've got leprosy."

"She's busy, Nick. I'll go to the bar. More of the same?"

"No," said DelCorso, rational enough to know that one more Jack Daniel's would carry him over the threshold. "Make it campari and soda."

Kaplan stood and weaved his way through the crowds of admen, lawyers, and publishing executives who were fortifying themselves for the ordeal on the Long Island Railroad. It was the day after DelCorso's reflective walk, and it again occurred to him that he wasn't very different from these men in three-piece suits—just another businessman trying to relax with a few drinks at the end of the day, but anxious about

■　272　■

getting home. He looked at his watch, like any commuter worried about making the train. Five-thirty. Another half-hour with Kaplan; then he would hop the subway for the Heights and be on time for dinner, which Margaret served precisely at seven. Finishing the mixture of whiskey and melted ice in his glass, he looked out the window at Manhattan, a jumble of Brobdingnagian IBM cards tented by a pollutant haze that made him yearn for places where you could see the sky.

Kaplan came back with two drinks.

"Be sure to leave me a tip," he said, straightening his shirt collar as he sat down. Since his divorce six months ago, Kaplan had undergone a renovation, losing thirty pounds while acquiring a hair transplant, a sun-lamp tan, and a new, casually fashionable wardrobe.

"Where were we?"

"You mean before you felt like taking out your hostility on the waitress?"

"Yeah."

"Basically that you're your own worst enemy. We don't play politics. You didn't get voted in because . . . I don't know how to put it . . . because of your style, the way you are . . ."

"What style?"

"Personal style. You're overly competitive, sometimes paranoid, with a tendency toward physical violence."

DelCorso, offended by the accuracy of this description, said nothing. He tipped his glass, the bitter campari cleansing the whiskey taste from his mouth.

"That's why those three guys voted against you. Not because they're old friends of Dunlop's."

"You can't tell me—"

"Yes, I can." Kaplan leaned forward, his artificially browned face only a few inches from DelCorso. "They would have done the same thing if you'd acted that way toward any other photographer. Add to that the letter we got last spring from Erinair's agency about that bullshit you pulled in Ireland. There're some members who think you ought to be put under observation."

"Maybe I'll do that. Go to the shrink the way you did when you were getting your divorce. Why is it, Al, that you needed a year of analysis to figure out you weren't in love with your wife anymore?"

"Let me give you some advice. I'm in your corner. Always have been. If you've got to be an obnoxious prick, be an obnoxious prick to somebody else. And while I'm handing out advice, I'll give you some more. We're all competitive, but somehow we manage to keep our little jealousies under the surface most of the time. The times we don't, we sure as hell don't let it drive us into delusions and then start slugging. And when somebody wins a Pulitzer or whatever, we don't go ranting and raving all over town that the awards committee was rigged."

"You know, maybe those guys are right. Maybe I do need to be put under observation. A crazy person usually doesn't think he's crazy, right? He thinks his delusions are real, am I right or wrong? And I think Dunlop hired the goon who did this." DelCorso put his finger on the small scar, just above the eyebrow, where the revolver's butt end had struck him. "As far as the Pulitzer committee goes, they do more politicking than Congress. I can't believe they gave it to him for that mediocre crap he did of the evacuation."

The Pulitzer. Though he liked to think of himself as a man with something more on his mind than winning prizes, DelCorso could not take a philosophical view about losing the Pulitzer this year. He'd been certain that "Death in Action," as he'd entitled the picture of the soldier in Xuan Loc, had deserved it. The prize would have confirmed the photograph as his trademark. It would have been the symbol of the world's applauding his work; and in that applause he would have heard the sound of final absolution and acceptance. The Pulitzer would have made him feel worthy of all he had.

"I wonder where it comes from?" Kaplan asked.

"What?"

"This anger. Did you inherit it? Order it from Sears Roebuck?"

"When I was ten, a kid three years older than me broke a clay sewer pipe over my head for no reason. That's when I figured out that the only thing life was going to give me was a ration of shit unless I put up my hands and started swinging first."

"You're not in an alley anymore and Dunlop isn't a juvenile delinquent with a sewer pipe."

"He's worse."

"Do you know what I think it is between you and that guy? It's a mentor complex."

"What the hell is that?"

Kaplan's expression had taken on a professorial gravity.

Having undergone a year of it, Kaplan now regarded himself as a minor expert on analysis and tended to hand out unsolicited opinions about everyone's subconscious motivations.

"Simple. Dunlop taught you the business and opened up doors for you. But that put you in his shadow, made you dependent. You had to declare your independence, like a son does from a father when the time comes. Because you grew up in a place where you get banged on the head for no reason, your way of declaring independence was to declare war."

"Thanks. Any charge?"

"No charge. But seriously, I think you should see somebody."

"Wait a goddamned minute. We got together for a few drinks so you'd explain why I didn't get membership. Now you're saying I ought to see a *shrink*?"

"I'm talking personal growth."

DelCorso groaned aloud. Personal growth—two of the buzz words Kaplan had learned on the couch.

"People can grow, Nick. They can change if they're willing to make the effort."

"Right. They can change their wardrobes and get hair transplants."

"You sarcastic bastard, listen to me. You know how things work at the agency. My suggestion to you is that if you want membership, you're going to have to change, knock that chip off your shoulder, and I don't think you can do it without professional help. A shrink can help put your head in a different space."

DelCorso remained silent, but had decided that if Kaplan used one more phrase like "put your head in a different space," he would put Kaplan's teeth in a different space.

"Well, what do you think?"

"Just what you'd expect me to think."

"Okay, I tried. Do me and yourself a favor. Try to mellow out. Don't get drunk and tell clients to shove fish up their asses, and don't go beating up Pulitzer Prize winners. If you mellow out, maybe you'll have a better shot next year."

"Mellow out, son, and Santa will bring you a present next Christmas."

"I didn't mean to sound condescending." Kaplan's attention was momentarily diverted by an attractive brunette, but he lost interest when he saw her take the arm of a man in a blue-vested suit. "You interested in dinner, Nick?"

"Should have asked me earlier. Maggie likes me to call before four if I'm not going to make it home."

"I guess that's an advantage of being single again. I don't have to call home anymore."

DelCorso sensed the loneliness in him and, for a second, considered inviting him to the house. He decided against it because a surprise dinner guest was the sort of surprise that made Margaret a nervous wreck.

The subway ride to the Heights did nothing to calm DelCorso's bad temper. The crowds, the smells, the graffiti splashed on the cars—"Latin Lords," "Satan's Disciples," "Tony C, A Living Legend"—markings of urban warrior tribes, kept his agitation simmering. Climbing out of the stale cellar of the station, he saw a black teen-ager sitting on a trash can, tapping his feet to the rhythms of the radio he held to his ear. Jivin'. A jive-ass spade. The music tells him he's alive, otherwise he's dead, you can see the deadness in his eyes, a dull film over them. The kid agitated him further, largely because he reminded DelCorso of himself fifteen years ago, a white version of this punk. He saw, under the dull film, the same anger in the eyes: street anger, which was a special rage in that it was democratic. It wasn't directed at a particular social class, race, sex, or nationality, though any one of these might serve as its temporary object. It was a feeling of being at crossed swords with the world, with rich and poor, white and black, with your own kind as much as with outsiders, with yourself. Where does it come from, Nick? It comes from the street, Al. Vietnam had heightened it, but it had been lighted in him long before Vietnam, maybe on that morning when a sewer pipe cracked his skull, shattering a lot of illusions and assumptions normally found in a ten-year-old boy.

But what should he do about it now? Kaplan was right—it was not an appropriate emotion for a man of his age and position and it was hobbling his career. Northstar, like Magnum, was a cooperative agency, owned by its members, a select circle of senior photographers. As far as prestige went, it played Yale to Magnum's Harvard; in terms of organization, it was as hierarchical as a medieval guild. You started as an associate, worked your way up to correspondent, and after two or three years were eligible for elevation to member, which entitled you to a share of the agency's profits in addition to your own fees and gave you first shot at the choicest assignments. Once a year the free-lance knights of this photographers' round table met to decide who, if anyone, would be admitted; selection was based less on merit and more on what Kaplan had called "your qualities as a human being." Del Corso took that to mean, if the members liked you, you got to be one of them.

He thought about this as he made a detour down Furman Street past the Brooklyn docks. He knew what had made his anger flare this afternoon: the recognition that he was disliked. It seemed an injustice to be voted down merely because a few of the knights didn't care for him. His work, he believed, more than compensated for his personality defects.

He continued down the street and, after making sure no one was looking, paused to dance on the balls of his feet and pop left jabs at imaginary jaws. The big-city desolation of the docks, the shards of beer and wine bottles glittering in the gutters, the metal containers stacked on the wharves, the old tires, cables, and oil drums littering the yards where freight cars hulked beside brick warehouses, the screeching winches loading freighters from the ends of the earth, the crew of off-duty longshoremen playing poker on a cable spool excited DelCorso's combativeness and love of self-dramatization. He walked a few more yards, stopped and threw a few more punches. Jab. Hook to the body. Side to side, up and down. He saw himself as the tough kid who'd battled his way to the top and was scorned for his raw mannerisms. A character from *On the Waterfront*. Couldda been a contender. Couldda been a champ. Left to the midsection, up to the face. Above him, traffic hummed on the BQE, but he could also hear the gulls, squealing over the green harbor, and caught the smell of the sea filtering through the odors of tar, diesel fuel, and brick dust. Two lefts and an overhand right . . . he's down! . . . eight, nine, ten. . . . It's over! Nick DelCorso is the new middleweight champion of the world! This old fantasy made the fire rise in him, but it was the fire of a rebellious pride, not rage. He would do nothing to knock the chip off his shoulder, he would strive to keep it there, even if it grew as big as Mt. Whitney. It was part of him, as immutable as the color of his eyes; and those who wished to like him would have to like him chip and all. The hell with the rest. Who did they think they were, what did they think the agency was? An exclusive men's club? A posh law firm? He would win them with his work. He was going to be so goddamned good that they would vote him in next year even if he revealed that he was an ex-con with a rap sheet for rape and armed robbery. He would do something extraordinary.

Lebanon.

He would go to Lebanon as he had gone to Vietnam in 1968—on spec. Goddamnit, if you were going to free-lance, then you might as well do it all the way, without the comfortable cushions of fat expense accounts and guaranteed daily rates. You surrendered those and received freedom in exchange, freedom from worries about deadlines and shipping film, from the necessity to conform to the tastes of whatever magazine was paying your fare. He would pay his own fare, shoot with total freedom, and shoot better material than anyone had over there. Which wouldn't be difficult—so far, most of the stuff he'd seen coming out of Lebanon was wire-service mediocrity. Besides, the war, from what he'd read in the papers, seemed tailor-made for the message he wished to get across. The horror that lay at the center of all wars was there, but it was not wrapped in gauzy illusions about duty and sacrifice, excitement and purpose. As far as he could tell, it had no purpose whatsoever.

He walked into the house, ten minutes late. Ten minutes fell within Margaret's zone of tolerance for tardiness, so he wasn't greeted with reproving looks. Dinner, as usual, was spectacular by the standards of most American households: baked snapper in an orange and lemon marinade, wild rice, asparagus with hollandaise, and a chilled Chardonnay. As usual, it began with Margaret saying grace. Danny mugged during the prayer, as usual, and as usual, Margaret admonished him.

"Daniel Francis, I've told you a thousand times to be reverent during grace. "

"Sorry, Mom."

"Not as sorry as you're going to be if you pull that again," DelCorso said in the tone of the paterfamilias. Although he did not believe in praying before meals—God hadn't put food on the table, he had with his hard-earned dollars—he felt compelled to support Margaret out of respect for her religious principles.

"How come you don't say grace, Dad?"

"Because Mom says it."

"That doesn't answer my question," replied the precocious Danny.

"I'll explain when you're older. Now eat and don't give me any more of your lip."

Margaret suddenly froze him with one of her cold stares. He recognized that look: a sign that the Ice Princess had been offended by something, but DelCorso could not imagine what it was. Did she find the phrase "don't give any more lip" impolite? Probably, but not so impolite as to warrant a glance that frigid. What? He took a bite of snapper, pretending not to notice but, unable to stand the suspense, asked:

"What's the matter?"

'Nothing. Why? . . . Angela, eat your rice."

"I don't like rice."

"If you don't eat your rice, you're not getting dessert."

"You just gave me the look of death."

"I did? You must be imagining things, Nick."

"I didn't imagine anything."

"There's nothing the matter . . . Angela, I told you to eat your rice or no dessert. I mean it."

"What's for dessert?"

"Your favorite. Fudge ripple."

With a sulky defiant expression that was her father all over again, Angela obeyed and took a spoonful of rice.

"How's the snapper, Nick?"

"Fine."

"I wouldn't mind getting a compliment now and then without having to solicit it."

"Is that what's the matter?"

"Nothing's the matter. I got the recipe from a marvelous woman I met this morning."

"Who's that?" DelCorso asked, his eyes on the wandering Jew hanging over the kitchen window, his mind elsewhere.

"Gladys Paige. She buys period furniture for museums and official residences, embassies, that sort of thing. In fact, she helped Jackie Kennedy furnish the White House. Her family and Jackie's had summer places in the Hamptons."

"One of those."

"What do you mean, 'one of those'? She's a very cultured woman. Refined in a way you don't see often anymore. There isn't anything she doesn't know about period pieces. Or art. Or plays. Her youngest son is with the Guthrie right now."

"What's the son of this cultured, refined woman doing with a hippie folk singer?"

Margaret suppressed a laugh.

"Not Arlo Guthrie. The Guthrie. The Tyrone Guthrie."

"What's that?"

"You're joking."

"No."

"It's in Minneapolis," she said in a lecturing tone. "It's an internationally known repertory theater."

"Never heard of it," he snapped.

"You're awfully touchy today."

The last thing he needed tonight was to be made to feel like a cultural boob by his own wife because he didn't know the Tyrone Guthrie was a famous theater. He poked at the snapper and, for an instant, with his whole heart and soul, with every cell in his body, he wished he wasn't married to this snobbish beauty.

"Got the word today. I'm not going to be one of the part owners of Northstar, at least for the next year."

"Oh, Nick, I am sorry. What was wrong? The way you've been working . . ."

"That doesn't count. I'm not charming enough. I've got a chip on my shoulder. Kaplan thinks I should see a shrink so I can mellow out. The greening of Nick."

Margaret said nothing, and DelCorso interpreted her silence as at least partial agreement with Kaplan's recommendation.

"Finished my rice," Angela chirped. "Finished my rice."

"Quiet, Angie," Danny said. "I think Mom and Dad are going to fight."

"We are not, Danny. And besides, your father and I don't fight. We—"

"I know, Mom." On his freckled face, Danny's grin was the grin of a slightly malicious elf. "You *discuss*."

Little smart ass, DelCorso thought.

"That's right."

"I don't care. I finished my rice, so now I can have fudge ripple."

"No. Now you've got to finish your fish. Then you can have fudge ripple."

"Mommy!"

"You heard me."

"I've got to make a phone call," DelCorso said, draining his wineglass.

"Aren't you hungry? I went through a lot of trouble to make this, Nick."

Good. Make me feel guilty about not eating. The fact is I lost my appetite because I don't like feeling I'm an ignorant slob and there are a few things I want to get off my chest but I can't do it with Angie complaining about her damned fudge ripple.

"I had a late lunch with Kaplan." It seemed an acceptable lie. He hadn't lied about the phone call, though he did not have to make it at that moment. What he had to do at that moment was leave the table before he tipped it over, threw a plate, turned on the kids, or said something truly offensive to Margaret.

In the living room, he took a bottle of brandy from the liquor cabinet and poured a double. The Tyrone Guthrie, he thought, climbing the stairs to the bedroom. She made it sound as though the Tyrone Guthrie was a household word, like the New York Yankees. Sitting on the edge of the bed, he dialed the number for IPS and asked for a copy editor he knew on the cable desk.

"Can you get a message to Bolton for me?"

"Yeah, sure," the man said. "What is it?"

DelCorso paused, composing the message in his mind, his ears open to the sound of Margaret's footsteps on the stairs.

"Make it as follows: 'Beirutwards asapest. With airport closed need info best way into country and any other tips you can give. Regards, Nick.' "

"That's short enough. I'll get it out on our next service message to him."

When he hung up, DelCorso had all the contradictory emotions of a husband arranging a rendezvous with a lover. He was excited and guilty, full of anticipation, and a little frightened. Kicking off his shoes, he lay back on the cool sheets and savored the brandy. Combined with the whiskey he'd drunk earlier and the wine he'd had at dinner, it made him drowsy.

He was on the edge of dozing off when Margaret entered the room, a high color in her cheeks. She did not look at DelCorso as she strode across the floor into the bathroom. When she came out, she called down the hall to Fiona:

"You can put the dishes in the dishwasher now."

"All right, Maggie," came Fiona's crisp, English voice.

"How come she wasn't at dinner?" DelCorso asked. Margaret was sitting in front of the mirror, brushing her hair, its russet filaments shining in the light.

"I guess she had a late lunch too."

"Maggie, I know you went through a lot of trouble—"

"It isn't that. It's that on top of everything else."

"What's wrong?"

"Did you make your phone call?"

"Yes."

The brush tore from the crown of her head to the tips of her hair, the static electricity crackling, like her voice.

"You come home late, you spend ten minutes with us, and then you go off to make a phone call, and I find you here, drinking by yourself. It's as though you can't stand being around us."

"C'mon, Maggie. You're making a big deal out of nothing. There's something else."

She laid down the brush and turned to him. There was something artificial in the movement of her head, like an actress responding to a cue.

"If you think your not paying much attention to us is nothing, then I suppose you'd think anything else I have to say is less than that."

Were all women this evasive?

"Try me."

"It's Danny."

"It had better not be problems in school, not with the money I'm laying out for that place."

"You saw it tonight. His irreverence. He was awful at mass yesterday, just awful. I couldn't settle him down and had to tell him to leave and wait outside. Then, today, I got a note from his Sunday school teacher and found out he's been misbehaving there as well."

"I'll talk to him."

"I don't think your talking to him will do much good." Margaret rose and moved to the french doors, where she stood with one hand holding the curtains, her movements again somewhat staged. "I think if you set a better example it would make a difference."

"I know what's coming."

"Nick, how much trouble could it be? Danny's at an age when boys imitate their fathers, which is why I think your example would make a difference. He's supposed to make his first communion this year."

DelCorso yearned for another brandy.

"How many times have we been through this? I don't believe in any of it, not a word of it, and I feel like a damned hypocrite when I'm in a church."

"I suppose I should admire your honesty, but I don't. I

think you're carrying it too far. I'm just asking you to do something that will do your son some good."

"What're you saying? That I don't do anything for him? What about that goddamned private school he's going to? He's in second grade and I'm already laying out tuition like he's at Harvard."

"I'm not talking about the check-writing variety of fatherhood."

"I know what you're talking about. You want me to start going to mass, not just for him. For you. Like you wanted me to go to that ballet last month, or that concert the month before or the opera. I'm not religious and I'm not a culture vulture. I'm not now and wasn't when you married me."

"I know." Her voice diminished. "I just thought . . ."

"Thought what?" Sensing an advantage, he decided to press it. "That you'd make me different? Little by little, year by year, and then one day Nick becomes a clone of those jerks who used to take you out and who you couldn't wait to get away from? Nick becomes the kind of man your father approves of—if, that is, he changes that funny-sounding dago name of his."

"That's unfair. That's really unfair."

"When it comes to your old man, I can't be unfair enough."

"I meant unfair to me."

DelCorso lay silent on the bed, thirsting for another brandy but too lethargic to go downstairs and pour one. He did not think he had been unfair to her; if anything, he'd been the opposite, protecting her from the conviction closest to his heart: he had not believed her yesterday when she told him she loved him for what he was; she wanted him to become the kind of man *she* approved of. If, in marrying him, she had had motives ulterior to love—he was a way out of a future she did not want but could not escape on the power of her own will—love had, nevertheless, formed the core of her attraction, the instincts of her heart telling her that he was her masculine counterpart despite their differences. She had escaped the future that had been laid out for her, but time proved she had not freed herself from her past and all it had taught her about which kind of man was the right kind for her. The lessons of her girlhood gradually overcame her natural impulses. Those old voices censured her for loving DelCorso as he was, commanding her to recast him into a model worthy of their esteem. On his part, DelCorso was at times attracted to the idea of being remolded by her. Perhaps the world would find him more acceptable if his tastes and manners improved, if he could discourse at length on ballets and operas, be seen at the theater, have a reputation as a devoted family man who accompanied his wife and children to church. Perhaps he would find himself more acceptable, able to look in the mirror and have gaze back at him a civilized man out of whom the grit of the streets had been refined at last. His pride, however, led him to resist Margaret's attempts at reformation; his pride and his fear that he would smother the angry fire that had driven him this far if he became someone else. A war photographer, like a professional fighter, could not afford to lose his demons. Overlying this anxiety was the worry that Margaret, who now loved but disapproved of him, would approve of him but cease to love him; and possession of her heart being more important to him than her approbation, he chose to remain as he was.

"Well, Nick? Wasn't that unfair? I *took* your name. I'm not ashamed of it. Maybe you are."

"Those guys at the agency think I'm a hot-headed wop with a chip on his shoulder. Your old man does, so maybe you do too."

Margaret made a start toward the dresser, then stopped and looked around, either for some activity to distract her or for something to throw at him.

"Is that how we sailed off on this tack? Because of what happened at the agency?"

"Maybe."

"You are the most defensive man I've ever met, I swear. I'm a Catholic, I want to raise my children as Catholics, and all I was asking for was a little help from you in raising them and you respond with this crazy idea that I want to change you so my father will approve of you."

"I'm not going to make a hypocrite of myself. What the hell good is that going to do for Danny? Seeing his old man genuflecting and making the sign of the cross when he knows it's a sham?"

DelCorso had forgotten his many foxhole conversions—those times of danger when he had knelt and crossed himself with a martyr's fervor.

"He doesn't have to know what you're thinking, Nick. He just has to see you there once in a while."

"Lie to the kid, in other words."

"You're impossible. I give up."

Margaret, though, did not give up, at least not immediately. The argument continued for another half-hour; because it was one they had had two or three times before, each could anticipate the other's responses, each knew which limits were not to be crossed, and so they were able to conduct the dispute without raising their voices or saying something that could not be forgotten or forgiven. Eventually the quarrel ended, not because any resolution had been reached but because it seemed pointless to pursue it any further. The house settled into its evening routine: DelCorso went down to the library and read a magazine over another brandy; Margaret and Fiona tidied the kitchen, then, at nine, put Danny and Angela to bed, making sure the children said their prayers.

By eleven, the couple were in bed. Their argument forgotten, they made love.

DelCorso did not experience with his wife the moments of ecstasy and total abandon he had experienced in his fantasies. He loved Margaret with a tender fastidiousness. Any man who saw her might wonder how he failed to be driven mad by her perfect beauty; but the lack of defect was the problem, for it made her appear like an artist's ideal conception of a woman, a masterpiece of human architecture so smooth and symmetrical that she aroused the stasis of awed admiration rather than the kinesis of passion. Margaret's body was the outward form of the purity DelCorso had seen in her that day on the tennis courts, all in white, the restrained caution of his lovemaking an expression of respect. He was afraid that if he released the wild desire that was in him and did what he wanted, which was to clutch her buttocks and lift them high off the bed, her back arching as he rose to his knees, thrusting into her until he wrung from her a cry of pain and delight, uniting in that suspended instant angel and beast, touching the hand of God by letting the devil loose, he would degrade her. A satyr raping a goddess. And so he kissed her gently, embraced her carefully, protecting her from himself.

Margaret fell asleep immediately. DelCorso lay awake, recalling the times he'd returned again and again to the Columbia courts, hoping to see her once more, drawn to the white vision of her. Then, on a warm afternoon in the early fall, she reappeared. Enchanted, he watched her rise on tiptoe and lob a serve to her partner's backhand side.

Her partner, the same one she'd had on the day he first

saw her, rushed in from the base line, crowded the ball, and caught wood with an awkward chop. The ball ricocheted over the fence, bouncing on the sidewalk a few feet from DelCorso before it rolled to rest under a car across the street.

"Game, set!" said Margaret, walking triumphantly to the net to shake the dark-haired girl's hand. Then she daubed her face with a towel, which was also white.

"Six-four that time, Maggie. I'm getting better. Let's try one more if you're up to it."

"After a break, Sharon. What happened to the one you knocked over the fence?"

"Went into the street somewhere. All the others we've got are dead, but I'll be damned if I'm going to crawl under cars for it."

"We can play with two if, Sharon, you learn to stop crowding the ball and catching wood."

DelCorso guessed they hadn't asked him to get the ball because they were afraid to speak to him: with his build, dark hair and skin, he probably looked like one of the characters Barnard girls were warned against, a Puerto Rican infiltrator from Morningside Heights named Angel or Rosario who dealt hard drugs and raped girls on an unmade bed under a picture of the Sacred Heart. And, as he crossed the street to fetch the ball, it occurred to him that the orbit of his life passed much closer to the world of the Angels and Rosarios than it did to whatever planet Margaret and Sharon had come from. Nevertheless, his instincts, always as true as a lensatic compass, told him something could happen between him and the red-head. Against all reason, they told him it *would* if he could think of a way to make it happen.

With the ball in his hand, he tried to devise a strategy. He could flip the ball over the fence and simply go on his way, a gesture of casual gallantry. Or he could walk boldly up to the gate and hand it to them, but he wasn't sure he had the nerve. He stood by the curb, pondering his options while the girls rested on the bench, their backs to him. For a few moments, he could not move at all. What conceit to think a woman like her would bother to speak to him; her slightly lazy, slightly breathless voice, the poise with which she moved around the court said money, a lot of it. Money, class, grace—in sum, everything he didn't have. To build his courage, he tried to inflate his self-image. He bloused his shirt to accentuate his broad shoulders and narrow waist; he tidied his hair, thick, black, and wavy; he looked into the sideview mirror of a car to convince himself that his broken nose was offset by his eyes, which tilted upward at the corners, and which some women described as sexy. He worried about his limp, which was pronounced in those days. If one of the women asked about it, he would have to come up with an alibi: an auto accident, a football injury, anything but the truth. The radicals who'd made Columbia a battleground weren't the only people who considered Vietnam veterans criminals; just about everyone did. DelCorso himself often thought he was one, though his shame was less for what he had done and more for what he had learned in the war: an ugly truth about himself and about human nature that he was not supposed to know. And his limp, like the scars on his leg, was an outward mark of this forbidden knowledge.

But the scars were also signs of another kind of knowledge that gave him the nerve to walk up to the gate and tap on one of the iron posts.

"Excuse me, does this belong to you?" He overenunciated to refine the staccato street rhythms out of his voice.

The heads of the two women turned as one. Through the fretwork of the Cyclone fence, DelCorso saw Margaret's eyes, an intense and promising green.

"Is it a Wilson three?" she asked, her voice rising a fraction of an octave on "three." DelCorso was encouraged; somehow he'd known she'd be the one to answer him.

"A what?"

"The ball. Is it a Wilson with three dots on it?"

DelCorso glanced at the ball, feeling that he looked as stupid as a monkey examining a strange object.

"Yes, it does."

"It's ours, then."

Sensing himself at a critical threshold, he hesitated for a beat, to see what she would do. His heart expanded, squeezing his lungs when, instead of asking him to toss the ball over the fence, she rose and came to the gate. A woman didn't learn to walk the way she did, it was born into her, a genetic memory. With the same natural, regal air, Margaret extended her hand after opening the gate.

"Thanks very much," she said. Struggling against an impulse to touch her white arm, he handed her the ball. She withdrew behind the gate. DelCorso imagined he was putting out signals strong enough to be felt physically, but as he stud-

ied her green eyes for a response, he saw none of the promise
he fancied he'd seen in them at a distance; they glowed as
emptily as radar screens when no planes are in the air.

Say something, say it now before she goes away.

"Shouldn't you be playing at Riverside?"

Her eyes registered only a question.

"Riverside? The courts there are full up. They're always
full."

"I mean, it could get dangerous around here."

Margaret's gaze drifted toward the street.

"Oh, I suppose it could," she said, her voice freighted with
assurance that nothing would happen to her. DelCorso immediately recognized her confidence as the kind that was created by a failure of the imagination; she sounded like certain
happy warriors he'd known in Vietnam, men incapable of be-
lieving anything could hurt them until something did.

"You go to Barnard or here?"

"We're graduate assistants here when the Leninists aren't
protesting something. We thought it would be fun to spend a
few months in New York."

"Yeah, sure. Fun City." Jesus, I don't believe I said that.
"Where're you from?" And I don't believe I said that, either.

"The North Shore. Marblehead."

DelCorso nodded knowingly, although the name meant
nothing to him then.

"What about you?"

"Chicago," he answered, excited that she had shown even
this perfunctory interest in him. Involuntarily, he inched forward until he was hanging on to the fence like a prisoner
in a detention camp. Margaret, only a couple of feet from
him, stood with her racket under her arm, one ankle crossed
over the other. She looked like a model posing for a resort
advertisement. Sharon, more wary or less innocent about
speaking to strange men this close to the frontier of Spanish Harlem, stayed near the net, holding her racket like a
club, ready to fend off the lustful lunge of Rosario the Rapist.
Sharon knows the score, Sharon thinks I'm a creep. I am a
creep, DelCorso thought, because, in fact, he wanted to lunge
through the gate, though not with the intent to commit
rape: he wanted to embrace Margaret, to immerse himself
in the whiteness of her clothes and flesh as in a baptismal
font.

"Chicago," Margaret said. "What brings you to Columbia?" She glanced at his camera bag. "Oh, you're probably in the journalism school."

"I'm past the J-school stage. I'm with AP."

Digging into his pocket, he produced a press card and passed it to her, this to establish that he was a respectable young man, legitimately employed.

"DelCorso," she said, reading the card. "There's a street in Rome called the Via del Corso. Are your people from Rome originally?"

"No, they're from southern Italy," he replied defensively. He hadn't cared for the way she said "your people," as though he belonged to some exotic Indian tribe.

"Ah, the *mezzogiorno. Forze Calabria!* Ah, Calabria, Calabria," she went on in a mock theatrical voice. "*Una provincia più bella.*"

What the hell is this!

"Where'd you learn to speak Italian?"

"In Italy. I studied at the Uffizi for a year. I'm in art history. I adore Italy."

"My grandparents didn't feel the same way about it."

"And you're a photographer," she said, ignoring his swipe. "That fits, Italians are a very visual people, you know."

"No, I didn't know that." DelCorso leaned against the fence post, thinking, I've got to go somewhere with this conversation or get out of here. "Are you teaching art at Columbia?" Beautiful, Nick. Real original.

"Yes. As a matter of fact, one of the courses is on the history of photographic art."

"That should be a pretty short course."

"Why?"

"Because photography isn't art. It's applied science. Any photographer who calls himself an artist is a fraud."

"Dr. Lawson would choke if he heard that."

DelCorso paused, seeking to draw encouragement from her eyes. Nothing.

"Do you live in the neighborhood?" he asked tentatively.

"In this neighborhood? Of course not. We're staying with friends on West Seventy-second."

"Maggie, for God's sake!" Sharon called in warning.

"What's the matter?"

"For God's sake." Sharon strode to the gate, brandishing her racket. "If you don't know, it won't do any good to tell you."

"Oh, that. There's nothing to worry about. This is Mr. DelCorso. He's a photographer, and he's got an opinion about art and photography that would make Dr. Lawson choke if he heard it."

"Really." Sharon's voice reminded DelCorso of the frozen-food department.

"He just told me that any photographer who calls himself an artist is a fraud."

"Is that right?"

"Dr. Lawson would gag if he heard that."

Sharon gave DelCorso a look whose disapproval had nothing to do with his opinions about art and photography.

"Thank you for returning our ball, Mr. DelCorso." Her voice moved out of frozen foods and into the meat locker. Any colder and he'd need a sheepskin coat.

"No problem."

And it wouldn't be any problem to tear a string out of your racket and strangle you with it.

"Maggie, don't you think it's time for the next set?"

Tell the bitch to go practice her backhand.

"All right. Let's see if you can do better than six-four this time. Very nice talking to you, Mr. DelCorso."

"Nick."

"Very well. Nice talking to you, Nick."

DelCorso would have lost his nerve if, just before she returned to the court, Margaret had not tossed him a crumb of hope with her eyes. The expression in them was more coquettish than it was seductive, a kind of girlish flexing of her powers to attract; nevertheless, it encouraged him, if for no other reason than it failed to discourage him.

"Could I call you sometime?"

"You could here. Just ask for me at the graduate school. Margaret Fitzgerald," she replied, eliciting a disapproving groan from Sharon.

DelCorso returned to his car in a euphoric mood, but his happiness was diluted by a peculiar thought in the back of his mind: for a woman like her to display any interest in a man like him was evidence that something was wrong with her.

THE ONLY LIGHT was the ghostly blue of the digital clock. Three A.M. DelCorso fumbled the phone off the hook. Margaret, a sound sleeper, had not been awakened by its ringing.

"Is this Mr. DelCorso?" asked a youngish male voice.

"Yeah."

"This is IPS. Sorry for calling you at this hour. We've got an urgent Harry Bolton has asked to pass on to you."

DelCorso told him to wait. Sitting up, he switched on the reading light and took a pad and pencil from the drawer of the nightstand.

"Okay, shoot."

"It says: 'Can't stay out of it, can you? Only two ways into country. Fly Cyprus, book overnight freighter passage Larnaca for Junieh, Christian port north of Beirut. Or fly Amman, hire one of the Lebanese drivers taking stills and TV footage Beirut to Jordan for satellite relay. Drive will cost two-fifty U.S. Will need transit visa through Syria. Have booked you room at Commodore. See you soon. Regards, Harry.' That's it, Mr. DelCorso. Really sorry to call you at this time, but it said urgent."

"Don't worry about it. Thanks."

A pleasant agitation would not let him go back to sleep. Taking an overnight freighter from Cyprus appealed to his romanticism, but hiring a driver in Amman sounded like a surer thing. He would need a visa for Jordan as well as for Syria and Lebanon. Get those at the consulates. Draw money from the bank tomorrow. Five thousand should do it. Pay for airline tickets with his credit card. He lit a cigarette, trying to order the muddle of thoughts and emotions in him. When that had no effect, he padded into the bathroom and sneaked one of Margaret's Valiums. Valium. Would she be all right? Yes, she would handle it. He could wrap this one up in two weeks, three perhaps. Lying down beside her again, he looked at her sleeping form with tangled feelings, excited he was leaving, wishing he could stay, wondering why he could not be the kind of husband and father she wanted him to be. He felt he owed that to her, because she was, in an uncertain world, the center of his life, inviolate and intact. Because, deep within himself, he agreed with what her father had said about him: he wasn't good enough for her as he was. Something wrong with her? No. With him. He didn't deserve this thoroughbred who could have chosen any man but had chosen him. The anger that sometimes caused their quarrels was, he saw now, an anger toward himself and whatever it was in his nature that prevented him from living up to her image of what he ought to be. Why couldn't he have bent his principles a bit and compromised on the matter of going to mass?

Self-criticism, however, cannot be sustained for long. As he lay facing her, there rose in him insensibly a resentment toward her for awakening a sense of his own unworthiness. It was not the things she said that troubled him, the subtle reminders of his ignorance or his failings; rather, the facts of her existence reproached the facts of his, forcing him to compare himself unfavorably to her. He contrasted his unattractiveness to her beauty, his high school diploma to her blue-chip education, his social awkwardness to her grace, the wealth of her family to the commonness of his, her virtues as a mother to his inadequacies as a father, his impulsiveness to her deliberateness, his infidelities to her fidelity. He wondered if he made an issue of her lapses with alcohol simply because it was the sole serious flaw he could find in her, and it allowed him to forget his own defects and his inability to correct them. Looking on her curving silhouette, he saw the fundamental reason why he had to leave, why he spent so much time on the road: to get away from her because he didn't like himself when he was around her. That realization had never come to him before, at least not this clearly. It confused and frightened him. He loved and needed her, and yet also needed to escape her and her rebuking virtues.

27

TEN DAYS AFTER the slaughter of Nabil, Bolton rode into the Holiday Inn in an armored personnel carrier the Phalangists had hijacked from the Lebanese army, now reduced to a force of night watchmen guarding embassies and a presidential palace where no government had functioned for months. The APC had clattered up a narrow back street in the predawn darkness, drawing spurts of rifle fire from insomniac Moslems, and stopped at the loading dock in the rear of the hotel. Where frozen steaks, fish fillets, and cases of French wine had once been hauled off delivery trucks, crates of small-arms ammunition, rocket-propelled grenades, and plastic explosives were pushed out of the APC and lugged into the building by gunmen wearing camouflage fatigues.

The ride up from the corniche had been no more than a few blocks, but to Bolton, waiting for a rocket to turn the APC into a crematorium, it had seemed like miles. Relieved to escape the vehicle, he followed his escort, Sami, a balding pudgy man who'd managed a furniture store before the war, across the dock into an unlighted corridor. Ruffles and flourishes. He had made it. The first correspondent to get inside the hotel that was described in every dispatch, including his own, as "embattled." He wondered why he did not feel the usual flush of victory. Maybe four-thirty in the morning was too early to feel triumphant about anything. Ahead of him, the *kataeb* carrying the ammunition formed a line of muttering shadows. They turned down another corridor, on whose wall Bolton made out an arrow and sign that read MAIN LOBBY. Sami led him in the opposite direction, into a glaringly bright kitchen that had been transformed into an urban guerrillas' cafeteria: a brawny man with a revolver on his hip was frying eggs while a dozen-odd *kataeb*, plates in hand, stood waiting under the stainless-steel pots that still hung from the overhead racks.

"You would like something to eat before we meet Major Yusseff?"

"Just coffee."

"Only tea is made."

"Tea, then."

Sami waddled to a large urn and filled two cups.

"You see? We have everything we need and more. Yes, and more. Ha! Last night we had ice cream. The freezers are full with enough to last us weeks."

"What're you going to do when that's finished? Order out?"

"By that time our brothers in East Beirut will have opened a corridor. Taking Karatina was the first step."

"Yeah, I was there. Some step."

"But if our brothers fail, we'll die here if we have to."

"Count on having to."

"What? Do you think the *fedayeen* have us trapped? No! How could we have brought you here in the armored car if they have us trapped?"

"Lucky."

The strong tea scoured from Bolton's tongue the coppery aftertaste of the fear that had gripped him in the APC. Sipping from the cup slowly, he laid his tape recorder on the countertop and tried to muster the enthusiasm he was supposed to feel. He thought about the long hours he and Raymond had worked, arranging to get him in here (and, he hoped, out), the chances he had taken to rendezvous with the Phalangists this morning. He dwelled on the rockets that would fly into the offices of the competition once this story was on the wire and on the air. On the air. Even the correspondents from the national networks would get a few blasts. *Bolton IPS on-scener inside Holiday Inn. Can you match!* He had always wanted to give those silken-voiced stars of the airways a whipping, but now that he was about to . . . *Beat! Exclusive! Scoop!* Shit.

Nothing, it seemed, could dissolve the fog of indifference within him. These journalistic triumphs were not worth the effort and the risk; and the longer he thought about this one, it appeared less like the fruit of initiative and enterprise and more like a stunt, a newsman's equivalent of riding a motorcycle over a pyramid of flaming fuel drums.

The *kataeb*, all with faces charcoaled by five-day growths, found places for themselves and started eating ravenously. The smell of the eggs making Bolton decide he was hungry after all, he asked for a plate.

"Of course. Of course. Major Yusseff may not yet be awake so we have time. How would you like them? Let me guess. Easy over. All Americans like their eggs easy over."

"Over easy."

"Ha! Yes! Over easy."

"Make mine scrambled."

Sami put in his order. While the cook was scrambling the eggs, three more militiamen stumbled into the kitchen, one of them a belligerent kid wearing a black beret, a gold crucifix, and a tanktop, over which was slung an AK-47 with a folding paratrooper's stock. He said something to the cook, whose reply sounded like an insult, though Bolton could not understand a word. The kid's answer was sharp, and the exchange, like most disputes in this screwball country, became violent in seconds. The cook, built like a bouncer, whipped hot grease from the spatula into the kid's face, flung him against the counter, and banged him over the head with an aluminum pot. The other two men seized his arms before he could swing again, but were wrestled off by half a dozen of the *kataeb* who had been eating. Outnumbered, the three were shoved out of the kitchen like rowdy drunks from a bar, the kid dazed and staggering, a river system of blood flowing down his face.

"What was all that about?" Bolton asked casually. He'd grown as used to these sudden outbursts as a tropic islander is to monsoon squalls.

"Chamounists," replied Şami, not without contempt. "The Chamounists sent us a few men, about a dozen, as a sign of solidarity, they said. But the real reason is political. They want to show the Maronites that they are sharing in this fight, to steal support from the Phalange."

"So what was all that over? Who gets the Christian vote in the next election?"

"Ice cream."

"Right."

"It was not over politics. It was the ice cream. The younger one told our man to cook them something for breakfast because last night none of the Chamounists got ice cream. Our man said he did not cook for Chamounists, who eat through their assholes. Then the younger one questioned the honor of our man's wife."

"Bet his wife would be happy to know how well he defends her honor."

"He isn't married."

The burly cook, gazing suspiciously at Bolton's tape recorder, handed over the eggs, next to the kid's skull the major casualty of the brawl: left on the grill, they'd burned to a cinnamon brown

"Yes, the Chamounists have been angry at us since last night," Sami went on. "We had only enough ice cream for our people. We had to think of our people first."

"Sure. Listen, not getting any ice cream is as good a reason as any to get your skull cracked open."

A faint vibration passed through the walls as an RPG exploded in one of the upper stories. It appeared to be a signal to the militiamen, who, as automatically as laborers responding to a factory whistle, slung their rifles and filed out.

"I think now we can see Major Yusseff."

Bolton traipsed after Sami into the main lobby, broken glass crunching underfoot like loose gravel. Beneath a chandelier hanging precariously from a circular molding, a Phalangist lay stretched out on the reception desk, behind him rows of mailboxes with room keys still dangling from the hooks. Another man slumped in a lounge chair near a counter marked with a sign INF MA N D SK. He would have looked like a shabbily dressed guest but for the Kalashnikov on his lap and the grenades hanging from his belt. Looking to one side, Bolton noticed that the three Chamounists had found solace after the loss of their kitchen privileges: they occupied the bar, the kid wearing a napkin around his head as a bandage, the other two seated on stools before a bottle of some kind of clear liquor, probably the potent brandy called *arak*.

The hotel manager's office had been converted into Major Yusseff's command post. Yusseff had held that rank in the Lebanese army before deserting to join the Phalangists, and still wore the insignia on his collar.

"Welcome, Mr. Bolton," he said, rising from behind the

desk. He was a man of average height with a sensual mouth bracketed by a drooping black mustache. "Welcome to the Holiday Inn." Square white teeth gleamed under the mustache. "We hope you enjoy your stay."

This turkey's got a great sense of humor, thought Bolton, setting his tape recorder on the desk. Major Yusseff looked past him toward the door.

"Where is your crew?"

"My crew?"

"You are with NBC television?"

"No."

"ABC? CBS?"

"No."

"I was informed you were with television."

Goddamned Raymond, had to push it.

"You were misinformed. It's radio."

"Ah, yes, NBC radio."

"No, not NBC radio. IPS."

"Excuse me?"

"I . . . P . . . S. The wire service."

"Wire service?" Major Yusseff asked, a little indignantly. "A wire service?"

"Yes, I'm afraid so."

The major sat down, crestfallen, his hopes of making John Chancellor or Walter Cronkite dashed.

"I thought you were network."

"Sorry, major, somebody misinformed you."

The major drummed his fingers on the desk, apparently trying to decide what to do. After conferring with Sami for a minute or two, he opted for half a loaf.

"Very well. The IPS wire service. Please. Proceed. Ask anything you wish."

Bolton switched on the recorder and recited a laundry list of routine questions. He had no illusions that he would extract any useful information from Major Yusseff. Or needed to. The major could have talked about anything—soccer scores, his children's grades, the price of tea in China—as long as he talked, his voice on tape being proof that IPS's man in Beirut had got inside the Holiday Inn and interviewed the Christian commander.

When the charade was over, the major gave him free run of the place so long as Sami remained with him; unescorted, he might run into trouble.

"Okay by me. I'm going to the roof first."

"The roof!" Sami's round, sleek face crinkled into an expression that was almost grief. "The roof!"

"Yeah, the roof."

"It is much too dangerous on the roof."

"Ya, Sami, no more dangerous than anywhere else." Major Yusseff's huge teeth showed again under the mustache. "It will do you good. You're too fat."

The generator didn't have enough power for the elevators, and Bolton, strained himself by the long climb, thought Sami was going to have a heart attack. Bolton had to carry his rifle the last fifteen flights. The former furniture salesman's face was a blob of scarlet, popping blood vessels by the time they reached the top. He collapsed in a corner, mumbling assurances to the snipers and machine-gunners, who appeared startled by the intrusion of a tall blond man packing a tape recorder.

Bolton surveyed the scene. A high concrete wall, with trash and debris piled up against it, encompassed the roof. The twigs of a dead plant fingered over the rim of a large cement potter. Three snipers sat resting against a circular object, probably a duct, beneath a garagelike structure that might have held the exhaust systems for the restaurant one floor below. Shrapnel and bullet holes were everywhere, bits of concrete strewn across the roof like rubble on a lunar plain.

In a half-crouch—the wall was not high enough to conceal the top of Bolton's head—he peered through a shell hole toward the hill that rose above the hotel, a density of apartment buildings climbing to the Moore Tower, atop which the twin barrels of a Palestinian anti-aircraft gun were silhouetted against the paling sky. Moving to the other side, he got a glance at the Phoenicia, almost within hand-grenade range, its east face all holes, chips, blast marks, and shattered windows framed by scorched walls. Good color for the print story, the esthetics of destruction. Now he needed sound for the roser.

But it was a quiet morning, and not having enough cynicism to ask the Phalangists to supply him with bang-bang by firing their rifles, he sat beside Sami and waited for something to happen.

All things come to he who waits. Sound. Noise. Noise that would delight the news editors on the radio desk. The anti-aircraft gun opened up, its 40-mm shells bursting in such rapid sequence the effect was that of a single explosion. The militiamen scattered to their firing positions, their AKs ripping the air apart. Flat on his belly, Bolton held up his mike. Gunshots popped from the Phoenicia, then an RPG went off, its roar like a man's cough amplified a thousand times. Overhead, things snapped, snicked, and hissed. Beautiful. The soundtrack to *All Quiet on the Western Front* couldn't have been better. A sniper atop the garagelike structure began shouting and signaling to the men below, whose fire slackened and stopped. The anti-aircraft gun kept on firing, and rifle shots continued to crack from the windows of the Phoenicia. Bent over like soldiers in a trench, several Phalangists ran to the wall nearest the leftist-held hotel, looked through the slit of a machine-gun emplacement, and started laughing.

"Hey, Sami, there's a joke here I'm missing."

"Joke? What joke?" Sami was pressed to the roof, the large cement potter protecting his head.

"What the hell are those guys laughing at?"

"At the Palestinians. They are doing our work for us."

Bolton sprinted to the machine-gun position and saw the 40-millimeter on the Moore Tower, like God's very own jackhammer, drilling holes into the walls of the Phoenicia.

"*Fedayeen*," said one of the *kataeb*, moving his forefinger in a circle over his temple. He had a superior grin on his face, as though the Moslems held a monopoly on insanity.

Bolton watched the intramural battle, wondering what had caused it. Dashing back to the other side of the roof, he asked Sami if the phones were working.

"Yes, I think so."

"Let's go."

More than happy to get back inside, Sami led him three floors down. Along the corridor, several rooms had been gutted, scorch marks darting out into the hall like black tongues. The doors to the others had been taken off or blown off.

"Ah, there." Sami pointed to the doorway of a suite on whose walls graffiti had been scrawled in lipstick: *Long live Lebanon, Long Live the Phalangist Party, Long Live the Blood of the Cedars.* "*Sabalkhair, bonjour,*" he said in a familiar tone as he walked inside. One of the most beautiful young women Bolton had ever seen sat by a window scanning over a sandbag barricade with a pair of binoculars. She wore a tiger-stripe camouflage uniform, starched and pressed to inspection standards, and a cartridge belt. A .30-06 Winchester leaned against the wall beside her chair, beneath which an attaché case lay on its side.

"*Bonjour*," she answered without taking the binoculars from her eyes.

"Leila, is your telephone in order?"

"Yes."

Bolton felt blood rushing into his crotch, a weakness in his knees.

"It's necessary for this journalist to make a call."

Only then did the beauty look at the two men. Her eyes, dark brown and hot, earth and fire, scrutinized Bolton with an expression he could not identify, a weird compound of lust and indifference.

"So. You are a journalist."

"Yeah."

"American?"

"Right."

"I thought so."

"What do you mean, you thought so?"

"I guessed you were an American."

"I don't get it."

"You live on the eighth floor of the Mazzan Building."

A faint, uncomfortable buzz traveled up and down Bolton's spine.

"This," she said, pointing with a lacquered fingernail at the scope of her Winchester. "There are all Moslems in your building. The first time I saw you, through the jalousies, I was that close"—the finger with which she'd pointed closed to within a hairsbreadth of her thumb—"but then I saw your light hair and how tall you are and I knew you could not be an Arab."

"When was that?"

"A week ago."

"You mind?"

"Not at all."

He went to the window and rested Leila's Winchester on the sandbags. The shutters to his bedroom window appeared within arm's reach through the twenty-four-power scope. Laying down the rifle, Bolton faced her.

"Last week a man was killed on the floor above mine. You?"

"Yes," Leila replied matter-of-factly.

"He was eighty years old."

"Moslem."

"You're quite the little lady."

Her eyes seemed to ravish him, seemed to be looking at him as he imagined they had when she'd centered the cross hairs on his chest.

You're sick, he thought. You're sick, this place is sick, the fact I'd like to screw you silly means I'm getting sick in it.

"Where's your telephone?"

"In the bedroom."

In the bedroom, Bolton asked Sami in an undertone:

"Who the hell is she?"

"Major Yusseff's mistress. Please do not think of making to her any love talk. He would kill you."

"Not before she does."

Sami had to make the call because the Phalangists' switchboard operator spoke no English. Raymond, who had gone to the bureau after Bolton boarded the APC, answered in a sleepy voice.

"Harry, you are inside? You are safe?"

"Safer here than in my own bedroom. It's pretty cushy, Raymondo. They even serve ice cream for dessert. Maybe I'll order a club sandwich from room service when I hang up."

"There is much firing, Harry."

"Tell me about it. Listen. It's the Feds in the Phoenicia and on the Moore Tower having a shootout. Find out what the hell's going on and call me back. I'm in room thirty-eighteen."

"Thirty-eighteen. All right."

While Bolton waited, Sami wandered around the suite, examining the furniture with a critical and practiced eye. This being the room of Major Yusseff's mistress, it had not been pillaged; but Sami began to take care of that. A brass bedside lamp caught his fancy; he unplugged it and placed it in a corner. Next to it he set a couple of ashtrays snatched from an end table; then he rolled the lamp and the ashtrays into a small oriental carpet "machine-made but good enough."

"What's the major's old lady going to say about you looting her room, Sami?"

"That whore's daughter won't notice the difference."

The whore's daughter, meantime, continued to scan the city for an available target.

While waiting for Raymond's call, Bolton noticed a copy of *Monday Morning* lying on the dressing table. The slick English-language monthly, which often confused degeneracy with sophistication, tastelessness with cleverness, showed on its cover the photograph of a statuesque model wearing a uniform and cartridge-studded belt similar to Leila's, the trousers tucked into a pair of spike-heeled boots. She stood in front of a bombed-out building, across which a banded headline read: SPECIAL FASHION ISSUE—DRESSING FOR URBAN WARFARE.

Bolton gazed at the magazine and thought, This is all really happening, and in a three-minute radio spot, in a six-hundred-word file, I'm supposed to make sense out of it.

Raymond called back.

"I got through to my Palestinian source, Harry."

Sitting on the edge of the bed, Bolton opened his notebook.

"The fighting is between the PFLP in the Phoenicia and the PDFLP. The PDFLP holds the Moore Tower."

"I already know that."

A familiar, acrid smell drifted into the room. An instant later, Bolton heard an explosion in the alley behind the hotel.

"There is also fighting in the camps."

"Which ones?"

"Sabra and Chatilla."

The smell hung in the air. Another explosion went off. In the other room, Sami and Leila were quarreling loudly in Arabic.

"What started it?"

Raymond told him, but with the poor phone connection, the hammering of the 40-millimeter, the explosions, and Sami and Leila's argument, Bolton had to ask him to repeat himself.

"I said, some of the men in the PDFLP did not get paid the last cease-fire. Last night, they asked all the Palestinian factions to call for another cease-fire so the banks could open and the men collect their money. All the factions agreed except the PFLP. They're always the most radical—"

"Hold on," Bolton said, writing quickly to catch up. "Okay, go ahead."

"So, one thing led to another, and in the Sabra camp, some PDFLP hotheads shot two men from the PFLP, and now they are at war."

"Anything else?"

Sami stormed into the room, muttering angrily to himself. He ripped another lamp from its socket and wrapped it in the carpet with the rest of his loot. At the same moment, the walls quivered from a shell bursting two or three stories below.

"Nothing else, Harry, except that the PLO is trying to stop

the fighting so the Palestinians can resume shooting Christians."

"Think they started already. An RPG just hit."

Sami tore into the other room and screeched at Leila. The sulfurous smell drifted into the room again. Another dull explosion followed.

"Harry, I don't think you should stay there too long. I can have the car ready for you right away."

"Give me half an hour, forty-five minutes."

After hanging up, Bolton tried to rough out a radio story in his notebook; but the bangs and crashes and Sami's shouts locked up his mental gears. Fragments of thoughts and phrases flew inside his head like shrapnel. *Bizarre scene here at Beirut's Holiday Inn . . . Phalangist Christians now under fire . . . PFLP in Phoenicia across street . . . but just moments ago . . . PFLP and PDFLP in gun battle with each other . . . explain why . . . Why? . . . Two factions dispute over calling for a cease-fire . . . Firing at each other because could not agree to cease fire with Christians . . . Can't make sense of this . . . Meanwhile, inside Phalangist stronghold saw a female member of Christian militia . . . No, female sniper . . . magazine issue with ladies' fashions for guerrilla warfare . . . Shit, nobody will believe this . . .*

Now Bolton heard bullets whacking into the walls outside. Sami, mumbling curses to himself, was back in the bedroom, tying his bundle with one of the lamp cords.

My escort, a militiaman who used to sell furniture, looted a room of lamps and carpets while . . .

He closed his notebook in frustration. Can't think in this madhouse. Do the roser at the office, splice in a few quotes from Major Yusseff, record over the bang-bang I got on the roof.

Sami cinched the lamp cord tightly around both ends of the carpet, then tied another length to both loops, forming a carrying strap. His face was flushed, thin ropes of blood vessels knotting under the skin of his forehead.

"Sami, what in the hell is going on?"

"What in the hell is going on?" he responded rhetorically. "Go into the other room and you will see what is going on."

Bolton went. Leila was carrying radical chic to its logical extreme. Having dressed for the role of girl guerrilla, she was now acting it out. Hunched down behind a sandbag barricade at the rearmost window, which faced the Phoenicia, she removed a fuse and blasting cap from the attaché case, inserted them into a baseball-size hunk of composition B, then got on all fours, the tiger-stripe trousers stretched tautly over her delectable ass, her back arched like a posturing cat in heat. Raising her head to look over the barricade, she flicked her Bic to light the fuse and casually lobbed the plastique bomb out the window.

. . . the Moslems in the Phoenicia started firing at us after the militiawoman began throwing bombs at their positions from the window of a suite in the Holiday Inn . . .

The bomb was answered by a spray of bullets, but a twisted fascination held Bolton to the spot. He watched Leila mold another piece of plastique. Her eyes met his for a moment, but he couldn't tell what she was thinking, if she was thinking anything at all. Expertly, she crimped another blasting cap to a short fuse, got back on all fours, and tossed the high explosive into space. The thought that this vicious and beautiful creature had once been a trigger-squeeze away from ending his life excited him anew and, looking at her buttocks, he wanted to rip her trousers off and take her from behind. Sick, sick. She's getting off on this and I'm getting off on watching her, talk about sex and violence, I'm going to get as sick as the rest of them if I don't get out of this city real soon.

"Goddamn bitch is drawing fire," he said to Sami.

"What do you think I was arguing with her about? She wants to. She's a fanatic. There is no fanatic like a fanatic with a cunt."

"It's check-out time, Sami."

They had climbed down about twenty flights when they heard an exchange of small-arms fire inside the hotel. Sami, the lampstands and rolled carpet slung over one shoulder, paused and unlimbered his AK from the other.

"What do you think?"

Bolton did not want to express what he thought: the only possible explanation was that the Palestinians had assaulted at street level, broken through, and were now fighting the Phalangists floor-to-floor.

"Only one way out, Sami."

They continued on down, Sami in the lead. The firing was very sporadic, but the closer they got to it, the more the furniture salesman's flabby body quivered with fear. Bolton was having a hard time controlling his own growing panic; he wanted to hide, under a bed, in a closet, but was driven on by a determination to escape this bullet-riddled cloud-cuckooland.

Sami had turned the corner to start down to the third floor when the door to the landing flew open. Bolton saw the bandaged head, the black beret, and the gold crucifix shining on the kid's brown neck; though his conscious mind registered no danger, his instincts told him to run. Sami, hampered by his stolen treasures, was not as quick. Bolton was halfway back up the fourth-floor flight when he heard the crash of an automatic rifle and the sound of a body tumbling down the stairs. Chunks of plaster, flying off the wall beneath and behind him, stung his back. Run. He lunged down the corridor, his tape recorder banging at his side, ducked into a room, and snaked under a bed.

He felt like a guilty lover fleeing a jealous husband—simultaneously terrified and embarrassed. Under a bed in the Holiday Inn. In all the other Holiday Inns of the world they're on the beds, watching television, sleeping, masturbating, making love, and I'm under one, hiding from a crazed kid tanked up on *arak*.

Someone ran down the hall. There was another burst of rifle fire.

They used to say I'd do anything for a story, but I'm not going to die for one, I'm sure as hell not going to die like this, not for three minutes on the radio and a few column inches on page one. More men came running down the corridor, Kalashnikovs rattling. Two grenade explosions made the floor vibrate. Bolton remained under the bed for several minutes, his legs drawn up so his feet would not show.

When he figured it was safe, he crawled out and cautiously looked down the corridor. Three men in green uniforms stood at the far end, near the fire door; another was dragging a body out of a room from which gray smoke billowed. Spotting the *kataebs'* cedar-tree patch on one of the militiamen's sleeves, Bolton started toward them, his thighs shaking, as though he'd just done fifty squat jumps.

. . . *my Phalangist escort was killed by a Chamounist Christian who had gotten drunk . . . angry because a Chamounist contingent was not fed ice cream last night . . . other Phalangists pursued him to a room on the fourth floor, where*

he was killed with hand grenades . . . if you believe any of
this, Mr. and Mrs. America, I could sell you a perpetual-
motion machine that also dices onions . . .

"Ah, wire service, thank God you are safe."

Major Yusseff shook his head, obviously grateful he did
not have a dead American journalist to account for.

"I was very worried about you. We found Sami on the
stairs."

"I'm all right."

The young Chamounist lay nearby, his body resembling
something that had been fed into a tree mulcher.

"I very much regret you had to be here when this happened."

"Not as much as I do."

"This drunk boy, down the stairs, he also killed our cook."

"Also, he killed my escort. You got another one? I want
to get out of here."

"I can get you out of here only. After that, you must make
your own way."

"It's all set up."

The car would be waiting on the Rue Pacha, hidden from
Palestinian guns in the Phoenicia. He would have to duck and
dodge a quarter of a block to get to it, and if he made it alive,
he would return to the bureau and file. He knew he would
file. The cassette in his recorder and the notes in his pocket
would haunt him till he did. Though the events of this event-
ful morning made no sense to him at the moment, he would
find or invent some thread of coherence to tie them together;
and he'd send out a story that would be rewarded with an ALL
PLEASED HERE AND SEND CONGRATS and orders to go risk his
life again. No. No more. BIBI bye-bye.

"Major Yusseff, it would be an embarrassment to the Phalangist party if I told what happened here, wouldn't it?"

"Yes, I suppose, but you are free . . ."

"This drunken kid killing two of your men, Sami looting . . ."

"Foolish of him to do that in front of a journalist."

"It would be an embarrassment, especially on the radio."

A nervous smile formed under the upside-down U of the
major's mustache.

"This is unusual, wire service. You're not . . . what's the
English for it? Making a setup for me?"

"No. I promise you that."

"It's very unusual."

"I know. I've got my reasons and it's not to set you up."

"Very well. Give me your tape and your notebook."

Bolton handed them over. The roser was now out of the question; as for the wire, he could write a piece from memory, but without his notes, the temptation to do so would be much easier to resist.

"Very unusual, but I thank you for this, wire service."

"Thank *you*, Major Yusseff."

28

"PLO SUCKS."

"Perfect." Bolton popped a few pellets of birdseed into the cage. Incoming dipped his white head and snapped them up with his beak. "Now try this. And . . . Christians . . . eat . . . it."

Incoming was silent. Bolton stuck a pencil between the bars and gave him a hard tap between the eyes. Reward and punishment.

"Try it again. And . . . Christians . . . eat . . . it."

"Christians eat it."

"That's the stuff. Now put it together and I'll buy you a drink. PLO . . . sucks . . . and . . . Christians . . . eat . . . it."

"PLO sucks and Christians eat it."

"*All right.*" Bolton tossed in more seed. Down went Incoming's white head, up went his square red tail. "Woody, buy Incoming a drink."

Woodrow Wilson Nazarian, the Commodore's Armenian bartender, shook his head in disapproval.

"To teach him such talk could cause someone to throw a grenade in here."

"That why you look as nervous as a whore in church?"

"Perhaps this war is funny to you now—"

"This war never was funny," Bolton said a little drunkenly.

"Buy Incoming a drink on me. He's a good bird. He's so good, I may take his act on the road."

"PLO sucks and Christians eat it."

"He's a great bird, an African Gray."

"I know what he is. Of the parrot family, African Grays are the finest mimics of the human voice."

"You're taking advantage of his talents for your own amusement."

"Buy him a drink on me."

"Incoming doesn't drink."

"Then I'll buy me a drink on me."

Nazarian splashed a short shot of I. W. Harper over the ice in Bolton's glass. Bolton objected, Nazarian replying that the American had drunk too much already.

"Who the hell are you, Woody? President of the local chapter of the Temperance Union? Your job is to pour whiskey. Pour it."

Angrily, the Armenian tipped the bottle until the glass was filled, the whiskey as golden-clear as the Horsepasture River below the pools at the Narrows.

"PLO sucks and Christians eat it."

"Incoming shut up," said the bartender. "It is Harry Bolton who eats it. Har-ry . . . Bol-ton . . . eats . . . it."

"Harry Bolton eats it."

"That hurts my feelings, Woody."

"You've insulted my religion. I am a Christian."

"So am I, you rug peddler. A Christian's Christian, a backwoods Southern Baptist Christian." Bolton beat out a rhythm on the bar with his hands, singing a phrase from an old hymn:

" 'I'm Baptist bred and Baptist born, and when I die, I'll be Baptist gone.' Gone, Woody, that's me, gone like a goose, gone like this morning's hard-on."

"I wish you were."

"I will be soon." He laid the telex message from New York in front of Woody. "And there's the proof. For the moment, I'll be gone to the head. Any calls come in for me, refer them to my press agent."

He negotiated an unsteady course to the men's room, observing the amateur brigade at work and play. At one table, Purcell and his gang of hacks were interviewing each other and deciding which rumors to accept as true. There was very little hard information to be had in Beirut, but these alche-

mists of journalism could take the flimsiest gossip and simply
by inserting the phrase "according to Western observers"—
according to themselves—turn hearsay into fact. Long-legged
Lizzie St. John, her posture suggesting she didn't know the
British no longer ruled the world or the waves, was seated at
another table with the same *Rolling Stone* reporter Bolton had
seen in Saigon. Beside them, a network leading man was scrib-
bling notes for his stand-upper. Pretty face. Wooden head.

Leaning over the urinal, Bolton braced one hand against
the wall. Pretty face, wooden head, amateurs, they can have
it all. There wasn't any room for a professional in this business; it was a business for stars and stuntmen. Maybe the
thirties and forties had been the golden age of war correspondents, an era when men and women could ply this trade with
some dignity. No more. He tried to imagine Edward R. Murrow
cowering under a bed, praying he wouldn't be shot by a hom-
icidal adolescent. BIBI bye-bye.

I wouldn't even accept an offer to be a network leading
man. I *couldn't* be a leading man, he thought, studying his
reflection in the mirror. Face too lined, neck too corded and
thick. No pretty face to earn me a hundred thou a year.

A hundred grand a year, that's what you expected to make
out of your real-estate scams, Dad, Smoky Mountain schemer
trying to get rich by hustling rich Floridians seeking to escape
the heat in the Carolina highlands. You tried to country-boy
them out of their corporate pensions and country-boyed yourself out of a thousand acres that had been granted to our family
by George Washington himself, George goddamn Washington
granted it to Isaiah Bolton for services rendered in the Battle
of King's Mountain, his services having been to lose a leg to
one of the British king's musket balls. He lost his leg and won
the land, you lost the land and yourself, but made me want
to win. I haven't given up on winning, I'm just quitting while
I'm ahead. I don't want to finish as a fifty-year-old bureau
bum, gone in the legs and winging stories until some young
wolf comes along and takes my job, hell, I'm only thirty-six
and I'm already winging. A hundred acres near Cullowhee,
you didn't lose that because it belonged to Ma's family. Just
below Yellow Mountain with good water running through it,
and I can build the place myself. I know how to peg, chink,
and notch. I earned spending money in high school splitting
logs for those rich Floridians. Loved the way I could split them

with one stroke and the ring of the go-devil against the wedge echoing through the mountains in the early mornings. With help, I can have the place roofed by the fall and then get down to work, and maybe the book will earn enough for me to buy back the thousand acres, I'll right your wrong, Smoky Mountain schemer.

Bolton returned to the bar to find Raymond there, well barbered and tailored, as usual.

"Everything is all set," he said, firing a cigarette with his gold Dunhill.

Bolton said nothing, hiking himself onto the stool and reading over the message Woody had left open on the bar.

281203 BOLTON: RE YR 271420 YR RESIGNATION ACCEPTED. THIS MONTH'S SALARY AND ONE MONTH BACK VACATION PAY OWED YOU. UPPICK COMMERCIAL BANK ATHENS. ALL MOVING AND TRAVEL EXPS YR RESPONSIBILITY. FYI MCDANIELS LETTING EVERY EDITOR IN COUNTRY KNOW YOU UP-FOULED HOLIDAY INN SNAP, SEZ YOU WON'T GET JOB AS COPY BOY IN FARGO NORTH DAKOTA BY THE TIME HE'S THROUGH. RGDS/HALPRIN/CABLES/NY.

Then Bolton's reply:

281750 HALPRIN: RE YR 281203 ONPASS MCDANIELS UNWANT COPY-BOY JOB IN FARGO. IN OTHER WORDS, HE'S GOT ME CONFUSED WITH SOMEBODY WHO GIVES A SHIT. BIBI. RGDS/BOLTON/BEIRUT.

These exchanges had been preceded by several others, beginning with Bolton's cable that he would not file his tapes and notes had been confiscated. Halprin then wanted a piece describing his mistreatment at the hands of the Phalangists. Bolton refused, using the excuse that such a story could get him into serious trouble with the Christians. Halprin countered with a request that he file a color story from memory. Bolton pleaded shell-shock amnesia. McDaniels, who still thought of himself as Lieutenant General McDaniels, then sent a message ordering him to file something. Never one who took orders easily, Bolton decided the time had come to quit playing games, with New York as well as with himself. To quit, period. Once and for all. It surprised him, even, for some perverse reason, wounded his feelings, when the home office accepted his resignation without a plea that he reconsider. YR

RESIGNATION ACCEPTED. The phrase struck him in the same way as his and Dorothy's divorce decree: he'd never wanted anything more, but its finality depressed him.

"So, Harry, everything's in order."

"Heard you the first time."

Bolton slugged down his drink and ordered another.

"Sarkashian bought the things you aren't bringing with you."

"How much?"

"Two thousand Lebanese."

"Two? The couch alone was worth two."

"That's all Sarkashian would give me."

Lying carpet-monger, you got four and pocketed half.

"What the hell, Raymond. What the hell." The I. W. Harper burned down Bolton's throat. "I'm not going to need a lot of money. I'm going to build the place myself. Cedar and yellow pine."

"PLO sucks Christians eat it Harry Bolton eats it."

Raymond turned his heavy-lidded eyes on Incoming.

"Don't mind him. To rephrase Marcus Aurelius, he speaks the truth, of which no man need be afraid. Except for the last part. I don't eat it. I'm through eating it."

"I've arranged everything else," said Raymond, attempting to keep the conversation businesslike. "You have plane reservations for the day after tomorrow from Damascus to Athens. I have a very good man who will drive you in the morning."

"Great." Bolton finished the whiskey and, catching Woody's eye, pointed to his empty glass. Frowning, the bartender filled it. "What time?"

"At six. There isn't so much fighting then, so it should be easier to get out of the city."

Drive to Damascus at six. Then to Athens by plane. Athens to New York, New York to Atlanta, Atlanta to Asheville, rent a car and drive to Cullowhee. I'm in the Middle East now and in a week I'll be in Cullowhee, North Carolina, beneath Yellow Mountain. Then, I'll—stop. Stop for good. Jesus Christ, he was going to settle down on one small parcel of this world that he had roved ever since he'd joined the army fifteen years ago. Settle down without the prospect that, in a week, a month, six months, some event would send him to a place he'd never been before. He would never know again the magic of a night landing in an alien city, of standing on the fantail of a ship steaming into a strange port at dawn, of riding a train through unfamiliar country. He would wake up every morning knowing he would wake up in the same place the next morning, and the morning after that. The thought of such predictability sent his stomach on a sudden, fast downhill run; it conjured a passing image of himself thirty years from now, a local character, peculiar in the way of people who stay in one place too long, an object of curiosity to the rich Floridians who would be driving past his cabin on autumn-leaf trips. Old Harry Bolton lives up there . . . Wrote a book in that cabin a long time ago . . . Used to be a correspondent back in the days when they had newspapers . . . Drinks a lot, they say . . . Stop. Holy Christ, he was going to *stop*.

"The tickets are in the office," Raymond said, studying the wristband of his watch. "So is the money from Sarkashian."

Bolton's stomach was still sliding downward at forty miles an hour. What would he do if he could not handle a normal life, a life lived on a level plane instead of a roller coaster? Pack his bags and go back to this? He took a generous shot of whiskey to slow his belly's descent. It was only fear, after all. Journalism, the little whore, was trying to win him back by inflicting him with fear of the journalist's natural enemy—the ordinary. Another shot of I. W. Harper halted the skid in his midsection. Rhinestoned slut, you won't manipulate me the way you did last year in Saigon. BIBI. There is magic in the everyday if you keep your eyes open.

"You convert the money into U.S.?" Bolton's tongue felt thick, his lips numb.

"Yes. I told you, Harry. Everything is arranged."

"You're a prince among men, Raymond. How're the streets?"

"Not bad here. There was much fighting near the port this morning."

"Guess I ought to go clean out my desk."

"PLO sucks Christians eat it Harry Bolton eats it."

He fed the parrot a helping of birdseed.

"Eat that, Incoming. And keep your head and ass down."

When he stood to walk out the door, he felt as if he were on the bow of a destroyer in a North Atlantic storm.

It was still pitching and yawing when he returned to the bureau, where he poured a cup of Raymond's tar-thick coffee.

DelCorso was in the newsroom, reading over the morning's file.

"Nick, you acclimated yet to the Paris of the Middle East? Three days should be enough."

"More than enough."

"Yeah, Nick. Ever think of how many 'Parises of' we've been in? Saigon, Paris of the Orient; Beirut, Paris of the Middle East; Algiers, Paris of North Africa. Never Paris, the Paris of France. What's next? How about, let's see, how about Bangui, the Paris of Bongoland. We have never been to Bangui."

DelCorso remained silent.

Bolton went into his office and started rummaging through his desk, but he was too buzzed to decide what was worth keeping, or to care if anything was worth keeping from this old life of his. DelCorso had followed him and, looking both sulky and solemn, stood in the doorway.

"You got something on your mind?"

"I was reading over the file. There was a helluva lot of fighting near the port. . . . "

"Yeah?"

"I'm going out that way this afternoon with Conklin and McCafferty. Heard Dunlop and Lutter are coming in their own car, maybe a French TV crew."

"Sounds great."

"I came up here figuring you'd want to go. We usually cover these dicey ones together."

"As you've probably heard, I'm all through rolling dice for my ass."

"Heard it from Dalman just now."

"Right. Bye-bye to bush battles and bongo wars, bye-bye to the Turd World."

"I wanted to hear it from you."

"Hear what?"

"That you're running out."

"I wouldn't call it that, Nick."

"I would."

Bolton was growing rapidly sober.

"Well, I wouldn't, Nick. I wouldn't, because if you call it running out again, I'm going to lock the door and you and me are going to have at it."

"Goddamnit, Horseman, you owed it to me to tell me about it before everyone else. Ten years. We've been together since the Iron Triangle. I can't believe this."

"Sorry for not checking in with you, but believe it. I'm all done. Period. Thirty. Ends all. Bye-bye."

Beneath the single black eyebrow, DelCorso's eyes shone with a weird intensity: he looked like a betrayed lover.

"You're one of the best, Harry. So am I. We've got an obligation—"

"Don't. Don't give me any obligation speeches. I've got an obligation not to bend over and kiss my ass good-bye trying to beat AP by five minutes."

"We've got an obligation to tell them what's going on in places like this."

"Hang on before you blast off to Saturn with this obligation talk. Let me show you something." Rustling through a pile of messages spiked atop his desk, he found the two he was looking for. "Here, read these. These are the first two queries Dalman got as the new Beirut bureau chief."

292020 DALMAN: KATY AND THE LADY SAYING ARAFAT DIRECTING MOSLEM FORCES FROM SECRET HQ IN WEST BEIRUT. CAN YOU GET INTERVIEW WITH HIM THERE? RGDS/LUCAS/CABLES/NY.

292150 DALMAN: THANKS YR ANALYSIS PREMIER'S EFFORTS TO FORM PEACE-MAKING GOVT. HAVE RCVD INFO YALE UNIV. CHOIR TO TOUR CHRISTIAN ORPHANAGES EAST BEIRUT FOR EASTER CELEBRATION. CLIENT NEW HAVEN GAZETTE WOULD LIKE 600 WDS ON THEIR ARRIVAL TOMORROW. RGDS/LUCAS/CABLES/NY.

"You still want to talk obligation?" Bolton asked, disturbed that amusement had not flickered in the intense, brown eyes.

DelCorso tossed the messages aside.

"All right. It's horseshit. That doesn't mean you have to quit the business. Quit this silly-ass wire service you work for. Free-lance, or, hell, you could get a bureau with one of the news magazines just by asking."

"They're all fucked up in their own way."

"If everybody in this business thought the way you do—"

"If," Bolton interrupted, "but they don't and won't. If, shit. If Miles Standish had shot a cat instead of a turkey, we could all eat pussy for Thanksgiving."

"Do you have to make a wisecrack about everything? I'm saying we've got an obligation to make them see what's going on."

"Who? Who the hell are 'they'?"

"Mr. and Mrs. Fat-assed America, sitting on their fat asses with their fat-assed kids, fat, dumb, happy."

"What's wrong with being fat, dumb, and happy?"

"Cows are fat, dumb, and happy."

Bolton spread his arms wide in exasperation

"Nick, I can't do it. All right. I just can't whip up the sense of mission you've got. Maybe it's because you're a photographer and a free-lancer. You don't have to deal with requests to find Yasser Arafat's secret headquarters or cover the arrival of an Ivy League choir in a war zone."

"Screw those jerk-off editors. What it comes down to is, when I look at shit like the shit that's happening here, or in Nam or Biafra, I feel responsible. I think I am, in a way. You, too. And them as well."

"Mr. and Mrs. Fat-assed America?"

"Yeah."

Bolton paused, looking at his friend. Suddenly, he realized something about this dark, passionate, temperamental man, something he should have realized years ago.

"Son of a bitch, I get it now. You want to make them feel responsible, the way you do."

"I want them to see the truth."

"I don't think so, Nick. I don't think you want to make them see. You want to make them pay."

"That's—"

"Not bullshit. You hate them, these people whose eyes you want to open. You hate them for living ordinary lives. You think they're complacent, so you're going to shock them out of it."

"Bullshit."

"Not bullshit. You want to make them pay. Earn their right to be fat, dumb, and happy by walking around with the cross you're going to put on their backs. Ever occur to you that it's all right if some people lead normal lives and worry about normal things, that if more people worried about their fat-assed kids and paying their mortgages and not about religions or ideologies or power or putting a few thrills into their lives, there might not be as many wars like this one?"

"How the hell did we get into all this philosophy? I'm talking about you quitting this business."

"You got into the metaphysics. Our obligation to bring the light of truth to the American breakfast table."

"Maybe you'd better lock that door because I'm going to say it again."

"Go ahead."

"You're running out."

"On what? My obligation?"

"That's half of it."

"What's the other half?"

"You're running out on me."

A newsreel of memories flickered through Bolton's mind, of the afternoon when he took a bullet pulling DelCorso out of the Iron Triangle, of the fear they'd shared in Kyrenia, under the Turks' machine-gun fire, of all the rotten, dangerous places where he'd stood beside him, never thinking about running out. Lodging his boots against the desk, he kicked it over with a single thrust of his long, powerful legs.

"Get the fuck out of here," he shouted, springing to his feet. "Get the fuck out before I rip that guinea face of yours apart."

DelCorso stood, fixed as a post, the faintest smirk bending the corners of his mouth.

"You coming this afternoon or not?"

Bolton had to hand it to him—DelCorso could be as cool as a glacier sometimes. He wanted me to do that. Blow my cork and then tag along with him out of some stupid, outdated, juvenile sense of manly honor.

"No," he answered regaining his self-control. "Hell no. Talk about paying, you owe me for that last one. You goddamn owe me. Think about it."

"I will. You do some thinking about what I said."

"I'm going to try not to."

29

THE DEAD HAD BEEN BURIED in the sewers beneath layers of garbage from the vegetable *souk* nearby. The grates and manholes, knocked ajar, exhaled the corpses' stench, the odor of rotting cabbages, beets, and garlic, and the sewers' own cool, rancid breath. The old dead lay under the street, the new, those killed in this morning's fighting, were still on the street, Moslems and Christians, men and women. Some had fallen singly, some in groups, some in the gutters, some in doorways. There seemed to be a body or a fragment of one every hundred feet or so. Sometimes the extent of the carnage was deceptive because this street was lined with looted shops and boutiques: on one block, DelCorso had seen a pair of legs as beautifully formed as Margaret's, legs attached to half a trunk, satiny high heels on the feet, and he thought he was going to get sick, seeing such a lovely woman mutilated so horribly, until he noticed that the legs belonged to a mannikin. There were almost as many mannikins as there were bodies, stripped of whatever fashion they'd displayed, decapitated, limbs torn off, wooden breasts amputated, abdomens shot to splinters. In the general mess, with storefront signs and window shutters scattered on sidewalks, bricks and rubble everywhere, mortar and rocket craters flooded from a morning rain, automobiles over-

turned and smoking, it was just as easy to mistake a corpse
for a mannikin as the other way around. The maimed, disfig-
ured dummies troubled DelCorso more than the dead. He
wasn't sure why. Was it because those images of the human
form looked more human than the humans, who, dead, looked
more like dummies than the dummies? Was that why the
corpses evoked no special emotion? The dismembered mannikins aroused a horror that was not the horror of death, but
of something he could not name. And what was this, to be
more appalled by the wreckage of life-size dolls than by the
destruction of people? He might have been led to wonder if
he had a crossed wire in his senses had Conklin not remarked
on the same peculiarity.

"Man, I don't understand these people," he said. "They've
got enough of each other to shoot at, so why do they have to
blow those things apart?"

"More you run and jump, more you want to run and jump,"
McCafferty replied.

"What the hell does that mean?"

"When they run out of flesh and blood to shoot up, they'll
shoot up anything they can. These people can't get enough of
killing."

"I wanna go home," Conklin sang quietly. "Oh, how I
wanna go home."

"Conklin, I suppose you're thinking of your summer with
those little kiddies of yours back in Baltimore."

Conklin gazed up the street, at the flattened, blackened
ruins of an old Mercedes taxi. He'd put on several pounds in
the past year, but this extra weight made him appear younger;
if he used to look like a flabby college boy, he now resembled
an adolescent who hadn't shed his baby fat.

"I'm thinking that this is the last shithole I go to."

"You and Deecee haven't seen the half of it yet."

"To paraphrase Spiro Agnew, 'Seen one shithole, you seen
'em all.' "

"This one's special."

"Too bad Wilson isn't here. Maybe he'd find something
funny to say about it."

DelCorso, still disturbed by the argument with Bolton,
snapped: "Do me a favor, don't mention Wilson again."

"Yeah, sure, Nick, I forgot."

"I haven't."

Hugging the walls, the three men moved up the street. On the opposite side, Dunlop, Lutter, and the French television crew resembled an infantry squad patrolling the ruins of a half-conquered city. DelCorso considered pack journalism to be to the practice of his craft what group sex is to the art of love, but he didn't mind the company in this instance. Even Dunlop's presence reassured him: here, *any* familiar face was reassuring. The past three days had taught him that fish who swam alone in this sea stood a far greater risk of being eaten than those who traveled in pairs or schools. That was the only rule that seemed to apply; otherwise, survival in this city was a game of midnight baseball played with a deck full of jokers.

According to the file he'd read in Bolton's office, the Phalangists had attacked from Karatina early this morning and tried to seize this district, somewhere between the port and the wreck of the Souk Française. Apparently, they were trying to open a supply corridor to the Holiday Inn. Apparently, the Moslems had beaten them back. Apparently—in the past half-hour, he hadn't seen a living soul on the street, Moslem or Christian. The only certainty was that the war had moved elsewhere for the moment. It might return here the next moment. It might not. That was another thing he'd learned about this war—it wandered around the city with the capricious vagrancy of a psychopathic killer, establishing no pattern by which a man of reasonable intelligence could forecast where it was likely to strike next. In this precarious atmosphere, DelCorso wondered if he ought to rely on even the rule of safety in numbers. It was based on hope as much as on fact, the hope that the various militias, who might be tempted to prey on a lone newsman, wouldn't dare fire on a crowd of journalists. But what was to stop some free-lance sniper from picking one of them off? Nothing except the conviction that a camera around the neck would have the same inhibiting effect as, say, a Red Cross armband or a blue U.N. helmet. It wasn't a conviction easily maintained in a war in which civilians were massacred in their doorways.

Two, perhaps three blocks ahead, a machine gun beat a long tattoo. Halting, the two files of men dropped to their haunches. The gun fell silent. Behind DelCorso, Conklin sang under his breath,

"I wanna go home, ohhh, I wanna go home."

"Conklin, for our kind, this is home. You can't go back to Baltimore."

"For your kind, McCafferty, not me. Hey, Deecee, this sucks. What's the point?"

"Photo opportunities," McCafferty said. "Point is, we're looking for photo opportunities."

"Shit, the only people who'd buy pictures of this mess would be the editors of *Demolition Digest*. Don't think there's a living, swinging dick inside of a mile."

"What fired that gun? A swinging dick's ghost?"

"All things are possible in this, the worst of all possible worlds. What do you say, Nick? Let's head back to the cars."

He said nothing, looking toward an intersection a quarter of a block away, until his glance was drawn to the opposite side of the street. His eyes met Dunlop's briefly in a silent understanding: though retreat seemed the smart thing to do, neither of them was going to turn back. DelCorso led off. Rising to a stance a little above a deep knee-bend, he advanced toward the intersection, pausing when the machine gun fired again, its irregular tapping like a loud telegraph key.

"Nick, I don't see the point of going any farther."

"Then don't go, Conklin. It's a free country."

"The intersection's as far as I go."

"Fine with me. I'm not your squad leader."

DelCorso went on ahead, Conklin and McCafferty behind, Dunlop and his kite tail abreast. Artillery and heavy rockets had bombarded the cross street, making it more of a shambles than the one they were on. In spots, the pavement had been ground into gravel, and the morning's storm had churned the dust into slush, the shell craters into jagged ponds. Houses smoldered, the smell of wet ashes in the air, a curse of smoke hanging over everything. An Ottoman-era villa that had taken a direct hit looked like a cutaway dollhouse smashed by a destructive child. An entire wall had given way, exposing the wreckage of the private little world it had once concealed—a brass bed in a bedroom, its spokes and bars twisted, a toppled refrigerator in the kitchen, a dining-room table leaning on two legs. Scattered over the crumbled sidewalk were the leaves that had been blown from the trees, as if the war had knocked the seasons out of joint.

The exposed interior of the house brought the same prickling to DelCorso's neck, the same nameless horror as the mannikins. Every species of fear had bitten him in the past several years, but this one belonged to a different order altogether. He wanted to name it, classify it, above all understand it, not because he had become a naturalist of fear or because he suffered from the illusion that understanding an emotion led to its mastery; rather, he believed that if he could understand why inanimate objects aroused the feeling, he would comprehend the truth of what was happening here, and that truth would permeate every grain of the images he made of this war. The truth, Harry, it's the truth I want.

He bracketed the house in the viewfinder of his Leica, expecting the narrowed field of vision to clear the circles of confusion in his mind. The shot was straight-on and conventional; had it not been for the cold crawling on his neck, he would have felt like a claims adjuster photographing wreckage after a storm. He moved off to shoot from a different angle, opening the lens as the smoke overhead thickened. Circles of confusion. What is this fear that is not the fear of death, disfigurement, captivity, torture, or pain? It had something to do with the transformation of the ordinary into the extraordinary, the familiar into the strange. He knew streets and cities; they were his natural element. But the streets of this city were more alien than all the deserts he'd been on, all the bush through which he'd stumbled and sweated.

Music. He swore he heard it on the breeze blowing in from the harbor—a high faint fluting and a couple of chords from a guitar. The sounds faded when the breeze died. Looking a block down the street, where it dipped toward the port, he saw half a dozen figures through a murk of smoke. They were moving in a circle, as in a primitive dance. The music carried on a fresh gust of wind and pulled him toward the circling figures.

"Hey, Nick, I wasn't kidding. This is dice city."

"No shit."

"I don't know who those dudes are and I'm not going to find out. Sticking right here."

"I don't need anybody to hold my hand," he said over his shoulder.

Conklin squatted at the corner, his chubby pubescent face showing above the pyramid of bricks behind which he'd found an illusion of safety.

"Nobody wants to hold your hand, Nick. You're bad luck."

The remark burned through him like a high-velocity bullet.

"Listen, asshole, listen good What happened to Wilson last year happened. It wasn't my goddamned fault."

"Didn't say it was. Just said you're bad luck."

"Conklin, you're spooked. Hell, Deecee, I'll tag along. Need a shot with people in it, live ones."

DelCorso continued toward the figures, now standing around with an idle restlessness that reminded him of the hours he'd wasted waiting on corners with his buddies, the big Chicago sky blackening and the lights going on in the city, waiting for something to happen and knowing that if it didn't, he'd find a way to make it happen. He sensed the same expectancy in the air, but there was no promise of adventure in it; a foreboding rather. McCafferty walked alongside, flat gray eyes never resting, seeking the sniper's shadow in the window, the flicker of movement on the rooftop. He's a whore of war, DelCorso thought, but if I have to have company, better the company of an alley-fighting whore than a suburbanite like Conklin.

He had other company. Dunlop had left Lutter and the rest of his entourage behind and was now on the other side of this street, glancing sidelong at DelCorso, like a runner checking his pace against an opponent in the next lane. All three of his cameras carried short lenses. What was the great man up to? It wasn't like him to work up close. Maybe winning the last Pulitzer had restored his guts. Stop thinking about him. Concentrate. Hard to concentrate when you've got two people with you, like three men making love to one woman at the same time. Regular gang-bang.

A distance ahead, the street ended in an escarpment of apartment buildings. The newer, higher ones had been punctured by rockets; the older ones, with their tiers of curving galleries chopped and chewed by countless bits of flying steel, looked like giant layer cakes gnawed by giant rats. DelCorso stepped over another mannikin, its dyed synthetic hair and blue eyes a little too lifelike.

Not far ahead, the woman with the doughy face and blimpish body did not look lifelike at all. She looked like a bloated dummy. Clad in a Moslem's peasant dress, she lay under a tree in a pile of shredded bark and leaves, her head, its eyes half closed and mouth half opened, propped against the trunk,

her ankles turned out at an odd angle. Death made everyone
double-jointed. Three brownish-red medallions were equally
spaced across her chest, ribbons of the same color hanging
from each as far down as her waist. DelCorso moved off the
sidewalk into the street, centering her in the viewfinder and
stopping down so the band of gunmen would be in focus.

What does he see? Dunlop, pausing to watch, could find
no journalistic or artistic value in a picture of a dead civilian
on a demolished street in a city full of demolished streets and
dead civilians. It wouldn't be a war photograph. The one he
had taken in Korea long ago, of two marines in a patrol action,
bearded faces under steel helmets, a quality in the play of light
and shadow suggesting the starkness of modern battle but also
man's capacity to transcend his circumstances—*that* was a
war photograph. But this? After a plane crash, did photographers take pictures of charred, dismembered corpses? Some
did, but even they blurred the details, knowing no newspaper
or magazine would have the bad taste to publish them. There
had been an uproar when some front pages ran pictures of
Jayne Mansfield's decapitated body after her car slammed into
a truck on a bridge outside New Orleans. If explicit gore was
taboo when it came to plane crashes and auto accidents, why
were images of war made an exception? What the hell does
DelCorso see beyond a corpse of a woman with three bullet
holes in it? Now, Dunlop noticed, McCafferty had raised his
camera as well. Perfect. The two dead-end kids at the front.
That was, he knew, an unfair comparison insofar as talent
went: McCafferty, like reporters whose capacities were limited to rewriting police blotters, would never rise above a basic
level; DelCorso worked on another plane altogether. He saw
something. And what is it he sees in this that I don't? Dunlop
had joined this excursion to find out. Since the incident in
Ashrafiyah ten days ago, his production had dropped to near
zero. Perhaps he was blocking his own talent, punishing himself for his complicity in the killing. He wasn't sure. Maybe
all photographers were accomplices to an extent. Whatever,
he had ceased to function, and the rockets *Time* had sent him
had scalded him with embarrassment and self-doubt. A man
with his credentials was not supposed to get complaints about
poor performance. He'd rehired Lutter to take the pressure off.
Lutter's job was simply to shoot as much film as possible for
the usual percentage, leaving Dunlop free to discover the secret to DelCorso's vision He would learn from the man he

had taught. He would learn how to molt the constricting skin of his good taste and save himself from extinction. No, he would go one better: to save himself from extinction would be merely to survive; he meant to triumph. If explicitness was the new wave, P.X. Dunlop would ride the crest.

Now he focused on the woman and, forcing himself not to listen to his censoring voices, made an exposure. He changed perspective by climbing atop a mound of rubble, made another exposure, climbed down and made a third; but without the spectacle of war, the drama and heroism, the reference points he was accustomed to, he felt as if he were working in a vacuum.

It might have surprised him to learn that DelCorso was also shooting blindly. If he had a conscious purpose it was to understand, and the woman lying in the street like some exterminated animal seemed one of the keys to the secret. The woman and her everyday dress, transmuted into something out of the ordinary by the bullet holes, which, with their trails of blood, looked like award ribbons pinned to her bosom.

When he'd finished the sequence, he continued toward the militiamen, who now saw the three photographers approaching, and, as if arranging themselves for a group shot, clustered near some object in the street. DelCorso counted six all together. They were about a hundred yards away, within range of a long lens, but the longest he'd brought was his 105-millimeter. DelCorso could sense a menace in their movements and postures. Approaching them as he might a pack of rabid dogs, afraid they would attack if he took his eyes off of them, he made his aperture and shutter settings without looking at his Leica. His and the footsteps of the other two men crunched against the broken pavement.

The prickling on DelCorso's neck spread to the back of his head, into his shoulders, and down his spine. Half a dozen men, five with Kalashnikovs, one with an RPG, were facing him, but he was not as afraid of the men and their guns as he was of something they manifested; for this prickling of the flesh wasn't the horror of anything so earthly and concrete as a bullet; it was more like a terror of the supernatural. St. Michael the Archangel defend us in battle, be our safeguard against the wickedness and snares of the devil . . . The Devil. It was a spirit he feared, a malignant spirit that inhabited these gutted buildings and deserted streets, howling its cry, audible only to the soul's ear, through the rocket holes in the walls,

round and black as chancres, expelling its breath from the
graveyard sewers whose stench made the nostrils burn, gazing
with the cracked doll's eyes of storefront dummies.

Another fifty feet and the militiamen would be within
range of his 35-millimeter; another fifty feet and the lens would
capture what his eyes now saw: six bizarre figures, extras in
a science-fiction thriller about some future age when civilization has tumbled and the world's cities are ruled by urban
savages. One gunman, with a mandolin strapped to his neck,
wore a mannikin's blond wig under his fatigue cap; another,
with a blanket belted to his torso, a flute stuck in the belt,
and skin-tight trousers tucked into high boots, looked like a
shepherd; a third had stepped out of a woodcut of Dickens's
slums—a high-crowned hat, threadbare suitcoat, and patched,
baggy trousers; a fourth, who looked no more than fifteen,
wore a woolen scarf despite the warm weather; the last two,
more conventionally garbed in makeshift uniforms orna-
mented with grenades, ammo pouches, and cartridge belts,
the bullets like rows of filed, copper-tipped teeth, had red
flowers stuck in the barrels of their rifles. The object around
which they stood, indistinguishable at a distance from the rest
of the rubble, was the spread-eagled corpse of a Christian, his
jaw propped open with the gold crucifix he'd had on his neck.

"This mob would make a South Bronx lineup look like
Camp Fire Girls," said McCafferty. Dunlop hung a safe distance behind.

"Who do they belong to?"

"We know they're not Christians. Looney Tunes by the
looks of them. Who gives a fuck anyway? They're all nuts."

DelCorso sensed that he and McCafferty had interrupted
something, a ceremony perhaps, some kind of black funeral
mass. Tentatively, he raised a camera to his eye. Mirror and
prism reflected the Christian's corpse in the foreground, then
the six freak-show militiamen, and behind them, the perspective of the street, so battered there it looked like a rutted
country road. A stratum of thick, gray smoke hovered between
the buildings, casting a shifting shadow, admitting just enough
light to make the crucifix glint. The smoke was the heart of
the photograph; pouring from the hulk of a jeep or pickup
truck in the far distance, so dense that the vehicle would not
be visible on film, it would appear, on the print, to be rising
from the earth. Satan's brimstone cloud, the outward image
of the spirit haunting every square block of this city. F-eight

at a two-fiftieth—two-fiftieth would fix the movement of the smoke. He took two shots. Then one of the gunmen, one of the two who had garlanded their rifles, pointed his weapon. The scarlet petals adorning its muzzle did not diminish its menace. The militiaman said something that neither McCafferty nor DelCorso understood, but his gesture needed no translation: you shoot another picture and I'll shoot you.

30

I'VE SEEN THIS MOVIE BEFORE, DelCorso thought. His movements as deliberate as those of a man face-to-face with a rabid doberman, he showed the militiaman the laminated press card issued by the Ministry of Information.

"*Sahafi*—journalist," he said, turning the red and yellow card over in his hand.

"That's right."

"*Sahafi Amerikai*." The man's lips angled into a demented smile. "*Sahafi Amerikai*."

Handing back DelCorso's card, he demanded McCafferty's and repeated "*Sahafi Amerikai*" in a tone implying that the words had a sinister connotation. Then he turned to DelCorso again and said with a jerk of his rifle:

"You. Pass."

"I just showed it to you."

"He means *their* pass."

"Who the hell are they?"

"One way to find out." Pointing his finger at the man, McCafferty asked: "Mourabitoun?"

"*Aiwa*."

"Looney Tunes, Deecee."

DelCorso reached into his right pocket, fumbling through

the folded passes for the correct one. When he found it, he held it out. The gunman glanced at it and returned it.

After examining McCafferty's, he waved his rifle at Dunlop, who was photographing the scene from about a hundred feet away.

"You," he called loudly. "No. You. Pass."

Dunlop either did not hear him or misunderstood; he cut to one side of the street and aimed his camera. Atomized flower petals filled the air when the Kalashnikov went off, its bullets ripping a wall over his head.

"You! No photo! Pass!"

Dunlop rose from the sidewalk on which he'd thrown himself and walked cautiously forward.

"What in the goddamned hell," he said, attempting to restore his dignity by speaking in his best command voice, which wasn't very commanding because of its tenor pitch. "What in the goddamned hell were you doing, you son of a bitch?"

"Cool your jets, P.X.," McCafferty warned. "Seems these dudes are a little camera-shy. They want to see your pass. Hope you got a Looney Tunes pass."

Dunlop, wrinkles rippling from his eyebrows to the widow's peak of his short gray hair, took it out of his pocket. DelCorso saw, not without satisfaction, that his hand was unsteady. The yellow bastard probably hasn't had a bullet come that close to him in twenty-five years. Doesn't have a battalion of his Hollywood marines around him. He was standing close enough to smell Dunlop's nervous sweat, beading in the creases of his neck and blotting the underarms of his shirt. The Pulitzer. This yellow son of a bitch had taken the Pulitzer from him. No other word for it. Taken it. The Pulitzer—what an intelligent thing to think about in this situation. He banished the thought from his mind, as a priest would banish an impure desire. He was here on spec; if he was captured, he would not have a powerful national magazine behind him, pulling strings to secure his release; if he was hurt, the hospital bills would have to be paid out of his own pocket. His only insurance was the protection of his guardians, who demanded as their premium an authenticity of motive. The purpose. The purpose above all.

Now, with his Kalashnikov, the Mourabitoun pointed down a side street so narrow it was more an alley than a street.

"I'm not following that moron down there," Dunlop said.

"Don't think he's giving us a choice, P.X."

"We'd be damn fools to follow him down there."

"If he wanted to blow us away," DelCorso offered, "he'd do it now. Nobody here would turn him in."

The Mourabitoun waved his rifle again, more insistently this time. There was no arguing with a man with a loaded gun. The three photographers followed him down the street. The other gunman, the flower still in his rifle barrel, trailed behind, which somewhat eroded DelCorso's confidence that they weren't being led to their executions. He looked over his shoulder, trying to read the Mourabitoun's intentions; the militiaman stared back, his dark eyes as expressive as the heads of tenpenny nails. In the distance, the machine gun tapped again. The stink rising out of the manholes congealed in the compressed space between the buildings on whose walls of golden stone shell bursts had chalked black powder burns. A man killed in this morning's fighting sat slumped against a lamppost, holding out a rigid palm into which some wit had dropped a few coins. Will I look like that in a few minutes? Will the bullets rip into me and will I be left in the street, human rubble, my corpse an object of mockery?

They were led off the street and through a passageway, a place dim as a cellar, with a cellar's moldiness, and the two rows of balconies above, jutting out to within an arm's reach of each other, were like the halves of a partly opened cellar door. At an arched wooden gate, the Mourabitoun in the lead told them to wait, then went inside. Several minutes later he emerged and ushered them into a sunlit courtyard.

The sight of the six corpses lying in the golden rectangle with their trousers pulled down to their ankles disoriented DelCorso for a few moments. There was a rocking motion inside his head, such as a person feels when stepping ashore after days at sea, and his eyes went slightly out of focus. The bodies did not smell and the blood puddled on the paving stones hadn't dried yet. He figured the Christians could not have been killed—no, slaughtered—more than an hour ago. He blinked, clearing his eyes, but they blurred again immediately, as if they were automatically censoring the more revolting details, as if they were telling him this horror was not meant to be seen with clarity.

At first glance each severed head appeared to have its tongue sticking out of its mouth; another look revealed that the organs were not tongues.

"God," Dunlop said. The gray in his hair seemed to be bleeding down his forehead and over his face. "God almighty."

Molding their youthful features into expressions that were anything but youthful, the gunmen struck conquerors' poses beside their trophies. The one who'd gone in first had made a neat display, standing each severed head in front of its corresponding trunk so that heads and trunks looked like parts ready for final assembly.

"Now," he said. "Now photo." The other one stood with his Kalashnikov at port arms, the flower sprouting from the vase of its barrel.

DelCorso, McCafferty, and Dunlop did not move. The Mourabitoun pointed his rifle and repeated, "Photo. Now. Photo."

"Fuck this."

"I thought you specialized in this kind of filth," Dunlop said bitterly.

"No fucking way I'd waste film on this mess. Nobody'd ever buy a picture of it."

"I should've figured that's why you wouldn't do it."

"Don't get preachy."

"We'd better do something because these two won't have any qualms about blowing us to hell if we don't play along."

"You got any ideas?"

"We'll fake it, you moron. We'll fake a few shots, make these butchers happy, and get the hell out of here."

Dunlop, fighting an upwelling of nausea, set his shutter at a second and opened the lens to overexpose the negative. Even so, he felt like an accessory after the fact when he looked at the atrocity through the viewfinder. It occurred to him that he was preserving the secrecy of the crime and that, perhaps, it would be more scrupulous to make a record of it, to present to the world testimony of what he'd seen this day in this place. On the other hand, three decades of photographing wars had not convinced him that giving even the most graphic evidence of man's barbarism encouraged civilized behavior; instead, by giving such acts a cloak of acceptance and by deadening man's capacity for outrage, it seemed to encourage more barbarism. Better to leave monstrosities like this in the darkness where they belonged. He took two or three false frames; then, at the periphery of his lens's field of vision, he saw DelCorso, squatting at the feet of one of the decapitated bodies, a camera trained on the head propped in front of it.

"DelCorso, for Christ's sake. . . "

The shutter clicked, then the advance lever.

He could not believe what he was seeing; if this grotesque was too much for McCafferty, even though his motives were mercenary, how could DelCorso find it worth the film?

Shutter and advance lever clicked again.

What does he see? What can he see in this? It required almost as much savagery to photograph this crime as to commit it. God almighty, only an hour ago he'd been eager to learn the secret of this man's vision. Fine. He'd learned: the secret was to shed all attempts at decency and discrimination and acquire an eye for brutality, the bloodier the better.

Filth.

"*DelCorso . . .*"

DelCorso ignored him. Clarity, the clarity that hurts, had been restored to his eyes and mind. He turned the Leica sideways, cropping out the other corpses and focusing on the one in front of him, its stuffed mouth bulging, its half-opened eyes, cloudy and colorless, looking at him over its trunk and the awful red blooming between its legs, like a mangled carnation. Another face of war for you, readers of glossy news magazines. A mangled carnation, a flower in the barrel of the gunman's rifle, the dead arranged around the well like the petals of a tattered flower. Yes, now he understood the nature of his fear. *Village.* The mannikins in the street, bullet-chipped, like the fallen buddha, shot to bits by men in a frenzy. *Village.* The soldier beside the buddha, doing to a dead Viet Cong what these men had done to the Christian militia. *Village.* The smoke whorling from the burning jeep like the smoke from the flaming huts, and the Moslem woman lying beneath the tree with her lips parted like the lips of the woman he'd photographed there, long ago, in that circle of light fenced by jungle. *Village.* Rach Giang.

DelCorso snapped a frame, then, still in a squat, duck-walked backward to encompass the entire scene—the obscenity of the bodies, the two proud killers, and the incongruity of the red blossom in the rifle barrel. He took half a dozen black-and-whites, then switched to one of his color cameras to catch the mellow gold of the light striking the stones of the courtyard walls. The ordinary turned extraordinary. He could imagine the courtyard as it might have been at this time of day before the war: neighborhood venerables sipping Turkish coffee in the glow of the kind old sun. Now those everyday rhythms and rituals had been shattered, but the warm sun shone all the same.

"Let's get a fucking move-on," McCafferty protested. "Nobody's going to buy pictures of this."

Maybe nobody will, DelCorso thought, but I don't care because I'm not selling. They aren't for the marketplace, these images are for myself. I might put them in a book someday, a collection like Goya's sketches, Nick DelCorso's own version of the disasters of war.

With his 50-millimeter, he bordered the faces of the Mourabitoun, whose eyes were like the eyes of the men in B Company after Rach Giang: eyes in which the fragile spark of divinity had been extinguished and replaced by a phosphorescence like the glow of animal eyes at night. That look is one of the disasters of war, as much a disaster as what has happened here. It's a look I know; it was in my eyes once. I know the dimension you're in, you two murderers; I have been there. He zeroed the lens so that the twin pair of eyes became the focal point of the picture, drawing toward their darkness the row of corpses and the line of chopped heads. Shutter and advance clicked, and clicked again. Yes, I know what dimension you're in—it wasn't enough to kill them, you had to do this to them—and I know each of your faces is more than a face of war; it is a face of the beast. The beast was loose in these streets—that was the fundamental truth of this war. It was the spirit of the beast DelCorso feared, not anything so occult as the spirit of the devil; the spirit of the everlasting beast in man.

DelCorso shifted to the right and exposed several frames, then to the left for several more, shooting color and black-and-white with every lens in his bag. Again, McCafferty protested, his head jerking on his stumpy neck as though he had a crick:

"What in the fuck are you up to, Nick? Let's get a move-on."

He paid no attention, afraid of breaking the magnetic field between himself and the militiamen, who seemed almost mesmerized by his cameras and his busy moving back and forth. He intended to make the most of this moment; his guardian gods required it. They had given him this chance to confront the beast once more without succumbing to it, to record cruelty without cruelty in his heart, to witness massacre and make the indictment he had failed to make long

ago. And with each frame exposed, he felt himself grow a little
lighter, like a diver shedding weights from his weight belt,
lighter and lighter, ascending toward the brightness at the
surface. It was, this buoyancy, like grace.

As he moved back to shoot a final sequence, stopping down
to increase his depth of field, Dunlop fell into his peripheral
vision. An expression of disgust sculpted furrows and lines
into the boxy face beneath the peaked gray hair. Sure, you're
disgusted, you disapprove, P.X. What I'm doing is in bad taste.
You faked it because you thought to tell the truth would be
in bad taste. Well, this abomination in front of us is in bad
taste. You poor blind old bastard, with all your Pulitzers, your
books and reputation, you can't see there is no drama any
more, no spectacle, and no heroes, only scum like these two
committing fiendish acts in their fiendish little wars.

Watching DelCorso, Dunlop more than disapproved. He
was in a state of repressed rage, both revolted and fascinated,
as if he were observing a man engaged in an unspeakably
obscene act. He'd seen his share of yellow-press photographers, but the worst had never gone about things with the
zeal DelCorso now showed. To describe him as a sensation-
alist would be too generous, to call him a disgrace to the
profession would be as mild as it was trite. *Filth.* What had
happened? He looked down at the cameras hanging over his
shirtfront, two Leicas and an old Nikormat, scratched, dented
here and there, their lens hoods bent at the edges, but their
inner mechanisms in perfect order. What had happened and
where had they gone, the decent, principled people who'd
brought dignity to this calling, the Margaret Bourke-Whites,
the Duncans and Capas? The Nazis had hired photographers
to take pictures like the ones DelCorso was taking, pictures
of proud SS butchers smiling over the mounded corpses of
slaughtered Jews and Poles. *Filth.* The Dickey Chapelles, the
Gene Smiths, where had they gone? DelCorso appeared to
have a fondness for genital wounds. The photograph—photograph, shit, the cheap snapshot he took of the groin-shot
American boy in Cambodia. Mutilation sells. *Filth.* Burrows
and Carl Mydan, what had happened to them? Dead or retired.
He was the last of that generation still in the field. Retired or
dead. Dead. It ascended suddenly from a hidden depth within
himself, a wish so powerful he thought he could will its fulfillment. He tried to expel the desire, which wasn't worthy of
him, but it had lodged in his heart and in his mind, where it

printed an image of DelCorso, lying on his back, his eyes still-staring beneath the single, solid brow.

DelCorso snapped his last frame and rewound the film, the break in the rhythm of his movements breaking the spell between him and the Mourabitoun. Like figures in a freeze-frame set in motion again, they abruptly stepped from behind the line of bodies and prodded the air with their rifles.

"*Yallah*—let's go."

"About fucking time," McCafferty grumbled as they passed through the gate into the musty shadows of the passageway. "Who're you going to sell that to?"

"I'm not going to sell them."

"Yeah," said McCafferty drawing the *h* into an *r*. "You go through all that and then you aren't going to sell. Maybe some-day you'll make sense to me, Deecee."

DelCorso did not say anything. He made sense to himself. He'd paid his final installment. He knew he had by the light-ness in his heart, which was almost a physical sensation; it was as if he were floating above the passageway, above the balconies that closed off the light, floating free as the clear air. It *was* grace. He had been released from the compulsion to shock and disturb, which had driven him for the past ten years to push himself to the farthest limits of risk, unmindful of those he dragged with him, like Wilson. Credit Bolton for being right on that score: through his photographs, he'd been trying to force the public to become a co-signer of his debt, shared guilt being easier to bear than guilt borne alone But the truth was, he'd had to bear it alone, just as, minutes ago, he'd had to relieve it alone. Bolton was leaving in the morning. He would have to see him tonight, tell him he was right, and apologize for that stupid accusation. Old Horseman, you knew me better than I knew myself.

Filth. Dunlop, walking behind DelCorso, felt tainted just being in his presence. An ulcerous pain sliced through his middle as he looked at the black, curly hair on the back of DelCorso's head, the wide shoulders that made him appear shorter than he was. Said he wasn't selling. Bullshit. What was he going to do with that crap? Put it in his family album? He'd sell, all right, because there was a market for filth, and there would be at least one critic who would praise it for its frankness. "Mr. DelCorso does not compromise in presenting the realities of modern warfare, however ugly and shocking." Yes, he would shock and the more the public was shocked, the more inured it became to shock and the more it demanded to be shocked further. In that way, the DelCorsos set the pace and determined taste, or the lack of taste, leaving the Dunlops nowhere. Quaint. Some of the people who wrote books about war photography already considered his work quaint, brushed with the sepia tones of the distant past, as though his images were to be lumped with those of the Crimea and Gettysburg. The vision flashed in his mind again, vivid, terrible, gratifying. It had the force and fervor of a prayer, a visual prayer. My God, I am praying for his death. Dunlop would have liked to deny this fact; to harbor such a desire was unacceptable to his view of himself. But DelCorso always had, somehow, some way, aroused the pettiest, basest aspects of his nature, and this mysterious power heightened Dunlop's hatred of him, intensifying the very desire he found so reprehensible.

They retraced their steps from the passageway to the alley, then to the street, where they found the other four Mourabitoun tying the dead Christian to the rear of a commandeered armored car. Its driver sat on the turret, one foot braced on the stubby barrel of the 75-mm gun, goggles pulled over the brim of his cap, his posture and manner reminiscent of a German tank commander in *The Desert Fox*. White blazed in the black of his unshaven face as he smiled for the French TV cameraman, one of those underfed European media types who wore denim shirts to claim membership in the working class. Conklin and Lutter snapped stills with their Leicas. Behind the armored car, the dead man was trussed up by his ankles. Someone had removed the crucifix from between his teeth, perhaps as a souvenir, but his mouth remained open, as though he were about to scream. Dunlop hoped the Mourabitoun were not going to stage a show like the one he'd seen a few weeks earlier—the body bumping down the street, shot at and stomped on until it looked like nothing more than a piece of trash that had got caught in the car's bumper. He rubbed his skin; dirt rolled between his fingers, the physical manifestation of the sordidness of this war. He wanted to scour himself in a scalding bath; he would be going home in a week, and didn't think he could touch his wife until every gram of this filth had been cleansed from him.

"Where the hell were you guys?" Conklin, lowering his camera, regarded them with his pink, adolescent's face.

"The Looneys had something to show us," McCafferty said.

"Yeah?"

"Nothing you'd want to see. It wouldn't sell in Baltimore, that's for sure."

"We saw that dude pop a few rounds at P.X., and then you guys disappeared, so we figured we had to see what was going on. Then the armored car showed up and these four assholes told us to stay put." The pink darkened a couple of shades. "I mean, there wasn't much else we could do. . . . "

"You don't need to apologize," DelCorso said.

He felt, on the back of his neck, the blue frigidity of Dunlop's stare.

"Conklin, you want to know what's down that alley, ask DelCorso."

"Hell, P.X., I don't—"

"Ask him." Dunlop's voice rose to a reedy, breaking tautness, each syllable like a note forced through a stoppered flute. "He'd be glad to give you all the filthy details. He's going to give them to the whole goddamned world as soon as he finds a market for his pornography."

DelCorso had heard that high, tight tone before, in Saigon years ago: *You've betrayed your country, your profession, and me.* It conveyed fathoms of anger deeper than the anger expressed by the words he spoke. A few hours ago, minutes ago, DelCorso would have reacted with his own brand of rage, but his feelings toward Dunlop had changed; if not exactly warm, they were at least free of their former rancor. He was one of the best in his day, he's still the best at what he does, but the blind old man can't see it's all so different now, that blood shed in battle is no longer sanctified, that the last quarter of the twentieth century cannot speak of heroes because it hasn't the right to them. We have lost something. None of us will ever photograph, with sincere pride and innocence, marines raising a flag on some future Surabachi.

Out of habit, he put one of his cameras to his eye, centering the lens on the Christian, the buff-colored armored car off to one side. This is the kind of thing we are fated to record, this and what we saw back there are the truths of war in our times. Shutter and advance clicked once more. When he focused on the driver, the gunman who'd fired over Dunlop's head batted down his arm.

"No! No photo!"

DelCorso drew back.

"What in the hell?"

"No photo. *Ruh—go—ruh.*"

"Cool your jets, Deecee."

"They're cooled. I don't get why he'd let us photograph that mess in the courtyard and then goes camera-shy over a routine shot of an armored car."

"They're not called Looney Tunes for nothing."

"*Ruh, ruh.*" The Mourabitoun, his emotional chemistry having undergone some inexplicable change, was now gesturing angrily at the entire crowd of newsmen, menacing them with his Kalashnikov. "*Ruh! Ruh!* No photo!"

The French cameraman unlimbered his 16-millimeter from his shoulder and gave the gunman a wan, placating smile. Then all, a little wary about turning their backs—Mourabitoun means "ambusher" in Arabic—climbed the street toward the intersection by the ruined villa. Dunlop and DelCorso lagged behind, Dunlop walking with the stiff, rolling gait of an aging athlete, DelCorso limping slightly, his bad leg beginning to react to the strains he'd put on it today. He tried to ignore its distracting ache, for he wanted nothing to dilute the joy of his release. Were it not for the hobbling pain in his calf and ankle, he would have leapt in celebration, a high, floating, graceful leap, like an astronaut on the moon. Threading his way through a patch of shell craters, each rimmed by dust and chunks of pavement, he took a painkiller from the first-aid kit on his belt and forced it down without water. Off by the curb, in a scattering of shredded bark and fragmented bricks, the dead Moslem woman censured his happiness, the bloody badges on her breasts like three reproachful eyes. The disasters of war. Could he use that as a title? Goya would not object, not if her photograph and all the others would serve as an admonishment. Yes, do a book when he got home from this. He would call it *The Disasters of War*. He would give himself six months to complete it, and to compensate for the loss of income, he could get rid of the loft and work at home. Home. There was another door open to him: he could live in the everyday without suffering the plague of restlessness because he felt worthy of Margaret now. Her virtues could no longer rebuke him. She filled his mind's eye then, eclipsing the damaged world around him, her heels lifted slightly off the court, legs stretched in a drawing of long muscles, arm held high, head raised to look at the ball, which, struck, angled over the net, her arm arcing across her breasts on the follow-through and her untouched whites brilliant in the sun.

It was like a violent gust of wind ripping rotted tent canvas. He and Dunlop had time only to flinch before the rocket burst behind them. The television crew, McCafferty, Conklin, and Lutter were already at the intersection, twenty-five yards ahead. DelCorso saw them throw themselves flat even as he rolled behind an anthill of rubble, the only cover he could find. Dunlop went down beside him, cameras banging against each other. A serpent of smoke coiled skyward from the street, roughly an equal distance between them and the armored car, which fired its gun. The little seventy-five piped overhead. Reflexively, DelCorso trained his 105-millimeter on the car and the Mourabitoun, scrambling behind a building at the corner of the street and the alley. Too far, a block at least. Another rocket erupted on a rooftop. The seventy-five answered again, its report and the whistling rush of the shell simultaneous. Dunlop took a 400-millimeter from his camera bag and bench-rested it atop the mound.

The next rocket toppled the armored car like a child's toy and set it afire. The hatch popped open. The driver squirmed out. A sheet of flame billowing from his back like a garish cape, he ran a few yards, fell, and rolled on the pavement, his arms and legs thrashing. If it isn't close, it isn't true. Impelled by his unquestioning belief in this aphorism, by his conviction that he had never been more blessed by his protective gods than now, by all the hot impetuosity in his nature, DelCorso rose and ran toward the twin beacons of burning flesh and burning metal. Running, he made his settings and calculations of time, distance, and risk. F-eight at two-fiftieths. A hundred yards more, roughly where the first rocket had burst, might put him in range. Too far and you don't have a picture, too close and you won't be alive to take it. Where was the invisible line between the extremes? The most likely danger was another rocket, but he would be relatively safe if he shot from the crater of the first one: shells almost never hit in the same place twice; besides, the distance between the crater and the target—the armored car—was another hundred yards, outside the killing radius of a one-twenty-two.

He could see the shallow crater, now about fifty yards from him, and the slivers of smoke rising from the asphalt melted by the blast. Beyond, the Mourabitoun in shepherd's dress sprang out from behind the corner of the building and threw his blanket over the driver, a squirming black form encased in flame. The blanket caught fire. The Mourabitoun leaped backward, helplessly watching cloth and flesh consumed. DelCorso stopped and took a quick snap. Winded, his hands trembling, he knew he had not held the camera steady. He jogged forward again, the pocked, debris-littered street reminding him of the broken ground over which he'd run in Ireland a year ago.

He knelt on one knee, bracing his left elbow on it to steady the camera and keeping his left hand free to focus and change stops. Another rocket sliced overhead to burst on the far side of the armored car, only its silhouette visible behind the flames. Quickly increasing the shutter speed with his right hand, he got a frame of the Mourabitoun running for the cover of the alley, his figure outlined against the cone of shell smoke. From the alley corner, one of the other militiamen let go with the RPG, its small projectile arcing overhead and crashing on a distant rooftop, the launcher's backblast kicking up a boil of dust and smoke. A second gunman, the one wearing the mannikin's wig, sprayed the air with aimless bursts from a Kalashnikov.

DelCorso panned in their direction, putting them at the extreme right of the viewfinder, the two fires at the left. The RPG fired again. DelCorso tripped the shutter as the backblast flung itself against a building wall like a wave against a breakwater. He was still too far, too far even to present the facts let alone the truth. Taken at this range, the smaller fire would not appear on a photograph as a burning human being; it would be mistaken for a hunk of armored car. He did not want ambiguity, but clarity. Twenty yards. He'd give himself another twenty yards. Ears tuned for the incoming hiss, nerves drawn taut, he moved forward in a slouch. Through the sooty haze now screening the street, he thought he saw the gunman with the wig swinging his rifle in the way a signalman waves a flag. Ten yards more. Doubt and fear assaulted his confidence: the gunman was signaling a warning. What am I doing this for? The purpose above all. He had been freed from the obligation to atone, but not from his obligation to tell the truth. This was an urban war, what was happening in front of him was street fighting, and he had a duty to record it as honestly as he could. That sufficing as a legitimate reason for the chance he was taking, he sprinted the next ten yards, or, rather, did a clumsy imitation of a sprint. Kneeling again to steady the Leica, he leveled the lens, through which he saw, like a mirror image of himself, the Mourabitoun kneeling with leveled rifle.

31

DELCORSO HESITATED a fraction of a second. Had he seen the pointed Kalashnikov with his naked eye, he would have taken cover instantly, but the interposing lens detached him from the reality of its danger. Framed by the viewfinder, gunman and rifle looked like a photograph.

Something clubbed him in the temple. The blackness seemed like the darkness of eternity, and he was suspended in a void where neither time nor space had any measure. He thought a bullet had pierced his brain and wondered why he still had the power to think. When would death smother the last flickers of his consciousness?

He saw again. He saw the gunman, still kneeling, and the barrel of the Kalashnikov climbing as it fired on full automatic. Rounds flew past him with a sound like the crackling of hot oil in a skillet. Blood leaked down the side of his face. Whatever had hit him, a ricochet or piece of flying pavement, had knocked him into a sitting position. Dazed, he hesitated another fraction of a second before spinning around to run. Weightless, defying gravity, he was floating through the air like Neil Armstrong on the moon. There was no pain, only the awareness of a tremendous impact that had lifted him off the earth, then flung him down on his back. One of his cameras jabbed his solar plexus as he rolled over. He tried to stand to make a dash for the mound of rubble, but his left leg folded under him. As he fell, he caught a glimpse of a red blot spreading across the front of his shirt and a huge, bloody rent where his left kneecap had been. Jesus, the leg again. St. Michael the Archangel defend us in battle, be our safeguard against . . . Dear Jesus, he would lose the leg this time. Struggling for breath, he belly-crawled toward the spot where he'd left Dunlop. He wanted to see how badly he'd been hit and staunch the bleeding, but he didn't dare stop: bullets were still cracking around him. The bastards were trying to finish him off. He kept crawling, dragging himself on his elbows and forearms, but the little pyramid of debris that represented deliverance seemed no closer.

"Dunlop! Jesus Christ! Dunlop!"

More rounds popped. Glancing over his shoulder, he saw two gunmen running up the street toward him, firing from the hip as they ran. He crawled faster than he thought possible, skittering like some kind of crippled land crab. Michael the Archangel get me out of here.

"Dunlop! Dunlop!"

It took most of his strength to shout for help. His lungs hurt, as if a tube had been cinched around his chest, a tube drawing ever tighter. His mouth was dry, his tongue sticking to its roof and tasting of old pennies. The faster he moved, the harder his heart worked, quickening the flow of blood out of the wounds in his head, chest, and leg. His heart was pumping the life out of him. A drowsy weakness began creeping through him. He fought against succumbing to it, like a spent fighter drawing on his last reserves of strength, but his will lost its command over his body. Unable to move more than a foot or two at a time, he waited for the Mourabitoun to catch up and make an end of it, regretting as deeply as he'd regretted anything that he would not see Margaret's face again. Regretting he didn't have a gun to take the sons of bitches with him.

Behind the parapet of crumbled bricks, Dunlop watched the prostrate figure less than fifty yards away. Several of the rounds carelessly aimed at DelCorso dug into the street in front of him. He did not move, but his paralysis was not caused by fear as much as by utter amazement at seeing his wish fulfilled. Or almost fulfilled. There was still life in DelCorso, but life would not be there for much longer. How to explain this fulfillment without his having done a thing to bring it about? He did not believe in voodoo; the answer had to be

coincidence, a coincidence of his wish, the inevitable arithmetic of the battlefield, and DelCorso's own rashness. It occurred to him, very briefly, that he now had a chance to be a
hero after thirty years of photographing heroes, but he could
not find enough proportion between risk and reward to justify
exposing himself. He would be putting his life on the line to
rescue a man as good as dead, to save scum. A bullet snapped
above his head. At almost the same instant, a rocket screeched
in and fountained with a sharp clap in the street somewhere
between DelCorso and the pursuing militiamen. Dunlop turned
and broke for the intersection, the rocket and rifle fire giving
him a legitimate excuse for his desertion.

Rounding the corner, where the others were crouched
alongside a building wall, he said,

"Let's get the hell out."

"Where the fuck's Deecee?"

"Dead, McCafferty." Dunlop sounded more out of breath
than he really was. "Shot him. Two of 'em coming up the
street for the rest of us."

"Dead? Just heard him yelling—"

"They killed him, goddamnit. They'll kill all of us if we
don't haul ass now."

"We can't leave him. You've seen what they do to the
dead."

Dunlop caught Lutter's glance momentarily. There was
hate in the gaunt face, and an implied promise in the eyes
that he would back up Dunlop if any questions were asked.

"I say P.X. is right."

With that, Dunlop, the TV crew, Lutter, and Conklin took
off for the cars, parked three blocks away. McCafferty lunged
and held Conklin back with his strong hands.

"You're not going back to Baltimore just fucking yet."

"Tim, he's dead. We'll call the embassy—"

"I'm not going to let them do to Deecee what I've seen
them do to others. You get that fat ass of yours in gear and
bring our car up here."

"It'd be suicide."

"It'll be your suicide because I'll kill you if you don't bring
the car. I'm going to get him."

The rocket had saved DelCorso from immediate execu-
tion. He did not look back to see if it had killed the Mourabitoun or just scared them off. Whatever had happened, they
weren't shooting at him anymore. A random rocket, but it

had landed so accurately it was as if someone had delivered covering fire for him. His guardians—they had not deserted him completely. What had deserted him was his strength. His breath came in rapid, shallow gasps, and when he tried to drag himself forward, he could crawl only a few inches; every inch was gained at the cost of enormous effort so that, crawling up the gently sloping street, lungs laboring, he felt like a climber scaling a sheer wall in the high thin air.

He was rising again, slipping the bonds of gravity. No. Someone was picking him up. Who? Dried blood from his head wound had glued his left eye shut, sweat blurred the vision in his right. Someone with powerful shoulders was lifting him in a fireman's carry. Slung over the wide shoulders, his head down, he thought, I'm going to live! To live! Maggie Fitzgerald, I'm going to live and see your face again, and Danny's and Angela's, I'll see all your faces again soon. Who?

"Dunlop?" he asked, his voice hardly more than a whisper.

"Dunlop shit. The motherfucker bugged out. Left you for dead."

McCafferty. He should have known. When you're in a whorehouse, count on a whore to do the right thing.

"Bleeding," he managed to say as McCafferty ran with him. "Got to stop bleeding."

"Stop talking."

Around the corner of the intersection, in the shelter of a doorway, McCafferty dropped to both knees and gently rolled DelCorso off his shoulders. Lying on his back, his head cradled in McCafferty's lap, he looked down the length of his body. Even through the blood and sweat, the sight of the damage terrified him: the front of his shirt was a slick, electric red, the calf of his left leg, attached to the rest of him by a few strands of cartilage, turned at a forty-five-degree angle to his thigh.

"Tim . . . I'm . . . all . . . *all* fucked up."

"You be easy now." McCafferty reached into DelCorso's first-aid kit, removing a packet of compresses and a roll of tape.

"All fucked up."

For sure he would lose it this time, oh, Jesus God, he would lose it, but he was alive and there was no pain. The pain would come, but if he was lucky, he'd be in the hospital when it did, sweet Mother Morphine coursing through him.

"Be easy when I do this, Deecee. Don't talk."

Be easy. Be easy, Mark. *Wilson.* Had this happened to him because of Wilson? Another debt to be repaid? Had he, in his blind drive to liquidate his original debt, incurred other liabilities, each of which would come due in its time?

McCafferty tore open the bloody shirt. Placing several compresses on the chest wound, he fastened them with the tape, wrapping it once around DelCorso's back, then crisscrossing it over his shoulders and tying it off behind his neck so that the dressing resembled the shoulder straps of old-fashioned infantry.

This could not be for Wilson. There was nothing he could have done to prevent Wilson's death. But if not for Wilson, for what reason had this happened? He hadn't been scratched in ten years of covering wars, each of his escapes from injury or death a sign of his gods' grace. Not an hour ago they had bestowed upon him their highest benediction, so why had this happened?

"You tell me if this hurts."

Gingerly, McCafferty began to straighten the twisted calf.

"Doesn't . . ."

"Okay."

"Doesn't make sense."

"Does it hurt?"

"No."

"Okay."

Easing DelCorso's head to the pavement, McCafferty gathered four slats of wood from the debris nearby. He placed one under the wounded leg, the next on top, the remaining two on the sides, lashing all four snugly with the tape.

"That hurt, Deecee?"

"Doesn't make sense."

"Goddamn you, do you feel anything?"

"No."

"All right then." McCafferty, using the last length of tape, tied a tourniquet above the obliterated kneecap.

"That too tight?"

"No sense."

"*Is it too tight?*"

"No . . . no sense . . . makes no sense."

"Never does when you're hit. Now stay quiet."

"Ten years never hit, never scratched."

"Listen, you pushed your luck and ran out of it. Your luck ran out. That's all, Deecee."

"Luck?"

For some reason, the word, or the way McCafferty had used it, frightened DelCorso as much as the sight of his injuries.

"Ran out of luck?" he asked, incredulous.

"Yeah. Now listen. I've done all I can. Conklin's getting the car. We're going to get you to AUB hospital, so maybe you've got some luck left. But if you keep up this fucking talk, you'll run out of that."

"Luck?" Panicked, he gazed up into McCafferty's wide face, seeking from the close-set gray eyes another, gentler answer. None came. He had run out of luck. Was it as simple and terrible as that? If that was true, then there never had been any guardian gods, no sacred mission, no sin, and therefore no redemption. Then this had happened to him because he'd mortgaged his luck, and luck alone. Then he would have lived the past ten years of his life by a myth. Now he knew why the word had frightened him: it had the sound of truth. He raised his head slightly, just enough to see the late sunlight, planing over the rooftops far away. It gave him hope. He knew he had to hope if he was to muster the will to survive. He had to believe in something beyond luck because he could not endure a day of facing danger without faith. Even if his faith in a personal set of deities, in holy missions and destiny, had been one intricately embroidered illusion, he had to find something else to believe in and he didn't have much time to find it. No time whatever. He had to find it now. *The truth.* Yes the truth. Even if it was plain, simple, ugly, disgusting, the truth was better than an elaborate and lovely myth, wasn't it? He could still believe in the truth and his obligation to pursue it. He felt calmer. Pursuit of the truth. Was there a better reason for coming to places like Beirut at the risk of his life? As for luck, he would have to be more cautious in the future and not push it.

He'd been damned lucky until now, lucky to have gotten as far as he had, to have married Margaret, to have fathered two fine children, to have survived a wall of automatic-weapons fire. All right, he would probably lose the leg, but he would compensate for it somehow. He was lucky to have had McCafferty here, lucky that Conklin was getting the car, lucky that he would be in AUB, pumped full of morphine before the pain started. No pain, please please no pain, St. Michael the Archangel defend us in battle, be our safeguard against pain.

I know what it's like, please no pain. He'd no sooner made this plea than, from the wound in his knee, a rotary blade sliced up his thigh, slashing every fiber of nerve and forcing a shrill cry from his throat.

"*Tim*."

"Be easy now."

"Hurt."

"There's nothing I can do. . . . Be easy . . . Conklin's coming with the car."

"Kit." His voice had the register of a small boy's. "Pills."

McCafferty got the bottle from the first-aid kit and forced two Percodans between DelCorso's gritted teeth. The thing spun through him, its edges honed as razors, as hot as white steel. DelCorso could not work up enough saliva to swallow the pills. He felt utterly abandoned now, utterly alone. No luck at all. All run out. Then he managed to roll the capsules into his throat with his sandpaper tongue and gulp them down. It would be a while before they took effect; even then they wouldn't do much. This degree of agony, beyond the imagination of anyone who has never felt it, required the pricking kiss of Mother Morphine. No luck at all. Shit. Curiously, he felt, in this bitter despair, a greater calm. Shit.

"Tim . . ."

"Don't talk, goddamnit . . . car's coming . . . you'll hear it in a minute."

"Tim?" It seemed he had something important to say, something he desperately needed to say. "Tim?"

"What? Damn it, what?"

"Shit."

He heard the car, but the sound of its engine filled him with terror, the terror of renewed hope. Hope that he was soon to be delivered from pain and death, terror that the hope was just another myth. The car would run over a mine or be struck by a shell before it reached him. Please get me out of here. Please please please. The louder the hum of the engine grew, the more he hoped, the more he feared, the more fervently he prayed. Please get me out of here. St. Michael the Archangel deliver me from pain and death, get me out of here. Louder and louder, the Mercedes diesel roared in his ears; then the leashes of gravity broke from him one by one. Conklin and McCafferty were raising him from the pavement to put him in the backseat, Conklin holding him by the ankles, McCafferty under the arms. The driver opened the door and just before they laid him inside, he swore he saw the sun as it shone at high noon—no, brighter, shining with a clarity so pure it blinded him. He felt the seat springs beneath him, the jolt of the car as it turned around and sped down the street, but he could not see anything. He heard Conklin say, "Tim, I got here as fast as I could," and McCafferty answer, "Wasn't your fault. His luck ran out, that's all," but he could not see them. The car was going very fast now, faster and faster, its velocity as gut-emptying as the nose dive of a plane. Please please let me make it, get me out of here, please get me out of here. Faster, too fast. A tremendous weight crushed him into the seat. Please get me out of here.

McCafferty had been wrong. DelCorso had not lost all his luck, his gods had not entirely withdrawn their benediction. They got him out.

32

THE FAMILIAR RITUALS WERE OVER. The flight attendants had explained what to do in the unlikely event of a crash (Die is what you do, Bolton thought), had shown how to put the oxygen mask over your nose and mouth, inflate the life vests, fasten the seat belts. The captain had welcomed everyone aboard, informed the passengers of their cruising altitude, speed, and estimated time of arrival in New York. He wished everyone a pleasant flight. Now the Olympic Airways 747 was somewhere over the Aegean, the no-smoking light off, and the attendants pushing drink carts down the aisle. Bolton, who brought his own, asked for a glass, no ice, thanks. He poured himself a double I. W. Harper from his hip flask and sat back trying to forget the past three days had happened.

"You know," he said, savoring the whiskey, "you don't have to do this."

"I'd do anything to get out of that fucking hole."

"Why do you always have to play hard-ass?"

"All right. I'm doing it because I want to. I was there. I figured she'd be better off hearing it from me than second-hand."

"You mean you have a heart after all."

"I've got common sense is all. If I was her, I'd want to hear it straight."

"If all you had was common sense and no heart, you wouldn't have pulled him out of there in the first place."

"Maybe. But you don't leave your own on the other guy's turf, especially when the other guys cut balls off."

"The embassy told me there'll be a State Department guy at the TMA cargo terminal to handle the red tape."

"What happens after that?"

"I guess she takes him home."

Neither of the men could refer to the cargo in the third person neuter.

Bolton drank half his glass, then refilled it. He had met Margaret only twice, and then briefly, so he wasn't sure what to expect. If he got himself good and loaded now, he would be able to sleep and numb his own pain before having to deal with hers. He should have gone when DelCorso asked him, once more unto the breach and all that. Maybe if he'd been there . . .

"I used to do this after I got back from Nam," Bolton said.

"What? Fly in 747s?"

"After the telegrams got sent, I used to visit next of kin and fill in the blanks."

"Must've been great duty."

"I guess it was better than a stake in the heart, but goddamn, I got to the point that I didn't feel anything anymore and had no patience. I remember this one woman kept pressing me. Was his body mutilated, will the coffin be closed? And I kept saying, no, he wasn't mutilated, and she kept asking, and finally I just said, 'All right, lady, both his legs were blown off if you have to know.' "

"What'd she do?"

"Slapped me."

"Well, we won't have to do much blank-filling. It's been in every paper and on every wire and every network. Felt real weird, me being photographed and interviewed."

"I guess so. How come you let Dunlop off so easy? You could have smeared his yellow ass from here to Christmas."

"Because I didn't want my Irish ass sued for libel. Anyhow, it wouldn't have made any difference if he'd stuck around. Deecee played the wrong card."

"She's still going to have some questions. Like how it happened."

"I told that to two dozen reporters, including you. He ran out there like he was bulletproof, caught one in the knee, and a piece ricocheted into his chest. I don't know if that's what did it or the loss of blood. Looked like a couple of gallons spilled out of him."

"That what you'll tell her?"

"Yeah, but not in those words. It's been in the papers."

"Funny. A hundred people die every day in Beirut and they're just numbers in the last paragraph. One newsman gets it and it's a banner headline."

"Yeah, like it isn't supposed to happen."

"What if she asks you the unanswerable one?"

"What's that?"

"Why?"

"Ran out of luck." McCafferty tipped his beer. "No other answer."

"I don't think that'll do."

"Then you'll have to answer it."

"I can't. I've been asking it of myself the last three days. I asked it when I heard about it, asked it when I saw him at AUB and that doctor was picking through him like he was a lab specimen, asked it every goddamned time I had to find some official with the right rubber stamp so we could get him out, asked it when they loaded him on that cargo plane. No answer."

"Maybe she won't ask."

Bolton said nothing, gulping the whiskey to dull the ache throbbing in that part of himself he had always sought to keep inviolate.

"This really it for you, Harry? You're going home after we get this done?"

"You bet the ranch I am, especially after this. I knew him ten goddamned years. My chopper pulled him out of the Iron Triangle back in 'sixty-six, when he was hit in the same leg. There's hardly an assignment we didn't cover together, and I keep telling myself, He's gone, your pulling him out of the bush didn't really save his life, just postponed his death a few years and he's gone and you've got to accept that. I know that's what I have to do, but right now I can't. Goddamnit I can't, just like I can't answer why and what for. Yeah, there's another one she might ask. What for? For a picture on page forty-six?"

"You'll have to answer that one, too."

"I've been thinking about it. Maybe I can come up with something. I've been thinking that he believed in what he was doing. He wanted to tell the truth, pass it on, that he was a kind of faithful messenger or an honest witness. Something like that. That he died pursuing the truth. How does that sound?"

"It'll probably sound okay to her. A woman who's lost her old man needs something to hang on to."

"How does it sound to *you*?"

"I don't need anything to hang on to."

"I think I do."

"In that case you don't want me to tell you what I think."

"Let's hear it."

"Listen, you and him were best buddies, so you don't want to hear what I think that sounds like."

"I'm a big boy, McCafferty. I can handle it."

"Forget it." McCafferty poured the rest of his beer into his plastic airline glass and drained it with one swallow. "But I will tell you the last thing Deecee ever said."

"What's that?"

McCafferty told him and Bolton saw in the oyster-colored eyes the same expression he'd seen in the eyes of some prostitutes: the twinkle of a cynicism so deep it delighted in itself.